PETALS OF PERIL

BRADY PHOENIX

To Josue,

Thank you for being the friend when I was coming into my own. Your kindness and joy was inspiring.

Rest peacefully.

Chapter 1

Thursday

CARS GATHERED ON THE hillside in late July, kicking up dust into the open air, twenty miles outside of Mabel, Nebraska. Kids skipped along the neatly trimmed paths with the tall grass guiding them toward the admissions desk. Sunflower petals drifted in the breeze, enticing toddlers to pursue the yellow fragments with glee. Two tractors hummed as they dragged trailers full of patrons enjoying the view of thousands of stems holding the beautiful fauna highlighted by the sun with faces peeking above the horizon from the playground.

The parents shouted at their children to stay close as the crowd continued to grow by the minute. The swing sets echoed with the laughter of children soaring above the flower patches. Teenage boys zoomed through the pathways, getting tangled in the maze of towering flowers, only pausing at the sight of homemade metal statues and intricate puzzles.

"Do we have another batch of burgers ready?" asked the older woman, observing the crew laboring over the grill.

"Yes, Gemma," said the head cook, flipping a pair of patties.

Gemma acknowledged the kitchen's update before telling the line of hungry patrons eager to bite in for some lunch. She witnessed the charred smoke envelop the sunflower fields, making it hard to see the central wooden tower in the maze. Whistles resounded in the field as the staff prevented a child from swinging near the deteriorating structure.

Gemma acknowledged the customers' compliments on her farm while static mumbled on her walkie talkie. The innocent children's joyful smiles made her crow's feet more pronounced. "Clear Blue Sky" by George Strait boasted through the speaker system, accompanied by faint scratches on the cassette tape. Despite the need for caution with her knee replacement, she paid no mind to the discomfort as they wobbled on the gravel. Since her husband's death, her business had been her primary concern. It was the sole memento of the connection she shared with Simon.

Chester Farms had enjoyed prosperity as a small business for several decades. What started as a simple tractor ride throughout their sunflower patch has grown into a complete empire with attractions to suit families throughout the state of Nebraska. It wasn't just the children who found joy in the wooden frames with holes for polaroid pictures. Feasts were arranged on the long table along the field's edge for a tea party surrounded by colorful blooms; the whimsical aesthetic was a popular attraction for arranging private meals for families of many sizes.

"Gemma, come in," her walkie said.

The removal of the chunky device brought relief to the sag in her overalls. Gemma pushed back her gray strands of hair behind her ears. Her focus became removed from the happiness that continued to grow around her.

"This is Gemma," she said, wiping the sweat on her forehead.

"The repair guys are here for the guest cabin. They're saying they'll have to shut the space down for a while."

Gemma's frustration grew as she glanced at the cabin at the opposite end of her property. Four-foot-tall sunflowers lined the mounded path to the home, which was larger than a glorified shed.

The absence of party venues and haunted mazes during October had made it challenging for her to earn revenue by renting out the space for evening events. A glint of a shingle dropped to the ground, its decay as if they were shedding tears of their own.

"I knew I should've been more firm with that damn fraternity," she said to herself, her grin tight to not show any sort of anger in front of her guests. "Bunch of fucking morons."

"What's the damage so far?" she asked her employee.

"The plumbing is shot, and there are several holes in the walls that messed with the electrical cords."

"Dammit," she growled. "And the carpeting? I knew that they shoved my flowers in the toilet. The flooding soaked up the carpet. Can it be restored?"

"Unrepairable. Too old and too mildewy."

"That carpet was recycled from my mother's old home. Are you sure there's no way we can fix it?"

"No, ma'am."

"I should've killed those kids myself," she said to herself, her teeth gritting.

At the apex of the field, the construction workers dragged planks into a pile. The foreman wrapped a cord around his arm, preparing to put the hand saw into his truck. Every person Gemma watched exiting the cabin brought an ache to her heart with the reminder that something that meant so much to her had now been reduced to filth.

"Okay, thank you for the update," she said softly to maintain her professionalism and not scare the children.

She covered her chest with an open red flannel, cradling her arms. Bubbles swarmed around her body from two siblings running around her path with hot pink wands; soapy water splotched onto her denim when they rested on her pant leg before popping.

She observed the growing crowd and smiled, proud of the success her family business had achieved. A tear formed along the underpart of her eye when she looked at the joy of the families; a sea of neon glowed amongst the yellow from the slew of color-blocked patterns on the wind breakers with each person enjoying the amenities of her farm.

A rectangular opening in a small shed had an awning to cover a wooden counter holding a pyramid of jars. Sunlight winked off the glass containers, exposing gooey tan substances within. With a smile, the clerk accepted the green slips of paper from thirty customers and carefully stored them in the metal lockbox, one transaction at a time.

"Hi Gemma," said the clerk after she dismissed the person in front of her.

"How's it going over here?" Gemma asked, exchanging a slight nod to the guest that was just dismissed.

With pride, they said, "We're getting close to being sold out. Your sunflower butter has become a hit!"

"I noticed," Gemma said, picking up a napkin that tumbled closer to her boots.

"Ever since you launched this, people would line up just to get a jar!" they praised. "You're such a genius for coming up with this idea."

"It was my kids' idea," Gemma said humbly. "I can't take credit for their ideas. I'm only responsible for the picture."

As she reached for the highest jar in her pyramid, Gemma couldn't help but chuckle. Placing the glass beside her face, she wore the same warm smile as the one on the label, as if she held a mirror.

"But you came up with the sunflower butter sandwiches!"

"Well, that *was* me. I figured everybody should have a taste of our pride and joy before they buy it."

A young boy of four years old approached her. Sunflower butter covered his mouth, creating the appearance of thick makeup on his cheeks. With the crust lodged between his two front teeth, he relished each bite of the sandwich.

Gemma walked toward her house; the crowd lessened, and the chattering minimized. Next to her gray pickup truck was a parked white van. Framing the woman's pale face was a perm of brunette hair. Resting on the shoulder pad of her pinstripe pant suit was a dead sunflower petal. The other person shut the rear car door and placed the camera gear near her feet.

"Where do you want it?" he asked, straining his back.

"Anywhere will do for now," the woman said, grabbing her compact mirror from her oversized pocket to check for definition in her thick, penciled eyebrows.

"Janice, how are you?" Gemma said, her smile glimmering with ease.

"Mrs. Chester! It's always a pleasure to see you too," Janice said, reaching her hand out for a shake. "I'm so glad you agreed to do this segment. We haven't had you at our station since Simon passed away."

"Yes, it's been a minute."

"Where did you want to do this? I would love to get some people here and get their take on the success of your farm as well."

"I'm sure there will be plenty of options," she said, her smile pushing past her tense lips with her arms ushering to showcase the crowd of people behind her like they were the supporting cast of a major production.

"Yes, you're right," Janice agreed, her cherry-red lipstick framed her polished white teeth. "Oh, I want to get a shot of those two! They look so adorable!"

She directed attention to the sandbox, which was not filled with sand but sunflower seeds. The bits trickled down the hands of the children and landed on their laps, bringing a sense of relief to the employee who had just directed a small group that was throwing them at each other. A mixture of various herbs permeated the air by the stand, where bags of flavored sunflower seeds were displayed. The presence of dill, cumin, and chili powder caused the fathers to gather around the counter with dollar bills fluttering in their hands like butterfly wings.

"I'll let you get acquainted with the guests. I would like to have a moment if that would be possible?"

"Of course," said Janice. "Take all the time you need."

As Wynona Judd started playing, the crew vanished into the crowd while Gemma made her way to the side of her house. A well-maintained mound featured lush, tall grass dancing in the wind while she ventured to the top of the hill. The hammock's white ropes swayed, awaiting someone to find solace in them. Adjusting the loops to flatten the seat, she settled herself onto the dissected tire strung up on thick rope. Clutching the swing, the rubber dug into her palms as she balanced her weight. The worn-out patch of dirt beneath her was marked by the indentations of her heels.

The sun illuminated the cumulonimbus clouds hovering over the sunflower field with scenery that took her breath away like a Thomas Kincaid painting. Every day, the foliage intertwined with her heart, filling it with joy. With each passing day, the lines around her lips deepened, evidence of her unwavering determination to overcome the challenges of running a business she and her husband started. A pit landed in her stomach, saddened by his absence once again, unable to enjoy the fruits of their hard work that brought both of them joy and sustenance.

THE LAST REMAINING vehicle left Chester Farms, marking the end of activity. At the bottom of the driveway, the employees gathered on the open patch of land to leave for the evening. As water flowed down the nearby stream, it drowned out the noises from the patrons, bringing a sense of peace as they started the transition back to lives of their own. Yawns became released from their mouths after a tiring day of providing entertainment. Zippers on jackets and purses securely held paper paychecks for recipients to cash and use for bills and living expenses.

Inside of the Chesters' family home were a group of ladies sitting around the kitchen table for their Thursday night activity: bridge. The flickering lights in the chandelier highlighted pastel hues of painted florals. Leftover beans and beef from the chili exchange were heated in the crock pots after their friendly meal. As the group shuffled their cards for the final round, the air became filled with the sweet smell of cornbread.

"Your turn to shuffle," said one lady, passing the cards to Gemma's space.

Gemma elongated her neck while turning around to acknowledge her turn. Soap suds pruned the tips of her fingers as she scrubbed each bowl in her sink.

"I think I'll sit this last round out," Gemma said, placing two spoons into the next sink.

"You can't just sit out of bridge!" hissed another one, straightening the sleeves on her shirt.

Sitting in the corner, Janice let out a chuckle. The linoleum tiled floor became sprinkled with crumbs from her chocolate chip cookie. She concealed her mouth with her fingers to avoid showing the food stuck in her teeth.

With sarcasm, Gemma asked, "Aren't you glad you came out to see this? Pretty lively bunch out here!"

There was a scratch on the record player as Neil Diamond's record moved to the next song. Low beats to "Sweet Caroline" grew with its crescendo; Gemma's head tilted back and forth to the sound, allowing her heart to fill in reminiscence.

"Yes, I am," Janice said as she patted the napkin on the corners of her lips, checking the paper for any lipstick that might've escaped her skin. "I always wanted to know what life is like behind the success of the farm."

With a touch of sadness, Gemma's friends exchanged a gentle smile, their lips upturned, hiding their teeth. Their fingers picked up the cards to move them closer to their faces like a fence; the queen of hearts couldn't keep her army strong enough through the sadness.

"I'm just your average farm girl," she responded, rinsing off the last of her dishes. "I eat meat and potatoes just like everyone else and keep myself entertained easily."

"What sort of entertainment do you partake in?"

"I have a never-ending pile of books to finish up in my library, for starters. I still have to finish *The Green Mile* before I dig into *The Game of Thrones*."

"That's quite a range of genres you read," Janice said, admiring the start of the plethora of books that were housed in her living room across the way. "What got you into that?"

"My granddaughter, Charlotte, introduced me to *The Green Mile*," Gemma said with pride. "She was always into the spooky reads. We watched *Carrie* together after we read the book!"

Janice removed herself from the group and headed toward the attached dining room. Light bounced off the white porcelain plates that were elegantly placed on the silky plum napkins and denim blue tablecloth. Her fingertips brushed against the shimmering spoons, flawlessly positioned alongside the forks and knives. The wine glasses caused twinkling fragments to fall onto a hand-painted mural depicting a charming cottage amid a rustic field, rich with textured tall grass.

Chesterfield couches in hunter-green formed a circle around the den, while one-inch squared tiles in charcoal and pumpkin adorned the fireplace at the center. The corner housed a single chair, surrounded by a multitude of books stacked from top to bottom.

C.S. Lewis had the children nearby with Aslan and the White Witch there for protection.

Shel Silverstein had poems ready for a whimsical beat.

Every Grimm fairytale was secured in their old, withered binding; their stories were ready to take her out of reality and into a world of fantasy.

A colossal bay window was located beside the chair. Sunflowers danced in the night sky, bidding farewell to the setting sun as it clocked out, just like Gemma's staff. Guided by the light, the bats chased one another to attract their meal.

"You have quite the space, Gemma!" Janice said, her hand wiped the surface of one shelf, finding not one speck of dust to cling to her fingers.

"Thank you," she said, talking over the ruffling of cards that were aggressively being shuffled by her pals.

Janice strolled along the subsequent hallway. Along the side door by the grand staircase, there were picture frames that lined the hall. The black-and-white images were distinct among the mixtures of sepia tones and colored photographs, all of which had similar faces throughout the decades. Perms were higher and fuller with the neon hues from the teenage girls; mullets were more defined and facial hair was becoming more darkened by the others.

"Your family is so beautiful," Janice said, observing the space between their eyes as a common denominator along with the bone structures.

"This place wouldn't be what it was without them," Gemma said, joining the anchor in her self-guided tour.

A tear shimmered in Gemma's blue eyes as she remained captivated by the breathtaking masterpiece at the foot of the staircase. The thick wooden frame of the structure had intricate carvings of vine patterns and was covered in pea-green paint. Behind the group of people, the sunflower field displayed a vibrant blend of yellow hues. In matching black outfits, a man and a woman stood surrounded by their children, with Gemma and her late husband in the middle. To highlight their connection, one group dressed in navy while the other group chose plum attire.

One girl stood on the outside, her orangish-red fishtail braid undone and contrasting with the others' polished appearance. The denim skirt had many holes and frayed bits peeking out, reaching her ankles. The crimson tank top straps peeked out from under her oversized, open knit sweater.

"That must be Charlotte," Janice said, pointing at the girl who stood alone. "I recognize her. My daughter went to school with her. Why is she standing by herself?"

"That is," Gemma said, her smile beaming. "You remember her father passing away shortly after Simon did. This was taken before Simon's passing."

"I'm so sorry, I completely forgot about his death. I was out in California that year. It was such a loss, him and his son," Janice said, cradling her arms. "It sounds like you've dealt with a good share of grief over the past few years."

"I have," Gemma said somberly. "James was my oldest. Charlotte came into the family when James married her mother. She can be a little different from other grandchildren, that little Charlotte, but I wouldn't have it any other way."

"Oh, my daughter has told me about her," Janice said, droning.

"She may not be blood, but she is still part of this family, and I'm proud to say that."

Janice noticed the laid-back nonchalant attitude portrayed in the picture. Charlotte's smile appeared more natural compared to the rest of her family. The smiles of everyone else seemed to be similar, their dimples defined and eyes vacant with pain as though strings were pulling the corners of their lips toward their ears. Gemma and Simon, standing side by side in the middle with mutual pride, Gemma's face the same as it is as she stands by Janice.

"It sucks that Simon had to go out the way he did. God, cancer can be quite the bitch!" Janice said.

The record player changed into the next song: "Cracklin' Rosie." With her eyes closed, Gemma's hand shielded her heart as she swayed in reminiscence.

"Neil Diamond was Simon's favorite singer," Gemma said, grinning. "I play him every night after work to remind me that the farm was a product of our love."

"That's beautiful."

"I feel like he's here with me when I hear that man's voice. All my worries about running the farm all by myself ease away with every song."

"Do your kids help you with the business?" Janice asked with concern. "Forgive me for saying this, but a woman your age should be careful about all the stress that comes with running a growing business such as yours."

"My kids are so busy with everything else in their lives. I don't want to burden them. I have a great staff that moves mountains for me. I get help from my grandkids whenever they have time to and I cherish every minute with each one of them every time they can help."

Janice examined the portrait, attempting to figure out which grandchild would be up for the challenge of helping her manage both the farm and the business. With all the kids resembling each other in appearance and demeanor, she couldn't confidently guess except for Charlotte.

Four additional figures in the portrait above the family created a small shadow in the sunlight. With bits of straw captured from a blow in the wind from their worn-out clothing, they were strung up higher than the rest. Each person had their own color palette, comprising a dark flannel shirt, oversized jeans, and black boots. Burlap concealed their faces, with buttons serving as eyes and stitched lines defining their mouths.

Scarecrows.

"Those look a little creepy," said Janice, her giggles were full of sarcasm. "Except this one. That one is a little cute."

She gestured toward the one located all the way to the right. Their attire consisted of various shades of red, complemented by a large black trench coat. Instead of buttons, two sunflowers were fastened on its face, unlike the other three; its eyes were so big it looked surprised.

"That's our suncrow!" Gemma said, admiring the piece.

"Suncrow?"

"Yes, suncrow. The grandkids made that one with me when they were much younger. The scarecrows out there were too scary, so they asked to make this one a little more fun. And the customers love it! They take their polaroids with them any chance they get."

"I see."

THUMP!

They returned to the kitchen to join the rest of the group. One of Gemma's friends slapped her handful of cards onto the table in frustration; the queen slid closer to the stack in the middle.

"This is horseshit," one hissed with anger. "They're cheating!"

"No, I wasn't," said another. "You're just bad at this game."

"Now, now. We don't get competitive in this house. It's all for good fun."

Neil Diamond finished his song. The record player changed discs with the needle navigating to the first track from War: "Why Can't We Be Friends."

"I think we should call it a night," Gemma recommended. "It's been a long day here and I think that tomorrow won't be much better."

"Yeah, I should head out too," Janice said, looking at her watch. "My cameraman must be snoozing in the van by now. I'm so glad you invited me over for dinner!"

"Any time, my dear," Gemma said warmly. "And bring back your little one next time!"

"I'll be sure to include all of this in my segment for next week."

"I look forward to watching it."

The group got up and headed toward the coat rack. One at a time, they individually donned their cardigans and slid into their penny loafers. Taking a last look at her compact, Janice applied another coat of lipstick. With their victory plans thwarted, the first pair stormed out through the entrance, slamming the door behind them.

"It's just a card game, geez," said Janice, shedding one last wink toward Gemma before following behind.

THUMP!

"What was that?" she asked Gemma, her eyes scoping out the room behind her.

"It was probably just something knocked down from the impact of the door," Gemma said dismissively. "Off you go, now."

To bid farewell, Janice subtly moved her head. She trailed behind the four who were making their way outside at a slow pace. Their shoes smacked against the garage floor, causing the cement to clap.

Gemma locked the door behind them, using both the knob and the deadbolt for extra security. Walking past her family, she made her way to the bay window down the hallway. The headlights illuminated the house as each car started, gradually fading away as they left, vanishing into the darkness down the gravel driveway.

Gemma made her way to the kitchen and grabbed a polka-dot mug for herself. When she turned on the gas, the stove emitted a click, ready to ignite the flame. With a firm grip on the handle, she opened the top of the tea kettle, allowing water to flow in from her sink.

THUMP!

Concern filled Gemma's mind. Doors stopped banging, and no irate players disturbed anymore. Before entering the dining room, she set the kettle on the stove. From the bay window, she viewed the deck encircling the entire side. The knick-knacks stayed in place, and nothing knocked over the chairs. Only the hammock moved in the breeze, swaying like a pendulum. Upon entering the den, every cushion remained in its proper position, and no books had fallen from their resting place.

THUMP!

With each passing second, the kettle's whistle became more and more aggressive. Gemma ran into the kitchen to take it away from the heat, pouring some water to soak the tea bag in her cup. Twirling the string, she made the bag bob along the surface like a buoy. A cloud of steam rose from her face as she blew on the mixture with force. She let the warmth soothe her chest as she gazed across the room. The issues of *National Geographic* were stacked in their typical fashion, with the latest edition placed at the top. Beside the stack, there was a brown circle that had seed fragments sticking out. Scattered on the ground are yellow petals, wrinkled from being removed from their stems.

A sunflower.

THUMP!

The floor became scattered with shards of glass. Churning in her stomach, Gemma's heart palpitated with a sudden jolt. Placing the cup on the counter sent a shiver down her spine.

"H-hello?" Gemma asked, her voice raspy from the water's heat.

She paced into the hallway. The pieces on the floor reflected light. Tiptoeing around the shards, her heart sank when she looked at the portrait. Cracked and broken, the remaining pieces of the family photo formed a spider web-like pattern in the center. Touched by the harm inflicted on her loved ones, a single tear streamed down her cheek.

Moonlight illuminated the gloss on the bookshelves with the plastic finish on some of her books absorbing it. More sunflowers were placed around the chair, with petals scattered near its four legs. Sitting upon the cushion was a man; his skin was palish-gray with bits falling apart. Insects moved within the decomposed wounds, revealing a protruding cheekbone.

Simon.

Gemma retched, her stomach tensed, and her legs grew weak. Despite the fatigue in her legs, she sprinted up her stairs, ignoring the need for rest. Running down the hallway, she passed by every room that once belonged to her children, doctored up and modernized to allow her grandchildren to stay, checking to see if there were signs of intrusion. She entered her bedroom and got down to the floor to grab a case hidden beneath the bed. Taking out a shotgun, she unfastened the case. While her fingers trembled, she struggled to load the shells into the barrel, her mind racing with questions about her deceased husband's presence in the house.

THUMP!

The record stopped playing; the needle fell off the track on the disc. Closing the chamber made Gemma's breath tremble. She cautiously descended the hallway, scanning for any signs of movement, but saw nothing. Peering down from the banister, her chin trembled as she gazed at the shards of glass below the stairs.

"I know you're in here!" Gemma said, her grip on the shotgun slipping from the sweat on her palms. "I'm going to give you to the count of three to get your ass out of my house!"

The silence in the room lingered. Absolute stillness reigned in the house.

"One!"

The pain in her chest intensified as her heart beat faster. The metal surface of the gun became fogged up by her breath as she held it pointing at the ceiling.

"Two!"

Getting a firmer hold on the weapon, she readied herself to defend what was hers. There were no doors flinging open or objects crashing to suggest a retreat.

A metal object penetrated her overalls, piercing her side. Catching her breath was impossible as Gemma screamed in pain. Pushed deeper into the blade from the other side, she felt the firm grip caused by a gloved hand. Down the stairs tumbled the gun, resulting in a discharge at the opposite end of the hallway. Gemma's ears were invaded by the sound of ringing moments before her attacker propelled her forward.

Wood shards broke off, causing slivers to embed in Gemma's palms. With each step closer to the bottom, her breath became shorter in shock. With her artificial knee detached, her bones snapped, fracturing through her skin. Slicing through her face, the glass caused her to tremble and squirm on the floor, desperate for an escape.

The creaking of the floorboards accompanied each step down the stairs under the weight of Gemma's unexpected visitor. Blood streamed from Gemma's sliced forehead, filling her eyes and making her vision blurry. As they approached, the silhouette became clearer, wearing baggy jeans adorned with patchy bandana fabric in various colors. With every stride, the boots would kick the hem of the black trench coat. Tattered and with straw poking out, the red flannel was in poor condition.

"W-who are you?" Gemma asked in terror, her grip slipping as she tried to crawl away.

The burlap draped over its face made its features more distinct in the light. In her eyes, two sunflowers greeted her as they removed their hat.

Suncrow.

Gemma's energy was depleted with nowhere to go; there was too much blood pooling around her body for her to get a good grip. As the business owner withered, the suncrow knelt down before them. The moonlight glimmered on the blade as it cut into her neck, causing more drops of blood to trickle.

Gemma felt uneasy as her artery opened, blood streaming onto the floor. Everything became lighter in her head; the room was spinning and becoming whiter but darker at the same time. The feeling in her fingertips and toes faded before spreading to her limbs. Blood filled the hallway as her life slipped away, forming her final resting place near the broken image of loved ones who had once completed her.

Chapter 2

S aturday

ON THE GRAVEL ROAD, the red station wagon meandered, raising dust that mingled with the cloudy sky. While driving through the countryside, the mother and daughter witnessed the fleeting presence of trees. James Galway's greatest hits playing on the cassette player had a hypnotic effect on the younger one, particularly the flutes. As the vehicle raced on, the cattle became a mere blur, while a young red-haired woman gazed out the passenger window.

"Don't you just love him, Char?" the mother asked, trying to gather the attention of her daughter, who was resting her head.

"Sure, Katherine," said the child.

"Please don't call me Katherine. I'm your mom."

Charlotte Rollins directed her gaze toward the sky. The sorrow burdening her heart caused a single tear to cascade down her cheek, as she discovered her grandmother's transition into the land of the dead. No more memories of enjoying coffee flavored ice cream after a dip in her swimming pool. No more book recommendations since she's the only one she knew that was big into reading, bigger than her. No more gathering the family together and being the person to keep everyone on track to being cordial with one another.

She was gone, and her life was over.

Click!

Katherine flipped the tape to hear additional symphonies on the second side. Charlotte usually enjoyed this music, as Gemma introduced both of them to James Galway; what got her hooked was that he played "Somewhere in My Memory" from the *Home Alone 2* soundtrack. She preferred *Home Alone 2* over the first because of her arachnophobia and dislike for Buzz, and the New York setting made it even more appealing to her since she had dreams to leave the Midwest.

Now her heart was broken, and watching either of the two was hard.

Katherine took every opportunity to look at her daughter. Similar to other parents, she would go to any lengths to comfort her child. They've lost enough people in their lives in such a short time with her husband and son, and later her father-in-law. After her mother-in-law left, she found herself unsure of what steps to take next.

TWO YEARS AGO, THE school convened for another day. Students diverted their attention by showcasing the latest fashion trends featured in Seventeen Magazine. *While some had a crush on Jonathan Taylor Thomas, others desired Sarah Michelle Gellar. Others focused only on movies starring the Olsen twins. Charlotte chose to be alone and disregarded the chatter among her classmates. She had no interest in any of their topics; in fact, she couldn't wait for Mary-Kate and Ashley to grow up so they would no longer be everyone's obsession. No one else had the same enthusiasm for talking about Green Day or Mr. Coffee as she did.*

The bell signaled the start of history, her most dreaded period. To make matters worse, today was the day the class would find out their grades for the test on the American Revolution they had taken the previous week. She had little interest in history from the start, knowing that her textbooks contained fabricated narratives that instilled false beliefs in her peers. Her assignments suffered because of the discrepancy between her researched answers and the teachings.

"All right, class," said Ms. Trapp, adjusting her thick spectacles along the bridge of her thin nose.

The class hushed, with murmurs dwindling to almost nothing. A final paper airplane soared through the air, performing a loop de loop before hitting Charlotte's head and breaking its tip. A lone spitball landed on the corner of the chalkboard with saliva splattered along the moistened paper.

"I'm sure you're all eager to find out how you did on your tests," Ms. Trapp continued, reaching for the stack on her desk.

A dry gulp escaped Charlotte's throat, leaving it scratchy. Anticipating her results, she picked at the flakes on her cuticles, trying to control her trembling. The thought of her grade dropping below a C-terrified her. While she had accumulated enough credits to graduate in the spring, her stepfather wouldn't accept anything less than average.

"Overall, you guys did okay. I think some of you need to apply yourself more."

As the teacher handed out the tests, the pressure mounted. A range of emotions were displayed as one student celebrated their perfect score, while the student behind them became deflated upon receiving a failing grade. The next pair displayed a lack of concern as they giggled at their mediocrity, comparing their incorrect answers written at the top of their desks.

Sliding along the surface of Charlotte's desk, a packet of papers came to a halt against her body. Red covered most of the front page with symbols catching any grammatical and spelling mistakes. She deserved that. Apart from that, the instructor graded her responses as incorrect because they contained inaccuracies related to the content covered in the lectures. Her answer about the result of slavery after the Revolutionary

War ended earned her a big "Wrong" written next to it; she stated that some were freed, but most were not. Ms. Trapp's eyebrow arched sharply when she read about owners breaking promises to free soldiers.

Charlotte's heart sank as she glanced at her paper and saw the capital 'D' etched onto it like a scar on her heart. Observing Ms. Trapp, the adult rolled their eyes in annoyance and proceeded to separate the pages by licking her finger, then handed the next test to the student behind her. She already knew what her stepfather's reaction would be.

MAKING HER WAY TO HER locker, Charlotte dragged her shoes on the floor. She experienced the defeat of having to reveal her grade to him, who had been eagerly waiting to find out. Her mind raced, trying to find any sort of reasoning to defend the grade. Regardless of her past statements, he was unwilling to acknowledge it.

Paper balls thrown into the air brushed Charlotte's cheek. Chuckles resounded in the hallway, overpowering the noise of screeching metal from the lockers. Disregarding their foolish behavior, she used her hair as a shield to isolate herself from her peers.

The sliding foot caused her ankle to twist, resulting in her falling to the floor. Grains of dirt and sand poked into her palms. Among the pocket lint and shedding hair from students, a solitary dust bunny tumbled near her face. The laughter grew louder and more powerful than ever. With an eye roll, she gathered herself and pushed through the knee pain from the impact on the cold, marbled floor.

"Sorry, I just noticed your hair was on fire," said one girl, her tone soft and innocent.

With an annoyed sigh, Charlotte brushed off the dust from her knees. Commentaries about the color of her hair were a constant burden for her every week.

"I didn't want to have it burn the brown marks on your face."

Or her freckles.

Charlotte proceeded further down the hallway, getting closer to her locker, accustomed to using the strategy of not acknowledging comments to steer clear of confrontation. Opening the door, a foot kicked her lower back, slamming her head with metal. Her forehead throbbed in pain, pulsating at the top. Frustration caused her knuckles to crack as she turned to see the same girl provoking her.

"Cut it out, Vanessa," Charlotte said, her body temperature rising.

"Or else what?" Vanessa said back to her, inching closer to Charlotte's face.

The girl's spit sprayed out of her mouth with force, moistening Charlotte's nose. Charlotte caught a whiff of the fruity Zebra bubblegum odor, tasting the warmth of saliva as it flowed into her mouth.

With a firm grip on a handful of her bully's hair, Charlotte took down Vanessa, feeling the sharp pain of her nails embedded in her cheek. Chants filled the hallway as others gathered around, exhaling cheers, hoping the popular one would make the victim falter. When Charlotte pulled the locks away from her scalp, screeches echoed in her ear. Ms. Trapp hurried toward the group, pushing aside any students in their path. Heels hitting the floor echoed like a Clydesdale's trot.

"That's enough!" she hissed at the students, tearing them apart from the group that huddled around the fight.

Peeling away the teenagers felt like removing layers from an onion; each row she went through ended up with an uglier reaction. Kids exchanged scowls and snappy comments, aiming to provoke the teacher.

As they got closer to Charlotte, Ms. Trapp reached out and grabbed her shirt from behind. Charlotte sprang back as if she had pulled a parachute's ripcord. As her fury dissipated, her skin cooled down from the calming effect of the adrenaline. Mucus built up in Charlotte's lungs as tears streamed down her face, unaccustomed to what she had to do.

"What on earth is going on here?" Ms. Trapp asked, fuming with curled ends getting more pointed.

Heads multiplied before Charlotte's eyes as the room spun. The classmates stifled their laughter as they watched the fight unfold.

"She started it," Vanessa said, catching her breath.

Seeking to emphasize her victimhood, she sobbed uncontrollably, her head buried in her hands. The onlookers showed their agreement by nodding to support the accusation.

"Miss Rollins! Detention! Office, now!"

CHARLOTTE RETREATED to her bedroom after she arrived home. Enduring the failing grade and hallway brawl left her feeling drained. On top of that, they tasked her with washing and erasing all the chalkboards in the school during detention. Layers of chalk left her hands raw as they formed a strange solution on her skin. Sweat had caused the tips of her hair to crinkle.

She turned the dial on her television, watching the last bit of Lag Wagon *on MTV. Getting out of this town became her primary mission. Graduation was within her reach, and she was determined to do whatever it took to reach the end of May.*

Charlotte's brother, Gabriel, walked past her open door, engrossed in his opaque-purple Gameboy. The speakers made tiny beeping noises every time Donkey Kong used a banana peel in combat.

"Can you play that somewhere else?" Charlotte asked, scooting closer to her television to tune out the noise.

"Like where?" he asked, his thumb pelting on the arrows.

"I dunno, maybe your room!"

Gabriel leaned his body, mimicking his character's movements on the tracks. He ignored her frustration; not a single sighing huff drove him away.

"Why are you so annoying?"

"Because I'm your brother, that's why," Gabriel said sarcastically, whipping his head back to flutter the blonde curls away from his eyes. "Now I died, dammit!"

"Serves your right, you twirp."

The sound of scuffling came from Gabriel's feet as he dragged them on the carpet. His Hanes socks created a burnt friction on his feet while he placed the device in his pocket. Charlotte passed his slow trot toward his room, guiding her hair behind her shoulders to go to the bathroom to scrub her face; the spit from her classmate made her skin irritated.

"Don't you have lines to memorize?" Charlotte asked as she turned the faucet on. "Your school play debuts in a couple of weeks."

"I know, but I don't want to do it."

Like a clumsy guard, he propped himself against the door frame using his lanky arms, his hands making only a slight contact with the top corners.

"I thought you loved to perform?" Charlotte asked, confused.

"I did at first, but once Dad got involved, it no longer became fun."

"I haven't seen Dad get on your case about the play."

"Every performance I've done before, he would pull me to the side before it started and tell me to not ruin it and that there are people that will look at me differently if I do."

"Really? Why am I not surprised?"

Charlotte contemplated, thinking back to the instances when he would behave similarly toward her. Whenever she ran cross-country in middle school, he would always say the same thing to her. She never saw his eyes widen in the audience during any concert she performed for band.

"Well, all you can do is your best and that's all that matters," she continued. "And if you don't like it, then you shouldn't have to be a part of it."

"Get real. You know he wants us to do something other than school. We are Chesters after all!" Gabriel said with defeat, tucking his hands inside the pocket of his hooded sweatshirt.

"We're not Mason or Alexandria! And we're most definitely not going to be like Olivia. Not even on a bad day."

Gabriel found amusement in comparing himself to the remaining cousins, apart from the obvious that he was thirteen while they were more in their late teens. They would never be like them, and this also applied to others like Noah or Lucas. They were never on the same wavelength, but when she stepped forward as the older sibling to offer necessary advice, they found a moment of unity.

DING!

Down the stairs, the dinner signal always triggered their hunger pains when it was time to take it out of the oven. On cue, their hands cradled their tummies, eager to nourish their growling stomachs.

"Time for dinner," he said, tossing his hair back once again.

Charlotte flicked her wet fingers over the bathroom sink after washing them, attempting to remove any remaining water after scrubbing. The plush fibers absorbed the last bit of moisture on her palms, gathering the yellowish-white chalk residue from detention.

She ran back to her room in order to turn off her television. Her arm touching the foil-covered antenna maximized the clarity of the picture. While returning it to its original position, music sheets fell onto the floor, covering her disassembled flute in its case. Her favorite piece, the one she had been working on all year for their graduation concert, was a solo rendition of "Memory" from Cats, the musical. Ever since Grandma Gemma introduced it to her, playing that song has always melted her heart. The sight of the aged cat wearing a torn fur coat on the video cassette, for some reason, gave her a sense of purpose and hope.

"Charlotte, are you coming?" her mother yelled from down the stairs.

"Yeah!"

Having closed the door to her bedroom, she started making her way to the dining room. She pondered over every memory that happened before the camera flash while gazing at the walls. By the fire on the camping trip, all four of them held sticks with flaming marshmallows lined up. Following her stepfather's desire for similarity, they managed to accomplish it on the fifth attempt, but one marshmallow melted off. The photo of her and Gabriel at the beach captured them lying by the shore as a small wave approached from behind, ready to attack them like a pouncing predator. Despite the freezing water and the risk of hypothermia, she persevered through four shots until she achieved perfection.

While descending the stairs, she noticed her calf muscles tightening and realized that their class photos were consistently chosen for retakes whenever there was a flaw or an awkward smile. Katherine sat at the head of the table; her face hidden behind the sheer veil of steam that rose from the bowl of spaghetti. Seeing Gabriel already digging into a piece of garlic bread from the basket next to him, she couldn't help but lick her lips.

Standing in the living room was her stepfather, his suit jacket still on as he dug his hand into the pocket. The jade carpet muffled his foot as he spoke with a man of equal refinement. The light bounced off the man's bald head, showing a touch of brunette that started growing from her stepfather's. Thick spectacles hid their eyes, except for a solitary eyebrow raised above the wire frame.

She appreciated the small radio playing music as she grabbed a plate from the kitchen. While she rarely enjoyed country music, there was one song that allowed her to appreciate it. Since it came out, Katherine would always play one of her favorite songs. Years after divorcing Charlotte's birth father, Reba McEntire was the one of the few who could empower her to move on from her funk.

"Fancy."

Her mother found renewed determination to carry on, thanks to something in the chorus. That song became an anthem after she recovered from her depression following her difficult divorce. The struggles Katherine had with dealing with Charlotte's birth father was hard on her; trying to maintain composure for her child that didn't know what divorce was or how he was when she wasn't around.

"Mom, did you notice the song?" Charlotte asked, a tiny smirk growing.

"Hell yeah," she said, elated.

"Honey, don't swear at the table," James hissed at her, interrupting the man in discussion.

Katherine suppressed a small chuckle. As she exchanged her happiness with her daughter, a wink escaped from her eye. She smoothed her blue scrubs and set a napkin on her lap. With spaghetti strands resembling chunks of hair, Gabriel pinched the tongs over his plate. Upon reaching for the garlic bread, Charlotte caused flakes to crumble onto the table.

"Charlotte, don't get too comfortable," her father said, his eyes gazing out the window behind the man.

Tomato sauce dripped down the ladle, causing Charlotte to freeze. The meatballs splattered onto the main course, causing red sauce to stain the woven, paisley floral tablecloth.

"If you haven't noticed, Dexter is here regarding you."

Dexter Munn was the family's attorney. James's parents' decision to open their farm to the public created the need for someone to handle the legal aspects of the business. With no hair on his head or jaw, his prominent feature was his bushy eyebrows. The flex of his muscular frame caused the seams on his impeccably tailored suit to stretch. Thanks to the money he received from his firm, and especially from the Chesters, he had the freedom to pursue his bodybuilding competition, a venture that always struck fear in those who dared to oppose him or his clients.

"H-hi Dexter," Charlotte said, rising from her chair, fighting back the teased growling in her stomach from being so close to eating her dinner.

"So, I just got back from the Cooper residence," Dexter said, his arms crossed over his pecs. "Care to share what happened this afternoon?"

Charlotte glanced at her mother, who propped her chin on her hands for support.

"Vanessa started it," Charlotte said, twiddling her fingers.

"That's not what she and your other classmates have told me."

"They're all lying!" Charlotte said in disbelief. "She tripped me and then spit in my face."

"Even your teacher said that you started it."

"She didn't see anything. She came over after it started!"

"Charlotte, I'm very disappointed in you," James said coldly, making his way closer to the table.

What else is new? *Charlotte thought to herself.*

"You need to be careful now that you're eighteen years old. The Coopers were considering pressing charges."

"They can't do that!" Charlotte said, a tear forming in her eye. "I was only defending myself."

"Until there is some sort of proof to work in your favor, you're the one that started it. Besides, they decided not to press charges."

I wonder how many times he flexed to scare them away.

"Well, thank you for your negotiating," her father said as he took his seat at the table. "I hope you have a good rest of your evening."

Dexter noted the dismissal and left through the door. With a gaze at Charlotte, he observed the innocence in her eyes, his lips pressed tightly together. A lone twinkle reflected from his eyes from the streetlight; there was one second where she saw he believed her, no matter how much was stacked against her.

Their lawyer closed the door as he left. The twirling of James's fork created a screech from the ceramic as it wound up the noodles. When he bit down on the meatball, his lips smacked and it wriggled between his molars. Charlotte poked around her plate, moving around the food; her stomach was no longer craving sustenance.

The rest of her family leisurely enjoyed their meal, filling the table with silence. Katherine and Gabriel refrained from making eye contact with Charlotte, who held their fascination by swirling the noodles in a linear fashion.

"So how did you do on your history test?" James asked as he reached for his glass of milk.

Oh, shit.

Charlotte expected that this news would be the final straw for him. The proof that he only considered what he sees and not the details was clear, even though she completed her work and answered the questions accurately.

"I-I got a D," Charlotte said, her eyes couldn't make contact with his.

When he poured a generous amount of milk, his throat made a click. With a forceful motion, he slammed the glass onto the table, causing white liquid to spray into the air like a bursting firecracker.

"I told you that you needed to pass this test!" he said, his tone growing more pointed with each syllable.

"I tried, Dad. I studied very hard."

"Not hard enough!"

"James, take it easy," Katherine said as she placed her fork next to her plate.

"No! I will not allow my child to fail her classes."

Katherine retreated to her seat, her hands running through her blonde hair as she sighed.

"I did my research."

"Oh, yeah. Here's that crap again. Was this test not accurate with what actually happened?"

"Yes!" Charlotte said, her hands sank into her pockets. "It's not my fault they're not teaching us the right information."

"Quit making excuses and take responsibility for your actions! Now everyone is going to know that you're failing. Have you thought about what other people are going to say when you tarnish the Chester name?"

Gabriel kept filling his mouth with noodles as she watched. While his cheeks were as round as a chipmunk, his eyes reflected the sadness he expressed in the bathroom. He is aware of the expectations established by their father.

"I don't care what others think!" Charlotte said, trying to hold back her anger.

"Why can't you be more like your brother?" James said sharply. "He gets good grades and is involved in many activities and doesn't get into any fights."

"Because I'm not him!" Charlotte said, kicking her chair into the table. The wood clunked into one another, sending an echo into the space that cut into the tension between the family. "And besides, I'm in band. Isn't that good enough for you?"

"Band is a class, not an extracurricular activity. Don't you think you should've done something more so that you can end up going to a good college?"

"I got into college!"

"Yes, some dinky little college. Look at your cousins. They all got into the university and are planning on making something out of their lives."

Charlotte's ears emitted a significant amount of warmth. The sound of crunching came from her clenched fist. Trying to resist the constant comparison, her knees shook with the effort to hold herself back. But this was the last straw for her.

"Then maybe you shouldn't have adopted me when you married my mom!"

"Charlotte, don't say that," Katherine said, grabbing her plate and taking it to the sink.

"No! It seems like I'll never be good enough for him. Why don't you just leave me alone and drop dead!"

In a fit of rage, Charlotte stormed out of the dining room. With each step, the hardwood floors echoed like a gunshot. She strained to hear James's ongoing bickering with her mother at the dinner table, as he desperately tried to justify his reasoning and comparisons. After slamming her bedroom door, she immediately collapsed onto her bed. Her eyes lingered on the framed photograph of the four of them, the singular picture that wasn't contrived. It was Christmas ten years ago. An abundance of fun and carefree innocence filled her memory. Instead, she had to defend against a different man she had always known. Defending herself brought forth a tumultuous blend of anger and pride in her stomach. She refused to apologize for standing up for what she believed was right.

Little did she know, those would be her last words to her stepfather. A collision occurred between his car and the ditch later that evening. The accident caused his vehicle to tumble endlessly with the front end and hood to be crushed, and it ended up upside down in the stream. To make matters worse, this was not only her last memory with her stepfather. James volunteered to be an extra chaperone at the school's play practice, taking his son to rehearsal and his final curtain call in Gabriel's life.

THE CAR ENCOUNTERED two hills steep enough to create a community sledding adventure. Air rushed into Charlotte's ears as it gusted through the cracked window. Guilt had consumed her every day since her stepfather and brother died two years ago, regardless of the urgency of her words. James tried his best to push her to be the best she could be, despite the complications in their love. He also was present in her life when her birth father wasn't during most of her adolescence, which was something that could make his frustrating qualities forgivable.

The player made a *click* as it finished ejecting another tape. Katherine reached inside the center counsel. Her face broke into a tiny smirk while she pushed the next cassette in. Guitars played before a familiar voice sang. When Charlotte understood her mother's intentions, a smile appeared on her face during her time of need.

"Fancy."

Chapter 3

The tape provided Charlotte with the perfect way to find her balance as the car drove past the nearby farms and up three additional hills. Before reaching the bottom of the driveway's steep slope, a cluster of pine trees greeted the car. Red paint was on a white sign, etched like chicken scratches the two words that no business wanted to see.

Closed Indefinitely.

With eyes darting in different directions, patrons queued up at the gate. They were eager to uncover the reason behind the closure of their beloved attraction. With tears streaming down their faces, the elders were determined to uncover the culprit and ensure justice for the victim.

As they drove up the gravel, they noticed two cars near the stream with cliffs looming above. As the wind blew, the sunflowers stooped, as if grieving with their heads lowered. Katherine waved at the worker operating the combine, noticing the fraying stems on its blades, and received a somber acknowledgement.

Gemma's house had two vans parked in front, one white and one black. A cord encircled her as she stood before a man with a camera perched atop his shoulders. She brushed her hair aside, letting the headlight illuminate every inch of her face.

"I'm Janice Cooper, reporting from the Chester farm," said the news woman.

Charlotte's body tensed as she pulled her shoulders closer to her chest. Running into this woman was the last thing she wanted, considering her mixed emotions. Since the altercation at school two years ago, Vanessa's mother has been the catalyst for escalating issues. Every time Charlotte strolled along the street, she always bumped into Janice and exchanged hostile glares. The local diner would fall silent as soon as Charlotte entered, disrupting Janice and her family's outing; her influence became contagious.

"It's been days after the untimely death of Gemma Chester, who was found brutally murdered in her own house. The face of the Chester farm is no longer in charge of the locally popular getaway with attractions and concessions the whole family could enjoy. There are no leads as to who could've committed this heartbreaking crime. The crime lab has painstakingly combed the house for evidence to close the chapter of this thrilling conclusion of Gemma's life. The family will close the business until the killer is found and new ownership is established. Action Three News has got you covered with all updates that come up."

The station wagon parked next to the black van. In a momentary glance, Charlotte and Mrs. Cooper locked eyes, revealing a hint of hatred in her hazel gaze. Despite the tension, Charlotte's motivation to reunite with the person she longed to see grew stronger.

There was a one-year age difference between Edward Chester and her stepfather. Even after James's unexpected demise, he continued to be the one who reached out to her every month. Even when James was alive, Edward would disregard his own aging to match her energy levels, making her experiences with the Chesters more enjoyable by chasing her around or dunking each other in the pool.

"Char!" Edward said, his crow's feet becoming more defined with his sparkling white smile as he met her at the passenger door.

"Uncle Eddy!" Charlotte's words were tinged with a melancholic joy.

He enveloped the young lady in warmth as he squeezed her in a tight hug. Through her denim jacket, she could feel his heart pounding against her chest. With no other father figure in her life, Katherine cherished their relationship, causing her mouth to tighten with a grin.

"How're you holding up?" her uncle asked, holding her biceps as he tried to gaze into the relief in her blue eyes.

Charlotte turned to see the patio by the side entrance. Twirling dead leaves covered the cobblestone, and a white wooden arch contained a growing assortment of vines. Amid the greenery, a strip of yellow plastic waved like a tiny flag. The loss became real as she read the black lettering, making her stomach churn. With her chin trembling, she became unstable and fell back into his arms.

Crime Scene Do Not Cross.

"I know, I know. It's going to be okay."

His hand delicately brushed against the top of her head, taking care to avoid the loops in her locks so as not to get entangled in the loose fishtail.

"W-why would someone do this to Grandma?" Charlotte said, choking on her tears.

"I dunno. We're going to find out who did this. I promise."

Agreeing with him, Charlotte nodded. With tears streaming down her face, she moved away from him and wiped them on the cuffed edge of her jacket, allowing the denim to soak up her heartbreak. Walking toward her, Edward leaned in to hug her mother.

"I'm so sorry for your loss," said Katherine, trying to remain strong for her daughter.

"Thank you. Yours too. How's everything been going for you?" James's brother asked Katherine, trying to steer away from further depression.

"It's okay," Katherine answered, her arms wrapping her cardigan around him.

"Don't worry," Katherine replied, holding her cardigan close to her blue-scrubbed top. "I've been working more shifts at the hospital. I can't ever say I'm bored. Got myself a shih tzu to help with the empty house."

"And how's Craig?"

"He's fine too."

Craig was her new boyfriend. Katherine struggled to talk to anybody after the death of her second husband, especially men. Her guard went up when any guy casually said a simple "hello." There was a feeling that she had a curse for the past two years, causing death for those she confided in. She proceeded slowly with Craig, giving him allowance to respect her grieving process and focusing on being there for Charlotte during significant moments like graduation and transitioning to college.

"That's good. You deserve all the happiness."

Katherine had a smirk on her face, grateful for his kindness. The brief moment ended as the door opened. A woman, tall and slender, appeared. Her gray turtleneck sweater matched the Coors Light can, and her high-waisted tight jeans had a light wash that was like the metallic mountain under the logo.

"Hi Marnie," said Katherine, softly.

With a dismissive wave, Aunt Marnie glanced out into the fields, her dainty French-tipped nails fluttering alongside her curly brown hair.

Charlotte made her way toward the rear of the station wagon. Opening the trunk, she greeted Janice, only to be met with the same insolence as Marnie was to her mother. The weight of her packed duffel bag caused Charlotte's shoulder to sag. Simultaneously, their doors slammed shut as they each walked to the opposite side to avoid crossing paths during their farewell.

Charlotte approached Katherine and hugged her mother, causing an interruption in her conversation with her uncle. Katherine planted a large kiss on the side of her daughter's head, then cradled it in her arm.

"I love you. Call me if you want to come home and I'll be over as quick as I can," her mother whispered in her ear.

Charlotte said nothing. She noticed the news van as it departed the area, ambling down the driveway. A veil of dust concealed the landscape of the sunflower fields, causing her eyes to water.

"And don't let your cousins get the better of you."

Those were the words Charlotte wanted to avoid thinking about. Despite the challenges, she trained herself to love her family unconditionally. The ride to the farm didn't provide enough time for her to ignore her feelings for them and hope they wouldn't remain the same people she knew from her childhood. It would be nice if this Cinderella could avoid dealing with the wicked step-cousins.

Despite being in the open air, she found the atmosphere stifling. She left her mother and Edward on the patio, placing her bag on the table as she walked away. She passed by Marnie, who took a big sip of her beer. The tall grass brushed the tips of her fingers as she distanced herself. Struggling up the hill, she felt her calves tighten, but the serenity of the sunflower fields made it worthwhile.

The aerial perspective revealed flowers that resembled corn rows, complete with meticulously maintained pathways crisscrossing the entire plot. From afar, the neighbor's farm appeared tiny, covered in thousands of yellow blossoms. With every hand-crafted attraction emerging from the foliage, memories from her childhood rushed back to her. Innocent giggles caused her heart to flutter delicately; every day with her grandmother was the best day she could remember.

She observed her mother's car departing the premises. Abandoned in the countryside, she felt like a child being left at summer camp with strangers for the first time. Even with Edward there, she felt like there wasn't somebody she could rely on with full confidence.

"Hi Charlie!" said a voice behind her.

A shiver ran down Charlotte's spine, causing her body to cringe as if icy water had surged through it. She released a small sigh, attempting to calm herself before the worrisome part of the moment she anticipated the least. As she turned around, she spotted the white-roped hammock swinging back and forth, bearing the weight of three bodies. Three smiles, just as radiant, expanded, revealing more defined dimples near their ears. These bodies contributed to three-fifths of her source of insecurity.

Her cousins.

Chapter 4

"Shit," Charlotte thought to herself, hopelessness approaching her like an iceberg to a ship.

With a deep breath, she sought to center herself and reinforce her inner strength by polishing her armor, her eyes fixed on the leaves hanging above her. A mother bird shielded their young, using her wing to cover them deep in their nest. Rabbits fled from their leaves, trembling to search for a bush further away.

"Hey!" Charlotte's words slipped out softly and lingered in the air, her smile strained with tension.

The trio of relatives swayed on the hammock, causing the rope to emit a faint creak under their weight. The girl at the end stretched herself as far as possible to distance herself from her brothers, particularly her twin, who was twice her size.

"Hi Olivia. You're looking so pretty today," Charlotte said, her voice shaky.

Olivia pushed her dark brown hair back, displaying her sorority's Greek symbols in the navy sweatshirt with pride. Sunlight bounced off her glossy lips as she pouted. The fluttering of the eyelashes resembled the wings of a butterfly.

"Are you kidding me?" Olivia asked, lifting herself from her seat in disgust. "We've been in the car for hours. I look like shit."

Just trying to be nice.

On the other side of the hammock, Olivia's brothers wobbled like a teeter-totter. Collapsing onto each other, they rolled away in revulsion from their touch.

"Get off me, Mason!" said the smaller cousin, trying to push the muscles off of his slim body.

"I'm trying, Noah!" Mason grunted, hoisting himself with his arms like he was preparing to do a pushup.

Charlotte gave a subtle smirk, careful not to provoke the three. Her family gatherings always meant one thing—making sure her cousins liked her. With Simon and Gemma out of the picture, the amount of people that fueled her soul had been reduced. With Marnie taking Charlotte's insecurities as fuel to expose her through Olivia and Mason, she wanted to tread lightly.

Noah and Mason dusted off the fragments of earth from their clothing. Mason plucked grass strands from his basketball jersey loops as if they were porcupine quills. Noah brushed his dark curls away from his face; the split ends of his curls puffed away from the humidity.

"So, how's school?" Charlotte posed a question to deter their frustration.

"We were so close to making the playoffs this year!" Mason said in defeat.

"Oh yeah. I was meaning to come to one of your games this year. Sorry."

"Don't hold your breath," his twin sister hissed. "If he doesn't keep up his grades, he'll lose his scholarship."

"My grades are fine! And what about you and all the frat parties you go to? Do you even go to class?"

The twins arguing reminded Charlotte of two feral cats fighting for a bowl of milk. Their fights always ended with a tantrum or outburst whenever one of them lost. Charlotte had to console Olivia many times when she was on the verge of tears, even though she would go back to mistreating her the moment she felt better. Marnie would always attribute Mason's wall-punching incidents to Charlotte, forcing her to disguise the truth as much as possible.

"I go to class!"

"Yeah, drunk! Laying in the back row passed out doesn't count for shit."

Prior to making eye contact with Charlotte, Noah rolled his eyes. With curiosity, his eyebrows, thick and bushy, raised up and down as he observed his siblings.

"And how have you been, Noah?" she asked the other cousin, ignoring their bickering as they stared daggers at another.

"I've been fine. I'm up for a promotion at Blockbuster Video." He straightened the top button on his royal-blue button-down shirt.

"That's great!" she said, sticking her hands into her pockets.

"I can't wait to be in charge. I need the money."

"Don't we all?" Charlotte quipped.

"Yeah, and when are you going back to school?" Noah said, his snarky persona snapping back as his siblings calmed down.

Charlotte's posture slumped, her shoulders drooping toward the earth. A gentle breeze tousled her hair, adding to her embarrassed demeanor.

"I-I don't know. When I'm ready."

Charlotte attended a college that was a three-hour drive from Mabel. The devastating loss of her brother and stepfather left her needing space. Finding her happiness again meant she thought she needed independence and a fresh start with a new group of people. She only lasted one year in academia before deciding to drop out, making her time there short-lived. Despite working tirelessly as a barista, her efforts resulted in homelessness and had to move back in with her mother because of unforeseen circumstances. Despite taking forty credits that year, she only had a mountain of debt to show for it, and not a degree.

Noah shook his head in disbelief upon hearing her answer. The twins crossed their arms as one of their eyebrows raised. Mason's bronze skin, along with the sun's illumination, highlighted their judgment as all three of their lips pursed.

"So, Mom's told us you work at the Dairy Queen again?" Olivia's smirk was evident as she spoke.

"Yes," replied Charlotte, attempting to hide her embarrassment by returning to her high school job, the scent of cooking burger patties lingering in her nose.

"Tsk tsk tsk. Our dad keeps talking about you and had such high hopes. It's a shame that you're wasting your life dipping cones."

I know. Don't need to rub it in. I'm doing the best I can!

A sudden burst of light blinded Charlotte, causing her retinas to become painful. She heard a small growl emanating from a device before her. As she rubbed her face, she observed Olivia holding a polaroid camera with the photo spitting out the front like it was sticking its tongue at her.

Fanning the photo in front of her face, Olivia burst into laughter. She sought to find the perfect photos for her collection. Her camera's luminous flash carried a techno-inspired energy that captivated the students around campus with every photo she took. Ink bled into the black, bringing vibrancy to the small, square image.

From the bottom of the hill, Edward's low voice echoed. "Kids, are you up there?"

"Yes, Dad!" Mason belted out like a quarterback.

"Come get your things out of the car already!"

Mason extended his arm across his chest to stretch his muscles. Noah trailed behind him, twisting his back to ease the strain on his spine, which had been tested during the long hours in the back seat of their van.

Olivia's eyes rolled and her feet scuffled, leaving her white jeans covered in a layer of dirt as a sign of defeat. She had no desire to engage in manual labor. Suppressing her tantrum, she flung the photo at her cousin, who picked at her fingers.

Charlotte breathed deeply, finding relief after her first battle against the words that weighed on her heart. No one was there to unite or support them in their distress this time.

Not her brother.

Not her stepfather.

Not her grandmother.

Charlotte took hold of the photo and gazed at the picture. The sunflowers had a hint of brown, which contrasted with the sepia undertone in front of her. Standing with her hands cupped, the young woman had a distant look in her eyes as if she were staring at a ghost. The yearning for normalcy in her family permeated her bones. A reminder that this weekend, the only person who had her back was the weakened person, whose face appeared startled in the picture.

Chapter 5

1985

THE STATION WAGON CONTINUED *its slow journey through the countryside. Despite the relentless snowfalls, the red metal remained free from rust caused by salted roads. Charlotte swung her feet above the back seat floor as the guitar played the beat of "Jet Airliner" by Steve Miller Band. Fidgeting with her brother's hands, she granted Gabriel a taste of the freedom with the air blowing in their faces. The electric guitar played its chorus as James tapped his hand on the top of the steering wheel.*

"Are you excited to see your cousins?" James asked, his hand wrapped around Katherine's.

"I am, I am!"

Charlotte hadn't been around her cousins for more than a couple of hours. Whenever she had the chance to visit the farm was rarely at the same time as the others. The times she would be in her birth father's custody would be the times that they would likely be around. She would envy the times her mother would have with his family while she sat in front of the television on Saturday morning, watching cartoons with an open box of Cheerios sprawled out on the coffee table. Katherine would spend time in the sunflower fields, while her father's girlfriend, who craved attention more than a child, overshadowed Charlotte's desire to play outside.

In 1980, Katherine and James met at the grocery store. James was at the C. W. Post Cereal while Katherine was checking out the newly launched oatmeal cylinders from Quaker, wondering if it would be suitable for her six-year-old. Katherine was knocked down by an elderly woman, causing a chain reaction of falling onto James and the stack of Bopperoos, Fruit Brute, and Magic Puffs cereal. As people rushed by, Corn Pops and Colorful Rice scattered on the floor, creating a crunch under their shoes. Embarrassed, they cleaned up scattered breakfast and filled the silence with small talk about Katherine's nursing career and James' accounting work. After completing the cleanup, James suggested grabbing lunch at the nearby Burger King, and that's when everything changed.

Katherine honored Charlotte's boundaries by arranging meet-ups only during her father's time. It took six months of dating, but eventually introductions became a possibility and Charlotte became smitten with James. Her attraction toward him was like how most children were drawn to his fun-loving spirit. He started spending more time with them and eventually moved in. Months turned into a year before Katherine became pregnant. James became motivated by her rounding belly to propose and promise a lifetime of happiness and love to his new wife and stepchild.

Gabriel's birth made Charlotte's life feel complete. When she turned seven, months of going to her father slowly disappeared into small visits of half a day. His devotion to his girlfriend eclipsed any hope of maintaining a passionate relationship during Charlotte's formative years. He had children with his girlfriend and visited only on holidays. Charlotte always wondered whether her father distanced himself or if his girlfriend influenced the decision.

Gabriel was the force that kept her new family united. He inspired James and brought out the best in everyone. Katherine's happiness and conflict resolution skills improved with James compared to her first husband. The sheer number of flower bouquets would make any passionate gardener jealous. Restaurateurs would be indebted to him for keeping their lights on by treating her to outings for celebrations such as renewing her nursing license or completing a marathon.

The car arrived at his parents' house and pulled into the driveway. A small sign near the gate confirmed the farm was closed. The hundreds of rows of stems brimmed with vibrant green, ready to burst into their joyful yellow petals. Two men cleared the roadside near the stream to prevent snakes from finding shelter in the long grass.

The property's beauty left Charlotte in awe, her eyes widening as she took it all in. The swing sets eagerly awaited her, anxious to be warmed up. Wooden boards featured characters with holes in their faces, painted in eye-catching pastel and electric colors, creating a whimsical backdrop for capturing humorous identities in photographs.

"Wow!" Charlotte said, the humming of the mowers calmed her down.

A smile spread across Gabriel's face, revealing seven gleaming little teeth in the sunlight.

There was a cluster of individuals standing in front of the house. Several children gathered in lines next to their parents, interrupting the game of tag. At the center were a woman and man in their middle age, their arms linked together, dressed in matching pairs of overalls and blue flannel shirts. The group's wave was a harmonious motion, like the soothing sway of palm tree branches.

James comforted Charlotte, saying, "Relax, there's no need to be nervous," as he turned off the car and unbuckled himself. "You met some of these people. You're going to love them."

Unfastening her seatbelt, Charlotte let out a smile of relaxation. Her brother's nonchalant wink provided her with the reassurance she sought.

"James, Katherine! How are you?" asked the oldest woman, who couldn't wait for the family to get out of the vehicle.

With a full and warm hug, she pulled Katherine from her seat to give her a tight squeeze. His father patted his back with love after James shook his hand. Charlotte's feet wavered on the gravel, accidentally submerging one of her shoes in the taupe puddle. She approached her and crouched down to her level.

"And how are you, Charlotte?" the woman asked, smiling. "Do you remember Grandma Gemma?"

Gemma's spouse approached her. When he bent down, his knees crackled. Reaching into his back pocket, he pulled out a flower that matched the size of Charlotte's head. The gigantic petals of the brown seeds appeared like a mesh, blossoming out in a radiant burst of happiness.

"And Grandpa Simon?" Gemma added.

Joy emanated from the little girl as she snatched the flower from his grasp and dropped it by her feet, where five petals grazed the puddle. Charlotte's grandparents each received a gentle squeeze on their necks, allowing them to give her a small kiss on both sides of her temple.

"I'm so happy you get to see the farm!" Gemma said with elation. "We're going to have so much fun!"

"And you'll get to play with all of your cousins," Simon said. "Just know that you are always welcome here."

"This place is amazing!" Charlotte said, her eyes admiring the flowers surrounding her. "Can I have this someday?"

"You sure can," Gemma said with a laugh. "You're the first to ask, so it's only fitting."

Gemma and Simon moved to the other side to greet the family's youngest addition, their laughter continuing as they played along with the joke. At this moment, Charlotte caught sight of the rest of the family, her giddiness at an all-time high with dreams of living at such an exquisite place. The kids who were around her age all had glazed expressions, their eyes widening to examine every part of the newcomer's appearance. The tear on her second-hand sweater was no longer endearing to her, as the two girls sneered at their own jumpers from C & C Children's Wear, which couldn't compare to any of her formal garments from Sears. Holding his football tight, the tall boy tapped with impatience, longing to play catch. The other two gripped their favorite army man by its plastic hands, letting the long rifle dangle by its strap.

"H-hi," Charlotte mumbled, slipping her clenched fist into the pocket of her stained denim skirt.

Not a single one of them uttered a sound. Charlotte was unsure if they were experiencing the same nervousness or if they had stopped accepting new members into their cousin's secret club. In the lineup, there were two adults from each side—a woman with blonde hair and two children, and a bald man with three.

"Come on, let's be nice to your cousin," the woman said, her hand gripping her daughter's shoulder.

With a flick of her ponytail, the bald man's wife reached into her denim jacket pocket. She tightly held onto a metal container and tilted its contents down her throat.

"Hi, I'm Lucas," said the blonde's son, reaching his hand out for an innocent shake; the ribbed cuffs of his long-sleeve shirt draping over his wrist. "And this is Alexandria."

Alexandria pulled her two icy blonde pigtails back and rested them on her shoulders. As she enjoyed her candy, she casually dropped the lollipop wrapper on the ground, letting the wind carry it away.

"And you remember Uncle Timothy?" asked their mother. "You met him before the wedding."

Charlotte remembered her Aunt Victoria and Uncle Timothy, along with Uncle Edward and Aunt Marnie. Meeting her stepfather's siblings was a wild combination of personalities. Edward was always nice to her, almost like he was an extension of James. Marnie was more bearable when she had water in her cup instead of the alcohol she enjoyed drinking. Their twins were distant with each other besides in the company of any newcomers. Noah played neutral to any of his siblings' antics. He would have to deal with either Olivia's tattling or Mason's punches whenever he stood in the way of their opinions. Charlotte vividly recalled their initial encounter at the local pizza joint, where Mason had established dominance over the rollerball game and issued threats to anyone who dared challenge him. The obnoxious scream and the ensuing ringing in her ears resulting from the claw machine's failure to snatch the desired teddy bear Olivia wanted to add to her collection. If Noah ever tried to be the older brother and offer comfort, Marnie would always turn against him and handle any disciplinary action.

Because of Victoria's role as a department supervisor at Montgomery Ward and Timothy's job as a travelling salesman, their availability was unreliable. Lucas and Alexandria were not around as often as the rest since their parents' work schedules were unpredictable. Charlotte's falling ill with strep throat on Katherine and James's wedding day ruined her chance to meet with Lucas and Alexandria, causing her to stay at her paternal grandparents' house. The times she spent with Victoria and Timothy were less cringeworthy than any other encounter with in-laws. Without work stress, they seemed more engaged in life beyond the time clock.

"James, I'm happy that you could join us," a voice from the crowd said.

A man stepped out as the handmade screen door groaned from the rusted hinges. Charlotte's outfit and the man's suit were equally shabby, featuring oversized sleeves that billowed from his arms.

"Dexter! How goes it?" James asked, waving his hand.

"Oh, you know. Just another day of work. I was told that the family was getting together, so I stopped by."

"Well, you know that you're a part of this family."

"The part of the family that pays you," Victoria joked.

The remaining members of the group giggled, then the adults joined him inside the house. Katherine reached her arm around Marnie, comparing notes about their admiration for Madonna and her release of "Like a Virgin." Katherine shared her story about her white costume at the Halloween party she attended with Marnie talking about her desire to fix her hair as the pop icon.

Side by side, the cousins looked like a baseball team with focus that wouldn't crack a smile. They swarmed around Charlotte; their shadows closing in on her. The door closing silenced Gabriel's cry.

"So, what were you playing?" Charlotte asked the group.

It took them a good minute to respond to her; the longest minute. Their lips remained parallel to the ground, showing no sign of curving into a smile.

"Yes, we were playing," Olivia said, her eyebrow raising slowly.

"Can I join?"

"Our mom says you're not an actual part of this family."

Charlotte defensively stated, "Yes, I am."

Mason clenched the pigskin and remarked, "We're different from them."

"You're not Uncle James's daughter," Noah said before looking at Mason. "You were brought to us."

"I know that. But Grandma Gemma says that it doesn't matter."

"Grandma's wrong!" Alexandria hissed, inching closer to the heartbroken outcast.

The icy blue eyes of Charlotte burned with both intensity and frigidity as she peered into them. Charlotte blinked quickly as the metal buttons on her overalls reflected light. As she observed, Alexandria's brother's eyes welled up in sorrowful tears. He clenched his fist and grabbed his jeans pocket to restrain himself from speaking up. Despite Lucas supporting her, the majority of children who shared their mutual rejection still overwhelmed them. As the door behind them opened once more, he bit his lower lip.

"Kids! Who wants to work on a project with me?" Gemma said, fluttering her fingers like innocent butterfly wings.

"I do, I do!" the children said with excitement, their energetic jumps covered over Charlotte, who sunk her head closer to her shoulders to hold back her tears.

"Let's go off into the barn!"

With the ball pelted to the ground, Mason said, "Race you there."

Sprinting to the other side of the farm, the group of cousins went past the closed wooden sheds that offered gourmet dishes to the establishment's customers. With each step, the children embraced the quiet with taking in the empty lot by running in circles and allowing the wind to caress their faces.

"Wait! Look at me!" Alexandria screamed, halting their venture when they crossed off the gravel onto the patch of grass.

She bent down toward the ground. With her shoes fastened by Velcro, she kicked her feet up into the air without a care for dangling shoelaces. When her billowing pant legs flipped down, it revealed her hot pink stockings. With the weight on her bent elbows becoming too much to bear, her arms buckled, and she crashed to the ground.

Gemma commended Alexandria and reached for Charlotte's hand to escort her. "Good job! You'll do the best cartwheels in no time!"

As they crossed the driveway, Charlotte squeezed her grandmother's hand with reassurance. Walking on the soft grass made her struggle to maintain stability. Wiping her nose with the cuff of her sleeve, she attempted to conceal her sorrow.

"I know they could be quite the handful, but they'll come around," Gemma said with her other hand brushing the top of the hedges like it were a railing.

"I know," Charlotte said in a solemn manner.

"Your mother tells me you love to read?"

"Yes, I do."

A smile brightened up Charlotte's face. She became more balanced in her energy, as if she had a conservative amount of caffeine. The colorful archways she passed by filled her with hope, encouraging her to integrate into the family.

"Perhaps I can read you one of my favorite books: The Lion, The Witch, and The Wardrobe,*" she said, Gemma's wink emphasized the love and sincerity that Charlotte eagerly sought.*

Both of them joined the others in the barn. Strands of straw, stacked a story high, fluttered in the air. The wet wood greeted them with moisture, showing the necessity of replacing the deteriorating boards holding the chipped siding. In the center of the structure, a lone table stood as Olivia and Alexandria skipped around it.

"Hey, be careful over there!" Gemma said.

Jumping back and forth on the guard that covered the rotating blades, Mason paused. Leaning against the equipment, Noah's hand came close to touching the faded red button at the center of the council. Positioned on the opposite side, Lucas sat on the sawdust heap, eagerly expecting the valve's release of more fragmented wood.

"Now, come along! It's time to make our annual scarecrow for the field."

The kids huddled around the table. Disgusted by the options, Olivia discarded the worn-out clothes, throwing them onto the ground. Every item Noah was intrigued by was dismissed by his brother.

"I think these pants will do the trick."

Gemma had a pair of jeans ready with ten patches, each in a different bandana fabric color, scattered around the denim.

"This color is the same as my dance costume!" Alexandria said, her hand patting the lavender swatch.

The hems of each leg had fluttering white and indigo strands from their cut stitches. Each child grabbed straw and stuffed it into the legs to give them more volume. Olivia clutched the grass, thoroughly inspecting for any bugs that could have taken refuge there.

"*Go ahead and grab some straw,*" *Gemma said, guiding Charlotte toward the stack with her hand.*

Mason's bony arm collided with Charlotte's shoulder, and she winced in pain. Brushing it off as unintentional, he shrugged his shoulders and Gemma didn't mention it. While tucking in the red flannel shirt, they proceeded to fill it. The volume around its torso expanded, as if it was inhaling deeply. With enthusiasm, the kids scattered around the table, each adding their personal touches to the collaborative masterpiece. Charlotte struggled with the black buttons, pushing them through the thread-stitched holes in the abundance of grass.

The figure had an arm that extended across the table, its muscles strong and well-fed from grain. Grasping the shoulders of a black trench coat, Mason vigorously shook it, as though removing dust from a rug. By hoisting it, the group helped to dress up the piece with the outerwear.

"*Almost done!*" *Gemma said.* "*This is turning out just wonderful!*"

Charlotte beamed as she observed her cousins' contented joy radiating from the group project. She held back from making creative additions because she hoped they would be more receptive to her if their headspace improved without compromising their vision.

"*Can we go out to the cabin now?*" *Mason asked.*

"*Can we, can we?*" *Noah cosigned.*

"*Yes, go ahead,*" *Gemma said, as she grabbed some brown utility gloves from the trunk she pre stuffed.*

The children bolted out of the barn. With a sudden rush of force, the children slammed the boards back into the frame, causing the plank to vibrate. Once more, Charlotte found herself alone in the company of Gemma and the scarecrow, her fingers picking apart the bits of straw clinging to her jeans when she shed a glazed look at all the details that came from everybody but her. The closest friend she had, other than Gemma, was just created on the table. The positive aspect is the inability to talk back and reject her with comments.

"Care to do the finishing touches with me?"

"Sure!" Charlotte said, her smile growing.

Charlotte dashed to the chest and rummaged through the items. The stench of mothballs wafted up her nose as she examined the vintage clothing spread out before her. Charlotte huffed on the dusty round gray hat from the 1920s, restoring it to its original shine.

"Perfect!"

They placed the head Gemma prepared on the stand. The red thread separated the fibers of the two large X's, forming multiple small ones that gave the impression of a mouth sewn shut. Another advantage of having a friend is that she can't talk back, even if they could speak. Placing the hat on top, the masterpiece was complete. The creation's human form had been completed with Charlotte taking in the warmth of Gemma's arm hugging her shoulders.

"All we have to do is string it up and it should be good to go in the fields."

"Wait, one more thing!" Charlotte said, racing back to the trunk with the most enthusiasm she'd had since arriving.

Two pieces made of yellow felt fabric, stiffened with starch, caught her eyes. Elaborate broaches were adorned with brown mesh in their circular shape. She placed two sunflowers gently on top of the eyes as she ran back. The striking color stood out against the plain burlap, resembling a surprised expression.

"Genius!" Gemma said with admiration, her eyes matching their creation.

"Thank you," Charlotte said, her stomach fluttering with happiness.

"I don't think that naming it a scarecrow would be fitting for this one. We need something more fabulous. Don't you agree?"

Charlotte pondered various ways to make it suitable for their creation. Nothing had a ring to it, not one word. But then it hit her. There was no need to completely reinvent the wheel. Sometimes, a small modification is all it takes to enhance a wheel's performance.

"I got it," Charlotte said, her hair bouncing as she jumped repeatedly.

"Well, come on then. What is it?" Gemma asked, chuckling.

"Suncrow!"

Gemma's face lit up with excitement. The connection for her project to her passion made the most sense. Admiring the figure, the name became the catalyst for the next addition to her business and progressing their relationship.

"Yes, suncrow. I love it!"

Chapter 6

The wooden stairs groaned under Charlotte's weight as she made her way down to the basement of the house. Various shades of blue created a calming atmosphere around the massive pool at the center. Mason thumped his chest, highlighting his toned pectoral muscles with repeated flexes. The reflection of light on the water's surface created shadows in the crevices of his well-defined six-pack abs.

Wrapping her robe around her, Charlotte found security in its coverage, safeguarding her vulnerabilities. The seersucker fabric got wet from the water drops caused by Noah's cannonball after he swung on the rope at the deep end.

"Charlotte, you made it!" Mason said, treading the water away from his body.

Olivia took off her black cover-up at a leisurely pace, revealing a fire-engine red swimsuit, much like Phoebe Cates in *Fast Times*, with no one around to impress except her family. The spandex hugged the curves of her slender body, with a high cut that extended over her hip bone.

Charlotte thought in disgust, *Look at her showing off,* as she saw her glide down the steps, her fingertips slowly moving along the metal railing.

Her skin became wet as the water rippled. Beads of water shimmered on Noah's dense chest hair while he drifted on the water, with his lower body submerged in the middle of the inner tube he swam to.

"Come on in. The water's fine," Noah said as he waved his hands to steer his device, his curls bouncing from the weight of the water.

Anxiety caused Charlotte's knees to shake. It has been years since she last went swimming, back when she was twelve during Christmas with the Chesters. When her body matured, her insecurities heightened. She was the last girl in her family to experience breast development, but hers were smaller than Olivia and Alexandria's. Her pride in her body diminished as she gained weight to shape her figure, with the fat accumulating in areas that were more toned in others compared to her. No matter what happened, she would not be better than her cousins, let alone in their league.

"I-I think I'll sit down for a while."

She walked over to the other side of the room, her pinky toe grazing the surface of the uneven cement blocks as she walked in her flip flops. Chlorine sprinkled onto her tongue from the twirling green and blue Nerf ball as it glided over the water, bouncing on the surface like a skipping stone. The metal pressed against her exposed thighs as she sat on the chair with chipped-white paint. Straightening her spine, she noted the firmness tight against her skin.

Every splash from her family brought memories rushing back to her mind. They may have all been adults, but they knew how to let loose and have some childlike fun when it mattered. Laughter filled her thoughts as she remembered a safe space where opposing sides could gather for an hour to relieve their stress. Fond memories for her involved racing to climb the rope to the top and gathering as many glow sticks in the deep end as possible with only one breath.

The glass on the metal table wobbled, spilling a bit of wine onto the floor. The following seat was taken by her aunt who slumped into it. With her arm resting on the surface, Marnie reached out for her niece's hand and saw the black polish twinkling in her eyes.

"How've you been, dear?" Marnie inquired while wearing a smirk.

Charlotte grasped the arms of her chair, saying with reservation, "I've been fine."

"Are you really?"

Charlotte was unsure how to reply. It was hard to predict how her relationship with Marnie would evolve. She needed to be careful with her words as Marnie could use them against her. Charlotte's comment on Olivia's revealing outfit one time resulted in a rumor that she called Olivia a harlot, and she didn't even know what that was. Marnie would occasionally confide in Charlotte to share gossip without fear of being judged. Charlotte found herself in a losing situation where nobody would believe her side, even if she chose to confide in someone.

"Yes, everything is fine."

"How's school been?"

You already know.

"I dropped out."

"Really?" Marnie asked, her tongue thickened with a slur.

"Yes."

"Why?"

Have you been living under a rock?

Charlotte's face stayed stoic, not displaying any vulnerability. Despite her best efforts, the bottom of her eyelid twitched as she tried to maintain composure.

"Did you fail out? I thought you were one of the best in your class."

I was. Just not good enough to land scholarships to pay for it.

"I didn't."

"Then what the hell happened?"

Charlotte watched as her cousins raced from one side to the other. Before diving underwater, they counted down and used the edge as a guide to propel themselves with maximum momentum. Three pairs of arms thrashed about as they moved their bodies forward like propellers in a motor.

"My loans didn't go through."

When her loans didn't process properly, she didn't have the time to get the payments squared away. With only a single parent's income, there wasn't a lot of support available for her, especially on a nurse's salary. Her savings were meager and with the Chester farm being such a success, Gemma offered only her sympathy and Charlotte didn't want to ask for anything more since she wouldn't help any other grandchild.

"Oh, honey. I'm sorry. You should go back."

"I told you, I can't until I pay off my unpaid balance. Plus, all my loans are in default."

"Look at Mason and Olivia. They're being responsible adults and managing their education just fine. Why can't you be more like them?"

Because they're getting a free ride off your dollar.

"Think of all the memories you can make with joining a sorority or going to a basketball game."

That's all they do, from what I heard. They don't even go to class.

It was as though Marnie was listening to be heard rather than hearing to listen. Regardless of Charlotte's response, she always had a prepared reply to reject the statement. Despite all attempts, her aunt remained steadfast in her conviction of her children's superiority.

"And don't you think that it would make the family look bad that you're not doing anything with your life?"

"I am doing things!" Charlotte raised herself from her chair, teetering it back from the thrust of her backside.

Marnie's olive eyes widened and twinkled as she looked through the sliding glass door. Worried about her drink being wasted, she reached for her glass.

Charlotte stormed off from her aunt, no more accepting her criticisms. As she turned to look at her, Marnie noticed a lone tear formed as a sign of her heartbreak. Trying to shield herself from others' unrealistic expectations was causing her armor to weaken and deteriorate. Even with the obstacles that marred her journey, many people were unwilling to approve of the route she took in life. Every insult felt like a hard slap in the face, eventually turning into a brick wall she walked into.

SMACK!

Her face landed amidst two muscular pecs, like a set of solid cushions. Her fingers contacted his washboard abs as the light above his bald, bronzed head blinded her, causing her fingers to slip into the thin side of a red speedo. While trying to assist her disoriented demeanor, Dexter's swimsuit slid down.

The blocks made her footing stumble with the shock of Dexter's body as she fell over the edge. With water rushing up her nostrils, the weight of her soaked robe made it challenging for her arms to stay buoyant. Inhaling chlorine, portions of the pool entered her throat. Dexter leaped into the water, extending his arm toward Charlotte like a hero from *Baywatch*. Trying to maintain her grip, her hands slid on his smooth skin while her feet brushed against his shaved thighs.

"Come on, Charlie! You know how to swim!" Olivia said, chuckling as she wrapped the towel around her hair.

Somehow, all the lessons Gemma taught her have flushed away. She thrashed in the water like a fish struggling in a small pool. The waves expanded, splashing beyond the edge and wetting the bricks.

Dexter steered Charlotte to the edge, saying, "Calm down, Charlotte. Let me help you."

To quell the hunger pains that were emerging, she coughed as her stomach filled with water. She felt like she was drowning on the inside, even with the offer of help. Despite being familiar with people, she felt the heavy weight of loneliness. Despite her hopes for a brighter future, days filled with depression and loss constantly overshadowed them, enveloping her like a dark cloud.

With the family lawyer's help, she was able to push herself onto the ladder, feeling the cold metal against her palms. After clutching it tight, she leaned her head against the step, shedding tears of shame that blended with the chemicals. She peeled off the soaked robe, watching it sink downwards just like a sandbag.

Dexter crawled out of the pool. Loads of water trickled from the small bits of spandex that were protecting his privates as he readjusted his swimsuit for coverage. After grabbing the nearest towel, he took Charlotte's arm and led her up to the main level. The water streaming down her legs from the black one-piece caused her pasty-white skin to glisten. The towel draped over her back as Dexter enveloped her in his arms. As her vision cleared, the first thing she noticed was the fabric clinging to his groin.

Charlotte wrapped the ends around her body as she said, "Thank you."

"Sorry to scare you," Dexter said as he grabbed another towel to wrap it around his hips. "I just figured you all wouldn't mind that I went for a dip."

Charlotte's body trembled from the sudden freeze of the water, feeling the chill. Positioned behind the bodybuilder, her aunt rested a hand on her chest to suppress her laughter and prevent the wine from dripping from her lips. Noah's gaze held sorrow as he disregarded his siblings' entertained responses.

"I told Eddy upstairs that I'll be back on Monday to read the will. I won't receive it until then, which should give enough time for the entire family to show up and make themselves at home."

Dust drifted from beyond the glass door, building up like a storm cloud with mix of smokey gray and taupe from the exhaust and gravel. At the top of the stairs, the door swung open and Edward's head appeared. Light above flickered, reflecting off his head.

"Aunt Victoria and Uncle Timothy are here!" he said, to rile the children's excitement.

Mason and Olivia ascended the stairs with jubilance. The last remnants of water hit the wooden boards of the steps. Noah reached out to Charlotte, gently patting her shoulders to offer his condolences for losing her balance. Removing the towel, Dexter bid farewell to Charlotte before diving into the water to resume his swim.

This was all too much, and that was only the first half of the family.

Chapter 7

The dust cleared up as soon as the crew went outside. Two vehicles parked parallel to one another; one hunter-green van and a white BMW. Charlotte nestled into her towel, clutching it like a child would a safety blanket. Suitcases tumbled out as the van's trunk sprung open. Arranged luggage stacked like a neat heap of clutter.

"Shit! Don't scratch my luggage!" screamed the young blonde woman.

Rushing to her suitcases, Alexandria ran her hands over them, inspecting for any dents or scratches. Like soldiers in formation, she lined them up next to each other, grunting from the manual labor.

"Chill out, it's not a big deal."

Lucas slid the door closed. He placed the cushioned pad on his trapezius before securing the strap of his black Nike duffel bag over his head. Ready to receive the family's warm welcome, he opened his arms wide for hugs. As she collected the rest of her things, Alexandria rolled her eyes. She pushed her hair behind her ears and used her plaid-blue pleated schoolgirl skirt to wipe away the dust off her hands.

Good god! You're only here for a couple of days!

The parents dashed over to the children, causing a bustling scene as each cousin greeted one another. Olivia sprung up to Timothy with her legs raised and her coverup moving upwards, displaying the contour of her rear. Mason's exposed chest caused Lucas's black t-shirt to become damp.

Victoria maneuvered her way out of the crowd to find her brother and niece. A warm smile that emanated from her lips enveloped Charlotte. Her hands stayed near her chest as she was caught off guard by the ambush.

"Charlotte, how've you been?" Victoria asked jubilantly, her smile full of warmth.

"I'm okay," Charlotte stated, detecting her aunt's heartbeat under her gray sweatshirt. "I'm so sorry for your loss."

"Yours too."

Victoria peered into Charlotte's eyes, seeing through her defenses to recognize the concealed sadness within. Victoria, just like her uncle, was open to including Charlotte in the family. Katherine, preoccupied with work to sustain her family, sought solace from anyone willing to be there for her daughter during her hardships. Even prior to James's accident, she was an excellent resource for guiding through life and providing a different perspective on changes in her body and feelings toward boys.

Following his wife's lead, Timothy joined in. His salt-and-pepper hair gleamed like scattered specks of glitter. Charlotte's ribcage cracked as he hugged her.

He acknowledged Charlotte with a solemn smirk, saying, "Good to see you."

"You too."

He provided a good balance for her aunt in both personal and professional aspects. Victoria would give advice on growing his salesmanship as he would be there for her during the store's difficulties, particularly during the holiday season and annual inventory audits. Knowing the importance of balance, they could switch between living in the moment and buckling down to work toward success.

Charlotte's body stiffened when Timothy brought in Alexandria, who then extended an arm over her shoulder. The cousin touched Charlotte's shoulder lightly as she patted it twice, their hands barely making contact.

"Hey booger," she murmured to Charlotte.

The nickname Alexandria gave her made Charlotte's stomach churn. While the other grandchildren went for alliterative names, Alexandria stood out by using embarrassing ones. The nickname "booger" has its roots in the time they spent playing in the barn, where Charlotte inhaled too much dust. After three episodes of relentless sneezes, she finally could join them once again, only to discover that her black shirt glistened with dried up bits of snot trickling down the neckline with embellishments of boogers at the end of each stream.

"How're you?" Charlotte inquired softly, attempting to steer away from the mockery.

"I'm good. Thanks for asking!"

They locked eyes in a tense standoff. Like Marnie, she possesses the skill of seeing through others, which she cleverly exploits. The silence was heavy, broken only by the chirping of orioles in the trees. With a raised penciled eyebrow, she relished ignoring her every second.

Timothy patted his daughter on the back and said, "Tell her about how you got into the nursing program, sweetie."

"Oh, yeah, I got into the nursing program at school," Alexandria echoed with enthusiasm.

She said nothing further. It was as though her uncle was talking to the opening of a cave with only darkness to talk with and nothing more to contribute other than repetition.

"And soon, you'll get to be like your Aunt Katherine," Victoria added.

"Yep."

Alexandria quickly joined the other children after leaving the group. Her energy spiked as she embraced Olivia and Noah tight, as if she had just downed an espresso shot. She shared the news of her acceptance into nursing school with her cousins, her excitement escalating with each repetition.

Charlotte ignored the mutual disdain and approached her cousin, whom she felt most connected to. Lucas and Alexandria, despite being siblings, have distinct personalities. While he joins in the activities with the other cousins, he always attempted to include Charlotte in any way he could. Just like their parents, the children seemed to be a balance of good and bad. Charlotte embraced Lucas, wrapping her arms around his body in the most genuine hug she had given since she arrived hours ago.

"Charlotte," Lucas said, echoing Charlotte's energy.

She was reluctant to release her grip. Her support network has shown up, and she wanted to absorb the inclusion for as long as possible.

"How have you been?" Charlotte asked, breaking away from him quickly, the wind slapping her bare skin.

"I've been good. I made the Dean's List at school."

He wasn't as enthusiastic as Alexandria would be when around Olivia or Mason. His lack of pride was clear in his tone, despite his accomplishment.

"That's great! Congratulations!" said Charlotte, grabbing his forearms and shaking them with a jolt of supporting excitement.

"Thanks. What about you?"

Charlotte glanced around as most of the group went indoors, with Mason and Noah carrying Alexandria's luggage. A slight flash of light winked at Charlotte as Olivia extended her arm to capture a snapshot on her polaroid camera. Alexandria and her had a close embrace, leaning their cheeks together with smiles showing perfect teeth framed by glossy lips.

"I've been working a ton," Charlotte told Lucas, with Victoria and Timothy paying close attention.

"That's great!" Victoria said with encouragement. "At Dairy Queen, right?"

Charlotte's fingers fiddled with each other. Her shoulders hunched, remembering her encounter with Marnie. She'd had enough opinions on where her place of employment would reflect the family's image for at least a couple of hours.

"Yes, I'm one of the shift supervisors."

"Nice!" Timothy said. "And you're going back to school soon?"

"Yes."

"Going to get good grades this time?"

"You know it."

Charlotte's eye twitched. She used a nudge of her elbow and a playful wink to engage with Timothy.

"I'm sure James would be so proud of all the hard work you're putting in for your future," Victoria said, tearing up with the reality of the absence of her brother not being around for this moment.

Victoria joined the rest in the house, accompanied by Timothy. His arm encircled her back like a comforting, weighted blanket, soothing the anxiety caused by ongoing losses.

"I think you should get settled in," Charlotte advised as she patted Lucas's biceps. "It must've been a long drive."

"Four hours goes quick when you sleep through most of it."

Lucas made his way into the house. The door hinges squeaked while the screen bounced against the frame and then came to a rest.

The sunflowers, affected by a strong wind, looked like they were expressing sorrow for Charlotte by pulling their petals toward the center in a melancholic way. Squirrels dashed through the yard, racing toward the trees, playing a game of tag like close cousins. The two hummingbirds sipped on the sugary water in the feeder, behaving as if they were having a casual lunch together.

Please let me get through this weekend alive.

RUNNING HER FINGERS through her hair, Charlotte untangled the damp strands from the pool. With each step she took downstairs, the ruffles on her black maxi skirt danced around her. Each picture she passed triggered memories of her late grandmother. Even ones Charlotte wasn't alive for, she could envision how someone captured that moment.

In one photo, Gemma, the same age as Charlotte, appeared in her late teens to early twenties. With her hands tucked in the pockets of her denim jacket, she displayed confidence with her shoulders back. Instead of gray hair, she had orangish-red styled in two ponytails with curly ends that fell onto her shoulders and chest. The dimples on her cheeks matched, creating half-circles, while she wore a proud smile next to the barn, which appeared in vivid red amidst the sepia tones of the photo. While Gemma may not be a blood relative, there were many resemblances. The only distinction is Charlotte's preference for the grunge movement rather than the sweet country girl aesthetic.

As she neared the bottom of the staircase, the smell of burnt oak filled her senses while Alexandria and Olivia conversed near the fireplace in the living room. Their fingers delicately moved across the pages of the teen magazines, marveling at the newest trends of cutouts and fringe with a touch of jealousy. A tiny shoebox was tipped over between them with polaroids sprawled out. Mason and Noah sat in the den next to the kitchen sitting in front of the Toshiba television, their fingers pelting the buttons on the controllers of their Super Nintendo to settle the score between who was better between Jax and Sub-Zero in *Mortal Kombat 3*.

The most recent family portrait in a black frame was obstructing her, lacking any glass for protection. Sunflowers seemed just like always, with their petals lifted as if posing happily for the camera's click. Despite Marnie's memory of pinching her shoulder to correct her posture, the family stood tall in pride, including herself. The only dialogue she could recall was her cousins complaining about wearing matching outfits within their family groups. It was as difficult as pulling teeth to capture that moment because of everyone criticizing each other. If it wasn't for someone's smile not being perfect, it was another one's posture. That one perfect moment appeared seamless, but it was anything but. Only the scarecrows behind them were free from anxiety. Suncrow's final touches made her smile, remembering the creative freedom Gemma gave her when the family did not.

As Charlotte walked past Mason and Noah, she spotted Victoria and Timothy in the kitchen. Chopping with a butcher knife, her aunt chopped the carrots. Rosemary stepped in the moment Timothy opened the oven to inspect the roasting chickens. Marnie half-heartedly tossed the salad, mixing the bowl of greens while leaning over the counter. Dexter bid farewell, fully dressed, while stretching his shoulder after his workout.

As Alexandria dashed into the space, she nudged Charlotte's back when Charlotte stopped at the shelving. Hundreds of videotapes covered the wall, sorted by genre, and organized meticulously in alphabetical order. The black cassette tapes in the bottom row were eager to find a home in plastic and paper cases, with only a strip of white tape for identification.

"You know, none of you guys could make it to my dance recital four years ago. I still remember that," Alexandria said as she traced her finger along the wall to find her match.

"So?" asked Noah, pelting the right arrow with his thumb.

"So, it's more meaningful than some stupid game."

I'd beg to differ.

"It's not like I care you didn't make it to a single one of my games," Mason defended, squinting at the screen.

"That's different."

"How so?"

"Just let me show you the recital, okay?"

"Nah."

Alexandria marched past the boys, who shifted their positions to get a better view past her muscular form. With a flushed face, she disconnected the cords from the console, sending the controllers flying from their hands like thin whips.

"What the fuck?" Mason grunted, pelting his fist onto the rug.

"Guys!" Timothy said, shaking his fingers from a tiny burn he sustained after not completely drying his hands off. "Just watch the show and then you can play your game."

"Screw that!" Mason hissed as he walked away, the bottom of his feet clapping onto the floor.

"Language, please," Victoria said, rolling her eyes as she wiped the celery remnants off the cutting board. "I know you guys are adults, but this isn't what Grandma Gemma would like inside her home."

Living in a silent household with minimal interactions with her mother, adapting to diverse personalities has been quite overwhelming. Although she knew them, it seemed as if she was a stranger to them, or perhaps they were strangers to her. Childhood habits can influence the peaks and valleys of personality types, leading to some qualities improving while most deteriorate upon growing up. Some of those qualities had even taken a new form.

Charlotte retreated, attempting to fade away. With caution, she turned the doorknob, ensuring her black nails didn't scrape the iron. While strolling through the garage, four moths were attracted to the fluorescent light. Their reflection was caught on the saw blades above, wings flapping rapidly and causing chaos. A hook had a thick rope wrapped around it, similar to a lasso.

She moved past the patio and started walking up the hill. Every step made her feel like a bird soaring above, providing a better view of the area. The hammock swayed, eagerly waiting for someone to come and enjoy its comfort. She reclined on the seat made from an inverted tire next to the tallest tree, using the loops as arm rests. As she moved the flames from the lighter to her cigarette, the fire's warmth reached the tip of her nose. She took a deep breath and let the nicotine circulate through her system. Orangish-red ash turned to gray, flaking onto her lap. The smoke descended to the foot of the hill, blending into the stationary cluster of flowers. Except for the patch across from her roughly fifty yards away. Black peeked through the yellow curtains of flora, with a head darkened from the sun casting a shadow of mystery.

Chapter 8

Around the property, the light posts started flickering, illuminating the well-kept paths in the sunflower fields. Dark clouds hid the setting sun, the temperature dropping to a comfortable chill. The empty trash bag danced around the driveway, determined to avoid being seen as litter. Employees finished their workday by aiding in the preparation for dinner.

A lengthy banquet table was set up at the beginning of the sunflower maze. Steam wafted from the back of a navy-blue pickup truck, delivering an assortment of dishes to the destination. The plates perched precariously on the uneven surface, almost tipping over toward the jello molds wrapped in saran wrap.

The family followed the truck in a procession, with Edward holding onto his wife and their three kids trailing behind. Olivia crutched around her brothers, permitting Mason's strength to lift her from the ground like royalty. Victoria placed her head on Timothy's, walking somberly, with Alexandria and Lucas following suit. At the rear of the crowd, Charlotte stood with her arms crossed and head hunched down, yearning for someone to console her.

Delicate blue floral engravings adorned white porcelain plates placed on the table. The stars above shimmered as they reflected off the silverware wrapped in forest-green napkins. The chairs, each distinct in their wooden finish and style, were collected from a variety of auction houses and estate sales, creating a whimsical atmosphere straight from Wonderland. Each member placed an entrée on the table with three chickens at each end.

Edward and Victoria occupied the middle of opposite sides, with their family encircling them until they reached the end, where Charlotte found herself alone in the corner, far from Noah. Two large, comfortable chairs sat at opposite ends, each with reserved signs on their cushions, awaiting the reunion of their absent owners. Victoria expressed her gratitude to the employees who brought out the last two pies, mixing the scents of blueberry and cherry.

"We left you another chicken and some side dishes for you all to enjoy back in the garage. Help yourself," said Edward.

The staff showed their gratitude with humility and warm smiles toward the family. While returning to the garage, they came together and clasped hands to express their shared respect.

Everybody sat; the air was open, enough to not let Charlotte suffocate from the lack of bodies around her that was once for James and Gabriel, with Katherine sitting next to her. In some sense, she was okay with this, since it gave her some room; at least that's what she told herself. Both Olivia and Lucas grabbed a water pitcher and noticed the condensation forming on the paisley tablecloth. Marnie yanked the cork off the bottle of Chablis before giving herself a generous portion in her glass with only a tiny meniscus touching the top.

"While we get ourselves settled, I wanted to thank you all for coming during the most depressing of circumstances," said Edward, his lips tight as he held back a tear.

Ice cubes clinked as they dropped to the bottom of the glass cups, ready to be filled with a stream of water.

"The Chesters have lost so much over the years. With Grandpa Simon, our brother, James, and nephew, Gabriel, and now Grandma Gemma. This is the part of life where we must part ways with the ones we love, the ones that love us. Just because they are not here in person doesn't mean that their legacy won't live on. We must live our life the way they would like for us to and treat others the way they would."

As if...

Olivia's eyes rolled around in her skull before fixing on Charlotte. With jade shutters banging against the siding, the cabin stood in the distance behind her cousin. The clapping of wood felt like thunder as Charlotte observed Olivia's disdain, causing her to clench the tablecloth to battle her nerves.

The group dug into the food while Edward stabbed the chicken's breast with a butcher knife. People passed bowls along the table. Mason's plate was full of scalloped corn, with no space for green bean casserole or fruit. Alexandria pinched the tongs, picking out the tomatoes in the salad bowl while Olivia wiped the juices from the proteins from her plate to prepare a picturesque image from her polaroid. Charlotte picked strands from a chicken leg, mixing it with her greens; the thought of Olivia making comments about what she chose to eat was not something she appreciated, so she was always careful with her portions.

Noah placed the napkin on his lap and remarked, "Everything looks so good."

"If you didn't know, this was all Gemma's favorite foods. They're all her recipes," Victoria said with pride, her lips forcing a smile.

A light blared from inside the field like a child's flashlight. Through the flowers, two individuals left with seeds sprinkling onto their tennis shoes. Using her hands, the woman shaped the curls of her perm to perfection.

Janice.

"This is great, guys!" she said, smiling with admiration as she left the flowers, her body nudging Charlotte's chair.

"What is she doing here?" Charlotte questioned, evading eye contact as the woman's smile extended toward the family while she walked around in admiration.

"I invited them over for a few clips for their segment," Edward said.

"And you all look great. This family has always been an inspiration to the community," the reporter said, her hand cradled over her heart.

"Are you kidding me?"

"What?" Alexandria said, moving a tomato seed to the rim of her plate. "Everyone needs to know that we are a tight family."

"We are, and they will," Mason agreed.

"Why do we need to show it to everyone?" Charlotte muttered.

Olivia and Alexandria shot her icy glares.

"Well, I'll leave you guys to it. Thanks again," Janice stammered, her hand adjusting her hair behind her ear to cover Charlotte's view.

The camera operator switched off his camera and placed it next to him. Janice approached the gravel, taking high steps to keep her feet dry and prevent the dew from soaking in. Charlotte perceived the uncomfortable silence as they entered the van at the hill's base, attempting to ease their displeasure with her emotions. With every passing second, it became increasingly difficult for her to argue her point.

"Chill out, Charlotte," Mason said, his mouth full of food.

"People need to be inspired to come support our family through this loss," Olivia cosigned. "We don't want her business to die off with her gone."

"Grandma was a loving person to everyone. Isn't her reputation enough?" Charlotte said meekly.

"Easy for you to say. You're not really a member of this family. So, you could give two shits about what happens to the business."

"Olivia, don't say that!" Marnie snapped, slurring after choking on a gulp while her smirk hid behind her hand.

"What? You're the one that said that she's not an actual Chester."

Marnie didn't respond; her glass tilted over her mouth to finish the last drops of her beverage. Disgust made Charlotte's throat thicken. The burden of her hunger pains lifted as she felt the desire to eat slowly fade away. This statement has been made by her cousin many times before. Such comments were common during their childhood, but never in front of any parents as they grew older.

"That's enough!" Edward's forceful fist made the liquid in the glasses tremble, forming shivering wave patterns. "Everybody at this table is just as much family as everyone else, blood or not."

"Oh! Look at that!" Noah said, pointing into his cup. "This reminds me of *Jurassic Park*! I got to rent it the minute we released it at the store."

The onlookers at the table were astounded by Noah's lack of reaction, while the rest scrutinized Charlotte for any sign of vulnerability in response to Olivia's comment.

A tiny bottle shook in Olivia's hand, releasing the sound of rattling pills. She poured two white supplements onto her palms while she fixed her eyes on her cousin.

"What the hell are those?" Charlotte asked, noticing their significant size from across the table.

"These are my supplements," Olivia snarled as she prepared to chase them with water. "Suzanne Somers recommends them to look young."

"You're nineteen!" Alexandria exclaimed in disbelief. "How much younger do you want to look?"

Fucking moron!

"Anyway, I think that what Uncle Eddie is trying to say is to remember all the good times we had as a family with everyone at this table present and those who are no longer with us," Lucas said, calmly looking at everyone as though they were landmines, and one misstep of a word would cause a detonation.

"The cameras aren't rolling anymore. There's no need to fake it for the public," Olivia muttered under her breath before taking a crispy bite of her lettuce.

"Cut it out!" Noah hissed, nudging her with his elbow.

Forks and knives scratched the porcelain as they cut the food. Wordlessly, they glanced at each other, waiting to see who would start the next topic. Both Victoria and Edward exchanged glances filled with mutual disgust toward their children.

Charlotte fixed her attention on her plate, stabbing her chicken with her fork to vent her frustration by breaking it into pieces. She envisioned Olivia screaming with every jab, hoping that the imaginary misery would bring solace; but it didn't.

"So, is that neighbor boy still a freak?" Alexandria chuckled while attempting to steer the conversation in a different direction.

"That's enough! Everybody just shut up and eat!" Timothy screamed; the contents of his plate toppled to the ground when he tipped it over.

FOLLOWING AN HOUR OF silence during dinner, the family went into the maze to allow the employees to clear the remaining dishes. The plates and bowls clinked together as they wobbled and stacked in the back of the pickup truck.

The sunflowers multiplied as they navigated deeper down the path, revealing a large circle with a bandstand where local musicians used to perform for public entertainment. Upon the wooden structure, Victoria and Timothy carefully set down bundles of fireworks. The family members at the bottom tapped their feet with impatience, feeling the cold making their bodies tremble. Rubbing her hands up over her biceps, Olivia pouted to keep warm. Charlotte was the only one not fidgeting, as her anger toward Olivia's complaints kept her warm.

"Okay, everyone," Timothy said, his palms rubbing together fast with enthusiasm. "Thanks to my business partner's side hobby, he's put together something for us to commemorate another one of Gemma's favorite things."

"God, he never shuts up about his business partner," Alexandria whispered to Mason. "If it's not the fireworks he's trying to upsell, it's their damn woodwork crap."

"I think this has been an exhausting day for all of us," Edward said. "Why don't we all take a moment and reflect on our own relationships in silence. Take your seats wherever, but try to take this as an opportunity to connect on your own."

Sparks cascaded from the wicks, landing on the soil below. Charlotte was no longer interested in being involved in this activity. Walking on the path, she made the choice to disconnect from her family, if that's what she wishes for them to be.

Years of oppression because of snide comments from at least one person, tainted every family event. Whistles gradually faded away into the sky, brightening the darkness with flashes of red, then blue, and finally green. She pondered what James and Gabriel would say if they were here.

"Forget them! Their opinions don't matter!" echoed Gabriel's voice.

"Don't let them get in your way. You'll lose all your hair like me if you keep worrying!" echoed her dad.

She wanted to leave so badly. None of this is worth it. All she could think about was running inside, calling her mother, and moving on from her family troubles. Fleeing from them would result in their victory and reinforcing their beliefs. And how would Gemma feel about that? She was always the one that would lift her up whenever she heard one of her granddaughters doing something that would boil her blood, knowing that she didn't have the authority to discipline them. She needed to show to Gemma that she was just as strong as she instilled in her. It was her support that motivated her to persevere through difficult times, especially in recent years. Charlotte's one determination was to never disappoint her, in this life or the next.

Charlotte felt her eardrums vibrate from the massive explosion in the sky. Looking inside the window of the cottage, the siding trembled. She caught a quick glimpse inside the building from the sudden flash. Beneath the sheetrock holes along the wall's base, she discovered heaps of ripped carpet. The trash bags gleamed in the dark plastic, with PBR cans spilling out from the top. Then there was something different; something out of place from the garbage and rubble. A head emerged from the dark glass's reflection, not with a rounded shape but showing angles from the outline of a hat positioned behind her. She gasped for breath while turning around. Her heart palpitated as blood flowed through her veins.

Nothing was there.

Chapter 9

Charlotte ventured to the barn; moonlight peeking through the chipped pieces of wood siding with her muscles weighing her down. The distractions of death has kept her mind racing, and she couldn't do anything to bring peace; not even a full stack of Christopher Pike books couldn't bring her comfort. The evening filled the air with a symphony of crickets and the sound of pebbles hitting the wood chipper blades as she shuffled her feet. With each step, the straw beneath her feet crunched like crinkling paper, dry as ever. As she slipped out the back door, the maze came into view. The mural of a jester balanced on one foot with an anonymous face while juggling balls in primary colors. Bats flew between light posts, scurrying through a hole in the face of a farming couple resembling *American Gothic*.

Each time the arches' shadows passed by, a momentary chill came from the shade. The blossoms were withering from dehydration and being crowded out by weeds. Nighttime slumber for the relatives began as the upper-level windows of the house darkened when the light shut off. The act of being teased by family can be draining and overwhelm even the toughest people.

On the patio, she sat on the chair and let her back become accustomed to the comfortable metal. Peace settled in her mind as silence enveloped the outdoors. Inhaling the nicotine from her cigarette, she found satisfaction in her addiction. Her tranquility remained undisturbed by any signs of life, enabling Buddy Holly's lyrics to loop in her thoughts.

"Can I have one of those?" asked a mature, feminine voice.

The sudden interruption made her body jolt and shake. The tranquility she tried to feel at her grandmother's property was disrupted by someone she had to act differently around. The cousins' intense scrutiny sufficed; she craved a pressure-free moment.

Victoria settled into the chair next to her. Her skin's pasty appearance glowed in the dark as she extended her hand for nicotine. Anticipating relief, she relied on her niece to help obtain the stick.

"I-I didn't know that you smoked," Charlotte said, dumbstruck.

"Only from time to time," Victoria answered, while reaching for Charlotte's pack on the table.

"Go ahead," she stated, unable to object as her aunt took one without asking.

"Thanks."

The lighter teased with a couple of flickers, producing sparks that hesitated to become a flame. After being lit, the cigarette burned with the light, Victoria's face glowing orange. Taking a deep breath, she reclined in her chair, allowing the drug to flow through her veins. She exhaled deeply while gazing at the night sky, letting the smoke form its own clouds in the vast darkness.

Victoria pointed out, "You understand that these are not good for you," while flicking a flake of her cherry onto the ground.

"I know."

"I have to say that I'm a little disappointed that you took this up. I didn't see you as the type to pick up such a nasty habit."

What are you talking about?

"Then why do you do it?"

Victoria justified with confidence, "I use it only when I really need it. You're lucky that Grandma Gemma didn't know that you smoked. She would've shit her pants."

Charlotte mentioned, "She did know," while trying to calm herself down with a hit.

"Really?"

"Yes. She caught me one night when I came to visit over Easter."

"Did she let you have it?"

"No. I mean, she wasn't happy about it, but she didn't let me have it. All she did was remind me of how bad they were for me and then told me I can make my own decisions."

"Wow," Victoria said with surprise, more smoke casually leaving her lips.

Victoria crossed her leg while relighting the stick. Neglecting the desire to indulge, she noticed the heat subside.

"And what did Grandma say about you smoking?" another voice asked as they made their way to the table.

Oh, great! Another one.

On the opposite side of Charlotte, Lucas took a seat. He rested his head on his cupped hands. His forehead now showed three distinct wrinkles. A slight breeze toyed with his mushroom cut, causing it to brush against his eyebrows.

"She didn't know. I'm glad I didn't tell her," Victoria said, exhaling another breath.

"Why didn't you tell her?" Lucas asked, his eyebrow raising with curiosity.

"Why would I? I don't want her to be disappointed in me. I don't do it when we're here, so I don't see the problem with it."

"You're upset with me for doing this, but you wouldn't mind if it was you," Charlotte whispered, expressing her frustration.

She pressed the cigarette's tip into the table's center, crushing it. Half of the white paper was still uncreased despite the fold. The metal scraped against the brick as she moved her chair. The sound of her sneakers tapping on the sidewalk accompanied her return to the yard.

She gently cradled her arms in front of her. The loneliness of the breeze heightened her sense of isolation. Plants tried to get her attention by sending a small wave in her direction. The emptiness inside her persisted, regardless of her environment. As she stared at the night sky, a tear rolled down her cheek. She needed some kind of sign that everything was going to turn out okay. She desired something that would enable her to make mistakes without being judged by others.

"Charlotte!" Lucas said, the grass muffling his stomps as he sprinted toward her to catch up.

"Please leave me alone," Charlotte softly said as her throat dried up.

"Let me walk with you," he said, trying to catch his breath as he slowed his pace. "I need the fresh air too."

"Fine."

Taking a deep breath, she allowed the nicotine to circulate in her body again. By buttoning up her denim jacket, she created a shield of armor around her.

"I know she's kind of hard on you. But she cares a lot about your well-being."

"Well, she has a shitty way of doing it!" Charlotte said, clenching her fists. "Why is it that everyone else can get a free pass here for doing something bad and I'm the only one that gets called out for it?"

"What do you mean?"

"I know I don't get involved in your guys' conversations, but I hear what they say behind closed doors. I know Mason got a DUI this year, and Olivia has been to the free clinic more times than I can count with the different guys she's slept with."

"I know about them," Lucas said as they passed by an opening to the fields. "They got to face the consequences of their actions."

"Then why is it not brought up when we all get together if it's always about making the family look good? It seems like all everyone talks about how great they are and how horrible I am."

"You're not horrible."

"And what about the time Noah accidentally burned down an abandoned house and Alex shoplifted and blamed it on someone else?"

"I-I dunno. Noah fessed up to the accident."

"None of these gets brought up. But everyone is fine with talking about how I dropped out of school or got detention."

"I'm sorry. I didn't know how bad that made you feel," Lucas said, his gaze becoming softened, his smile small as he became saddened by Charlotte's isolation.

"I know *you* are. You've been the nicest to me this whole time. If it weren't for Grandma Gemma and you, I probably would've cut you all from my family tree."

"Don't do that. We care about you."

"I don't think so. If the shoe was on the other foot, I feel like they would dismiss me in the drop of a hat and not think twice."

They proceeded through the following opening. Their feet navigated the softened ground. While walking into the dense vegetation, the house faded away, overshadowed by sunflowers. Stems thickened like a wall, making their grandparents work more admirable with a definite labyrinth. Two wooden braces secured with twine and sticks in the first clearing greeted them, forming a triangular base for a plank suspended by two ropes.

"I'm sorry you feel that way about us," Lucas said with a thickened throat.

"It's not like I feel it all the time. You all had great moments; it was just when Grandma Gemma wasn't around."

"Yeah, she kept us all in line."

"It was as if she was glue to have us forget about each other most of the time and enjoy what we have as a family."

Lucas flashed a little smirk. His body trembled at the memory of their lost family member, leading to a sniffle as tears welled up.

"Even when James died, she made me feel like one of you guys."

"She did."

Charlotte settled onto the swing to relax. Dust from the ground gathered around her calves as she moved. Tears trickled onto her lap, moistening the material of her skirt.

"She didn't have to do that; her or Grandpa Simon. They could've cast me to the side like some others. Instead, they made me feel wanted and appreciated for being myself."

"They did that for all of us," Lucas agreed. "Grandma Gemma was even understanding when I told her I was having second thoughts about college."

"You do?"

Charlotte abruptly stopped like a record player's needle being lifted. Her jaw dropped with dirt particles getting a better chance of making their way inside.

"I thought you liked college?" Charlotte asked, shocked, as she turned the ropes to face her cousin.

"I do. I just don't know what I want to do with my life."

"I thought you wanted to work in advertising and help with Uncle Timothy's business?"

"I want to help them. I want to help both my parents. I just don't know if this is the way to do so."

"What do you mean?"

"I want to run a business, but I want it to be mine. I don't want to have strings attached and work under someone. I want to have people work under me."

"Oh, the bossy type. I didn't think you had it in you."

With a wink and a chuckle full of sarcasm, Charlotte tried to revive her spirits by bringing some lightness back into her being.

"Not really," Lucas said, clarifying. "I want to inspire people to be the best versions of themselves in the work they do. I want to be in the trenches with them instead of sitting behind a desk and calling the shots."

His proclamation made Charlotte grin. She knows the struggle of working under a micromanager without the adequate knowledge. All the jobs she's worked in the past had plenty of people that knew how to sit in an office and bark an order, but couldn't get up and help the team do what they asked.

"I want to be a leader and not a boss."

"Good for you. And a leader is what you will be!"

Lucas's eyes lit up as he straightened his posture, saying, "Thanks. I just don't know how I'm going to break it to my family. They are going to have a bird when they find out."

"Why? I think they'll be just fine."

"Have you seen the way they treated you when they found out you dropped out?"

Charlotte stopped brainstorming when he brought up a valid point. For some unknown reason, a portion of the family believed that attaining a college education was synonymous with achieving success. Throughout her time in school, she felt pressured to do well, despite the emotional burden of losing her brother and stepfather.

"Good point."

"Can I ask you something, and feel free to say no," Lucas said, tentative.

"Sure."

"Why did you drop out?"

Charlotte's noisy gulp was obscured by the plant leaves swaying in tune with the wind's music. She stood still, suppressing her fear.

"You don't have to tell me if you're not comfortable," he reassured, nuzzling her shoulder for comfort.

"Something happened to me that made me not want to go back."

"Like what?"

Charlotte's mind tried one last time to prevent her from confessing. Charlotte kept her mother uninformed about the events of the past year. Despite the loss and heartbreak, she aimed to not add to the family's sorrow. Yet, something drove her to have the urge to speak out. Lucas was very honest and confided in her, making her feel like they were sharing mutual secrets.

"Well, I worked at the coffee shop on campus."

"Yes, I remember you talking about that, and you really liked it."

"It was a great job. I loved helping the people, and the discounts weren't bad, especially when I had to study for tests late at night."

"I could've benefitted from a freebie for sure. Everyone at work nice to you? Were you all like a team?"

"Most of us."

"Bad bosses? Every place has one."

"Not as bad as this one."

"What, did he yell at you guys like a dictator? I've had my share of those."

"Worse."

"Then what?" Lucas asked, noticing her glazed expression and retreat.

There was no turning back. Her heart raced and her stomach churned fiercely, as though dinner was eager to leave. The only reason she thought she should talk is that maybe his influence could change the other's perception if Lucas did choose to tell them.

"Well, there was a holiday party that we all went to. My boss went all out with treating us. He rented out a space in a warehouse and had all the other employees from the region join with a live band and drinks."

"That sounds like my kind of boss."

Despite her strong urge to yell, Charlotte controlled herself as her eyebrow raised.

"Not if he drugged you and took advantage of you in the woods..."

Lucas's jaw hung open. He looked deep into Charlotte's troubled soul, noticing the suppressed sorrow she had been carrying. The truth became painfully clear as she wept, understanding the abuse her cousin endured from her boss. The man who managed the company she recommended as the ideal workplace turned out to be her personal nightmare.

Lucas spoke softly, making sure not to cross any lines, while retracting his hands. "I-I didn't know that you had to deal with that."

"It wasn't your job to," Charlotte said as her tears grew by the second of her resurfacing pain.

"Did you report it?" he asked with concern. "I would've gotten his ass fired if it was me."

"Easy for you to say. He was the district manager. Besides, it was my word against his. By the end of the day, I'm more easily replaceable than he was. He told everyone that I was the one asking for it, and then word spread like wildfire. And the police wouldn't do anything about it because they thought I was freaky based on the way I looked."

Charlotte's head hung low with shame. Her agony was so deep that even the sunflowers could not provide her with comfort.

"That's messed up!"

"It was. I couldn't focus in school because every class I would have to deal with someone glaring at me like I was some monster. I quit my job, and I couldn't afford to pay my own bills, so I got kicked out. He ruined my life."

She wept into her hands. The weight of her judgment has engulfed her in pain. She felt like she was back in one of those classes, being judged by others with the memory of eyes glaring at her.

"Well, I don't know how you could've done it. I don't know if I could survive."

Charlotte rolled down her sleeve to dry the tears on her cheeks. Wet eyeliner coated her cuffs, leaving them black.

"And then coming here, I get Olivia and Alexandria on my case about not being a real member of this family. Every time something good happens, I get overshadowed by their behavior. And I can't tell you the amount of times Aunt Marnie slapped my hand when I reached over for seconds and then looked at my figure. Why do they treat me like I'm a piece of shit? Somehow, I'm the bad guy when I'm just dealing with my life the way I know how."

"You're probably the toughest person I know," Lucas said as he crouched down to her level. "I don't know anybody else that has gone through the amount of shit that you have. You haven't taken that crap and let it ruin you."

"Look at me. I'm ruined," Charlotte stated, gesturing for her cousin to look at her.

"You haven't been to jail. You aren't some addict or criminal. There are many people that would take something like what you dealt with and cope with it differently. I think you turned into a pretty decent person, given the circumstances, if you ask me."

Charlotte laughed quietly, mouthing the word "decent" to inject humor into her sadness.

"I'm serious," Lucas said while guiding her to stand up. "Don't be so hard on yourself. You're better than these people, and you shouldn't let them get to you."

"I know what you mean, but it's easier said than done."

"I know."

The cabin, buried in the distance on the other side of the maze, emitted creaking from its wooden structure. A shingle dropped, making a family of birds fly off.

"I think we should get back. It's been a long day, don't you think?"

Charlotte was more depleted than she had ever been. The act of reliving the trauma has had a negative impact on her psyche. She desperately needed water to quench her dry mouth and rejuvenate herself.

"You're right."

"Okay, let's go."

Charlotte and Lucas exited the field. As the grass transitioned away from soft dirt and dew drops fell on her toes, her sneakers got cleansed. It was like she released herself from the baggage that had weighed her down over the past months with nobody to talk to; nobody to believe her.

"I think I want to be alone for a minute. "You go on without me," Charlotte said to Lucas, bringing herself to a stop.

"Sure."

Charlotte observed Lucas walking back to the house. Her stomach eased from the twisting and turning of her inner turmoil. While she wasn't looking forward to being at her grandma's house with the rest of the family, she cherished the time spent with her cousin, especially on this night.

She grabbed one more cigarette and lit the end. Allowing the nicotine to circulate through her system once more, she found solace after a day filled with difficulties. Though she lost the one who provided relief, she discovered someone who will support her unconditionally, unaffected by external influence. With a flick of the ash, she smiled, watching as the moon winked a small twinkle into her spirit.

Another familiar voice behind her remarked, "You know those will kill you."

"What the hell are you doing?" asked another, more youthful, more pubescent.

Charlotte stood frozen, her mouth agape in disbelief. She watched in stillness as the cigarette fell from her hand. The dew cooled down the heat, leading to a small sizzle close to her toes. She looked behind her toward the field's entrance. As she gazed at the two of them, shock washed over her, and she became motionless. His bald scalp gleamed under the moonlight on the top of the older man's head. His red polo was polished to perfection; not a single wrinkle, even with it tucked tight into his khaki pants. The teenager stood beside him, with the top of his head meeting the other person's chin. His shaggy hair was full and just about covering his eyes, framing the rest of his face with curly ends floating away.

"Dad? Gabriel?"

Chapter 10

James and Gabriel stood before Charlotte in the grass, causing her to gasp in disbelief. Bathing in the moon's light, their bodies glowed, revealing complexions that were pristine, unlike their appearance described to her before burial. She was face to face with two people she knew who had passed away. This was something unimaginable, like getting to meet Kurt Cobain in person.

"What the hell is wrong with you?" Gabriel asked. "You look like you saw a ghost!"

Charlotte was dumbstruck. She saw them both get buried at their funeral. Since quitting college, she may have done a drug or two, but not any time recently; there were no hallucinogens in her system to explain this.

"Is it really you?" Charlotte asked, her chin quivering.

"It's definitely us," James replied, a subtle smile playing on his lips.

"I can't believe it. I thought you were dead."

"We are dead. Don't get any ideas," Gabriel teased.

Charlotte let out a tiny sigh. The possibility of them being alive was something that could have existed. She might have found a fresh start with her family, complete again, and let the pain of their leaving fade. But that wasn't the case; they were still dead.

"Then what are you doing here?"

James shrugged and said, "Honestly, we have no idea either."

"We've been back at the farm ever since that night," Gabriel added. "We've been here every day, watching Gemma and the rest of you come and go with their visits. It's like this is where our spirits can roam."

That couldn't be. Spirits haunting their family farm felt like something out of a movie. This wasn't *Beetlejuice* or *Poltergeist*; this was real life. Charlotte didn't know of any other cameras around here, apart from Olivia's polaroid, that's not around at the moment to prove her hypothesis that a movie was being filmed.

"I don't know what to say."

"You don't have to say anything," said James. "We've been right beside you the entire time."

"Watching your every move!" Gabriel said, his arms raised like a menacing monster. "Even when you go take a piss!"

"That's enough," James said, revolted.

A tear, thick enough to flow on its own, trickled down Charlotte's cheek as she chuckled. She missed everything about her brother, especially his humor.

"I'm just kidding!" Gabriel said.

"So, you've been around to see how everything has been over the past few days?" Charlotte asked.

"Yes, and we know how hard it is to be around some of your relatives," James confirmed. "I must admit that Olivia wasn't my favorite niece. She can be quite the little bitch sometimes."

"See! I told you this so many times!" Charlotte said as she threw her arms up hopelessly.

"I know you have. I just didn't believe you."

"Well, that's apparent."

"I knew it all along!" Gabriel admitted. "They treated you differently than they did with me. Remember that year when they all gifted you socks and underwear at Christmas and all of us got toys?"

Charlotte recalled all the years she received gifts she needed and continued to feel grateful, acknowledging their necessity. As a kid, though, it would've been an enjoyment playing with the newest doll or toy that everyone else had. Mason and Noah got games for their Nintendo, while Alexandria got Barbies and Olivia received expensive makeup. When unwrapping was over, all the kids got to play with the new gifts from their relatives, while she had to fashion a sock puppet from the fresh pair of Hanes.

"And I'm appalled that Olivia didn't consider you family," James said in disgust. "You are just as part of this family as the rest of us. I hope you didn't feel that way from me?"

"I-I mean, you did put a lot of pressure on me to be the best. I know you know I was trying, but it seemed like you were competing to have the best child in the family."

James's eyebrow cocked closer to the top of his head, his hand resting under his chin. Gabriel looked up at his father's inquisitive glance, twiddling with his fingers at his sister's confession that he shared mutually.

"Was I really that hard on you?"

"Yes! You weren't always like that, though. It just seemed like it was closer to holidays or visits that you would push me."

"I'm sorry. I only wanted what's best for you."

A squint in his eyes reflected contemplation. A raspy edge cut through the gentleness of his voice. There was sincerity in his apology; it wasn't like he had to put up a front in front of anybody else.

"I know you did, but you know you had your foot on the gas way too hard at times. It made me feel like I wasn't good enough or something."

"Oh, but you are good enough." James walked closer to his daughter; his arms reached out to her, wanting to cradle her and bring security back into her damaged insecurities.

Charlotte reached out as well. She missed her family dearly and hoped for a hug after being apart. One touch from them would fill her with pure happiness. Her hand touched his, but she felt nothing. She shoved it into his hand, but his skin became translucent and felt cold and light like air. The moment her hand went straight through his arm, she knew for sure they were ghosts.

"Cool, huh?" Gabriel asked as he punched his sister in the stomach, his fist surfacing out of the lower part of her back.

"Knock it off," James commanded.

He saw the disappointment on Charlotte's face. This reunion could be exactly what she needed. It felt like he was in prison, separated from them by glass and relying on a phone for communication. There was no connection, just words.

"I want to give you a hug so badly, honey," James said, a tear glistening on his face.

"I know you do," Charlotte said, cradling her arms. "You know, I've never seen you cry in all the years I knew you."

As James wiped the moisture from his face, she couldn't help but laugh. The humanity for all the guilt he experienced was quite ironic being that he is alive or human. Gabriel smiled at Charlotte, satisfied that she got through to him, after all the years of being tentative to express their concerns to be the best for him.

"I miss this side of you. I miss you."

"I miss you too," said James.

"Me too," said Gabriel.

"I guess one regret in my life was to not be more appreciative of what you both did. You guys tried your best, and that's what matters."

Charlotte became warm from his confession, which was appropriate because a giant gust of wind swept across her face, knocking one sunflower down to her with the stem not being strong enough to stabilize their plant; it bent at a ninety-degree angle.

"I don't want you to think that you were a shitty father," Charlotte clarified as they continued to walk the outskirts of the field. "There were a lot of great memories that I cherish. You weren't horseshit like my birth father was."

"Yeah, he's a piece of work all right."

The three continued to laugh. Gabriel extended his hand toward the field. Even though a human hand could feel the flower stems and maybe break some, the force of his push was restrained. The petals fluttered, as if ridiculing him for failing to crush them as his hand appeared through the plants.

The stars glistened in the night sky. Tiny specks of white and gray shimmered against the dark blue sky. As they reached the top of the driveway, the view from the threshold of the Chester farm was quaint, overlooking the open countryside. Against the backdrop of the now-darkened yellow fields, tree silhouettes emerged. The cows were small, grazing the pasture in the distance, their harmonious herd bonding peacefully in the silence. Charlotte felt a warmth spread through her, knowing the quiet could bring her contentment. Although she had a rough couple of days, she wished the night wouldn't end.

"I wanted to tell you something," James said, his hand hovering over Charlotte's shoulder.

"Sure. You can tell me anything."

"It's not like you have a choice. He'll haunt you until you listen!" Gabriel joked, enjoying every second of his sister's widening eyes.

James looked back at his son. A glare so fierce it could make a misbehaving child compliant. Even in death, Gabriel's silence deepened, reflected in the widening terror of James's gaze.

"I know you've been struggling with feeling like a part of the family."

"I have."

"Just know that a family tree can have branches pruned if they aren't keeping it healthy."

"You want me to kill them?"

"No, silly," James said, chuckling at her sarcasm. "I'm just saying that a family doesn't have to be blood to be considered one. It could be those that fill your heart with joy and fuel your soul. And know that your mom and I love you so much. Remember that."

"I do too," Gabriel chimed in.

Charlotte let her father's words process. It would be so easy to sever the ties with some of these people since they wouldn't bat an eye if they had the choice themselves. It's common for individuals to leave behind those who show little concern for their well-being. Each of them had a sense of potential, a shared spark ignited by Gemma and her legacy. She wasn't ready to give up on these people, not yet.

"I know, Daddy. I just can't."

James said nothing. Only the faint tickle of a breeze on Charlotte's neck broke the tense quiet in the air. Annoyed by her hair falling into her eyes, she pushed it behind her ears. Her gaze drifted to the hilltop across the path, where the tire swing swayed in the wind, like unseen forces were at play. The realization that she was no longer alone brought a smile to Charlotte's face. She had people that were on her side, agree or disagree, dead or alive. Driven by curiosity, she looked behind her, hoping one of them would offer a wise response. Only the silent flowers stood, taking a break from the wind.

They were gone.

BACK INSIDE, CHARLOTTE found it hard to fall asleep. While James's old room had fresh bedding, everything else was a reminder of his childhood. With bits of paint flaking from its edges, the rocking horse wallpaper strip loomed above the crimson coat. There was an old toy chest in the corner, handmade by Grandpa Simon; it was identical to the one he made for her and Gabriel when they were brought into the family. This one, once cobalt blue, now faded from years of neglect and chipped corners. A stain from spilled green paint lingered in the corner, a reminder of Gabriel's mishap on the carpet.

The room where her stepfather had grown up made her uneasy, particularly after his death. The experience of seeing his ghost and talking to it was even stranger. Was she just losing her mind with all the loss? Her conversation with the one she missed dearly was a pleasant break from her troubles, and they were starting to resolve some outstanding matters.

As her eyelids grew heavy, she couldn't stop thinking about him and their shared memories, eventually succumbing to sleep and sinking into the comfort of her mattress.

CHARLOTTE KEPT TOSSING a rubber band ball at the wall. The dinner table altercation faded, replaced by calmness with each toss. Her day went downhill fast, starting with failing the test and ending with a fight. To make matters worse, her stepfather wouldn't give her a chance to explain what happened. She wanted to be better, but every step she took was met with disappointment.

If only he would understand.

With static fuzzing her TV screen, she moved the antenna closer to her head, hoping to improve the signal. With the "Waterfalls" music video playing, it was hard to hear TLC in the background. She waited for the next musician to play amongst the popular hits that continued to be played from the popular demands to satisfy the majority. Charlotte only wanted to play Green Day, but it was always something else.

After throwing the ball again, she had no other distractions to take her away from her book report she needed to finish for next week. Her English class had decent reads, but they didn't have the same adventurous spirit as Narnia. Narnia offered a wonderful escape for her when times were tough, through the journey of Diggory and Polly in The Magician's Nephew. *Exhausted, her arms seemed to lose their connection to the rest of her. Charlotte grabbed a book from her dresser, taking out the red, fringed bookmark to resume reading the last pages of* To Kill a Mockingbird. *She'd rather write about C.S. Lewis for a book report, but the syllabus required them to read* Heart of Darkness *after this assignment. While not bad, the other books lacked the adventurous spirit of her childhood favorites.*

Hours slipped away unnoticed, and her head found a cozy spot in the book's crease. The television commercials featured clips from Spring Break, with young women competing for the camera's gaze, hoping to launch their acting careers. Gabriel usually woke her from her trances, either by doing it himself or by shouting at his video games when he lost. Her startle was not even affected by his rehearsal of his lines; no grunts from King Lear to scare her.

She checked her book with a nervous hand, wiping away drool, fearing her saliva had seeped into the pages and drowned Atticus Finch. As she walked down the hall, she wiped away the glossy film in her eyes to check on Gabriel. The wires of Gabriel's gaming system were a jumbled mess, and the console remained off. His backpack remained in the corner, buried underneath his hooded sweatshirt; his homework neglected to be completed.

Charlotte walked down the stairs, the floorboards groaning with every step. Through the reflections of picture frames, her face was obscured in the portraits of her family's adventures. Through the open doorway, blue and red lights bounced off the top of a bald head. Curious that James was in trouble with the law, she stopped at the threshold before the wall disappeared and only the banister would expose her presence.

"How am I going to tell her?" Katherine asked, her voice thick with sadness.

"She's going to find out somehow," said the man.

"I know, but she's already had enough in her life. Her birth father hasn't spoken to her for almost two years. James was pretty much her father for most of her life."

Charlotte's throat thickened; her stomach churned. What could've possibly happened to her stepfather? She may have been angry with him for not seeing her perspective, but it was all just a big misunderstanding; every family goes through their shares of disagreements.

"Find what out?" Charlotte asked, revealing herself to the group.

Tissues covered most of Katherine's face as she gazed at her. Dexter tried to ease her pain by rubbing her shoulder. With their hands in their pockets, the two officers stood outside on the sidewalk, somber and heavy, as if the air itself had grown thick with despair.

"Oh, honey!" Charlotte's mother cried out, rushing toward her daughter and wrapping her arms around her in a snug, snake-like hug.

Resting her head in her hand, Grandma Gemma sat on the couch. Her eyes held a distant look as she surveyed the space that offered her son serenity. The news left her speechless, unable to understand what was happening.

"Can somebody tell me what happened?" Charlotte asked, trying to break free from Katherine's grip.

All eyes were on her. It was as though she was having an encore presentation of her adventures in the hallway in between her classes. Tension gripped her shoulders as the television displayed the news. A stony bridge in the countryside was where a young, male news anchor stood, only a couple of miles from Gemma's farm, which made it a familiar sight for Charlotte. By the ditch lay a vehicle, similar to the one

James drove. The moonlight reflected off the broken windows, revealing the front end that was smashed to a fraction of its original size. Three police cars parked along the road behind two ambulances. The peak's stone wall reflected the bouncing light. A soft breeze tousled the man's combover as he stood within the camera's frame.

"This is Robbie Rice reporting just outside of Mabel. An unfortunate turn of events has resulted in the untimely death of local family man James Chester and his son Gabriel. The vehicle raced down the road, careened into the ditch, and landed into a stream. Police have determined this as an accident, but we won't know the full details until the investigation is complete. Let our thoughts and prayers be with his family as they process this devastating news."

Charlotte's knees gave way, throwing her off balance. As she processed the news, her head felt lighter and her breath grew shallower with each passing second. This couldn't be real; this has to be some kind of prank. James was always a skillful driver. Some would argue, even too good. He'd scrutinize her practice sessions for the test in an overly controlling manner. He'd be ready to fix any sudden wheel movement as if he had a whip.

Dexter steadied her by reaching out an arm and placing a firm grasp under her armpit. Katherine found comfort in Charlotte's embrace, burying her face in her shoulder and letting out another wave of heartbreaking sobs. The events were so unbelievable that Charlotte's body became numb with shock. Their deaths couldn't be the ending, especially not after dinner. Tears flowed as she understood her final words to James were beyond recall. This branch of the family tree was cut, but not by choice. Fate cut down this one and then burned it in front of the base, taunting the family for their victory over death.

Dexter patted Charlotte's back and said, "I'm so sorry."

Charlotte was at a loss for words. Whenever she had something to say, her tongue felt too thick to speak. The little food she'd eaten at dinner was making her feel sick, and she desperately needed to throw it up.

Standing up, Gemma felt her knee quiver. Her warmth spread through the hug when she joined in. Any bit of comfort was what she needed, but it wouldn't take away the pain of her loss, or anyone else's.

"Come sit with me, dear," Gemma told Charlotte, gesturing toward the couch.

Another officer escorted Katherine to the kitchen, followed by Dexter and the sheriff. She leaned onto the counter, pushing aside her cup of tea and filling a small portion of bourbon at the bottom of a tiny glass; James's glass.

"I don't know what to say to make this go away," Gemma said, her hand resting on Charlotte's.

Charlotte bowed her head, her nose was runny with snot trickling out of her nostrils. The final bit of the news segment featured two stretchers carrying black body bags. The bags' volume made things more tangible, even more real than they already were.

"James and your brother were most definitely taken away from us too soon. I wish I could take that pain for you, but I can't. It's the unfortunate part of life, and it can be quite the bitch."

Charlotte's frizzy hair covered her face, hiding her sadness like a wall of bushes. If only that could be a possibility.

"All we can do is remember them for how much of an impact they had on our lives. They may not be here, but their legacy will live on."

I hope that the impact doesn't include our argument.

There were so many memories she could revisit, each one reminding her of her admiration for James and the happiness he brought to her and her mother. No matter what she thought, their conversation from earlier consumed her mind. She felt burdened by his concerns and accusations, which pressed down on her like a heavy cloud. All she could imagine was Gabriel's last glance at his older sister, filled with anger and heartbreak because she felt misunderstood and unheard.

"I know what you're thinking. What about all the times he wasn't the best?" Gemma added.

She's right.

"I know my son can be quite the pain in the ass. I can say that from firsthand experience."

A quick nod from Charlotte contained the giggles that threatened to erupt, as she recognized the truth in her grandmother's words.

"Do you remember the time that we went fishing, just the four of us?"

Charlotte's mind drifted back to their visit to the lake where Grandpa Simon took James and her on a fishing trip in a boat he borrowed from a friend. This was one of the first times they got to know each other better. Even then, James wouldn't stop complaining to his father about speeding, even when trying to avoid anyone who might have let go of their water ski rope, even if they were a long way off.

"He was quite the little shit," Gemma said, chuckling in reminiscence.

"He was," Charlotte agreed, a tiny smile lifting her lips.

"But all I can think about was how much he made you laugh. You have such a pretty smile, like the sunrise. He sure knew how to make your face light up!"

A tear welled in Charlotte's eye, not from sorrow, but because Gemma was correct. James helped her remove the fish from the hook after she caught her first one. Before tossing it back in the water, he couldn't resist moving its lips to make the aquatic creature speak with her. He even gave it a voice, sounding like he had inhaled a whole tank of helium.

"He did."

Charlotte pressed her face into her hands. The tiny meniscus of tears grew into a puddle in the human cup. The joy he brought completely overshadowed her worries. It was as though he were a warrior fighting off an army of negativity.

"And I remembered when he took you out to the farm for the first time. Do you remember that?"

"I do."

The memory of her cousins clouded the introduction. Though she often found good in her memories of some people, she had difficulty finding it in others.

"Do you remember the suncrow?"

Especially when they made the suncrow.

"Yes."

"After you were all done making the suncrow, James came up to me and asked how you were doing since he knew that this was a big step for you to meet your new cousins."

And? she thought to herself.

"I told him of all the additions you made after Grandpa Simon took everyone else to the pool. He thought you had quite an eye for creativity.

"He did?"

"Yes, he did. He loved you so much. I was always the first to know about your B honor roll, after your mom, of course. He made sure that we all would show up at your band concerts. He was so proud of you."

This came as a surprise to Charlotte. Despite being critical of her, he was surprisingly proud of her dedication. It made little sense as to why he pushed her so much, but the result of his appreciation for her dedication and trying attitude was all she longed for.

"Did you know he has that picture of when you were lead in the church play on his desk at work?"

"I didn't."

Charlotte slumped against her grandmother, resting her head on her shoulder. She was about to lose control. It dawned on her that the man she considered her worst critic was actually her most ardent fan. Even though he was a pain, she never got to acknowledge his intentions and offer thanks.

She never would.

THE SCRATCHING ON THE wall startled Charlotte. Checking the alarm clock, it was only a couple of hours after midnight. The burden of her emotions has left its mark on her body. Each joint in her legs ached as if they were rusty and needed lubrication. Her throat was scratchy and needed moisture.

With effort, she rose from the bed, stretching her spine toward the ceiling, striving for a more tolerable posture. Looking out, she spotted the sunflower field, a reminder of the feast she'd had earlier at the dinner table. Weighted down by sand-filled tea kettles, the edges of the gingham tablecloth fluttered in the wind. The trees waved their leafy branches, swaying gently in the breeze as if they were saying a friendly greeting.

A line of figures extended along the edge of the field. Their arms and legs oscillated with each huff of mother nature's breath. A sliver of moonlight pierced a dense cloud, illuminating their flannel shirts. The one in red stood out to her. A tiny speck of sunflowers was paired along the center of the burlap face, reminding her of the first time she spent out at the farm. It was a poignant reminder of James's unwavering love for his stepdaughter, regardless of his unconventional ways of showing it.

It was a sad sight, the cottage standing there across the way, its neglect a stark contrast to the life it once held. Charlotte wanted to help preserve the space, but her limited time and resources made her feel powerless to do so. She noticed movement near the house, hidden among the sunflowers. The movement forced the plants to the ground, creating a path. This wasn't like a coyote or any other animal—a round shape, like a head, popped up between every flower.

Someone was out there.

Chapter 11

What could it be?

The head swarmed around the patch, knocking down more of the yellow and brown beauty before disappearing out of her sightline by the hill. Charlotte removed her oversized band t-shirt and buttoned up her flannel shirt; the placket was misaligned, which caused an unflattering drape between her breast and stomach.

Pulling her baggy jeans higher, she exposed her knees through the ripped fabric. She made her way down the hall, tiptoeing to avoid waking up any of the grownups; she remembered where those sensitive spots were from all the other times she would sneak out to follow her cousins when they would go play in the dark in years past.

One foot caught on the other, and she wobbled toward the accent table. Her grandparents' portraits swayed precariously, threatening to fall onto the gleaming surface. The central image showcased their three children, all young and around the same age as Charlotte when she was first introduced to the Chesters. Their identical overalls, filthy on the bottom, looked dark in the sepia tones. She'd never seen James or her uncle Edward with real hair, but they both had the same shaggy style that reminded her of Gabriel's. Victoria's photo depicted her blonde hair as washed out, styled in two pigtails that fell below her shoulders. It was as though Alexandria took a step back in time and ditched her attitude and decided to help around the farm for a day, or at least for that moment in time for the photo to capture it. Another group of kids, most enjoying themselves, played at the newly opened farm, which at the time had fewer attractions than it does now. A time of less excess where the outdoors was the only entertainment for kids, keeping them active and away from television screens.

A wicked set of snores, escaping from beneath the neighboring door, rumbled through the room from Timothy's persistent struggle with sleep apnea. Passing by the next room was Marnie and Edward's room. Their white noise machine recreated the lively sounds of the jungle with cassette tapes; moving prey fleeing from a jaguar was calming to her aunt. There was one time Charlotte woke up to a sabretooth mauling a little one; she couldn't sleep the rest of the night.

Passing into the last room was Gemma and Simon's room. Charlotte didn't know why all the cousins agreed to sleep in their room. It was unsurprising that Olivia and Alexandria decided to share their bed and make the boys sleep on the floor. Opening the door, she noticed a chiffon fabric draped along the frame, adding a romantic and delicate touch.

With her luck, Charlotte had to navigate to the other side of the bed. Duffel bags were stacked along the perimeters of the wall with Alexandria's suitcases piled in a generous part of the corner next to the closet. With the open window beside him, Lucas lay near the window, half-covered by a worn Toronto Raptors comforter to cool down. Mason turned to the side, causing his silky boxer shorts to ride up higher, which made Charlotte feel sick when she saw a brief glimpse of his privates. In the cozy confines of his sleeping bag, Noah appeared like a chrysalis undergoing a metamorphosis.

"Hey, Lucas," Charlotte said, nudging him in the shoulder. "Lucas, wake up."

With a groan, Lucas rolled away, trying to get back to his peaceful slumber.

She grabbed his shoulders, gave him a shake, and said, "Come on."

As his eyelids lifted, his neck popped, and the icy moonlight enhanced the blue of his eyes. A network of prominent, red veins surrounded his irises.

"W-what," he muttered, pulling the blanket over his head in frustration.

"I need you to come with me. I saw something."

"Can't it wait?"

"No, it can't."

Charlotte had a hard time staying silent. Her words were fraught with anxiety, fearing she'd disturb the many people who could waken by a single syllable. Mason let out a sigh, extending his arms and resting his head on his bicep. Olivia laid motionless; her eye mask concealed herself away from the rest of the world. Alexandria made a pained face, almost like she was trying to imitate a dog's half-hearted bark.

"I really need you to come with me."

Lucas slammed his fist into the pillow, frustrated and longing to hit something more substantial. Rubbing his face, he let the energy flow back into his body.

Charlotte let her cousin have some time to get his bearings. The blanket went flying toward the window, and the wind, in turn, brought the curtains back, almost touching his exposed and lean abdomen. He snatched his *Beavis and Butthead* t-shirt, then walked toward Noah, stepping over the brown bag as though it were a log. Olivia let out a small snore, a slight noise escaping her as she moved her pillow to find a comfortable angle for her neck. Mason's foot twitched, accidentally bumping into Lucas. He stumbled, unable to catch himself before falling forward. Lucas grunted when he collapsed onto his cousin; his toned muscles were solid as a rock and allowed no cushion. The collision was like a bag of bones against a brick wall, followed by a wheezing inhale. His gasp echoed along the wall, making Charlotte's heart pound against her chest. Mason's sudden movement sent his cousin flying off his chest, causing Lucas to fling onto his legs.

The remaining children stirred like a chain reaction, Noah expelling a groan with his body wriggling in his sleeping bag to try and go back to sleep. Olivia let out a yelp that pitched higher than a yorkie with her arm slapping Alexandria, causing her to gasp with shock that sounded like she was informed of the juiciest gossip.

"What the hell?" Mason growled, shoving Lucas away from his crotch.

Olivia's eye mask landed on the floor after she threw it. The green mud on her face seemed to enhance her anger, making her resemble a vicious ogre as she furrowed her eyebrows.

"So much for keeping quiet," Charlotte mumbled under her breath.

With deliberate steps, she walked to the door, closing it quietly and straining her ears to see if their parents had heard their sudden fright. Timothy was still snoring; nothing had changed.

"I'm sorry," Lucas said as he got back to his feet. "Charlotte saw something."

"No, don't tell them!" Charlotte thought.

Charlotte slumped, observing the irritated expressions on everyone's faces, including Lucas, who felt embarrassed by his accidental contact with Mason.

"Here you go again, Charlie. Trying to get attention," Olivia hissed, removing the comforter from over her.

"I'm not looking for attention, Olivia," Charlotte retorted, her fist clenching.

"Listen, Booger, I'm tired after the long drive and hearing Dad sing oldies for hours. Can't this wait until morning?" Alexandria said, rubbing her eyes.

"Yeah. Nothing's going to happen," Mason agreed. "Not while we're all here."

Charlotte was gradually coming around to their way of thinking. After embarrassing herself by waking everyone up, she didn't care if it was George H. W. Bush himself in the fields. Nothing was worth it anymore for her to pursue her curiosity.

"Come to think of it, don't you remember when we would sneak off into the fields when we were younger?" Noah asked, peeling himself from his sleeping bag by slowly unzipping himself out.

"Yeah!" Olivia remembered, her enthusiasm piqued. "And remember the time when—"

"Let's not get into what happened," Charlotte cut them off, her right temple suddenly pulsating.

Sneaking off into the fields was a favorite pastime for the cousins when they were kids. Because she would be left out of the adventure, Charlotte stealthily followed them, wanting to find out what they were doing. Following them through the tall plants, her ten-year-old self was terrified. The only companions she had were the gentle breeze and the wild creatures, as she stayed hidden and out of sight. It wasn't until she lost them deep in the brush where she started to panic and forgot her way back to the house; it wasn't in view. A figure in a burlap mask chased her, leading her to run into a tower and hit one of its legs, resulting in a serious gash on her head. Every day, the sight of the two-inch blemish below her hairline in the mirror filled her with the memory of her terror.

"Screw it," Alexandria groaned, rising from the bed with a dramatic sigh. "Let's go check it out. It would be like old times."

As Charlotte watched them all put on their slippers, she let out a nervous sigh. Noah zipped up his black hoodie while Mason slipped on his white beater.

Mason felt a sense of security as he cracked the door open, letting his gang know the coast was clear. Olivia tied her pink, plush robe to cover her silky pajamas, using her sleeve to rub off the mud. Noah trailed Charlotte, meticulously mimicking her footsteps to avoid making the floorboards groan. Olivia and Alexandria trailed behind them, closely like the twins from *The Shining*; their hands grasped tight and had no interest in breaking apart. Lucas followed next; his lips were tight, full of apology as he sensed Charlotte's reluctance to have anybody else join them in her plan.

Mason and Noah went down the stairs ahead of Charlotte, who watched them go. The family portraits in the glass showed their reflections. Seeing her aunt and uncle's doors, she regretted the choices that had led her to this point. A single thought crossed her mind about waking them, but she dismissed it. It wouldn't differ anymore, they were grown adults now. The worst part was that they could torment her without limit if they repeated their past actions.

"Shit."

THE QUIET WIND HELD the landscape frozen in time. Not a leaf stirred on the still branches. There wasn't a single sunflower that was dancing; all were standing still like they were being ordered by a drill sergeant.

The full moon glowed with its usual brilliance. The sky was clear, offering an unobstructed view of the bright path the children walked on. Alexandria skipped down the path with newfound energy, her steps mimicking Dorothy's journey along the yellow brick road. With his biceps bulging, Mason asserted his leadership, sending a warning to any who dared to challenge him. Noah and Lucas had their heads tilted, looking into the stars that were dazzling in their eyes; the busy city life was nothing like complete silence and serenity in the open country, away from traffic, away from school, away from people.

Two roads diverged, offering them a choice, with Mason stopping to gather the troops. Olivia pulled her robe higher, hiding her chest beneath the collar. Alexandria huddled closer to her brother, waiting for the warmth to beat out the chill in her body.

"I feel like we should split up. What do y'all think?"

"I don't think that's a good idea," Charlotte said, her voice quiet and meek.

"Well, where did you see this thing?" Noah asked.

"Over there."

Her finger gestured toward the highest tower. Telescope lenses winked back at them with a sliver of reflected light. The rope, undisturbed and arrow-straight, dangled over the edge.

"Don't you think it could've gone anywhere?" Alexandria asked.

"You're right. I think we should split up," Noah agreed.

No, Charlotte thought to herself.

"Okay, then that's what we'll do. How do we want to do this?" Alexandria asked.

"I can take Noah and Alexandria," Mason volunteered.

"And why them?" Olivia's eyebrow arched as she asked.

"You can take care of yourselves," he said with a chuckle. "Plus, Noah needs a big, *strong man* to protect him!"

Noah's head was enclosed in his arm, anticipating a noogie. His chin pressed into Mason's bicep as his muscles contracted. A whiny sigh escaped Noah's lips, overwhelmed by his power but finding humor in his cynicism.

How chivalrous, Charlotte thought apathetically.

"Okay, then let's go!" Olivia said with dread, scuffling her feet when she veered to the left.

Putting distance between herself and Charlotte and Lucas, Olivia crossed her arms and walked ahead. With a shared chuckle, Mason, Noah, and Alexandria took the other trail. Lucas, walking past the first attraction, crossed his eyes as he poked his head through the sunflower graphic.

"C'mon, smile," he urged, sensing Charlotte's absentmindedness.

Charlotte's eyes were blank, a reaction she'd trained herself to use over the years. Despite any situation that might elicit joy or sorrow, she could maintain a perfectly impassive expression.

"I said I was sorry for getting the others involved."

"I know you did."

"She just doesn't like being out here, isn't it?" Olivia contributed, her voice whiny.

Olivia picked the flower, severing it from its stem. One by one, the yellow petals flaked onto the ground by her fingers, pinching them away as though she were plucking an ingrown hair.

"I don't blame you," Olivia continued. "This is really stupid anyway."

"Then why did you agree to come out here?" Charlotte asked, confused.

"Sometimes we do things to make other people happy."

"And you're not happy?" Lucas asked.

As a gentle breeze swept past, it stirred the plants, scattering petals near her slippers. Seeds sprinkled on top of her toes, tapping on the plush tops.

"The whole thing is stupid," she confessed, grabbing the remaining flower and squeezing it tight. "Grandma's dead, and I'm stuck here with you guys."

"What's that supposed to mean?" Lucas asked.

"You know what I mean! I find it ridiculous that you're here and you get special treatment when you're not one of us."

"What kind of special treatment do you think I get?" Charlotte asked, bewildered once again. "You've treated me like shit ever since we were kids."

A snicker escaped Olivia's lips as she looked up at the sky. Her face radiated joy as she inhaled deeply, lost in the blissful memory of her years of tormenting.

"And I would do it all over again."

Charlotte stopped moving, keeping her emotions hidden. Olivia's lack of remorse for her comments over the years was unsurprising. It didn't make it any easier for Charlotte to hold herself back from punching her in her face. The urge to grab Olivia's hair and yank it was a fleeting fantasy for Charlotte, but she opted for a more dignified course of action.

"What the fuck? Why are you such a bitch?" Lucas asked, irritated.

"Why is she such trash?"

"Excuse me?" Charlotte asked, her nostrils flaring as she narrowed her eyes. A sharp crease appeared between her brows, her lips forming a thin, tight line.

"You know, you don't have to be a part of this group. If you're going to act like a brat, then you can walk your ass back to the house."

"That or I can take you back myself," Charlotte mumbled.

Olivia felt her stomach twist in knots as her cousin's threat hung in the air. Her hand fluttered against her chest.

"I don't want you here just as much as you don't want me," Charlotte said, walking closer to Olivia, who stood rooted in place. "We can at least be cordial to each other this weekend while we settle everything that Grandma and Grandpa worked their asses on until their deaths."

With a gasp, Lucas leaned on a wooden stake, moving cautiously to avoid shattering the Christmas lights that circled overhead.

"I don't want trouble, so you can either just keep the shitty comments to a minimum or stay the hell out of my way," Charlotte continued. "Either way, if you keep up this crap, I will make sure everyone knows about the perfect little angel being anything but that!"

Olivia was at a loss for words. The pink in Charlotte's skin turned a purplish shade in the darkness, causing her to flinch. Those she victimized over the years are finally speaking out against her behavior. Thoughts of what she might say made Olivia tentative, at least for the moment that she was outnumbered in the middle of the field.

"Do you understand me?" Charlotte said, now inches away from her face.

"Fine."

ON THE OTHER SIDE OF the field, the remaining cousins walked along the path. Mason plucked a sunflower from the base, waving it like it was a sword; its stem was flimsy as it considered breaking in half with the petals and seeds unbalancing the weight. Alexandria looked in every direction; the moving plants startling her with every small breath of the wind. Noah's arm wrapped around her, soothing her nerves and chasing away her shivers.

"Why did I sign up for this?" she asked herself, cradling her arms over her chest.

"Don't you remember how fun it was when we were kids?" Noah said, hoping to spark her enthusiasm.

"Yeah, we were exactly that: kids."

"Don't be such a party pooper!" Mason hissed, tossing the plant back into the field, leaving the sunflower's fellow plants to deal with the loss.

As they rounded the corner, the path grew narrower. The flowers were reaching heights that even surpassed Mason's six-foot frame. A nearby cutout, its planks weathered and loose, groaned as the wood creaked on its rusty hinges.

"We're not kids anymore," Alexandria told her cousin, letting him warm her up.

"Why do you have to act like such a grown up?" Mason joked, putting his hands inside the pockets of his basketball shorts.

"Why won't you grow up?" she joked.

"We have the rest of our lives to do that!"

"And besides, it was only fun when we were pranking Charlotte going out here."

Noah persisted in his silence. Watching the amused expressions on Mason and Alexandria's faces as they lit up in reminiscence made his blood boil. The longer Mason reminisced, a more quiet chuckle bubbled up from within him.

"She's not *really* that fun anymore," she continued.

"Was she ever, though?" Mason agreed.

"Give her a chance, she's not that bad," Noah chimed in, hesitantly.

"Don't give me that," Alexandria hissed while she ran her fingers through her hair. "I still don't understand why she gets to come here."

"God, you're starting to sound like Olivia," Noah said, cringing with his lips tightening.

"She's not wrong with what she said."

"That's because you're girls and need to stick together," Mason joked with his hands swinging around his shorts to swish the fabric.

"No! I agree with her because I don't see Charlotte as a Chester. I never did."

Noah recoiled, saying, "That's harsh," and removing his arm from her.

"Well, she isn't! She was only brought into this family through marriage. It's not in her blood."

"Wow! You *really are* sounding like Olivia," Mason said with a chuckle as he kicked the dirt, causing a cloud to float around his knees.

"Yeah, and you're being a real bitch about it, too," Noah said, pursing his lips with eyes piercing into her bitterness.

"Shut up!" she said, fumbling her words as her hand reached for a flower with fingers pulling out the petals. "Watch her take Grandma's money from the will and never speak to us again!"

Silence descended, engulfing the air and the other two with pieces of the flower trailing behind them. Each yank made a crunch that felt like the fauna was pleading for Alexandria to stop with the torment. Her cheekbones bathed in the soft glow of the moonlight, causing her blonde eyebrows, one raised in suspicion, to fade into the shadows.

"Who cares if she gets anything? Why is it about money with you?"

"You should be worried! Grandma and Grandpa worked hard for everything they had. I'd be damned if I will allow some mutt to come and take that from me!"

Noah's lip curled up in revulsion. After all the years of hanging out at the family get-togethers, this side of her was not one that he ever saw, nor appreciated. I guess they weren't kids anymore; some people grow up to be more mature and responsible adults, while others grow up with more of a colder outlook on life, and sometimes blended with a bit of selfishness.

Noah stood up, his face nearing hers, and declared, "Charlotte isn't a mutt."

Alexandria's face burned with the increasing heat of his suppressed anger. His heavy breaths sent shivers down her spine as it touched her neck.

"Why are you standing up for her? You didn't like her either."

"She may not be close with me, but she is a human being and deserves the same amount of respect as the rest of us."

The whites of her eyes, stark against the darkness, revealed her grimness as they rolled. The blonde strands of her hair, swaying before her face, added to the emotionless and zombie-like quality she exuded.

"And besides, we don't even know who's getting what. For all we know, it could go to charity."

She had her arms folded across her chest. The ground beneath her feet gave way, accepting the tap of her toes as they dug into the soil. Another gust blew, and the flowers perked up with movement, with flowers bowing their weight toward them as though they wanted to touch him.

"I hope I get that Nintendo," Mason said, his shoulders slumped in a shrug.

His comment, meant to add to the conversation, left them both speechless. Both were annoyed with one another. The air crackled with unspoken tension, each word a loaded gun. Their growth and grief put pressure on their bonds and ties, testing their relationships. They felt the same way when they spoke in unison.

"Shut up!"

AS OLIVIA FELL FURTHER behind Charlotte and Lucas, she continued scuffling her feet along the ground, her steps becoming slower. As they met each other's eyes, Charlotte's eyes twinkled with relief that her dreaded cousin had been put in her place, making a sense of ease settle between them. It was even more satisfying to see her take charge and fight her own battles. It was on her own she stood up for herself. And because of it, her posture straightened with confidence.

"How much longer do we have to be out here!" Olivia whined, her hand slapping one stem.

"I don't know," Charlotte answered. "Until one of us finds something."

"That could take all night!"

"I don't want to be out here either," Charlotte agreed sharply.

They arrived at the cabin, the moonlight shimmering through the mud-caked windowpane. Charlotte thought back to earlier, when she stormed out on her family after Olivia's tirade, remembering she had seen something moving in the flowers. A thought flickered through her mind—could the mysterious being be living in the abandoned house?

"Do you want to go look inside?" she asked the group.

"Do you think it's safe?" Lucas said, his hand tracing the bare siding, brushing against a rusty nail, almost touching it.

"You're not scared, are ya?" she joked.

"You're starting to sound like one of us now," he said with a laugh.

Olivia wiped the dust off her robe with her fingers, declaring, "I'm not going in there. It's gross!"

Olivia's choice to stay out has fueled Charlotte's determination to go inside. Perhaps this is the farm adventure she's always wanted to experience with her cousins. Her favorite cousin being there would make it even better.

"Fine, keep a look out. Scream if you notice anything," Lucas said.

Watching the two approach the door, Olivia rolled her eyes. Her robe would now be sullied by the earthly delights, but she crossed her legs and sat on the ground, regardless.

Lucas paused at the door, absorbing the message conveyed by the DO NOT ENTER signs and the crumbling duct tape that shimmered. By tearing down the barrier, Charlotte enabled her cousin to begin their search. He turned the knob, its texture rough against his palm. The door was stuck because of the warped wood. He heaved his weight into it, nearly losing his balance and falling to the floor.

The air felt stagnant and smelled like mildew. Rolls of carpet are stacked along the edges of the walls. With ripped edges flapping in the breeze, the blush-pink wallpaper, a familiar sight for years, has come loose from the wall. Each step on the creaking floorboards brought them closer to the lounge, and with it, disrupting their childhood memories.

Fluffy stuffing billowed out from the tears in the brown paisley couch like pus from an infected wound. A mix of ash, burnt wood, and blackened garbage clogged the fireplace. Now covered in soot, the books that towered above it have their titles obscured. Brown water from the roof leak filled the gaping hole in the bathroom floor where the toilet once stood. The water had run down the walls, turning the pastel blue paint into a more earthy tone.

Charlotte's heart ached. One person's treasured spot had been carelessly destroyed by another. The place she used to go to as a child during her outings had fallen into complete disrepair. Memories had now become just that, with the place of inspiration completely ruined.

"What the hell happened here?"

Charlotte's eyes welled with disgust as she noticed someone had burned Gemma's Narnia book, a single tear tracing the curve of her eyelid with *The Silver Chair* now scorched.

Lucas was equally astonished. His gaze fell on the bedroom door next to them, bringing back memories of the blanket forts they'd built with Mason and Noah. A gaping hole had been punched in the center of the door, with light-brown splinters jutting toward him.

"I think my mom said that there were some frat boys that rented the cabin out."

Charlotte's stomach queazed. The memories of serving fraternity brothers at the campus coffee shop came back to her. Either they lacked decisiveness, making her feel like she was talking to a hungover brick wall, or they were just being jerks to impress the sorority sisters in a belittling demeanor. Their attitude toward other women, in any scenario, caused her to recoil.

"What a bunch of heartless pieces of crap!"

"I know," Lucas agreed, shaking his head. "I would kill them myself if I had the chance to."

A gust of wind caused the door to rattle against the wall. Straw fragments scattered across the ground. The chilling thought of the shadow pursuing her plagued Charlotte's mind, causing her to stand behind Lucas. The broken porcelain on the mantel shuddered as three heavy thumps echoed from the adjacent bedroom.

"What was that?" she said, gasping as she inched closer to her cousin.

Three more thumps came. It was as though a beast was knocking on the door, demanding to be let in. Lucas felt Charlotte's black-painted nails digging into his arm, scratching his skin.

"I think we should go," he said, grabbing her arm.

The two ran back outside. With no pause, he seized the door and slammed it closed. The awning of the roof trembled from the force of his pull, causing a shingle to flake onto the ground, landing a mere four feet from their right.

"Olivia, we should get going,"

Their eyes darted around the cottage, yearning for an answer, even a whimper. Only the sound of birds departing from the lampposts gave their ears a tingle. As they circled the area, the only indication of Olivia's presence was faint indentations in the dirt.

"Where the hell did she go?" Charlotte asked, her breath becoming heavy with each second.

Her mind whirled with questions about the woman's whereabouts. Olivia wasn't the brightest, so she knew Olivia couldn't find her own way back, even though she had been in the maze many times. She also wasn't brave enough to go hide in the middle of nowhere, wanting to do some sort of prank to create any jump scares to her.

"Dad, Gabriel, do you know where she went?" Charlotte uttered a whisper to the plants.

Silence met the rattling leaves. The heavy silence and her increasingly labored breathing underscored Charlotte's search for her family.

"Who are you talking to?" Lucas asked, his eyebrow lifting in surprise as he startled Charlotte.

Charlotte's heart skipped a beat when she saw the look of worry on his face. The timing wasn't right for her to confess she speaks to ghosts, even if it's her family.

"N-nobody," Charlotte said hastily. "I was just talking to myself."

As Lucas searched for their cousin, his ragged breaths became more audible. He ran to the other side of the building, then back, and over again. The moon vanished behind a gathering mass of clouds, becoming more dense with each passing second. His fingers trembled as he delicately brushed the petals, praying she might be beneath. She was nowhere to be found.

"Olivia!"

Chapter 12

With the tower in view, Mason sprinted along the next path. Each turn fueled his motivation, like the clock was ticking down for his half-court hero shot. Noah quickened his pace, arms pumping, breaking into a sweat as he followed. With her hand shielding her jaw, Alexandria pretended to yawn, masking her shock as she maintained her stride.

"Come on, guys!" Mason said, his lungs lightly panting. "I heard Lucas from over here!"

As they headed toward the tower, they saw two more cutouts, one depicting a picnic being rained out. One captured a three-year-old with a tilted birthday cone hat dropping a scoop of ice cream on the ground.

"Looks like someone's been on the juice for too long," Alexandria remarked, her hand grazing the image and pushing the board away.

The giant hole in the ground made Mason stop. As the others drew closer, his smile became brighter. He stood with his hands on his hips, waiting for them to catch up.

"Do you remember this?"

Upon the others' arrival, they gazed into the pit, a good ten feet in depth. Sunflower seeds took up close to half the space in the hole. Two ropes suspended planks in place to make a bridge, and two additional strands acted as handles for support. The bridge, with two ropes, one above the other, on each side, made crossing a challenge for the children.

"You couldn't make it across, Noah," Mason said, chuckling.

"I told you I had a stomach ache!"

The memory of his cousins watching him struggle on the ropes brought laughter echoing back into his mind. His body mimicked their swaying, the fibers digging deep into his hands, burning his palms as he struggled to regain his balance. The kids watched with amusement as he landed face-first in the seeds and struggled to climb the wooden ladder. His childhood had many embarrassing moments, but this one stood out, especially with his family.

"Bet you can't cross now!"

His stomach lurched, the remnants of their dinner eager to make their way out of his body. The pit appeared less daunting now, as he was three feet taller than before. He was not interested in dwelling on the past, particularly to impress his cousin.

"Maybe next time."

"Wimp!"

"Yeah, what's the matter? Chicken?" Alexandria contributed, her tone antagonistic.

"We've got to find Lucas, along with everyone else," Noah said, hoping they don't see his excuse.

"Olivia!" Charlotte's voice echoed from the unknown.

"See? Let's get going!"

Mason and Alexandria scoffed. Noah sped ahead, abandoning the other two and becoming the first to cross a different bridge. The planks teetered in every direction; his balance became wobbly. His ankles got out of alignment when he reached the middle. With each lift of his leg, the wood swayed in all directions. Mason made things worse by shaking the ropes and laughing as he almost fell into the pit. Alexandria's eyebrows furrowed along with her chuckles; the shadows of the night made her more menacing.

"Cut it out!"

He heard his knees crackle as he walked closer. The strain of his calves dispelled any lingering grogginess he might have felt. He needed a moment to adjust to the solid ground beneath him. He headed for the tower, disregarding the fact that the others hadn't crossed yet.

"Hey! Wait for us!" Alexandria said, her balance shaky as she tried to find her center of gravity.

Her plea did not matter to Noah at the moment, especially when her laughter cosigned the joke. Mason's antics weren't funny then, and it's still not funny now. His brother often reverted to their childish games and jokes, which was what they needed as they transitioned into adulthood during stressful times. What Mason struggled with was finding the right time to stop. Going overboard was typical of him, and it would often result in someone yelling at him to understand their limitations.

As he neared the tower, it seemed to grow taller, eclipsing his initial estimate of twenty-five feet. Two shadowy figures, their arms flailing, stood along one of the legs, calling his name.

"Noah!"

"Noah!"

Mason's weight caused the planks to creak as they struggled to hold him over the decaying foundation. Under the weight of his steps, the ropes sang with tension, their cries echoing his progress. As Noah tipped over and fell into the pit, a grunt escaped him, eliciting a chuckle of irony and an eye roll.

"What's going on?" Noah asked, confused. "Where's Olivia?"

"She's disappeared," Charlotte said, anxiety etched on her face as her eyes darted around, desperately searching.

"Where's the others?" Lucas asked.

Noah pointed behind him. Like a plant growing taller, Mason's silhouette became more defined as he crawled out of the space. A loud laugh erupted from Charlotte, echoing within the structure as she reveled in her contentment before joining them again. Alexandria's braids swung behind her as she listened, eyes narrowing in disdain.

The three met up with Mason and Alexandria. Mason brushed away the seeds clinging stubbornly to his dark, hairy legs with little football shapes marked on his skin.

"You saw nothing, understand?" Mason said as he adjusted his white beater over his shorts after wiping his face; the crevasses of his abs were more defined in the darkness.

"Why does it matter?" Charlotte asked.

"Because everyone knows that I'm king of the maze!" he hissed with seriousness. "I hold the record for the annual race, and everybody knows about my perfect run!"

Despite their efforts, the three couldn't deflate his ego. Why does it matter that he's the champion of a children's race that happened ten years ago? Why did he worry about others judging his imperfect run? Ever since Mason joined the basketball team in ninth grade, the team nurtured this type of behavior to the point that he never did anything wrong.

"Whatever. Olivia is missing," said Charlotte.

"Wait, what?" Mason asked.

"Do you know if she told you about this being some kind of joke?" Lucas asked, inquisitive, as he looked at their reactions for any clue.

"No," Alexandria and Mason replied together, their voices empty.

A whisper of wind grazed the back of their necks. With increasing force, the gusts pushed Alexandria toward the flowers, one threatening to shove her in. They protected their eyes from particles whipping toward their faces by shielding them.

"Well, we need to find her, then," Charlotte continued. "Let's check the tower to see if we can find her from above."

Their eyes grew wide as Mason and Alexandria met each other's gaze. This was the most direction Charlotte gave to them. While her serious demeanor made them want to laugh, her leadership entertained them and held back their judgment.

"Come on!"

Lucas walked beside Charlotte. Noah trailed close behind her, as the others followed. With a self-assured stride, Charlotte walked, drawing amusement from Alexandria and the other person who mimicked her with mocking hip-swaying.

Charlotte heard their laughter, but the comments were just muffled mumbles to her. None of this was new, so it was easy for her to ignore it, especially when it wasn't about her or them; this was about finding Olivia.

As she ascended the tower, each step brought a chill, the air sharpening with each breath. Their resting place disrupted, the black birds flew away from the railings in annoyance. The stars grew in size, their twinkle more vibrant, like they were climbing toward the heavens.

Reaching the highest point, she started strolling along the platform's edge. With a firm grasp on the railing, she tried to hide her fear and maintain her composure. Her weight caused one board to buckle, and her foot sank deeper into the floor. Alexandria, her body resting on one of the chairs, found a place to sit under the gazebo at the center. Scarecrow decorations stood watch at every corner of the structure, their emotionless eyes making her cringe.

The sunflower field, now closer, revealed intricate patterns and clearly plowed pathways, a contrast to the view from the hilltop or her stepfather's bedroom. The rows, defined, exposed even the smallest details of the stones and the trash the guests had discarded.

Nothing seemed out of place.

No sign of Olivia.

"Can we go back? I'm sure she just went back to sleep," Alexandria complained, stretching her arms in annoyance.

The scarecrow behind her swayed, its straw shifting. Fibers from the frayed plaid shirt danced around her face. A sudden movement of a hand caused Alexandria to gasp and flinch. Inching nearer to Charlotte, the scarecrow slowly shifted. Turning its attention to Alexandria, it lifted a finger from its withered glove, the hand covering its stitched mouth.

"Shhhh."

Alexandria's fear turned into laughter, holding herself back from the huffs to be noticeable. She rose from her seat and strolled toward Mason, who was gazing out at the other side, away from Charlotte and Lucas. She gave him a light tap on the shoulder, silencing him as he spun around. Seeing the scarecrow creeping toward Charlotte, Mason's face lit up, finding it even funnier that Noah and Lucas hadn't noticed the floorboards creaking.

"Any sign of her?" Charlotte asked, combating a yawn.

"None here," Lucas replied.

"Nada!" said Noah.

Charlotte moved along the banister, rounding the corner. A shadow was stealthily making its way toward her, which she caught sight of in her peripherals. The moonlight was being blocked by the dark clothes. The shadow startled her as she turned around, causing her stomach to clench and her knees to give out. What began as a small screech escalated into a fearful scream that resonated throughout the maze.

When their arms extended toward her, the scarecrow emitted a grunt. Charlotte flinched, stepping back to avoid touching it. The railing splintered, poking her back and causing her to wobble.

"W-woah!" she yelped, her arms flailing.

"Charlotte!" Lucas and Noah said, screeching as they shoved the scarecrow away from her.

The banister separated from Charlotte, leaving the rod to drop onto the ground. The plank broke, dislodging the nail, and she fell under the force of gravity. With a grip on the structure, she looked down at the terrifying distance, her stomach twisting, desperate not to lose her hold. Her tears fell, despite the pain of the splinters on her fingertips.

"Grab our hand!" Noah said, wrapping his around hers.

"We won't let you go!" Lucas cosigned.

Sweat slicked onto their skin as they both leaned back, using their strength to pull her up. With only her legs dangling, Charlotte was hanging halfway back to the top. The scarecrow's presence, amidst their laughter, shifted her fear into anger as Mason and Alexandria mocked her.

She kicked her feet up onto the structure, but a slipper slipped off and fell, forcing her to find another way to reach the top. As she reached safety, her body felt heavy, causing her to sink into the supporting boards. With each breath, she felt her heart quicken, echoing the laughter from behind the burlap. The fabric covering Olivia's face fell away, revealing a mole on her chin.

"Gotcha!" she said as she removed the gloves from her fingers.

"That wasn't funny!" Lucas said to her as he inched closer to her face.

"She could've gotten hurt!" Noah said.

"Relax, she's fine. Isn't she?" Olivia said, unbuttoning the shirt.

As it swirled through the air, the garment plummeted from the tower's side, hitting the ground. Removing a straw from her pajamas, she examined her fingernails for grime.

Charlotte was rendered speechless, completely lost for words. She clutched her arms to her chest as she shivered. Avoiding any boards that might creak like the last, she moved with hesitant steps.

Her expression was seldom the further she made it from her. The confidence she had grown to embrace had become shattered, broken back to the submissive fear.

"You've taken it too far!" Lucas said, following behind her.

Noah looked at his sister, also with no words to say. The disappointment was in his eyes as he shook his head, reflecting the sadness.

Alexandria and Mason high-fived Olivia, and the three laughed in satisfaction, while the other three scurried down the stairs. Another successful prank, and it wasn't even intentional. Only Olivia knew the secret, and she wanted revenge for Charlotte's actions. Charlotte may have grown up and started to speak for herself, but nobody crossed Olivia and got away with it.

As they sat on the picnic table, they breathed in the fresh air, taking in the view and watching Charlotte put her slipper back on. Noah and Lucas tried to calm her shaking by wrapping their arms around her and offering comfort. The farther they walked from the house, the smaller their silhouettes became on the path. Olivia smiled, finding a strange pleasure in her suffering. As the trio passed another light, the flowers beside the path moved with unusual speed. These were swinging from the force of another body; a figure, creeping away and meandering the fields.

Chapter 13

S unday

THE SUNRISE OVER THE fields roused the birds from the slumber. No longer hidden by darkness, the flowers burst with vibrant color. A gentle melody filled the air as the wind chimes swayed.

Her adventure with her cousins had kept Charlotte up, her eyes revealing red veins from the lack of sleep. Her mind fixated on the prospect of falling with no one to save her. Even worse, nobody really to care. When she wasn't thinking about that, the horror of the last prank they did to her would haunt her. The right side of her head throbbed from the scar that haunted her to this day. All she could remember was exactly what happened last night; Olivia starting the joke with Mason and Alexandria co-signing in on her humor, and Lucas and Noah staring blankly at her misery.

Despite running back to the house to stop the bleeding, only James and Katherine rushed to her side. Her mom, with her medical training, stopped the bleeding and rushed her to the emergency room for three stitches. Marnie's presence completely consumed Edward's attention, causing him to miss her injury. While Victoria got everything ready for inventory, Timothy focused on budgeting in the office. Gemma and Simon would have been there to help, but Charlotte recalled the door being shut, and they were having a serious argument.

Stretching her arms, she allowed her shoulders to emit a loosening crack. Sleep deprivation was nothing new for her, but it's not something she wanted. She grew accustomed to the rhythm of pulling all-nighters, studying and then working early mornings at the coffee shop.

Her muscles ached as she went to grab her black and yellow flannel shirt. Her biceps protested in agony as she buttoned her placket, clenching from the effort of grabbing the planks when she dangled from the tower. Instead of wrestling with her jeans, she chose to wear her denim skirt, which allowed her to hike up her legs with ease. Her braid was more disheveled than usual, but she didn't seem to notice. She embraced her unkempt look, finding comfort in the wild strands of her peeking hair.

The hallway was filled with open doors, yet not a single sound escaped from the rooms. All she could hear was the chatter coming from down the stairs. Laughter filled the corridor as Olivia and Alexandria talked about Charlotte's desperate pleas for help when she dangled over the edge.

She entered Gemma's bedroom. A wrinkled heap of paisley bed sheets lay at the foot of the bed. Noah's sleeping bag laid spread wide, as if a butterfly had just broken free from its chrysalis. Clothes laid scattered on the floor, abandoned, as if someone expected them to be picked up and cleaned.

A breeze wafting through the open window caused the closet shutters to rattle, trembling along their tracks. The door's hinges allowed the planks to come closer together, forming a triangular shape at each end as she opened it. Overalls hung on the hangers along with tattered flannel shirts; ones that were on the verge of being recycled for future scarecrows. Her fingers brushed through the sleeves of each one that dangled in front of her; each shirt brought out a memory of her legacy in the family and the farm.

Above the closet were little shoeboxes; she was never the type to throw anything away. She pulled one down and looked inside. Photographs were piled in there; colors blending in with the black and white with hints of brown and sepia tones. Seeing the images, she choked back tears, particularly when she saw a picture of Gemma at the same age. A year after graduating, she found great joy in her current path. She stood tall in front of the chicken coop on the grounds. With her chicks scattered across the land, she beamed with pride.

The next image was of Gemma and Simon. Smiling at the end of the driveway, they cut the giant ribbon, their thirty-year-old selves holding onto the scissors. The grand opening of Chester Farms was a sight to behold, with children brimming with joy, their happiness clear as they ran and played on the newly opened grounds. James and Victoria, both wearing plaid button-down shirts, looked alike, but Victoria stood out with her plaid skirt and knee-high socks. Edward stared off into the distance, his eyes avoiding the camera, as Charlotte recalled the mailbox's location across the street.

Each photograph ignited her imagination about life in those times. Without technology's intrusion, navigating the world was easier, as people found entertainment in the natural world. There wasn't an economical shift, or the fear of needles being shared if you chose to take injectable drugs. The seventies appeared to be a more liberating period, less superficial and less driven by pressure to conform.

Among the photos at the bottom of her stack, one stood out as more recent. Charlotte stood quietly at the end of the tea party table, listening as her cousins chatted among themselves. She fidgeted with a spoon in a teacup as Mason, arms spread wide, dramatized his gains during flag football. Alexandria's eyes were wide, waiting for the conversation to change and Olivia peering at one of the other children playing; her envious glare was toward the girl in the frilly dress that she desperately wanted to add to her closet. A small mound formed a barrier between the two boys, who sat together amidst the young customers on their business day. They stared intently at the camera, their eyes burning with concentration. Their jealousy stemmed from the cousins' possessions, a feeling no one should have, or perhaps they were focused on what was happening behind the camera. Charlotte tried to erase certain parts of her memory, and this was one of them; she didn't remember who was taking the picture.

Before closing the box, she wiped her face with her sleeve, placing away the things she hoped would be happier memories, even if some were fabricated. Her arms once again cringed as she reached up to put it away; the pain was a bit much for her as it was like she was lowering a casket into the ground.

"I miss you."

HUMMINGBIRDS BUZZED around the feeder, enjoying the sugary treat as the sun's rays filled the room. A solitary monarch butterfly danced around the patio before settling on a chair. Charlotte walked into the den, where she saw most of the crowd going about their usual routines.

Mason was discussing the playoffs with Noah.

Marnie was diving into a glass of water to combat her headache.

Olivia was checking her makeup in her compact mirror.

Alexandria was searching for another home movie of one of her activities.

Edward was discussing the day's plans with Victoria and Timothy.

Seated in the corner, Lucas looked out the bay window, the view a stark contrast to the sunflower vista. A bowl-shaped incline anticipated snow, ready for children's sledding adventures. The forest was a tapestry of vibrant green maple leaves, surrounded by miniature pines that acted as a border.

"Hey, Charlotte," he greeted, his smile strained.

"Morning," Charlotte said, settling into the chair next to him, paying no heed to Alexandria's attempt to sit in the same spot, which resulted in her crashing to the floor.

"How'd you sleep?" he asked, concerned as he noticed the bags under her eyes.

"Not too well."

"I'm not surprised, after the crap they pulled on you."

Surveying the space, he observed the cousins glaring at her. Noah concealed his shared annoyance at their behavior by hiding behind Mason. A wave of satisfying grins spread across their faces as they celebrated their victory by scaring their cousin.

"I'm not surprised they did it."

"Really?" he asked, eyebrow raising.

"Well, I'd like to think that some people would grow out of their crap, but I guess sometimes it's what makes them comfortable."

Charlotte pressed her lips together, hiding her disappointment. Olivia's chuckle, sharp and piercing, grated against her ears.

The clatter of pans in the sink marked the completion of Edward's cooking. A thin veil of smoke, laced with the alluring scent of bacon and sausage, hung in the air. A towering stack of pancakes, two feet high, awaited Victoria's hungry gaze as Timothy, clutching syrup and butter, prepared for the feast. Marnie took three pitchers of juice and one of the water, half of which she'd already drunk.

"Okay, who's ready for breakfast?" Victoria said after setting down the plate, the top flapjack hanging over the edge.

Mason barged into the dining room, knocking Alexandria backward onto the couch as he shoved past her. A suppressed laugh escaped Noah's lips as he winked at Charlotte, savoring their karma's return.

"I'm not that hungry," Charlotte said, holding her arms across her chest for protection.

That was a lie. She was starving. Marnie and Olivia's micromanaging at dinner had already frustrated her, and the anxiety from her fall made her crave comfort food.

"You need to eat," Lucas said, putting his arm on her shoulder. "We have a busy day today."

The sound of Mason's fists hitting the table made Marnie massage her temples in frustration. The clatter of silverware accompanied the morning ritual of preparing for nourishment. Unable to hold back any longer, Mason speared the pancake pile and retrieved three giant flapjacks. A generous pour of syrup created a cascade over his breakfast, engulfing the three strips of bacon in sugary delight. Olivia meticulously picked through the stack, choosing the thinnest and smallest piece, which she handled with delicate care, earning an eye roll from Noah.

Everybody took their turns with dishing up their breakfast. Marnie rushed back to the kitchen, grabbed a small, sharp knife, and began carving the green-skinned apple she had taken.

As everyone devoured the adults' work, Charlotte watched the portions shrink. Her eyes tracked her cousins, engrossed in their meal, oblivious to her grabbing. She disregarded her earlier comment, then helped herself to two pancakes, two sausages, and bacon.

With her chair settled, a silent exchange of glances passed between the people present. His advice validated, Lucas winked at Charlotte, amused by the amount of food on her plate. As mouths snapped, food being chomped with each bite, she was free to eat without restraint.

The bacon was crispy, just the way she liked it. She scarfed it down in two bites before shoving the sausage patty to join it. Her body felt a jolt of energy with every morsel she consumed. The pleasure of being full lessened her physical pain, giving her a respite from the emotional burden.

"Mason, you ass, you took the last of the pancakes!" Alexandria said as she craved seconds; the tiniest one was just not enough for her.

Mason disregarded her anger, shrugged, and stared at her while taking a huge bite and devouring it with the intensity of a lion tearing into an animal carcass.

"So, how's everybody been holding up?" Edward remarked, seeking to shift the conversation toward a brighter outlook."

Nobody responded right away; their mouths were full of food, and only Noah let out a tiny cough to clear his throat before shoving food down it.

"I know that this has not been the easiest week for any of us," Victoria added as she gently placed her fork onto her plate. The clanking made Marnie cringe once again. "But they say that with death, it brings an opportunity to reunite and mend relationships."

Olivia scoffed in disbelief. She patted her lips with the napkin, trying to keep her rouge lipstick perfect.

"You've got to be kidding me," she hissed as she threw it onto the table.

"I'm not," Victoria countered, raising her eyebrow. "I know you're all close already, but isn't it nice to be together as a family?"

"That's true," she agreed. "But not all of us here are family."

Charlotte stopped, nearly gagging on the pancake in her mouth. She reached over to her glass of orange juice, and the acidity burned the inside of her mouth from the bites on her lip from her nervousness.

Edward said sharply, "Olivia, we will not talk about this again."

"Yes, we are!"

As Olivia rose from her chair, her hip bumped Alexandria, causing a sticky substance to brush her cheek.

"Watch it!" Alexandria said, wiping it away, the fibers of the napkin sticking to her.

"How come she gets to come here and get what's rightfully ours?" Olivia carried on, as if Alexandria wasn't even there.

"Yeah, I think that only anybody that has been in this family from the start should get it," Mason added, his mouth full of pancake.

"Well, that's not your say, is it now?" Lucas said, staring daggers at him.

"What is it with you guys and money?" Edward said, his tone raising. "Is that all that Grandma meant to you?"

"No, but it would be nice if she gave us a little something," said Alexandria, dipping her napkin in her glass of water to dab onto her syrup stain.

With each mumbled word circling the table, the voices grew more insistent. The family members were having conversations that felt like alliance negotiations. Everyone except Charlotte, who gazed at Edward with sadness. With wide, disbelieving eyes, Victoria scanned the table, her chin twitching as family members voiced their thoughts.

"You don't deserve that!"

"Uncle James is dead. Why is she still here?"

"Mutt."

"I really want that Nintendo. I call dibs if it doesn't go to anybody."

"Enough!" said Victoria, her fist pounding on the table, causing the glasses to teeter.

The water in Alexandria's cup spilled onto her lap. A grunt escaped her as she rose from her chair and stormed out of the room. Her anger was palpable as she stomped up the stairs, her every step shaking the light over the dining room table, silencing the complaints.

"I can't believe what I'm hearing!" Victoria hissed, her fist trembling. "I thought you were joking last night, but I guess you all feel the same way."

Mason and Olivia lowered their heads, shrinking back as if they were a dog being reprimanded for ruining furniture.

"If Grandma saw the way you're acting and how you view her, she would have an absolute cow! How dare all of you treat Charlotte this way? She is family, regardless if Grandma said it or not."

Victoria grabbed her plate and ventured into the kitchen. The redness in her face faded away as she turned her blonde hair to face them. She hurled the plate into the sink, sending it crashing into a pile of shards. A slamming door followed shortly after the jingling of keys as she reached for her purse.

With a raised eyebrow and hands cupped around his mouth, Edward said, "I'm very disappointed in all of you."

Noah and Lucas were consumed by guilt as they saw Charlotte's hands trembling under the intense scrutiny of half the room. Anger flushed her cheeks, making them warm. The hurtful things they said about her belonging to the family became too much for her to keep quiet.

"I'm done with your crap," she growled, silencing Edward before he could say anything. "You all have had such a problem with me even before my stepdad died and Grandma kept me in the family.

You think you're all so perfect, but nobody talks about Mason's DUI or Olivia's shoplifting; no, it's always what I do that's never enough. If belittling people is what you want to do, then maybe this isn't the family I want to be a part of."

The chair fell as she got up. With her plate in hand, she went to the kitchen without acknowledging her cousins.

"What'd I miss?" Alexandria said as she appeared in the doorway.

Charlotte had no time to stop herself. A gooey mess of leftovers from her plate was shoved against Alexandria's chest, ending up near her feet. Seeing the opaque brown stain on her new sweatshirt, Alexandria's jaw fell open, and she whimpered, "It's ruined!"

Like her aunt before her, Charlotte crashed the plate into the sink, making more pieces go airborne. She stared at the porcelain; the fractured bits were as broken as the family was, even before her grandmother passed.

Leaving, she slammed the door behind her with her denim jacket slowly covering her like a security blanket. With her cigarette in hand, she walked past Victoria, who was inconsolable, her face buried in her hands in the front seat of her car. The sun's warmth kissed her face as birdsong filled the air. The sunflower's green leaves rustled in the wind, waving at her as if to encourage her. Her heart pounded, fueled by the adrenaline of confronting Olivia and the entire family. She usually regretted being outspoken, especially if she risked upsetting them, but she didn't mind this time. This time, she smiled wider, relieved the weight on her shoulders was gone.

The lines had been drawn.

VICTORIA TOOK A COUPLE of breaths; the windshield fogged while she concealed her hair into a bun. Stealing a cigarette from Charlotte's pack earlier, she lit it up and puffed, sending ash flakes onto her jeans. Her hands couldn't stop shaking; the family was acting out of character, or at least she's catching wind of how they really felt.

"This isn't right," she said to herself.

A tear formed in her eye as she saw her niece walking beneath the arches, her fingers trailing along the leaves.

"Poor girl."

Turning the ignition, she heard the keys jingle. The engine's desperate rattle signaled the need for a fresh oil change. Changing gears, she backed up out of her parking space and then shifted to drive to go down the hill. A drive was what she needed to feel like herself again. She didn't know what came over her to yell at the children over money; there must be a more logical way to address their concerns.

Dust swirled around the car when she came to a stop at the bottom. A crunching came from the gravel as the black rubber tires moved over it. She turned the wheel right and sped up to thirty miles an hour. As the sunflowers shifted to green maples, the breeze dried her sweaty palms while she held her hand out the window. This wasn't the way she wanted this weekend to go; she wanted things to go by more smoothly, like shooting fish in a barrel.

As the car drove away, she tossed the cigarette out the window, the stick landing on the pebbles, left behind. The cassette tape struggled to play as she inserted it. Guitars and violins became an upbeat melody with Tim McGraw saying the first lines to "I Like It, I Love It." Her hand beat onto the steering wheel, trying to keep up with the rhythm.

A figure appeared out of nowhere and ran across the road. Victoria slammed on her brakes, her heart stopping as the car skidded five feet before coming to a halt. Her eyes widened as she observed the person running farther into the woods, their jeans and flannel becoming a blur in the dusty air. To find out who was there, she parked her car on the road's edge.

"Hey!" she said, clearing her throat.

The person didn't stop. Branches cracked under their feet, echoing in the forest.

Victoria sighed in frustration, unprepared to run after having a cigarette. Her ankles trembled as she balanced on the loose gravel before descending the steep drop into the ditch. Her lungs felt heavy, struggling to keep up with a full stomach and racing thoughts. Regardless of her emotions, the person pressed on, their presence diminishing to a mere speck.

With quick movements, Victoria made her way into the forest, avoiding each branch that aimed for her face. A sharp pain ripped through her thighs, making a cramp seem imminent. The once defined grain of the bark has now blurred together. With the incline growing steeper, she decided to stop and rest, especially now that the person was gone.

At the base of the incline, a huge, withered tree trunk lay covered in mold. She leaned onto the wood; the bark flaked to the ground next to her heels. Her hair, disheveled from her messy ponytail, frizzed in front of her face. It was as messy as what Charlotte would prefer. With wings fluttering, birds chirped in the surrounding canopy. Looking down at her hand, she waited for her double vision to disappear. Next to it was a hollowed opening. Her interest heightened, she glanced inside to find something strange. Chips marred the corners, and the navy paint was worn away and faded. Rust covered the clasps, indicating they had not been polished or cared for.

A chest.

A twig snapped behind her, causing her to gasp for air. When she turned around, the filtered sunlight, already dimmed by the leaves, was completely blocked. The figure, with its red flannel shirt torn at the elbow, stood in front of her. Mud stained the denim jeans, covering most of the shin. A stick, capped with a polished, bent metal plate, rested in its hand.

Before she could speak, the shovel hit her face, sending her tumbling to the other side of the trunk. Cool leaves, damp with moisture, touched her face while mud marked her forehead. Her eyelids sank deeper, plunging the shaded space into greater darkness. The spinning intensified, draining her energy and pulling her into unconsciousness, leaving only the figure raising the weapon for another strike.

Chapter 14

The room was thrown into chaos. Lucas glared at the others while Edward and Marnie cleaned up the dining area, consolidating leftovers onto one plate so they could stack it to the kitchen in silence. Alexandria descended the stairs in a fresh shirt for the third time, and it wasn't even ten o'clock yet. Seeking respite from the tension, Noah stepped out onto the patio, hoping to clear his head and gear up for the upcoming day. When Charlotte reached her limit, he couldn't stand to see his family.

"Hey, man. I'm sorry about all that," Mason said to Lucas, recognizing his frozen expression of judgment.

Lucas's gaze met his brown eyes. Sunlight filtering through the window cast an olive-like hue on his skin. His smirk, though slight, illustrated his conviction about Charlotte's role within the family.

"You all need to cut the shit out," he retorted, heading to the den.

"I know we do," Mason agreed half-heartedly. "I've never seen Aunt Victoria be so angry before. And she does have a point. Why does it have to be about money? Grandma meant so much more to me than that."

As Lucas observed the remorseful expression deepening on his face, he eased his guardedness, recognizing a break from his usual condescending manner. Olivia was in the corner, recapping her feelings for Alexandria, so he didn't have his strings pulled to go along with their feelings about the matter; perhaps this is how he really felt.

"Just think of how much Grandma meant to all of us. That includes Charlotte."

"You're right. I'm sure she meant a lot to Charlotte when she needed someone to be there for her. I know Grandma was there for me when I needed someone."

"See? Sometimes it's more than blood when it comes to family."

Mason may've started to get the picture. Charlotte was a part of the family because of the bond with Gemma; something that doesn't require the same blood to run in their veins. There was a connection in his eyes, a shared understanding of his cousin's struggles.

Water gushed from the sink, clearing the syrup that coated the porcelain. Reaching into the other sink, Edward gathered the broken pieces of plates. With his fingers, he pressed against the base, hoping to not find a sharp point to stab his hand. Marnie took a break from cleaning to rehydrate, filling her glass with water. Despite Charlotte's absence, there were no signs of joy.

"What do you say we play a game of *Donkey Kong*?" Mason asked. "I haven't beaten that, even after trying so many times."

"Sure. You go ahead and get started. I need to take care of some things upstairs."

With a nod, Mason took his leave from Lucas. He approached the television, adjusted the input before turning on the Nintendo. A vibrant jungle scene with two monkeys chasing bananas filled the screen as the intro played.

Olivia moved toward the door, her sandals slipping with each step. Around her neck, resting on her stomach, hung her polaroid camera. Alexandria did the same, tying her white sneakers in place.

"Well, at least the kids are busy now. Do you think we should wait for Victoria and look over the bills?" Edward asked, wiping his hands on the worn towel.

Timothy put the leftovers in the fridge and sighed, "I don't know when Victoria will be back. When she has these moments, it's best to let her be."

"Okay, I'll see you on the patio."

OLIVIA AND ALEXANDRIA made their way over the gravel, taking in the fresh air that opened their lungs. Little toy tractors sat in the grain boxes, taking a rest from the days of toddlers' playtime. To avoid further staining, Alexandria took relaxing breaths after ruining her clothes, hoping her palazzo pants would stay clean. The wind rustled the sunflowers, and the camera's flash illuminated them as it took a picture. Petals fluttered with anticipation, eager for their turn for a capture from Olivia's device.

"Do you ever put that down?" Alexandria asked, tucking her hair behind her ears.

Olivia brushed pollen from her eye, dabbing it with her sorority sweater. Aiming the camera at her cousin, she took another picture, hoping to catch her stunned reaction.

"Should I?" she asked, the light flashing again. "We need to capture life's beauty. Did you see the pictures I took of Charlie last night?"

"No, but maybe you should just take in the fresh air. It'll be good for you."

The tea party table was behind them as they walked onto the path. A slight gust caused the tablecloth's corners to dance anxiously on the surface. The rustling leaves whispered an invitation to the silence, encouraging them to leave behind their usual selves and simply enjoy the beauty of the place.

Olivia placed the photographs in her bag, saying, "I need to show my friends this place."

"Why?"

"I can't let my sisters know how boring my life is. I have a reputation to live up to. Half of them have lakeside cabins!"

A roll of Alexandria's eyes conveyed her displeasure. Her patience is dwindling because of a lack of sleep. Despite the fun they had together, she couldn't tolerate Olivia's antics indefinitely.

They encountered the first fork in the road. Following Olivia's instructions from the night before, they took a left. A piece of siding hanging from the window, the cabin appeared dilapidated in the distance, as if sending a greeting.

"Ugh, why can't they just tear that shit down?" Olivia whined. "Why make it such an eyesore for all of us to see?"

Alexandria couldn't respond to that. She couldn't fathom tearing down something so meaningful to her and her family, overwhelmed by the memories that filled that space. Every Christmas in their childhood, Dexter would put on a beard and a white wig and act as Santa Claus, handing out presents to everyone and bringing them joy. Reading *The Night Before Christmas* at the fireplace the night before was something she was fond of; has she forgotten about that?

As they walked along the path, Alexandria brushed her hands against the young sprouts, her touch light and fleeting. The open plot they came to next was reminiscent of the bridge they'd seen the night before. They encountered a stretched net taut across the hole, mirroring its size, creating a trampoline. Alexandria recalled her childhood, bouncing lightly despite the aging knees, reminding her she wasn't a child anymore.

"I could never stand this one," Olivia murmured, slinking through the flowers to avoid the attraction.

Alexandria let herself drop, her hair cascading over her face. The impact of her body becoming limb was relaxing and nostalgic. The clouds above her were perfectly aligned, and one looked like an elephant with a trunk so long it could wrap around its own body. A memory surfaced of her and Simon enjoying an afternoon in the fields, snacking on Little Debbie cakes and gazing at the clouds.

His encouragement of imagination inspired her, and she carried that feeling with her, taking time to appreciate the serene beauty of the sky.

"Why is it so cold?" Olivia asked, stomping her foot onto the ground in frustration, dust forming around her sneakers. "Can we keep going so I can get warm? I also need to get back to take my supplements."

A sigh of annoyance escaped Alexandria as she sat up. Olivia's complaints made her realize she was still the same immature person she always was. She's still the same, unable to find anything that brought her joy. No matter how hard people tried, she always found a flaw in them.

Using the trampoline's bounce, Alexandria was able to get off. The path grew narrower as they continued. Flower stalks touched their shoulders, reaching up to the same height as their heads. Sharper, more frequent turns demanded, swerving around every corner, intensifying the maze.

"What did you think of the crap Char pulled out at breakfast?" Olivia asked, her smile more menacing.

The breaths Alexandria took became shallow. Olivia's comments continued to interrupt her chance to relax. Gemma's peaceful flute music would be playing, then a cranky child would mess with the needle, scratching the record.

"What's your problem with her?" Alexandria's voice was sharp as she asked.

They made it out of the path, where the space was bigger with another patch of land. Two sets of swings and a slide that was one story high met them, along with a merry-go-round. Sand mounds, confined by a wooden frame, provided resting spots for the toy tractors. Two picnic tables sat forlorn, their emptiness crying out for company.

"The same as you?" Olivia hissed, startled by what she heard.

"Which would be?"

Their gazes met, and they stopped to look at each other. The blonde eyebrow on Alexandria's face rose closer to her hairline. She clamped her lips shut, barely able to contain her frustration. The flowers arched back from the tickle of the wind, fearful from their tension that continued to rise.

"It seems like you always have something against her," Alexandria continued. "Yeah, she's not my favorite person to be around and can drive me crazy, but give her a break and try to make the most of the weekend. We're all going through some shit."

"Bullshit," she responded, rolling her eyes. "You've told me all the crap that drives you nuts about her too!"

"Yeah, but why so much?"

A flush crept over Olivia's face. She set her camera on the picnic table; the strap hung over the edge. As she got closer to Alexandria, her rage intensified. One of her supporters was backing away from her feelings. She treated her college friends similarly; if they didn't agree with her or support her beliefs, she'd end the friendship and their reputation by spreading the worst of rumors.

"Because everything about her is so pathetic."

Olivia's cold disposition intimidated Alexandria, making her freeze.

"Ever since she got out of that car on the first day, I knew she was pure trash. I didn't like the way she talked, the way she walked; nothing about her. It's ridiculous that Uncle James found those two and married her mother. She doesn't belong here, and never will."

A stronger breeze blew toward them. Alexandria felt a cold shiver run up her spine when the hem of her pale blue shirt danced in the air. Olivia's declaration made her stomach churn, driven by a desire to stay distant and avoid any involvement.

"You know, it was fun to pick on her. But she isn't *that* bad of a person, or at least I haven't given her the chance to prove me wrong. You have had tons of chances to do so. You're the one who's pathetic if you want to keep thinking that way, especially when we should be thinking about Grandma."

"What are you talking about?" Olivia asked, grabbed Alexandria's shirt to prevent her from walking away. "You've done the same shit. Don't act like a saint now."

"Bullshit!"

"Have you fallen too many times, you stupid bitch?" Olivia continued, her grip slipping from Alexandria's resistance. "Don't make me out to be the bad guy!"

Ignoring the maze, Alexandria pushed her cousin aside and damaged the flowers. She couldn't stand the sight of Olivia, and no matter what she did to leave, she would follow and find a way to rebuttal back to justify her means.

"Stay away from me!" she said, her silhouette disappearing. "I'm not like you!"

Gathering her bearings, horror struck Olivia. She adjusted her hair, attempting to position the ends correctly. A slight tightening in her throat made swallowing difficult. Inhaling deeply, she attempted to quell the tremors in her fingertips.

"Screw you!"

She shut her eyes to regain her composure. The wind returned, the flowers rustling. A soda can somersaulted into a hole in the ground. Approaching the picnic table, she turned her camera so it was facing the field. Her finger pressed the timer, creating a ten-second window to compose herself for the moment to capture.

Ten.

The loose dirt yielded beneath her feet, mimicking the feeling of walking on a sandy beach.

Nine.

She made it to the flowers; her breath became short.

Eight.

One last pat smoothed her hair, securing it against the wind.

Seven.

Her hand on her hip, she squeezed her stomach, highlighting her waistline even under the baggy sweatshirt.

Six.

The timer ticked on, and she waited patiently.

Five.

The flowers shifted behind her, their stems parting.

Four.

A figure's outline emerged through the opening, just a short distance from Olivia.

Three.

The lighting struck Olivia as odd, the shadows not aligning with the cloud positions.

Two.

She turned around. A tiny gasp escaped her as her jaw dropped to her chest, caught by surprise.

One.

With a forceful strike, the silhouette used a wooden plank to knock her unconscious, sending her sprawling to the ground.

FLASH!

The photo ejected from the front. As the grey haze faded, the image gradually came into focus. The ink brightened the yellow, highlighting the central area. The red flannel shirt, peeking out from under a black trench coat, was a bright contrast against the floral background. Patches in a variety of colors adorned the dirty jeans. Taupe enveloped its face while it fixated on Olivia, whose face connected with the plank, hitting her on the side of the head and rendering her unconscious on the ground.

ONLY DRIED-UP STEMS, mere nubs less than a foot high, dotted the barren fields. Gemma and Simon's house was in sight, with only the attractions blocking the path. A three-layered, icy figure stood in the field, its face adorned with misplaced coal by the children and topped with a slanted hat.

Small snowflakes drifted down, creating a thicker blanket on the cabin's roof. Flickering lights surrounded the windows as smoke blanketed the white and gray sky. The man approached the door. His red and white outfit, full and puffy around the middle, caught everyone's attention. Dexter hauled a bundle of presents over his shoulder with ease; his last body building championship gave him plenty of practice to allow the toys to be child's play compared to the dumbbells that would challenge the strain in his muscles.

Preteens huddled near the fireplace, their hands wrapped around steaming mugs of hot chocolate. Positioned at the front, Gemma showcased her newest nutcracker to everyone. The purple jacket hid a small, chipped piece of wood by the epaulette, and gold glitter coated its pants and cheap trim. The whimsical decoration sparked excitement in Charlotte's eyes, and Gabriel was eager to try it out, peanut in hand.

"Grandma, have I told you how beautiful it is out here," Charlotte said, her eyes admiring the flakes drifting in the wind.

"Once or twice," she answered, nudging her shoulder.

"I would love to live in a place like this when I grow up. It's so quiet and peaceful."

"You can do whatever you put your mind to."

"Can I just have this place when you don't want it anymore?" Charlotte asked, her hands covering over her tiny giggles.

"Well, I don't think anybody else has asked. So, I guess it's yours!"

Gemma shed a wink to James, causing her son to smile with warmth. Katherine fell back into his chest, allowing his arm to wrap around her body as she took in the acceptance of her daughter into the family. The glow on her daughter's face was something she would always remember as she only recalled her being quieter and more somber.

"I believe someone's here," James said, pulling himself up from the couch as he looked over Charlotte's head.

Katherine trailed behind, heading to the kitchenette for a supply of garbage bags. Marnie placed her empty eggnog cup on the side table, wiping away the tiny mustache above her lip as Edward snuggled closer to her.

"Ho, ho, ho. Merry Christmas!" said Dexter, his hand on his plush belly.

As their presents neared, the children's eyes sparkled with anticipation. The burning sensation in Charlotte's arm grew as Gabriel refused to release her hand. Alexandria scooted behind the group, resting her back on the foot of the couch in between her parents. Lucas joined Noah and Mason, who were moving their baseball card collection into a neat pile to make room. Lucas admired Noah's newest addition of Mark McGwire while Noah and Mason whispered a plan to convince him to trade their bent Barry Bonds for Ken Griffey Jr..

"Look everyone, it's Santa!" James said, his eyebrows continuing to bounce up and down.

Gemma and Simon drew their chairs closer, their hands clasped tight, their love strengthened by their family. Leaning against his shoulder, she let him kiss her forehead gently.

"Okay, everyone. Let's give some room for Santa," Katherine said as she grabbed another chair from the dining area.

The children were eager to make him feel at ease. Only a foot from his black boots, they scurried closer to him. The silhouette of a monster truck, visible through the thin fabric of his sack, made Gabriel bounce with excitement.

"Have you all been good this year?"

All the children bobbed their heads wildly. Charlotte got a small glimpse at Olivia, who pushed her hair behind her shoulder, knowing that she wasn't and secretly wished for a lump of coal for her or a good kick in the pants.

"That's not what I heard!"

Santa winked at the parents, who were laughing together as they enjoyed watching their children's fear. To tease their children before giving them something off their Christmas list was what they needed to make their spending more worthwhile, in addition to making them happy.

The children lined up to take turns sitting on Santa's lap. Olivia pushed past her twin to grab hers before he could. She was full of glee to get the newest hair crimper and ran to the nearest outlet to warm it up next to the fireplace; she played with every strand of her hair, eager to pick out which ones she wanted to experiment the device on first. Mason and Noah ripped open their new handheld gaming systems with excitement to start playing their racing game. Alexandria got a cassette player to put in her Madonna's Like a Prayer album; she couldn't get those headphones around her head fast enough. Lucas was excited to get the newest Hot Wheels remote controlled cars; he ran to the kitchenette to gut out the utility drawer for batteries to power up the remote.

Gabriel jumped for joy when it was his turn. His bouncing on Dexter's knee resembled a bumpy ride in a buggy on an open dirt road. As he swayed precariously, Dexter recoiled from a child's hand that tried to grab his beard for balance. Gabriel ripped through the green plaid wrapping paper, adding to the growing pile of shreds on the floor as Katherine continued to clean up while Victoria captured the moment on her Polaroid.

"Look, Mom! I got a nerf gun!" Gabriel said, admiring the ten pack of foam darts.

The adults, amused by his innocent belief, smiled at him. While the older children were questioning Santa's authenticity, he remained a true believer.

"Charlotte, this one's for you," Dexter announced, handing her a small, rectangular present, and signaling Gabriel to leave.

He hurried over to James, who leaned forward on the couch to assist with opening the package. To read the instructions, James put on his glasses, and Katherine looked over his shoulder to scan the fine print for any safety warnings.

Gazing at the beaming faces around her, Charlotte pulled herself up from the floor, witnessing the happiness their new gifts brought. To avoid getting tape stuck to her socks, she tiptoed across the living room, carefully avoiding any loose bits of wrapping paper. Dexter let out a small grunt as he struggled to keep his balance when her weight settled onto his knee.

"Be careful, Santa. That might be a little too much weight for you," Olivia whispered as she hovered her fingers over the iron plate to check for warmth.

Everyone was so engrossed in the moment, they didn't hear what she said. Victoria and Timothy paid attention to Alexandria and her gift, while Mason and Noah were comparing their racing experiences and working to avoid collisions. Only those whose jaws had dropped could hear it. Gemma looked at her granddaughter in disbelief. Dexter was startled and rubbed his white-gloved hand over Charlotte's back as she retreated into herself.

"T-thank you, Santa," Charlotte mumbled, grabbing the present and dashing away from the crowd with haste.

She sought cover behind the unlit floor lamp, blending into the darkness. Her movements were deliberate as she tore the paper, minimizing the mess she made. As she peeled the tape off the paper, she tucked away the pieces, trying her best to keep it all intact.

The cover, which showed two children riding a winged horse over a lush green landscape, brought a subtle smile to her face. It was her very own copy of The Magician's Nephew, *by C.S. Lewis. She looked over to Dexter, who gave her a warming nod of encouragement, and Gemma, who smiled at her with love. She opened the book, losing herself in the story and devouring the words on the pages.*

Dexter received a handshake and a cup of coffee from Simon. The kids were entertained by their toys and the adults were satisfied with the result. As Victoria looked at the photos she'd captured, a warm smile spread across her face, highlighting her dimples.

"Olivia, honey. May I have a word with you?" Gemma said as she got herself up from the chair.

"Can it wait, Grandma?" she asked, pinching the clamps to prepare herself for a test round.

"Actually, no. It can't."

A dart slapped into Olivia's face. Gabriel let out a playful laugh while Mason paused his game to point at her and enjoy her irritated, glazed expression.

"I think it can."

A sigh of frustration escaped Gemma's nose. Her face turned pink. Her fingers fumbled with the cord as she reached for the outlet. A single eyebrow arched as she tugged, letting the two prongs drop onto Olivia's lap.

"What did you do that for?" Olivia said in shock.

"Now," her grandmother said sternly.

Olivia got up from her seat and walked into their room. The three sets of bunk beds had blankets scattered across them. The room's center resembled a giant hole because of the sprawling collection of open sleeping bags. Duffel bags and suitcases had clothing exploding out of them with dresses and t-shirts intermingled with the jeans and khakis.

Gemma closed the door and said, "Have a seat."

Olivia's throat tightened, and she played with her fingers. As her grandmother's shadow engulfed the room, her shoulders slumped with dejection. Her knees locked as she landed, the metal springs of the mattress creaking under her weight.

"I heard what you said out there," Gemma stated, her legs crossed as she sat on the floor.

"Yeah, and?" she asked dismissively with a confident smile.

"That wasn't a very nice thing to say to your cousin."

"She's not related to me," she stated, folding her arms.

"Yes, she is. She is just as much family as you are."

Olivia said nothing. Her eyes darted around the room, avoiding contact with Gemma's.

"And even if she wasn't, saying something about one's weight isn't appropriate toward anybody."

"Well, she is bigger."

"That doesn't matter. She is just as beautiful as you are."

Olivia rolled her eyes. The idea that anyone would link her beauty to the one she loathed was something she never imagined encountering in her teenage years. It was unbelievable to her that someone would put her on the same pedestal as her.

"Are you hearing me?" Gemma asked, crawling closer to Olivia, her hand touching her knee.

Olivia wanted to be anywhere but there. She wasn't happy about being told what to do, especially if it was to consider someone as pretty as her. Gemma seemed set on delivering her lecture, regardless of what anyone said.

"Could you imagine if someone did that to you?"

Olivia couldn't help but to think that it would never happen. Her beauty was so undeniable that no one would dare challenge it. The conversation was going nowhere, and she yearned to leave the room.

"Yes," she agreed, monotone.

"So, can you promise me that you'll be kind to your cousin and keep the mean comments to yourself?"

Olivia hesitated, her gaze finally meeting Gemma's. The fluorescent bulb's yellow glow created reflections on the irises. A gust of wind blew snowflakes against the window, causing it to tap. She loves her grandma, but doesn't want to agree with her. Olivia smiled at her and gave a nod of her head.

"I promise."

Gemma's face lit up. Olivia received a tight hug from her, her grandmother's heartbeat felt strong against her nightgown. With a tentative pat, Olivia acknowledged her promise, but was unsure how to proceed. No other options remained. There was nowhere to escape.

Gemma opened the door and ushered her with the rest of the group. Breaking his focus on his coffee mug, Dexter quickly glanced at her. A satisfied smirk appeared behind his beard, knowing that Gemma had given her a lecture. Plugging in her crimper near the fireplace, Olivia stared at her cousin. Charlotte's actions made her want to scowl, but she kept her composure as promised.

THE WORLD WAS SPINNING as Olivia's eyes started to open. Her blurry view of the sunflowers cleared after she woke up. Her head pulsed with agony as she regained full awareness. Getting her hands out from behind her back became impossible, making any movement difficult. As she looked around, she noticed the rope binding her wrists to the merry-go-round handle.

"Help!" she said, her mouth dry and raspy.

Every fifteen seconds, the device spun faster, showing the same sandbox appearing and disappearing. Her shoulders popped as she desperately tried to escape her bindings. As tears streamed down her face, the eyeliner on her cheek smudged. With nowhere to turn and nobody to help, her heart hammered in her chest, consumed by panic.

A shadow emerged, making its way through the patch of flowers. The black trench coat almost grazed the ground. Olivia gasped and bit her lip when she noticed the burlap sack over its face; the mesh on the sunflower eyes twinkled in the light. The basket dangled in its hold, swinging rhythmically like a pendulum, while tiny, unintelligible whispers came from its mouth. As she spun, Olivia's body moved away, creating tension as she faced the opposite direction.

"Why are you doing this to me?" she said, panicked.

The attacker placed the basket on the picnic table close by. The polaroid camera was worn around their neck, with the lens resting on a bit of straw. Another turn sent Olivia spinning, her chest exploding with a scream as the camera captured her terror in flashes of light.

"Please stop!"

She flinched, her body jerking as the suncrow's hand moved to stop the contraption. Gazing into its dark eyes, she found nothing there. No remorse. No mercy. Reaching into the basket, they grabbed a small bottle with a hose attached. Olivia's brow furrowed, bracing for whatever mischief might follow. Before firing the trigger, the suncrow stopped to appreciate her fear, allowing the contents to spray out.

The liquid splashing onto her face made Olivia flinch. Drops fell from her forehead, dripped down her chin, and landed on her lap. A tingling sensation set in on her skin, causing irritation almost instantly. Her eyes, burning with pain, caught a fleeting glimpse of the label, which read "pesticide." They placed the bottle on the ground to give her another spin.

The wind intensified the chemicals searing her skin, forcing a primal scream from her very core. Red welts have erupted on her once perfect complexion, creating a mottled appearance. Her eyes, red-rimmed and filled with pain, seemed to scream for relief as the whites grew dark with strain. The rough ropes dug into her skin, causing her shoulder to dislocate as she struggled to break free. She wasn't going anywhere, and neither was her pain.

The contraption stopped again. She was struggling to breathe, her breaths getting shorter and more difficult. Blood oozed from the corners of her lips, leaving welts behind. Relishing in her pain, the suncrow moved back toward the table to get something else. Sunlight reflected from the blue plastic with a cone shape. It bent from the figure's glove pinching it.

"Please, make this stop," Olivia said, muttering, her mouth drooling bits of red.

The suncrow grabbed a hold of her face. With the earthy taste of the glove pressing into her mouth, Olivia's jaw clenched as she fought the urge to yield. Like a worm seeking refuge, her tongue twisted and turned with no escape. Tickled by the funnel's tip, her throat triggered her gag reflex. As crows flew overhead, the sight of the bottle being unscrewed made her yelp.

Trickling down her throat, the remaining pesticide was ingested. Olivia struggled to cough up the liquid trapped in her mouth as the suncrow's hand pressed against it. The acidic burn swelling inside her caused her windpipe to constrict. Rage bubbled inside her, threatening to boil over like a simmering pot. As she strained, her muscles twitched, attempting to relieve feeling something clawing its way out of her gut. Blood-tinged foam flowed from her nose, leaving a pink stain on the glove that grew increasingly darker. Trembling feet kicked up dust clouds, growing fainter with each passing second. Her head became limp, falling over her shoulder as her hatred became silenced, and her comments were no longer toxic.

Chapter 15

Charlotte emerged from the barn. The door shivered from her slam; the boards were loose and unable to stay put. She went for the closest bench with a view of the fields. A vibrant wash of marigold and pewter spread across the sky as the sun peeked over the horizon.

The wind had done its job and took a break. Nothing was making the flowers flutter. She stopped to think about the two years she had, taking a moment to herself. She faced a series of devastating events: losing her stepfather and brother, enduring the trauma of a workplace assault, and making the tough choice to withdraw from college. Such situations would leave anyone feeling terrible. Despite everything, she felt a renewed sense of hope. She would prefer none of those things had happened, but she feels a stronger sense of resilience now. If only her family knew the depth of her life, instead of judging her by appearances and assumptions.

"Everything okay?" James said as his spirit took a seat next to her.

Charlotte had a whirlwind of thoughts filling her mind. Maybe something really happened last night, not just her imagination. Maybe these spirits are all legit.

"I will be," she said, releasing a breath of contentment.

"You always say that."

Charlotte chuckled at his observation. Those words were a common phrase for her, but she hadn't noticed. This helped her believe the storm would eventually subside.

"I guess I do."

James put his arm around Charlotte's back. Even though she couldn't feel his warmth, she did have some sense of security. It's like he never left.

The flowers shifted unexpectedly, and a shadow appeared within the stems. Charlotte's pulse quickened. It was too early in the day to endure another scare, especially after last night; the tower was in the distance, and she could still see the broken banister that caused her to teeter.

"I should've gone out here more often!" Gabriel said, skipping through an opening.

Charlotte took a sigh of relief. Gabriel's love of nature was out of character, but his happiness was contagious. He was free from the influence of video games and the demands of extracurricular activities. With time on his hands, he found himself surrounded by the vastness of nature.

"Yes, you should've!" she said, smiling.

James' eyes flickered with admiration as he looked at his son. The lines around his eyes became more pronounced as he radiated pure joy. He felt the freedom, his hand drumming on his thigh.

"Gah, I wish I could've seen more of this," he said, remorseful.

"I know, me too," Charlotte agreed. "I got so caught up in surviving school and doing all this extra shit, I forgot to stop and smell the flowers."

A small laugh escaped James' lips as he enjoyed her sarcastic tone and her hand gestures toward the field.

"I know that's partially my fault for pushing you two."

"Yeah, it is," she said, her voice becoming raspy.

James's smile vanished, his lips forming a straight, thin line. The true nature of his parenting was becoming increasingly clear.

"But it wasn't all you, not always," she said, looking into his teary eyes. "You were a great dad. You were fun when you needed to be. It's just when it came to this family, you wanted to impress them or something."

James nodded in agreement. Gabriel scrambled through the bushes, jumping over the bent stems close by.

"I love my family. I mean, you can't pick and choose where you're born. But for some reason, this farm brought the worst in all of us."

"Yeah," Charlotte said, her gaze dropping to the dirt.

"Eddy, Victoria, and I weren't always like this. We had a lot of fun as kids. Once we grew up, it felt like every day someone had to be the first to have a child or get married. It always seemed like a contest, no matter what it was about."

"Well, you lost on both counts."

"And no matter what I did, it seemed like there was some sort of competition as to who would be the better child or most successful."

"I can see that."

Charlotte recalled a family dinner they had to suddenly leave. They argued about who had the more prestigious job behind the barn. She remembered birds scattering into the sky as Edward's voice, deep and angry, defended the quality of his nonprofit work. It was a side of Edward she didn't like to see and she failed every time she tried to remove it from her memory.

"So, I felt like I had to push you to show them I can be a good parent, instead of pushing you into being better versions of yourselves."

"I know you tried. There isn't a perfect parent out there. I try to forget about the times when you made me want to rip out the last bit of hair on your head and only remember the times when you made me smile."

James felt a sense of warmth coming from her sincerity. Charlotte smiled, attempting to mask the tear welling up in her eye. Her mouth began to hum "Jet Airliner." The vivid memories of the music-filled car rides left a lasting impression on Charlotte, a legacy James longed for others to cherish. He didn't have to worry too much about being thought of as the stern father when he needed to be and an even pushier one when he wanted to be. The joy he brought to the people who cared about him drew him back to his unfinished business.

"I wish I could hug you right now!" James said, wiping the tears from his face.

"Me too," Charlotte said, regaining her composure.

The grass rattled behind her, and the winds strengthened again. Her fluttering heart stalled, consumed by paranoia, as Charlotte realized someone must be there. Someone was eavesdropping on her conversation with thin air. Her biggest fear was that her family would discover she'd been communicating with what she thought were spirits, and the news would spread.

When she turned, the young man's hair, a mass of curls, fell over his face, blocking his eyes from view. Plastic crinkled in his hand as he held onto the bottle of water. He looked at Charlotte, eyebrows raised in concern, her arms crossed. Charlotte looked around, realizing her stepfather and brother were gone, leaving the seat empty.

"Hey, Charlotte," said Noah. "Who're you talking to?"

Chapter 16

Charlotte's heart dropped. Words failed her, and she couldn't figure out how much she had to explain to herself. Telling him the truth would surely make her family think she was troubled.

"I-I was just talking to my brother."

"Your brother?" he asked, concerned.

"Yeah. I was reciting the monologue from his play. *King Lear*."

"Really?"

"He practiced it all the time in front of me, so I pretty much knew it by heart. It's my way of connecting with him, I guess."

Charlotte clenched her fist, hoping her excuse would be considered valid. At that moment, nothing else occupied her mind.

"You know, that's a pretty thoughtful way to tribute them."

The warmth of Noah's smile soothed Charlotte's anxious heart. She stood up from the bench, craving a desperate change of scenery.

"Wanna go for a walk?"

"Sure. I could use it after their crap."

They strolled through the patch together. Ignoring the designated pathways, they opted for a direct route, unconcerned about damaging the property. The black birds scattered whenever one of them approached the flock.

"I'm sorry you had to experience that," Noah said, trying to avoid damaging the surrounding flower stems.

"It's not your fault, but I appreciate your apology," Charlotte said gravely.

"I know that you and I haven't had the closest of relationships growing up, but I will be the first to say that picking on you back then was fun. I just think there's a time when it should've stopped."

Charlotte didn't know if she should agree with him for it not being fun anymore or slapping him for thinking that it was in the first place.

Her raspy voice conveyed, "I don't think it was fun back then."

"You got to admit some of it was."

"Maybe. But when it comes to how I look or where I come from, then that's maybe when you should've thought about stopping."

Noah lowered his head, overcome with shame. The periods she was mentioning were familiar to him. There might have been a time when she tripped so comically she found it funny herself. Once it got to the comments, the laughter stopped, but the harm behind the words she always knew was intentional.

"I know. I wish I could say that it's Olivia and Mason's fault for making me. But I can't blame them for my actions."

"Well, Olivia is kind of a Grade-A bitch. And Mason is such a meathead."

The two laughed as they broke through one of the open patches, dodging the set of bridges. As Noah gazed into the pit, the sounds of his childish screams haunted his memory. Time hadn't healed the sting of his embarrassment. The flowers tipped forward, their seeds scraping Noah's face as Charlotte pushed them out of the way.

"Don't get me wrong. I love my brother and sister. But that doesn't mean that I don't think that they suck."

"I had that same thought about Gabriel," Charlotte agreed with an empathic chuckle.

Minutes of silence passed, and the flowers started to dwindle. After passing the tower, Charlotte craved only silence. Her head buzzed with the lingering frustration. The unwelcome thoughts that had plagued her since her arrival left her utterly dejected.

"Why is it that the rest of the family gets away with shit?" Charlotte asked, stopping to take a deep breath.

"What do you mean?" he asked, doing the same.

"It seems like I'm the bad seed of the family because I smoke and I dropped out of college. But nobody even mentioned the crap everyone else pulled. I think that breaking the law is much worse than making choices someone might not agree with."

Noah grimaced with concern. Noah remembers both times when they got reprimanded for their actions. Once the issue surfaced, family gatherings immediately squashed any attempts to talk about it.

"I don't have a problem with what you do."

"Thanks. But do you get what I'm saying? Ever since I dropped out, all I get asked is when I'm going back. I have unpaid tuition bills to pay off before they'll even let me back in."

The amount of times Victoria and Timothy have asked her seemed like a toddler constantly asking for their mother's attention. At first, there was some sense of concern involved, but then it got to where it made someone question their intentions. No matter how many times she explained to them that she couldn't go back until her financial issues were settled, they seemed to think she could just wave a magic wand and fix it overnight with money that grew from the trees in her backyard. Paying off debt to them seemed easy, as though it was a couple hundred dollars as opposed to tens of thousands.

"I just think that there's a lot of hypocrisy going on here, and I don't like it."

"I know," he agreed somberly.

They made it out into the open patch. The majestic hill reminded them of sledding adventures during the snowiest of winters. Charlotte even cherished the time they shared, riding a toboggan over a mound, almost breaking her arm when it tipped over.

A fence, with its wooden planks decaying, stood at the foot of the hill. Across the way, the cows grazed lazily on the taller grass. The barn, painted a dark rusty-brown, mirrored their grandparents' weathered appearance. Next to it was a little white house, about the size of the cabin. Curiosity etched on their faces, the cousins exchanged glances.

Charlotte's smile was sly as she admitted, "I never got to sneak into Grace's yard like you guys did."

"I haven't in so long. It was always Lucas and Mason that would do it."

"Shall we?"

"We shall."

THEIR SNEAKERS BECAME slick with each step through the moist, piled mud. The cows' monotonous chorus, a hypnotic drone, filled their ears as they gave their general talks. Mason's flatulence made the manure easier to acclimate to the slight sting creeping up their nostrils. Noah never cared about it, not since he did an atomic sit-up at a sixth-grade sleepover where he was suddenly woken up with his head meeting his brother's bare behind.

A gentle breeze brushed against the barn's foundation, causing the metal siding to rattle. The John Deere green of the tractors has faded, replaced by rust and exposed metal. Not a single soul dared to disturb the peaceful swaying of the tall grass. Charlotte recalled the farm's bustling activity, mirroring the Chester farm, with the husband operating machinery and his two sons aiding his efforts. The tomatoes were delicious in the homemade salsa, especially with the incredibly delectable sweet corn.

Not today.

"Gee, everything changes when you grow up," Noah said, the screech of the shed door hinges becoming hypnotic.

"Or maybe you start to notice the truth when you're not a child anymore," said Charlotte.

Small pebbles peeked through the muddy surface, dotting the gravel path they traversed. Tips of earth poked into the soles of their feet. The house was being put to shame by the size of their grandparents' house, being a fifth of the size and humble as can be. The off-white siding, chipped and faded, barely held the wooden shutters in place with rusty hardware. Shingles tumbled down, a piece landing on the roof of the 1987 Ford truck with a resounding slap.

"Have you been here a lot?" Charlotte asked, curious because she hadn't been invited to join her cousins in sneaking over.

"At least once or twice a year when we were kids. Once we got older, the others would do it without me."

Charlotte's stomach lurched, remembering her first visit to this place as a new addition to the family. Mason suggested sneaking onto their property to steal something and getting her into the group to help. She went to the chicken coop without being seen and took the biggest egg she could find. As she ran back through the sunflowers, Alexandria startled her, wearing a burlap mask. The scare caused her to fall, smashing the egg in her pocket. Jokes about the wet spot on her backside became a constant in the house for the next year, a playful way of acknowledging her accidental urination, a topic everyone found amusing even though she was supposed to be too old for such things.

"Why haven't they kept up with the place?" Charlotte asked, her gaze drawn to the nails, all covered in rust.

"Ever since their father died, the boys couldn't keep up with the work. Don't you remember Bennett?"

There were two sons in the family. Bennett was the eldest and had a good head on his shoulders. As the second-in-command, he fully dedicated himself to the success of the family business, willing to do whatever it took. The one time he came over shirtless to borrow a scythe, Charlotte found herself having a tiny crush on him, regardless of being over fifteen years older than her. His toned, sun-kissed physique, glistening with sweat, caused an unexplainable reaction in her. Austin, the youngest, showed great promise as a workhorse. Bennett took him in and made him his right-hand man. His burly build would help with the more arduous tasks. He tossed hay bales over the fence one-handed, without breaking a sweat. Whenever Charlotte ran away to escape the family drama, Austin would be there to support her. While he wasn't a talkative person, he was an excellent listener.

"What are you doing here?" said someone from the other side of the house.

Charlotte and Noah trembled from the sudden appearance of another person. His blonde hair, slightly unkempt, concealed streaks of gray, which also showed in his chinstrap beard. His green eyes had a reflective quality, similar to the surface of a pool.

"Hi Bennett," Charlotte said, forcing a smile as she observed the pitchfork in his grasp.

"Charlotte, what a pleasant surprise. And Noah."

Noah's tension eased, his shoulders returning to their usual relaxed state. The chirping of a pair of robins flying by distracted him from the tension he felt.

"How've you been?" Noah asked, his hands trembling. "It's been a while."

"Could be better. It's hard to keep up the farm without the proper help."

Finances became difficult following their father's passing. The life insurance provided temporary relief, but managing a farm and a business was demanding. Broken machines and costly repairs only added to their misery and debt. Eventually, they had to let go of the farmhands because they couldn't afford them either; the last three were let go right before Charlotte graduated.

"I'm sorry," said Charlotte. "I know it hasn't been easy for you guys."

"It's not your fault. Accidents happen."

"I know. You were almost like a second family to Gemma and Simon," Noah said with a smile. "I'm sure that there's something we can do with some spare money depending on the assets."

"I won't hold my breath," a higher-pitched, more feminine voice interjected.

Charlotte and Noah turned back to the steps. An elderly woman occupied the doorway. Her pink apron's doily trim, tattered and stained, hung precariously, shielding her prairie dress. The German shepherd sat beside her rain boots, which were caked in dried mud.

"Hi Frieda," Charlotte mumbled, her eyes cast down as she noticed Frieda's stare through her wispy, gray hair.

"Hi Charlotte, and Noah, is it?" she said.

"Yes, ma'am," he said, equally nervous.

"Sorry to intrude on your property. We were just venturing around for old times' sake. We needed to get away from the house."

"It's all right, child," Freida said, as she lowered the cleaver, revealing their reflections in its blade. "I'm so sorry about the loss of your grandmother."

"Thank you," they both said in unison.

The silence was palpable, broken only by the intensity of their stares. Charlotte couldn't think of anything to keep the conversation from dying. Their struggle for survival was evident to her. The heavy bags accentuated the lines on their faces, etched with grief under their eyes. Bennett was so weary that he appeared to be considerably older than her.

"Did you want some help with those bags?" he asked Bennett, noticing the pile of black garbage bags behind him.

"Sure," he answered, smirking.

Charlotte didn't mind helping. The physical work provided a distraction from her grief. Plus, all the fresh air was something she could use. She needed to get back to her cousins to regain her focus and make it through the weekend.

The chickens scrambled around the backyard, fleeing the rooster's attempt to establish his dominance. Another breeze sent the wooden fence door swaying, knocking it off its hinges. Lush green leaves, trapped within the chicken wire fence, fluttered in the garden.

Scanning the property, Charlotte sought any other people. Nobody else hid in the shadows. Not a single piece of equipment was in use; it was just the four of them hauling the bags to the back of the pickup truck.

"Frieda, what did you mean when you said that there is no chance of us helping you?" Charlotte said, concerned upon reflection.

Frieda's brows crinkled tighter toward her eye sockets. With a resounding sigh, she released the air from her lungs. The plastic crunched as her grip grew firmer.

"Don't make promises you can't keep," she warned, her voice wavering.

"We've had little help from your family before, and we aren't getting it now," Bennett added.

"I'm sorry," said Noah. "I thought you were getting some sort of help."

"Yeah, I thought you guys were good friends with our grandparents," said Charlotte.

"We were," said Frieda. "I've just been burned before by people. I'm just saying that you can't make those types of promises. I've hurt them and they've hurt me. It's just a never-ending circle."

"Okay."

The awkwardness reappeared in the space. The vastness of the countryside seemed to shrink around her. Looking back at the farm, she saw the sunflowers like distant yellow dots. The tree perched on the hill swayed.

"So, how's Austin?"

"He's been okay," said Bennett, brushing the grime onto his jeans.

"Is he still, er...?"

"Quiet?" he finished. "Yes."

"The doctors said that he will recover when he's ready," said Frieda.

Austin's exuberant spirit and love for life were memories Noah and Charlotte treasured. While Gemma, Simon, Frieda, and her husband played cards, he would always join Noah's cousins for games in the yard full of enthusiasm. He was talkative at times, always finding something to discuss and relating to each of his cousins. His father's death plunged him into a deep silence, shrouded in grief. Not a single word came from his lips. It was as if his tongue had been taken from his mouth. Throughout the later part of his teenage years, he largely chose isolation over engagement, making him absent from many things. His gaze was vacant, as if he existed only in the present moment, lost in his own thoughts.

"Where is he? I would like to say hi to him," Charlotte said, curious.

"I don't know," said Frieda. "He hasn't been home since yesterday."

Chapter 17

Ice cubes in a glass of freshly squeezed lemonade clinked as spoons mixed with them. Around the back patio, hummingbirds buzzed, anticipating their sweet snack. With Earth, Wind & Fire's "September" playing on the record player, Lucas tapped his foot to stay in rhythm with his gameplay as though it were playing on the racecar's radio.

"I've always loved this song," Edward reminisced, his head tilting down.

"Don't you remember the time when Simon and Gemma had a little dance party?" Lucas asked, pressing hard on the left arrow on his controller.

Mason didn't acknowledge the memory. Losing wasn't something he enjoyed, especially not to his cousins. To feel most valuable, he strived for excellence in areas outside his academic weaknesses.

"Remember when Alexandria hit her head when Mason dipped her?" Timothy asked, chuckling as he placed the spoon in the sink.

"Not funny," said Mason, still focused, eye twitching.

Marnie's head sank further into her palm as she nodded off. A wide yawn escaped her lips as her mouth hung open. The bags under her eyes were more pronounced, and her eyes were bloodshot.

"So, when are we going to get to all the assets?" she asked while fluttering her eyelids to moisten her dry eyes.

Her husband, stroking her forearm, said, "As soon as Victoria gets back."

"We don't even know where she went. She could be gone all day!"

Edward's eyebrow raised toward the stubble on his scalp to where his hair was desperate to grow through his bald shape. The memories of his siblings being better than him at hide-and-seek where it would take hours to find them in even the most precarious of nooks and crannies; it was a benefit for Gemma and Simon since it kept them out of their hair for the whole day.

"You're right," he said, sighing. "Maybe we should get started. You can fill her in on everything, Tim."

Ignoring his nephew's suppressed growls of frustration, Timothy nodded, watching him wrestle with the urge to chuck the controller.

The screen door swung open to the back deck. The lovely smell of flowers couldn't distract them from the grim task of dealing with their loved one's possessions, especially their mother's.

"We can't really do much of this, anyway. We have to wait for Dexter to come with the papers on Monday," Marnie said, stretching, her cup of tea tipping close to releasing a couple of drops.

"I know, but we can at least chat about what to do with it," Edward said. "I want us to at least be on the same page."

"So, what are you thinking we should do?" Timothy asked, both his hands clasping his glass.

"I think we should sell it," Marnie interjected.

"I don't think so," said Edward, his eyebrow cocking.

Spouses exchanged glances. Edward couldn't believe this conversation was so common, even before his parents died. Marnie always conceded to Edward's arguments about preserving their family legacy whenever they disagreed.

"I told you, the people want this business to continue," he continued. "There's no need to shut it down."

"We could always use the money. Think of the kids' education."

"We had to work for ours, and so should they."

"The house needs repairs."

"There's a plan to have it worked on. Be patient."

Marnie had no other justification for cashing out their earnings. She desired financial security to leave her job and live a more luxurious life. During her visits over the last five years, she'd bring catalogs, circling her most expensive wants. She depleted her red markers from circling so many items on the pages.

"Timothy, what do you think? You've been quiet," said Marnie.

Timothy's gaze darted between the pair. The challenge of pleasing both was something he wished to avoid. He and Victoria had discussed their contingency plans for situations like this, but the weight of his decision's reality overwhelmed him.

YEARS BACK, THE WHOLE family gathered for Thanksgiving, their annual reunion. A perfect line of cars lined up opposite the snack stations. The last bit of patrons gathered their children that were throwing their tantrums to not leave the playground behind; arms and legs flailed to get out of their hold.

Workers turn off the attractions' lights to signal closing time. After a challenging day managing parents and many relatives who came to witness the business excitement, employees breathed a sigh of relief. The amount of times they dealt with cranky mothers that wanted to capture the perfect polaroid of the group and blaming the staff for the child not holding still created pounding headaches.

"Good to see you!" James said as he reached over to his siblings.

All three embraced in a group hug. Their months-long absence was keenly felt as they held tight. Tossing his bag onto the lawn, Gabriel raced toward Olivia and Alexandria, engrossed in their compact mirrors. Alexandria got a swipe of lipstick on the apple of her cheek when Olivia's screech nudged her.

"Gabriel, you pig!" Olivia hissed, the compact slamming shut.

"Look what you did!" Alexandria said in disbelief, her hand hovering over her mistake.

"I did you a favor," Gabriel said, holding back a laugh. "This is the best you've ever looked!"

"Drop dead!" they both said in unison.

The girls returned to the house. Alexandria whined to Olivia as they scurried through the garage, hoping her cousin's skills could correct the mistake and improve her appearance. Running back to his sister, Gabriel gave Charlotte a little wink, causing her to stifle a giggle that tickled the back of her throat.

Dodging Mason and Lucas's playful swats, the sunflowers swayed in the cooling breeze along the path. They strained to outrun the setting sun, desperate to reach the tower before nightfall.

"I bet you can't cross the bridge," said Lucas, turning the corner. "You never could!"

"Watch me!" Mason said, his eyebrows furrowing to prove him wrong.

Pulling Katherine in, Marnie guided her inside with a hand on her arm. Retrieving a PBR, they readjusted their grip from the condensation on the can.

"Have you heard Madonna's new song yet?" Katherine asked, pulling the tab back on her can.

"Duh!" Marnie proclaimed; her energy was full of passion. "I got tickets to see her concert next month."

"Jealous!"

In a race to the record player, they dashed inside. The needle hit a scratch on the black vinyl before Get into the Groove *began. Their bond deepened as they clinked cans in a toast, smiles radiating pure joy.*

Noah's yo-yo moved between his index finger and the ground. Swirling in the air was the marbled, purple epoxy. Creating a bridge, the toy whipped in front of Dexter, who was half a foot away from getting a bruise next to his eye.

"Hey, be careful, kid," he said, coming down from his shaken demeanor, allowing the slight tremble in his fingers to take their course.

"Sorry, Dexter," said Noah, winding up the string. "I'm trying to perfect this new trick the guys were doing at school."

"Well, practice makes perfect. Don't be hitting anyone or I'll sue you."

Dexter's wink at the juvenile showcased his bright white teeth against his tan complexion. With his arms folded across his chest, his growing biceps twitched. Noah's head sank closer to his shoulders; the mere thought of going to court for an accident was something he didn't know how to handle. He retreated, glancing back to see if the other man would change his serious expression.

"Cool it with the threats, man. You're going to give the kids nightmares," said Timothy, trying to keep his chuckling to a minimum.

"This will help me with all the cases of defending them when they actually break the law!"

Startled by Mason's grunt of defeat as he recovered from tumbling off the bridge and into the pit, they both saw Mason's and Lucas's heads appearing over the horizon. Distant scarecrows watched departing cars, leaving the family alone.

"Dexter, thank you for helping us today," said Gemma as she allowed Simon to shut the shed door behind her. "This time of year is always so difficult."

"Any help is greatly appreciated," Simon said as he patted Dexter's shoulder.

"Anything to help the business."

"It's the least I can do for you for letting me stay with you while my house gets fumigated."

Timothy observed the news van as its engine roared to life. Finishing her segment on family holiday celebrations for the nine o'clock news, Janice adjusted her hair once more before taking a seat in the front. Grinding her cigarette into the ground with her shoe, she extinguished it in the gravel. With disdain in her eyes, Janice's daughter rolled her eyes, kicked the baby sunflowers, and glared at Charlotte as she headed up the hill to the swing.

"I'm glad we had a moment alone before we all got together," Timothy said, twiddling his shaky thumbs.

"Yes, Timothy? What's going on?" asked Simon.

"Victoria and I were going through our finances, and we were wondering if there was any way that you could help us."

Observing Simon's son-in-law's uncertainty, Dexter's eyes grew wide with concern. The shame of asking for help sent an icy shiver down Timothy's neck. His pride prevented him from seeking help, a prospect he found undesirable.

"Why do you need the money?" Gemma asked. "I thought you said that everything was going okay."

"It is. It's just that Victoria has put in so many extra hours at the store and I'm taking cuts in my business just to catch up on bills. And we don't even have anything set aside for the kids' college fund."

"But you went to Disney World last summer?" Simon said, his eyebrow cocked.

"We did. We just didn't plan on some other expenses that came up. I don't want to trade in Alexandria's car for a beater."

A look passed between Gemma and Simon. The silence following the last guest's departure held their focused attention, leaving him defenseless. The last rays of the sun marked the end of joy, surrendering to the night's embrace. With the beer and duffel bag in tow, Dexter excused himself and headed for the cabin, the cooler rolling onto the grass.

"Listen, I understand everybody needs help when they need it. But this is something you got yourself into, and I think you and Victoria could benefit from learning by bailing yourselves out of this one."

"But you guys have money," Timothy said in disbelief, his frustration growing with the reality of his spending no longer justified in investing in the business. "I'm sure you guys got help to get to where you are today."

A frown creased Gemma's and Simon's faces. As the moon climbed higher, its shadow stretched, engulfing Timothy. A powerful gust of air expelled from their nostrils. A cloud of smoke drifted from the side of the barn; Victoria's color blocked windbreaker appeared through the cloud after every exhale from the cigarette that she was hiding from her parents. Every time he saw her, her despair was clear in her expression; her mind consumed with worries about their mounting debt.

"We worked for every penny that was placed into this business," Simon said, grunting.

"We never asked for help one time, even when we've had our struggles," Gemma added.

Timothy's pulse quickened. His gait was unsteady as his feet crunched on the gravel. The record finished, and the resulting silence was so awful it upset his stomach.

"I'm sorry, but you'll have to work this one out yourself," said Gemma. "If we didn't think that you couldn't handle it, we wouldn't challenge you to rise to the occasion."

"Now, I don't want this to ruin the memories we're going to have this week. I think we made our point," said Simon, his hand reaching over Timothy's shoulder, the warmth wasn't enough to cheer him up from his defeat.

As his in-laws approached the house, Timothy remained frozen in place. Their innocent light couldn't make him feel loved or valued, not now. Tears welled in his eyes as he watched Victoria gazing longingly into the distance, hoping for financial relief.

MASON JUMPED WHEN THE screen door slammed, yanking the controller from the console and sending it flying off the entertainment center. Robins chirped on the patio arches. Two stray cats, oblivious to the butterflies, frolicked toward the barn in playful pursuit.

Timothy, captivated by their innocence, walked behind them. His longing for a cat led him to them as Victoria developed cat allergies in her thirties. Yellow petals showered down, landing on his toes. The muted thud of her steps betrayed the volcanic eruption of fury within her.

"Everything okay, honey?" Timothy asked his daughter as he noticed her brewing anger.

"Yes, Daddy," she muttered, blowing a bit of hair that wisped in front of her eyes.

"You don't look like it."

"It's just that Olivia can get on my nerves."

"Yes, she can be quite the handful."

With hands clasped to her chest, Alexandria's eyes widened with nostrils flaring. As a cat crept through a gap in the building's siding, its meow echoed.

"Yeah, she can be rude at times. But she's my cousin and I have to love her because she's family."

A smile spread across Timothy's face, filling him with warmth. His family's open and honest communication was his proudest aspect. His financial difficulties, however challenging, did not diminish his humility.

"Oh, yeah, now that I have you alone, I wanted to ask you a question."

"Sure, what is it?"

"So, everybody at school has been giving me crap for that car you bought me. Is there any way you could lend me some money for an upgrade?"

Blood surged through Timothy's veins. In his ears, the birds' chirping has faded to an echo. The sunflowers remained motionless, cowed by his inner turmoil.

"It's always about money with you!" he hissed, his lip curling.

"But, Daddy—"

"But nothing! You're an adult and can get yourself that stuff on your own."

"You're seriously going to make me have this car in this shape? People are going to think of me as a low life, like Charlotte."

Timothy's knuckles cracked as he squeezed his fingers. His palms were slick with sweat. A hush fell as the wind's playful touch faded, mirroring Mother Nature's strained gasp.

"You can be so ungrateful," he said softly, cold.

He resisted the impulse to unleash more criticism on his daughter. Such gratefulness and openness were as infrequent as a full moon. Like the phases of the moon, Timothy periodically exhibited uncharacteristic behaviors, including materialism and demeaning comments.

Stunned by her father's departure, Alexandria couldn't speak. She hated being denied, which made her pull at the grass. Nature's green confetti, from flung blades, landed atop the vibrant blooms.

Fresh air did nothing to soothe his frayed nerves. Financial instability plagued his mind, causing his hands to tremble. The worst part was that his grown kids, living independently, didn't value money and his own belongings were on the brink of foreclosure and repossession.

He persevered up the incline, ignoring his calf, hoping the cats would bring him some joy. Despite his efforts, the door remained shut. A gust of wind teased him as he struggled with the jammed entrance. While touring the structure, the weight of his unpaid bills burdened his thoughts. What made him more suffocated was the secret he'd kept from Victoria about the business going under; he lost control of the business when he became overwhelmed with where to start. It became neglected without the proper knowledge to keep it afloat. From finances to marketing, his lack of experience wasn't enough to keep it strong. His fears of telling the truth buried him deeper in his lies, making the mess only more difficult to manage.

All of this made his head split in pain. As he turned the corner, a flat board struck his nose. Upon hitting the ground, blood flowed from his facial wound. The white sky darkened as he let his eyelids droop. A tingling sensation erupted in his feet as the blood drained from his legs while he was being pulled into the barn.

Behind him, the door closed. The twine's itchy fibers digging in irritated his wrists. Strapped to a sawhorse, his heavy muscles struggled to move. As the suncrow watched his body shake, his fear intensified.

"Help!" he screamed, his tongue dry and throat raspy.

A yellow funnel rose from the ground, its opening approaching his face. His lips fought the plastic's intrusion, its ridges scraping his tongue as it pressed into his mouth. Mumbling, the suncrow pressed against the wall, its gloved hands trembling as they reached into their trench coat pocket. Black specks scattered across Timothy's lap, then the floor.

Sunflower seeds tumbled down the funnel and into his mouth. With kernels accumulating on his tongue, they inched toward his tonsils. Suncrow crammed another handful into his mouth, causing them to jab his throat as he swallowed. He gasped for air, each breath shallower and weaker than the last, stifled and strained.

His eyes, bloodshot and faded pink, showed red veins bursting. Each handful sent down the chute further drained his strength. The seeds mingled with bile in his mouth, a revolting combination. With its gloved hand over Timothy's mouth and nose, the figure let him suffocate in his own fluids. His life became shortened from the seeds overwhelming him; just another thing that had him drowning in dependency.

Chapter 18

Sweat poured down Charlotte's and Noah's foreheads as they trekked through the fields. They let out one last wave of farewell to Bennett, who was wiping his face with the bottom of his flannel; his chiseled stomach peeking out. A golden retriever running circles around chased a rabbit visiting their garden from their shed.

"I haven't seen them in ages," Charlotte said, pushing aside some flowers to make a way through. "It's strange that Austin has been acting weirder than I last remember."

"Really? I saw them last fall when they came to visit Grandma. And Austin still runs around and hides. He's no different," said Noah.

"Yes, I don't go with you guys when you go out, remember?"

Noah reflected on their past conversations. He couldn't come up with a single event where Charlotte joined them for fun in the fields; ones that didn't result in her being the butt of the joke. In fact, this was the longest that he'd hung out with her ever. He didn't usually experience such ease during his conversations with her. He always seemed to maintain a pretense, to impress or deflect negativity.

"I'm sorry about everything," he said with sorrow, his face straightened with guilt.

"I know you are," Charlotte said, expelling a tiny smirk.

The wind began to pick up. Dirt swirled at their feet, creating a growing haze. Specks of dust fell into her eyes as the clouds gathered. She stumbled on the exposed roots protruding from the earth mounds, the air rushed from her lungs in her fall.

"Noah," she said, coughing.

He didn't respond. The wind picked up, making the cabin seem to float in the air. She wasn't ready to change her persona into Dorothy Gale and fly off to an unknown land; she knew how to navigate Olivia's antics and she was in no mood to deal with a new witch.

"Where are you?"

With trembling arms, she pulled herself back up. Strands of her hair blew into her mouth, clinging to her wet lips. With tears streaming down her face, she stumbled as she tried to move forward. The multitude of yellow flowers blurred together, overwhelming her vision.

Make it stop! she thought to herself, her misery growing.

To avoid the dirt, she shielded herself with her arm. In the open space, a shadow emerged straight ahead. With no sign of wavering, the stance showed a courageous defiance of the wind.

"Noah! I'm glad you're okay!"

The shadow didn't move.

With the blast over, the flowers ceased their agitated movements. The petals, battered by the chaos, could no longer hold their upright position. Charlotte breathed deeply, relieved no dust or debris entered her lungs. She dabbed at her wet cheeks with the inner hem of her jacket.

The playground became defined, with the swing set no longer being a simple line. The merry-go-round was no longer an oversized dot. Also, the shadow was no longer her cousin. Tattered, patched jeans revealed swaying black fabric at their bottom. Straw oscillated from the hat above the burlap mask.

"Very funny, Olivia!" Charlotte said, coughing. "Freaking hilarious!"

Memories of the beginning of her relationship with the Chesters overwhelmed her. The act of placing the sunflower brooches on her face symbolized her strong connection with Gemma. Unlike the suncrow, which was initially lifeless upon creation, this one projected a more sinister aura. Its gloved hands were clenched with fury; its gaze could see right into her soul through the mesh.

"I'm not playing your games."

Proceeding down the path, she went in the opposite direction. The shrill squeak of rust assaulted her ears on the swing set. Sinking deeper into the earth, her feet dug into the loose dirt. The leaves waved a warning, fluttering their green arms to get her attention. Upon turning, her creation was still behind her, at the same distance.

Following her.

Charlotte's fingers trembled through a rapid heartbeat. Assuming it was another prank, her cousins were succeeding at freaking her out. Her intense focus on the object's labored breathing unsettled her.

The house was in the distance, so she disregarded the path, going straight through the flowers. As she charged into the undergrowth, seeds struck her face. With unsteady ankles, she navigated the plants, careful not to break any stems or harm them. Every couple of yards she turned to look behind her; the black trench coat appeared through the yellow and orange like a blob.

With each faster step, her breathing grew shallower, her lungs burned, and her wheezing intensified. With a crackling of cartilage in her knees, she sprinted as fast as possible. As she neared the driveway, the green became more dominant. Her mind echoed with the memory of her cousins' successful pranks and their laughter at her fear.

Upon exiting the labyrinth, the air improved in quality. She fell into the grass after tripping over her foot. Shielding her face, she flinched for protection. Opening her eyes, she observed the flowers in the field moving as one.

Calmly.

The suncrow was gone.

To avoid swaying, she steadied herself with a hand on her belly as she rose. With the world's spin ending, the clouds became motionless. A second shadow emerged near where the patch opened. This one lacked a flowing trench coat. This one had their plum sweater over their periwinkle button-down dress shirt. The khaki pants reminded her of her departed stepfather. He looked at Charlotte with distress; his breath was scant, and his hands rested on his knees when he took a break from his walk. The sun peeked for a wink of reflection on the top of his head as she passed him.

Edward.

Chapter 19

Noah emerged from the flowers. A layer of clinging dust coated his sweaty brow. With a hacking cough, he ejected a mass of phlegm, ridding his lungs of the wind's lingering particles.

"Charlotte?" he cried out, only to hear his voice echo in the fields.

There was no response. Mother Nature's frightening tactics caused the flowers to tremble in fear. The weather's break was enough for them to act more like themselves; not bowing in shame from the power.

Where'd she go?

There are many places to find protection from the harsh wind in the abundant fields. He even thought of the idea that she found her way out; she is smart enough to run for shelter and probably went back to the house.

The gravel crunched under his sneakers as he ascended the driveway. On the hilltop, he spotted Alexandria swinging on the tire, her blonde hair flowed behind her like a pendulum. Up the incline went two tabby cats, wanting her attention. The basketball's rhythmic bounce resonated on the cement. Mason took a practice shot after jumping back; the ball missed the ragged net and didn't make it to the hoop. A smirk played on his lips as he took another shot at victory.

"Mason," Noah said, relieved to have company.

"Hey," he responded, shooting again successfully.

"That was quite some wind."

"Tell me about it! It threw me off on my three pointers."

A spring fraternity party fight left his wrist needing time to heal. Drunken fights over which house was better, resulting in some brothers getting punched, only made things worse. His outcome could have been better if he hadn't punched the walls in frustration. Conveniently, it happened as the season ended, giving him enough time to take it easy, but at the price of his skill; he had only mere months to get his shot back to the precision that landed him the scholarships.

"Have you seen Charlotte?" Noah asked, looking around the property for any indigo denim that stood out.

"No. Where were you two anyway?" Mason said, twirling the ball in his hand.

"We went out for a walk."

"Lame."

"We visited the neighbors."

"It feels like forever since I've seen them!" Mason said, the ball pelted at the rusted backboard. "How are Bennett and his brother? I forgot his name."

"Austin."

"Austin. That's right. Is he still weird?"

"He hasn't changed, if that's what you're wondering. Besides, he wasn't there."

"What even happened to him? Isn't he thirty or something and still living at home?"

"So?"

"I just think it's strange. He wasn't always so quiet. I remember when we were kids, the guy wouldn't shut up."

"I dunno. They won't tell anybody."

"Maybe he saw Charlotte's face, and it scared him shitless!" he said, laughing to himself.

"That's not funny," Noah hissed, ignoring the ball that bounced in his direction after another shot. "I thought you were going to cut the shit with that."

"Come on. They're both freaks. You've said it too!"

"Yeah, back when I thought it was funny. We're grown-ups now, and some things are just meant to stay in the past."

"Whatever," his brother said, rolling his eyes.

"Besides, if you gave her the time, you would think she was a good person."

"Just like Austin? You thought he was cool when you were pulling pranks on him, too?"

"We all did it! He enjoyed it!"

The two stared at each other. Above them, three birds flew in a circle, trying to calm their escalating fight. A sigh of frustration escaped Noah; his marble-like exterior remained unbroken.

"But there was something off about Frieda," Noah said, his voice trembling as he composed himself.

"What was wrong with the old bag this time?"

Noah took a deep breath, striving for composure to prevent another dispute. His curiosity was in dire need of being explored. Bickering as though their ages were in the single digits again. His plan to compare notes with Charlotte fell through because of bad luck.

"She mentioned something about hurting grandma."

"So? People get hurt."

"She had sadness in her eyes, full of regret."

"How could you see those things? She's a bag of bones!"

As Noah walked through the garage, he shook his head. The look Mason saw in his brother's face made him follow with curiosity. Mason threw the ball behind him, the sphere bouncing down the hills as though it slowly was sinking into a putting hole. Noah's furious shove sent the screen door bursting open. "Clear Blue Sky" skipped on the record player from his stomping feet. Mason cringed from the trembling fixtures, hoping that the wrath wouldn't wake their mother from her nap.

"Where is everybody?" Noah asked, checking to see if anyone was there.

"Beats me," Mason said as he wiped his shoes on the rug. "I was just going to ask you if you've seen Olivia. She hasn't taken her supplements."

"Maybe she went with Alexandria or Uncle Timothy. I haven't seen them in a while either."

"I just saw Alexandria. She wasn't with her."

Noah moved faster once he was in the hallway. In the family photo, he glimpsed his sister; her smile was strained, but her eyes betrayed annoyance. Looking more at the forced nature of the expressions, a sense of mystery started looming. There had to be more to Gemma's murder, and nobody was talking about it. If nobody was going to be open with the children, then it was time for him to look into it himself.

Upon passing the game closet, he opened the adjoining door. The little room had a string dangling in its middle. He switched on the light, but the room remained poorly illuminated. Precariously stacked papers covered the mahogany desk. In the center, a row of pencils displayed bite marks on their erasers.

Noah removed the files from the drawers one at a time, the papers shuffling as quietly as he could. Noah looked through the documents for anything unusual. Yellow sheets with scribbles overpowered his eyes from the number of written monthly invoices, reminding him of the paperwork he filled out at Blockbuster; he couldn't help but think of ways to organize the clutter better like he did there. At the back of one drawer was a metal box. Taking the key from the center console, he unlocked it; colors fluttered from the over-packed container with every assortment of greeting cards that could've stocked an entire Hallmark end cap. Every 'thank you' from all the guests that enjoyed her business made his heart flutter with satisfaction. There was even one he gave her after her knee surgery.

"Get well soon, Grandma! Love you lots."

A single tear formed at the corner of his eye. Those words remain true even now. Not visiting enough caused regret, but it didn't provide closure. She was gone and only his memories are what's left of her. Aside from her material possessions, the kindness she endeavored to cultivate is her true lasting gift; the beneficiaries of her possessions remain unknown.

Inside a handmade card from Charlotte, nestled an envelope. The ivory coloring was dirty and smudged with dust. Opening the flap, a flimsy piece of paper slid onto the desk. He carefully unwrapped the folds; yellow flakes toppled next to his feet from the metal ring punctures. He lifted it closer to the light, reading the blurry cursive and trying to avoid mispronouncing words marred by water damage:

DEAREST SIMON,

Words cannot explain the gratitude I have for your kindness in helping Eustace and me at the farm over the years. And Bennett still talks about the time you took him on your tractor when you were carving out the trails for spring. That joke you made about those scarecrows coming to life when he's a bad boy has made him think twice about acting up!

I know that these past few years haven't been the easiest on your marriage with Gemma. She is such a dear friend, and I feel horrible about what we did to her. As the saying goes, "we made our bed, and we have to lie in it." I don't want what happened to ever happen again. We made commitments to our spouses to love them through thick and thin, and what we did showed our weakness. What we need to do moving forward is to keep our relationship professional, so I ask that we keep our distance from each other for the time being. My feelings for you keep getting overshadowed by the shame of betraying my Eustace.

I hope you will understand. I know we will remain friends again after the dust settles.

Sincerely,

Frieda.

P.S. I don't want to be a pain, but is there a way you can make sure your guests don't trespass while you run your business? My poor horse got spooked and nearly hurt my dear Bennett.

NOAH'S EYES WIDENED in shock. He held his grandfather in the highest regard. He wished for the lasting relationship his grandparents had.

It was all just a façade. Grandpa Simon had cheated on Grandma Gemma.

He moved the paper down; his vision was blurry as it refocused on the space. Mason's lips sank into a frown with mutual disappointment. Shaking his head, he faced their family's secret. Behind him was a third person with an identical expression; liquid soaked into the cuff of her sweater, dripping onto the linoleum floor and puddling close to her socks.

Marnie.

Chapter 20

30^{years ago}

BUSINESS OPERATIONS had ceased for the day, and the last passengers disembarked after the tractor switched off. Construction workers completed the cabin's roof and gathered their tools. With the business booming and more customers than help, the five employees stretched, weary from their long day.

"Good job, everyone," Gemma said, though her smile couldn't hide her exhaustion. "I know it's been pretty busy with the traffic growing."

"It looks like twice as much as last weekend," remarked an employee, heading to the dumpster with a trash bag.

"It would be nice to have an extra set of hands," said another employee.

"Or at least pay us a little more," said the other.

A slender man appeared, walking from the fields. A touch to his date's back had her blushing.

"I'm afraid you may have to worry about a few other things before hiring more people," said the man.

"Yeah, like what, Dexter?"

The crew walked away; their heads bowed in defeat at the realization that they weren't getting their demands met at the moment. Their minds raced with questions regarding their future employment under the Chesters. Burnout had cast doubt on their commitment, though they were once very loyal.

"Well, for starters, some of those new structures have nails sticking out of them."

"Okay, I'll go over them with a hammer," Simon said with a sigh.

"Some of the holes may be a little deep. I almost twisted my ankle in there a few times."

"Me too," said his date.

"I'm sorry. Who is your friend?"

Gemma regarded the brunette with trepidation. Her patience had run out, especially with opinions from people who weren't involved in the company's creation.

"Oh, I'm sorry," Dexter said with a chuckle. "This is Janice. She's visiting here from Kansas City."

"Pleased to meet you."

"You have a lovely place, Mrs. Chester," she said, her eyelashes fluttering. "I did a story for my old news station on a farm just like this one. It had just the same charm."

A slight smirk played on Gemma's lips. A new customer brought her immense satisfaction and joy. Despite early financial struggles, dedicating both her and Simon to their business has brought them happiness.

"I just don't want your farm to end up like the other one. They had to shut down from all the lawsuits that were brought onto them."

"I beg your pardon?" asked Gemma, perplexed by the rerouting of her intention.

"There were too many injuries for them to keep up with."

A sigh of disappointment escaped Gemma's lips. All the concerns are piling up, and there's no way to prioritize them; they all need to be done sooner than later.

"Oh, by the way, how are the littles?" Dexter asked.

"They're not so little anymore, but they're quite the handful. Holidays become a zoo over here."

"I bet."

"It's still so rewarding. They won't be that demanding for long once they grow up."

Chuckles of agreement rippled through the group. Gemma strove for a complete commitment to the lighthearted mood. Their ever-growing workload consumed her mind.

"Well, I should get things closed up. I'll see you all around," Gemma said.

With a small wave, she went back inside. Nerves churned in her stomach. She was worried about meeting the next weekend's business deadline.

Sonny and Cher was playing softly on the record player. The paisley wallpaper glowed in the light of three candles on the kitchen table. Next to the refrigerator, Simon smiled, his hands on two wine glasses of burgundy, the liquid swishing around with ease.

With a "Hi, honey," Simon swayed to the music's gentle rhythm.

A smile played on Gemma's lips, acknowledging his gesture. She deserved a small drink after everything she went through today. Her aching knees desperately needed a respite, hoping to delay the inevitable need for replacements.

"Hi, dear."

She picked up the wine glass; the contents swirled, forming patterns as she brought it to her lips. The small amount she drank trickled down, quieting the growls in her stomach. Despite everything, she remained preoccupied.

"We should probably get to work," she said, taking a seat at the table.

"The day is done," he said, joining her. "The kids are asleep. Let's relax for a bit."

"Didn't Dexter tell you about his concerns?"

"No."

"There is a list of safety concerns that we need to get to sooner than later. Nails need to be double checked, and the fence over at Frieda's needs to be patched up. There are holes growing throughout the maze that need to be covered."

"That can wait until tomorrow."

"No, we should do it tonight."

Simon's eyebrows furrowed. He sighed deeply, his hold on the glass growing stronger.

"Why do you always have to do things right away?" he hissed, chugging the last gulp in his glass.

Gemma's forehead wrinkles deepened. A tense expression formed on her lips.

"I want this business to succeed," she replied, her boots tapping a rapid rhythm against the tiles.

The sun inched toward the horizon's edge. A heavenly light, born from a mix of blue, purple, orange, and red, countered the dark, serious mood Gemma maintained.

"But it's always about the business. You never make time for yourself; for us."

"And I wish you would put the same amount as I do."

Simon's heart sputtered. He moved his chair away from the table with a scoot, and the glass hit the sink with a loud bang. Glass rained onto the counter and floor after exploding from the metal. The bits shattered into smaller pieces under the force of his boots. His hip bumped the record player, causing the needle to skip and fall off the record.

"I work hard!"

The screen door slammed behind him, leaving Gemma in silence. Her arms strained as she lifted herself from the chair. She fought back a rising tide of worry, her eyes welling with anxious tears. Grabbing the broom, she swept away the glass along with her feelings.

HIS HAMMERING REVERBERATED through the labyrinth. The sunflower petals bent in the wind, appearing to cower from Simon's anger. His brute force caused the structures to sway, frightened by his grunts.

"Put in the same amount as I do," he said, nasally mocking her.

The nails became addressed in response to one of the listed concerns. In fact, they were embedded into the planks past the surface. He stamped his boot on the disturbed earth, making the mounds firmer.

"I told her we should hire more help so that won't be an issue, but no!"

Even the brisk, fresh air couldn't clear his frustrated mind. He had no interest in going back into the house; he couldn't even bother looking at his wife if she wasn't able to see the hard work he'd put into the farm. It was her idea to create the business, but she couldn't do all the manual labor all on her own. The office's organization relied heavily on his contributions to shelving and document management, preventing widespread disarray. The cabin wouldn't be what it was without him helping the construction workers to help cut the labor costs.

The aches and pains in his body disagreed with Gemma's proclamation.

As he looked, the barn seemed bigger, while the sunflowers appeared less dense. Simon strolled along the fence that marked the business's boundaries. A solitary light pulsed above a garden on the other side. The thirty-five-year-old woman's rake, metal prongs digging into the earth, was firmly in her grasp.

"Evening," said Simon, the hammer waving in the air.

"Oh, hello Simon!" Frieda said, her white teeth glistening in the dark.

The rake, now resting on the fence, tapped the wood of its handle. As she beat the gloves on her thighs, a cloud of dirt puffed from her jeans.

"What are you doing out so late?" he asked, making his way closer to her.

"I could ask you the same," she retorted sarcastically.

Simon's chest heaved, letting out a chuckle. He wiped his brow, the flannel cuff of his shirt absorbing the sweat. The wind felt like a fan blowing on him, cooling him down.

"Work never ends around here," he said, eyes rolling.

"Same here. Eustace always seems to find things for me to do."

"Gemma too."

Sitting on top, they caused the fence to sigh. His palms felt the fibers' bite, ready to splinter. Cows sang a mournful song to soothe their young.

"She on your case, too?"

"It's not a real marriage if there isn't a good ole' ball and chain!" he joked.

"That's right. They keep us in line."

"No matter how they tell us."

"What's that supposed to mean?" Frieda asked, her raised eyebrow casting a darkened shadow over her eye.

"Gemma thinks I don't work as hard as her."

"But you do work hard. You're the hardest working person I know. Even more than Eustace."

Simon felt a fluttering in his stomach, like a butterfly emerging from its chrysalis. The growing smell of manure near his nose went unnoticed by him. As his chest rose, his spine straightened.

"You really think so?" he asked, readjusting his balance on the fence.

"I do. I know Gemma can be a tough businesswoman, but I think she should take a breath and see what you both have done for the farm."

"Well, I couldn't do it without a wonderful support system. I mean, my neighbors were so kind to let us have so many people come and go."

His arm nudged hers. One of his eyelids shut for a little wink.

"I mean it. She doesn't give you enough credit."

"Kind of like Eustace?"

It was hard for Frieda to reply to his accusation. A wave of empathy washed over her as she understood the other person's experience. A tingling sensation ran down her spine, with a tremor running through her fingers.

"I know he pushes you so your business can thrive. But he needs to see what you do for you and your family. I know Bennett would be proud of your hard work. I'm proud of you."

Their eyes met. Moonlight glinted off a single tear. Their lips moved closer, as if pulled by a magnet. Pink tinted their cheeks, highlighting freckles. When she embraced him, his temple felt her chilly hand. His calloused fingers snagged on her sweater as he put them around her. The kisses multiplied with each passing second. Guilt gnawed at him, though flattery and appreciation masked it. He knew what he was doing was wrong, and he was certain that she felt the same, but the desires inside of him took control and it wouldn't stop when they laid out in the sunflowers for more.

Chapter 21

"Mom, what all did you hear?" asked Noah, the paper shaking as he slowly placed it next to his side.

Under the bright office lights, Marnie's eyes, a hazel so dark they appeared black, were immense. The final drips of her drink ran onto the floor from her pinky finger.

"Are you okay?" Mason asked, nervous, as the only other time she'd acted like this was when a Madonna concert was cancelled that she waited so long to buy tickets for.

"Y-yes," Marnie stammered, her hand shaking as she desperately tried to finish her now empty drink.

"You don't look okay," said Noah.

Slowly, Marnie retreated to the hallway, disregarding their observation as if it were just a murmur. Tears formed in her eyes as she gazed at the family portrait. Although the image showed only what they intended, far more secrets remained hidden than it depicted. Seeing Gemma's joyful face pained her heart; she knew that everything that had built their family was now destroyed, and her mother-in-law was dead and couldn't face it.

"Mom, will you please talk to us?" Mason said, concerned as he placed his hand on her back.

The refrigerator door flew open, the handle slamming against the cabinet. With a powerful shove, the jars of pickles and olives shook. Having finished her morning drink hours ago, she picked up the vodka next to the orange juice. As she slowly filled her glass, she added a splash of Coca-Cola to the top. The spoon stirred the contents of the glass container, creating a cloudy tan hue with each metallic clang.

"I-I don't think you should have any more," Mason said, reaching out to grab her drink. "Maybe a nap would make you feel better."

"Get your hands off of me!" Marnie hissed with more of her drink toppling over the rim and onto the top of her hand.

"We're just trying to help," said Noah.

"Help by keeping your noses out of people's business."

"You were going to find out one way or another," Mason defended. "We have to go through all of this shit at some point."

Marnie paid no attention to her son's rationale. With a swing, she opened the door leading to the back patio. Quickly setting the drink down, the uneven legs on the metal table caused the glass to tremble. She collapsed onto the worn cushion, sending a puff of dust into the air from the embedded gravel's air.

A look of concern passed between Mason and Noah. While they knew their grandmother's death would bring sorrow and the unexpected, its impact was far beyond their comprehension.

"Where's Dad?" Noah asked as he grabbed a towel hanging from the oven's handle. He reached to the floor to wipe away his mother's mess with fibers slowly getting dampened.

A pull on its hinges made the screen door slam. Edward cleaned his shoes to avoid getting dirt on the linoleum. Noah and Mason took another look at each other, trying to read each other's minds to find the way to ask about his father's affair. Telling him felt impossible without upsetting him.

"Hi Dad," said Mason, his grin forced.

"Hi," Edward said faintly as he made his way into the kitchen.

He reached for the faucet to turn it over to his side of the sink. Captivated by the water's hypnotic flow from the tap, he stared for a couple of minutes before wetting his palms.

"Are you okay?" Noah asked, now disturbed by both of their parents' distraught nature.

Edward said nothing. A deep breath preceded his pressing the soap dispenser. He watched the goo slowly transform into a sudsy substance that coated his hands.

"Dad?" asked Mason.

They alternated glances between his and Marnie's vacant expressions. Every time their mother appeared, she was taking a large drink, and their father was carefully cleaning under his fingernails.

"Please answer us. We need to talk to you."

Edward shut off the faucet and snatched the towel from Noah. The clash of vodka's stench against the clean scent of milk and honey went unnoticed by him. He tossed it on the counter and went to the back porch, sitting beside his wife. Their eyes looked tired, with nothing to say to each other; not even an acknowledgement of one another.

"Dammit, Dad, answer us!" Noah said, frustrated with his hands leaning on the edge of the table.

From their father's eye socket, a lone eyebrow rose gradually. Noah's heart pounded in fear from the intense look in his eye.

"Did you know that Grandpa Simon had an affair?" he asked tentatively.

Marnie drank much of her beverage, leaving only two-thirds remaining.

"Did Grandma know?" asked Mason, taking a seat to get to their level.

Marnie began to reconnect with reality. She was now as curious as her children as her hand went to rest on top of his. In frustration, she squeezed it tight, trying to force it from him.

"Please answer us," said Noah.

"Come on, answer them!" said Marnie with impatience.

Her hand flung the glass, which shattered upon hitting the siding. Sunlight glinted on the fragments atop the vines around the kitchen's window shutters. Marnie's anger surfaced, her breathing quickening.

"I know you're hiding something from me," Marnie continued. "After all the shit I do for this family, this is how you repay me?"

Edward said nothing.

"I've never lied to you about anything. Just tell us if you knew about the affair!"

"I did," he answered, his voice raspy. "We all did."

THE DAY CONCLUDED WITH just a few cars departing. Little Edward joined James and Victoria in getting into their pajamas. Racing down the hall, they hurried to the bathroom to be the first to reach the toothbrushes, with James slipping on a sock near the shower.

"Ouch," he said, chuckling before he quickly got back onto his feet.

Victoria chuckled while rinsing her toothbrush. She soaked the bristles, squeezed the tube of paste, and then shoved it into her mouth. With forceful scrubbing, each of the three's gums bled. Their innocent fun made Simon smile wider as he stood in the doorway.

"Be careful with those things. You may be doing more harm than help on those little guys," said their father.

Simon's words held no interest for the three. James and Edward resented their sister's consistent victory in their bedtime competition, a contest they viewed as solely focused on the final tally.

"You guys sure know how to keep yourselves entertained."

Victoria rushed past her father with her locks trailing behind her. After she jumped, the mattress springs let out a squeal. Quickly, she arranged blankets around her before her brothers put their brushes in the cup.

"I win again!"

Edward reacted to his sister with an eye roll. Given the opportunity, he'd shorten his brushing time, but Simon ensured full compliance because of past cavities and the dentist's emphasis on efficiency.

"I guess you do," said their father, walking into the kids' room.

"I always win," Victoria said, sticking her tongue out at James, who ignored her on his way to his bed.

"Maybe you can share with your brothers?" Simon asked, winking. "You're all winners to me and your mother."

"When is Mom going to say goodnight to us?" Edward asked as he hoisted himself onto the mattress.

"Yeah, she never comes up anymore," his sister agreed.

"She does too. She just has to close up shop, and then she'll be right up."

"And we'll be asleep by then," said James somberly.

"Why can't she close the farm earlier so we can spend more time with her?" asked Edward.

"She works really hard to provide a good life for you guys. You'll understand when you're older and have families of your own on what one must do to provide for them."

Simon attempted to restrain his mutual annoyance. The disappointment disturbed him on his children's faces. Although they signed up for this to provide for the family, he wished she'd pause and appreciate the present moment. The weight of their farm's commitment led to his persistent hope that the business would thrive, enabling her departure to be more available.

"She'll be up when she can. I promise."

WITH THE SUN DESCENDING, the children were in a deep sleep. Dreams about playing in the fields could never leave them; if they weren't doing it in real life, they were fantasizing about it. The discrepancy between the group's reality and their perception stemmed from a missing member.

Their mother.

Edward, alone among the three, found his mind in turmoil. Even a minute with Gemma was something he desperately craved, just to connect. He longed for the days when he'd scrape his knees on the gravel, and she'd rush to his aid. She would also make time for him to talk through any of his nightmares that haunted him in the dead of night; the boogeyman couldn't scare him any more with the words of encouragement that nurtured him.

He rose from his bed, moving softly so as not to disturb Victoria and James as they adjusted. He passed by the credenza, looking at their family photo that was full of joy and laughter. Seeing everyone smile made his stomach flutter; he couldn't wait for another one. As he neared the banister, their voices rose, their conversation becoming sharper and more pointed.

"Why do you always have to do things right away?" Simon hissed; his tone made Edward cringe.

"Because I want this business to thrive," she answered, the bottom of her boots tapping on the tile.

This was no surprise to Edward. She used this excuse whenever anyone questioned her absence or priorities.

"But it's always about the business. You never make time for yourself; for us."

"And I wish you would put the same amount as I do."

With a scoot of the chair, Simon slammed the glass into the sink. Glass showered the counter and floor after exploding from the metal. Bits crunched under his boots, breaking up into tinier ones. A scratched record caused the needle to skip, making an unpleasant sound that disturbed Edward.

"I work hard!"

The slamming screen door left Gemma in silence. Only the fading sniffles reached their son's ears in the silence. Their child sighed as the broom's bristles scraped across the linoleum floor.

A touch on Edward's shoulder made his breath catch in his throat. His heart pounded painfully in his chest as he clutched his left side. In front of him were Victoria and James. Their eyes were droopy with grogginess, but their smirks were growing from the fear they cast onto their brother.

"What are you guys doing here?" Edward said, moving back into the hallway's darkness.

"We heard broken glass and thought something was wrong," said Victoria, stretching her back.

"Mom and Dad got into another fight."

"Another one?" asked James, saddened.

"Maybe we should check up on Dad. He just stormed out," Edward recommended.

"Are you crazy?" Victoria asked, walking in front of him to stop him. "You know they said that we shouldn't be out there this late."

"Yeah, we'll get in trouble," said James.

"I don't care. I'm going to check on him, with or without you."

From their bedroom window, James and Victoria gazed outside. Their stomachs churned as they witnessed their father's head bowed in shame. They hated to see him like this; they hated to see both of their parents like this. Trying to console his sister, James grasped her hand, squeezing it gently to stem her tears.

"Okay, let's go."

TWENTY MINUTES OF FAKE sleeping bought them some precious time with their mother before she retired for the night. She kissed each child on their forehead, leaning over them one at a time.

"Sweet dreams. I love you very much," Gemma said as she shut the door behind them.

Moonlight bathed their window, which creeping leaf shadows surrounded. From his bed, Edward leaned against his door, waiting for Gemma to close her door and start reading before falling asleep himself.

"Okay, the coast is clear," he said as he heard the doorknob click into place.

With three pairs of silent feet, the group gingerly moved across the hallway and went down the stairs. The family photos on the wall filled them with hope of returning to their former life of fun and happiness. Victoria hoped they could even take a trip back to Mount Rushmore as she saw the shadows defined in the rock of Lincoln's chiseled cheekbones.

James gently closed the screen door behind him, being cautious not to let it slam. Slippers echoed on the cement before running onto the grass. With a slight wind rustling their leaves, the sunflowers greeted them. The rhythmic hammering of metal against wood guided them toward their father, dictating the paths needed to find him.

"I hope he's okay," Victoria said, her breath getting shorter as they picked up their pace.

Every path they took made their world feel smaller and smaller. The plant shadows created the illusion of an endless corridor, making them feel trapped. As they entered the clearing, the pounding had stopped. A solitary tower stood unoccupied and remote. The trio gasped for air, their anxiety growing with every moment spent away from the house, fearing discovery.

"What was that?" asked James.

Rustling came from the flowers in the distance. To reach their father faster, Victoria cut in front of her brothers, taking shortcuts across the field.

"Victoria, slow down," Edward said, dodging flowers that were mere inches from swinging toward his face.

Victoria wouldn't listen to him. Each plea from her brothers pushed her to greater speed. Her short stature made sprinting through the patches easier. The loose dirt swallowed James's foot, making him grunt as his ankle almost twisted.

Fewer flowers meant the clearing was more noticeable. A nearby wooden fence marking their neighbor's property line screened from view the farm's lushness. Two cows huddled together for warmth, anticipating the quiet of sleep. The stars shone above, winking a greeting that promised more glittering displays.

Victoria stood frozen; her eyes widened as she took it all in. Admiring the scenery, Edward gently placed a hand on her shoulder. Because outside time is limited, doing it without their parents' knowledge was thrilling. James joined the group, stretching his calves to ease the bothersome tightness.

"It's nice, isn't it?" Edward asked, the tall grass fluttering in waves.

Victoria said nothing. Her tongue was tied.

"Come on, you have to find something that's beautiful about this," James added.

Still nothing. All she could do was raise her arm and point ahead.

Her finger drew the boys' attention to something closer to their neighbor's farm. The light was flickering badly and required a new bulb. Gravity overcame the rake's precarious balance, causing it to fall. On the ground by the fence were two people. Their garments separated from their bodies as if a snake were discarding its skin. Victoria couldn't believe her father was kissing a woman other than her mother. Edward and James shared in the shock, giving Victoria the chance to escape the group and disappear into the patch.

"Victoria, wait," said Edward sharply, trying to remain strong as their heartbreak consumed them.

With an angry shove, Victoria sent the plants sprawling onto the ground. The children's chase of Victoria's weeping sprint caused scattered seeds to fall onto the dirt like tears from broken stems. The wind's force shoved the swings at the park, their hinges sadly squeaking as they passed.

After a good five minutes of chasing after their sister, she started to slow down. Running through the sunflowers was enough of a workout in addition to sobbing in between each labored breath. The run across the road resulted in sore muscles as the terrain shifted from open land to a thicker wood. The relentless downward slope of the ditch left their muscles aching and near exhaustion. As they neared her, the bare branches scraped against their arms; she began to slow. Leaping over bushes, the pursued deer vanished into the silence.

"Can you stop?" James said, annoyed as he let out a generous wad of spit.

Victoria collapsed next to a tree. Its base was so thick; the biggest tree in the woods. Her heartbroken sniffles interrupted the tranquility of the flowing stream. James and Edward sat next to her to take a break, all three of them broken.

"W-why would he do this to Mom?" Victoria asked, sinking her head into her arm as they hugged her knees.

"I dunno. It's a shock for me too," said Edward, wrapping his arm around her.

Her brother gave her support as she leaned on him. Despite his best efforts, he couldn't calm her down.

"Maybe this is a good thing?" James said.

"How can this be a good thing?" Victoria said, sniffling in pain. "He's cheating on her!"

"Yes, that's not that great. But maybe if Mom doesn't know, then things will be okay."

"What makes you think we won't tell?" asked Edward, dumbstruck.

"Hear me out. Maybe this is a one-time thing. Maybe a couple more. As long as the work gets done, then Mom doesn't need to know."

Edward and Victoria inched closer, their anxiety growing as they struggled to understand his reasoning.

"Just give him a chance. We can't afford for this farm to fail. It would kill the both of them. It would ruin us."

Those words were essential to understanding James's point. Their parents' sacrifices and hard work to improve their lives shouldn't be in vain. There was some hope in thinking that this could perhaps be a one-time mistake. Simon's many declarations of love for Gemma might excuse this as a minor lapse. They were committed to protecting the land's beauty, and the work done to maintain it.

"I don't want them to separate," Victoria said, her breath calmed down.

"I don't want them to lose what we have," said Edward.

"Well, then it's settled. Hopefully, this only happens once," said James, his confidence shaky. "It will be our little secret."

THE SCREEN DOOR OPENED. Strands of Charlotte's red hair escaped her braid, leaving it disheveled. Chunks of dirt fell to the floor, releasing themselves from the frayed fibers of her denim. The sun kissed her cheeks, leaving them pink and flushed.

She passed Edward once again, his head bowed in shame as he spoke with his wife and two sons, without acknowledging him. Noah and Mason glared at their father as though they were the parent scolding their child; the roles were reversed.

As she paused before the family photo, she studied her family once more. Alexandria subtly positioned herself in front of her brother, vying for attention within her family. Mason stood with chin held high, a cocky stance, and pursed lips, radiating confidence and skill. Both of those two were an extreme opposite to the genuine calm and happiness that came from Lucas and Noah's beaming smiles.

Next to her grandmother was Simon. She has viewed this photograph many times since its creation, and even more today. His prominence is more significant now than she's ever witnessed. She found something unsettling about his blank stare. Although he forced a smile, his eyes hinted at a secret.

But what?

Down the stairs went Lucas, where he met his cousin. A relieving smirk crossed Charlotte's face after her disorienting trek through the fields. She felt her muscles growing heavy from a level of inactivity she was far too familiar with, even in her younger years with gym class in the mix.

"Lucas," she said, readjusting her jacket. "I'm glad to see you."

"It's been a while," he said, observing her filth. "You must've been really mad to be gone for this long. Are you okay?"

The door slammed from the kitchen. The sound of shoes clapping on the linoleum and a long sigh broke the silence.

"Where'd you go?" he asked, softer.

"We went next door."

"Oh, really? How are they?"

"Nothing different, I guess. It's been a while since I've seen them last."

"I bet. The last time I went over there, Frieda wasn't doing too well. Bennett has been doing double time to maintain the farm."

"Yep. He's still working his butt off."

"And how's Austin? Is he still quiet?"

"Austin wasn't there."

Lucas's eyebrow began to raise. His arms crossed over his chest with concern.

"Strange. Austin never leaves the farm. Not for years."

Charlotte's thoughts accelerated. Throughout her acquaintance with Austin, she remained puzzled by his silences. Upon first meeting him, she found him to be exceptionally outgoing. There were moments when the only way to silence the child was with a smack on the head. The reasons behind his abrupt personality change and reclusive lifestyle were unknown. Yes, when a child loses their father, a part of them dies with the parent. His consistent lack of presence was strange unless Frieda summoned him.

"Do you know why he became so quiet?" Charlotte asked with curiosity.

"I don't know. From what the others say, he saw his dad die, and it screwed him up royally."

"How did he die?"

"Nobody knows. I don't think they've told anyone."

The den emitted hissing whispers. The mutters faded as Charlotte's interest piqued. With careful steps, she reached the hallway's end for a last glimpse of her family in the picture. Her proximity to the room amplified the whispers, making them more distinct.

To avoid drawing attention, Charlotte quietly peered around the corner. The quaint space featured pristine couches, their cushions fluffed as if untouched. The books in the library were put away with stacks adjusted and no sign of gravity pulling them to the floor. Standing by the window was someone sitting in one chair. Charlotte could only make out occasional curse words amongst the gibberish as the woman muttered nonsense with unwavering eyes.

Marnie.

Penny loafers stomped on the floor after another screen door slam. Heavy steps caused the overhead light to tremble as they shook the house. A flash of a bald head zoomed past the opening as Charlotte turned to look. She followed behind her uncle, passing by Lucas; an overwhelmed look of confusion was mutual in both of their eyes with too many oddities going on.

Running from the garage, Charlotte tried to catch Edward. As he neared the station wagon, gravel clung to his feet, the dust rising to meet the twilight sky. With the heat lessening, the cicadas' frenetic chirping faded, giving way to the pleasure of the evening chill.

"Uncle Eddy!" Charlotte said, breath shaky.

He didn't stop. He pulled the keys from his pocket, the sound of them jingling filling the air. The cacophony of metals created a confusing jumble, making it difficult for Edward to select the correct one.

"Please stop!" she commanded, more firm.

Edward let out a huge breath. His niece's frightened tone jolted him back to his humanity. Noticing Charlotte's longing for answers, he turned back to her.

"What's going on?" she asked him, noticing the red in his eyes from the tears that created a trail down his cheeks.

"I need to get out of here," he said, choked up.

"Why?"

"Because I ruined this family."

"What do you mean? You didn't ruin this family."

Everyone else has done their share more than you.

"There's something I should've told you all a long time ago, something I should've told my mother."

Charlotte's heart raced. Her stomach knotted, suppressing her appetite. Her starved fingers trembled, desperate for sustenance.

"What is it?"

"Your grandpa wasn't as faithful to this family as you think."

"You mean he cheated on Grandma?" she asked, nervous to face the truth.

Edward nodded in acknowledgement of the guess. The ongoing pain that shattered his heart was clear in his pained expression. His trembling fingers and jingling keys betrayed his lack of self-control, as Charlotte observed.

"Ever since we got here, I felt this presence. I don't know how to explain it," Edward continued.

Me too.

"I think I'm going crazy, but I thought I saw my brother a little bit ago in the fields."

No, you're not crazy.

Charlotte contemplated the idea of telling him that she was seeing her stepfather and brother as well. Noticing the fear in his eyes, she didn't want to take away from his concerns. Regardless of their spirits now haunting more than her, she couldn't believe that her grandmother had been deceived. Even worse, she couldn't believe that it had been by her uncle.

"Just take a breath," Charlotte recommended, trying to hold back her betrayal of the façade revealing its true self. "Remember what you kept telling me whenever I would have a breakdown?"

A chuckle escaped Edward's lips as he wiped away tears of reminiscence, calming himself. Every time her sadness overwhelmed her, he remembered needing to help her find relief. It was time for the student to become the teacher, no matter if Charlotte believed in the practice or not; it was the only thing she could think of to try to maintain peace.

"Let's take a deep breath together," Charlotte said, her smile becoming softer and more genuine as she took in his calm.

"Okay," he said as he walked back toward her.

He extended his hands toward hers, maintaining a distance of a couple of feet.

"That's the spirit!"

The country's silence calmed their nerves as they both closed their eyes and listened. Charlotte's biceps were even sorer than this morning after that first breath relaxed their muscles. Her breath left her lips drier, emphasizing their chapped state. Another breath led to their shoulders relaxing. Giggles filled Charlotte's mind as she recalled her childhood adventures running through the fields with her uncle.

Her eyes opened, bringing her back to her love for her favorite relative. Euphoria calmed her racing thoughts and brought her ease. She could feel better; she could even see how better she looked. A curved metal blade, fixed to a long wooden rod, was positioned behind Edward. The scythe's downward movement made her jaw drop. Years of giving advice culminated in Edward's acceptance, a smile gracing his lips as he took a nice, long breath.

"Watch out!" Charlotte cried out, letting go of his hands.

The scythe sliced across Edward's stomach. The upper half of his body fell, gravel digging into his face, eyes wide from the impact. Blood gushed from his ruptured stomach and spleen like uncorked champagne. His legs swung to the other side, twisting his limbs as he staggered. Frozen in terror, Charlotte remained unmoved by the blood covering her, eyes locked on the suncrow's chest as it rose and fell with rage from behind. The figure watched Edward to enjoy his last breath leaving his body that was no longer calm, but full of pain and despair.

Chapter 22

Charlotte and the suncrow exchanged intense stares with her urge to blink, making her cheek muscles shake. The setting sun's sparkle reflected off the broken trim surrounding the mesh eyes. Each patch brought back joyful memories of her and her late grandmother. The symbol of their love had now become the cause of a rift in the family, resulting in a pool of blood at her feet.

Charlotte ran toward the house, sprinting away from her frozen trauma. With each step, the gravel crunched louder as they ran faster, making Charlotte's ankles unstable. The scythe connected with her arm as the suncrow was almost within reach. A tear ripped along the seam of Charlotte's jacket sleeve as she pulled the weapon free, the fabric resisting and causing her muscles to tense. Tears streamed down her face as the blade's scrape on her tricep inched closer to her elbow.

Slipping off Charlotte's arm, the sleeve detached from the armhole and fell to the ground. As suncrow struggled to regain his balance, Charlotte dashed inside.

The screen door slammed and Mason's bag of potato chips burst open, sending crumbs everywhere. Panting, Charlotte slumped against the door, then onto the floor, hoping to avoid suncrow. The doorknob was slippery with blood from her hand as she fought to keep the door closed.

"What the hell is going on?" Marnie asked impatiently as she emerged from the den.

Lucas and Noah soon followed into the kitchen. Noah's eyes widened as he watched blood drip from Charlotte's elbow onto the rug. He ran to the stove to grab a towel from the oven handle and scurried past Alexandria when she came in past Marnie.

"What happened?" Noah asked, dabbing Charlotte's wound.

"I-It was," Charlotte panted, wincing in pain from the towel. "It was the suncrow."

"You mean that stupid scarecrow?" Alexandria asked, rolling her eyes.

Lucas's eyebrow rose as he stared at his sister in disbelief as he helped his cousin back onto her feet. Each time Noah and Lucas tried to pull Charlotte away from the door, she'd race back to check the lock. Charlotte's fearful eyes made Lucas uneasy.

"What're you doing?" he asked, pulling her away like a cat on fancy furniture.

"It's after me."

Charlotte's demeanor left Marnie and Alexandria looking at each other in confusion. Because the kids often teased and tormented Charlotte, they couldn't understand her intentions.

Was this another one of her antics?

"Where's Ed?" Marnie asked, moving past Charlotte's attention.

As Charlotte wept, the terrifying memory of her uncle's death and their separation overwhelmed her. The sight of his exposed intestines on his chest made her ill. As the adrenaline subsided, his blood dripped into her mouth, giving her a taste of his insides.

"He got him," she said, chin quivering.

"Who got him?" Mason asked, grabbing a glass of water.

"Suncrow."

"Oh, for heaven's sake!" Alexandria hissed, her hands raised dismissively.

"What's your problem?" Lucas asked his sister, letting go of Charlotte to allow Noah to help her to the chair.

"My problem? What about hers?"

"She doesn't seem to have a problem. You seem to have a problem with her," Noah added.

The sun descended toward the horizon. Blue and violet tones subdued the orange and yellow into darkness. Charlotte's blurry eyes prevented her from seeing the moonlight peeking on the green grass.

"Olivia was right. You're so desperate for attention," Alexandria proclaimed, crossing her arms.

Charlotte noticed Marnie's smirk growing and the arch of her eyebrow making her stare more intense. The deniers brought memories of every time she hurt herself when she tripped on the gravel and resulted in their distant behavior. She reacted to Mason's scares with consistent apathy. The only change from before was Olivia's absence; she wasn't there to fuel the fires.

"I'm the one that's desperate?" Charlotte asked, her knees trembled when she got back onto her feet. "Have you looked in the mirror lately?"

Alexandria moved closer to her cousin. The attempt at a disdainful glance didn't go unnoticed by Charlotte. She didn't have the support from Olivia to cosign any disdain. Charlotte's throbbing arm distracted her from her usual discomfort with allowing their statements to be said.

"You've been fighting for attention for years. If I'm the one that supposedly takes it away, then why do you always cry out for someone to care about your life so much?"

Tears welled in Alexandria's eyes, and she bit her lip from nerves. Charlotte's flushed face, spattered with blood, caused Alexandria to clench her fist.

"Guys, I tried to call for someone to look at that cut. The phone lines are down," said Mason as he rushed back into the space, breath quivering.

The lights flickered without warning, widening their eyes. With the fridge's hum gone, silence filled the space. Mason let out a small, high-pitched shriek that startled everyone.

"What's going on?" asked Marnie, ushering Noah closer to her for protection. Every flicker made her muscles tense.

"I told you. It's the suncrow!" said Charlotte, sharply.

"Let's go," said Noah, his hand grabbing his mother's tight.

Marnie held Mason's hand to link up with her family. Lucas steered Charlotte behind him and his sister, their shared look expressing disappointment at the sister's hateful expression. The sight of her brother defending Charlotte more than he ever had for her in years past caused Alexandria to cringe.

With the lights flickering once more, the music blared in and out of power, causing them to congregate closer together, Alexandria trailing behind. A gloved hand seized her from behind, silencing her cries for help. An arm encircled her, squeezing her stomach as it pulled her back. To prevent being taken, she frantically tried to grab at anything; she couldn't even shake the portraits before clutching the closest door handle. The figure released his grip on her at the top of the stairs. Step-by-step, she tumbled down closer to the pool, catching bits of straw that became illuminated from the lights. Her head hit the cement floor on the bottom, with the silhouette of a trench coat and straw hat to fade away from her consciousness.

EIGHT YEARS AGO, EVERYONE was finishing up their Easter lunch. Victoria splashed the ham with a final glaze. Marnie took a scoop of mayonnaise to add to the creaminess of the pasta salad, burying the cubed cheese. Timothy, sunglasses perched on his nose, prepared to hide the plastic bag full of eggs, each a different pastel hue.

"Why do we have to hunt for Easter eggs?" asked Olivia, flipping through her Teen Vogue.

"Aren't we a little old for this game?" Mason added.

"This is what Grandma Gemma and Grandpa Simon want," said James, stirring the potato salad.

"I don't mind it," said Gabriel. "My stash is getting low."

Charlotte chuckled at her brother, knowing that she was partially responsible for the sugary famine under his bed. All those times Gabriel would skip out on dinner whenever green beans were served, he would pretend to not feel well so he could get out of eating it and then having candy to fill up his stomach. She noticed Lucas's smile and realized he felt the same—that extra sugar wasn't needed.

On the dining room table, Edward put a stack of plates. As he took apart the stack of porcelain, the pieces clattered together before being put in their places. Katherine helped set the silverware on the mats, creating a soft jingle on the placemats.

Closing his briefcase, Dexter bid farewell and departed from the den. Shaking Simon's hand, he said his goodbyes and acknowledged every child he passed by on his way out the door.

"So, Charlotte, I heard that the knowledge bowl team at your school made it to state," Edward said.

"That's amazing! Way to go!" said Victoria.

The flattery warmed Charlotte's heart. The countless hours spent studying random facts for trivia were worth it. It brought a surge of joy after celebrating Mason's basketball victories and Lucas's perfect GPA.

"Thank you," said Charlotte, trying to remain modest as Olivia stared with envy across the room.

"We're so proud of you," said Gemma, her smile growing.

"Mom, did you bring the tape from my recital?" asked Alexandria, looking around the room for anyone's interest to pique.

"No, I didn't," said Victoria, grunting as she lifted the dish.

"I told you to bring it!"

"Well, it looks like I didn't," her mother said, lips tightening.

Alexandria plopped down on the chair, with crossed arms and furrowed eyebrows. A blue fire ignited in her eyes as she fixed Charlotte with a furious glare, attempting intimidation while her cousin looked away.

"How about last year's?" Alexandria asked, pouty. "Grandma, I know you have a copy here."

Approaching her granddaughter, Gemma felt the heat radiating from the teenager. Alexandria's flushed face unsettled Gemma, recalling past instances where it foreshadowed an emotional collapse.

"I do, honey," Gemma said, squeezing her shoulder to transfer the love.

A smile spread across Alexandria's face as she prepared to showcase her work. Examining the extensive cassette tape collection, she navigated past the Disney cases to the Star Wars tapes. The bottom sides featured blue marker scribbles on white labels. She reviewed recordings of all the Christmas parties, Mason's basketball games, and Noah's theatrical performances in church. Alexandria noticed the amount of recordings being more than hers. There were only two cassettes that contained something that featured herself as the main focus; even Charlotte had more.

With a light push, she inserted the tape into the VCR. As the player's gears whirred, her excitement mounted. She wondered if recounting her steps was necessary, as she recalled each one.

White fuzz covered the television screen to better highlight the stage details. The audience took their seats, with the camera shaking after Simon heard a joke that was told from Timothy about the movie "Constipation" not coming out yet. Victoria silenced the guys, directing their attention to the opening curtain signaling the show's start.

"Do you remember this?" Alexandria asked, scurrying to the chair, sitting on one of her legs.

Conversation continued among the rest of the group. Gemma, captivated by her granddaughter's talent, kept her eyes glued to the TV. Even her brother was too busy with shuffling the deck of cards to prepare for a game of slapjack with Gabriel and Charlotte. Mason led Noah to the den to set up a game of Perfection for them to play after lunch.

Alexandria's hands fidgeted with her jeans, pinching the seams as her annoyance grew, making her blood boil. Her only clear memory was how supportive her family was of Charlotte's knowledge bowl achievements. She felt like she had to take a backseat to everyone's attention for so long; the dance recitals weren't enough for her.

The sound of magazines toppling as Alexandria rushed from the room startled Gemma. Upset about the damage to her collection from falling, Olivia slammed it down.

"What the hell?" she said, flicking her hair behind her head.

Olivia trailed her cousin, running after her up the stairs. Only the sound of Alexandria's breath, growing faster and heavier, reached her ears. Alexandria's sighs evoked sympathy in her.

"Can you just chill out for a second?" she asked her as they made it into their parents' childhood bedroom.

Alexandria fell onto the bed, sobbing into the comforter. The lack of attention made her ears steam with anger. She got some sense of fulfillment that at least one person took their time to check in on her, even if that person sucks the air out of the room.

"Why the tantrum?" Olivia asked, petting Alexandria's hair.

"That wasn't a tantrum!" Alexandria hissed, her mascara smearing on her cheek.

"Then what the hell was that?"

Just then, an idea came to her mind. If Olivia was the one that liked to deliver the bad news, maybe the blood wouldn't necessarily be on her hands. Her grandparents may be the ones that mastered the art of gardening, with the sunflowers blooming to perfection, but that didn't mean that they could be the only ones to plant seeds.

"I-I just think that it's annoying that Charlotte gets all the attention."

"Yeah, it's stupid."

"Why do they care about her more than us? She's not even a part of this family!"

"True."

"She even told me you need to fix your eyebrows."

"What's wrong with my eyebrows?" Olivia asked as she touched them with concern.

Olivia's nostrils flared with growing anger. Alexandria held herself back with wanting to crack a smile, knowing that the fish had taken the bait. With Olivia now strung along, Alexandria had the chance to prolong the situation.

"She told my mom that she doesn't understand why you care so much about your beauty and that there's nothing special."

"No, she did not!" Olivia's face was getting pinker by the accusation.

"She's said so much shit about you. It's not even funny."

"It's not!"

Olivia launched herself from the bed. The family photos vibrated on the wall as her stomping feet rocked the building. Silence descended upon the downstairs room; the TV crackled with static, then Alexandria's solo started. Olivia stopped at the doorway, her lip snarled at Charlotte as she slapped the top of her brother's hand, with Alexandria standing behind her, with teeth glowing with a growing smile.

WITH THE LIGHT FLICKERING, Alexandria strained to see the shadowy figure at the top of the stairs. Shortening breaths accompanied her struggle to stand. As she tried to leave the figure, the uneven cement bricks hampered her progress. The planks groaned under the measured, heavy tread of the suncrow's boots. Stepping onto the slick plastic, the world kept turning.

I can't see! she thought as the covering gave into her weight, entangling her in the pool. *I can't move*!

The frigid water stinging her eyes with chlorine, jolted her from her daze. With her blonde bangs stiff and covering her eyes, she pulled them back to glimpse the table's edge. White static filled the television screen at the table's edge, widening her eyes. Her solo flashed onto the screen; a mass of extension cords connected to an electric generator made her spine tingle after she blinked.

"What the hell?" Alexandria said as her limbs treaded heavily with the plastic peeling away from her body.

Having reached the bottom of the steps, the suncrow strolled to the table. In her attempt to swim away, Alexandria expended all her energy. Every step the suncrow took was a flailing attempt to get closer out of the pool. A large gulp of water, taken in a moment of panic, choked her as she began to ascend the ladder.

"Please, don't do this!"

The suncrow's hands went to the table's underside, then they lifted the edge, causing the television to tip off the side. Alexandria let out one last gasp before catching the glimpse of her beaming smile on the screen as it touched the surface of the water.

Alexandria's body reacted violently to the electric current coursing through her. Numbness started at her extremities after an initial tingling sensation. She struggled to escape the water; her mind and body were disconnected. Her temples throbbed with a rhythm like a child's drumming. Smoke rose from the water and into her head. Alexandria's eyes captured the last bit of the suncrow enjoying its victory with her demise being herself.

Chapter 23

A collective gasp arose from the family when the lights flickered before going out once more. Birds stopped chirping, and the bugs ceased buzzing; it was as though the world stopped moving. A pause in the wind left the trees and their leaves unmoving.

Charlotte felt Mason's breath on her neck, and moisture collected there as he quivered. Lucas and Noah's eyes widened as their nerves rattled. Pinching her sweater sleeves, Marnie bit her lip.

"What's going on?" Mason asked, scooting closer to his brother.

There was no answer to his concern. There isn't a single justification for the events unfolding at home.

"And where's Alexandria?" asked her brother.

Through the window, Charlotte tried to pierce the darkness with her gaze. He couldn't find anyone to answer his question. Only the rushing water from the sink's spigot showed any movement.

"We have to go find her," said Charlotte.

"Maybe she's just throwing another tantrum," Marnie said dubiously. "She's probably the reason the power went out."

"What?" asked Lucas.

"I swear that her and Olivia always keep everything plugged in."

"That can't be it," said Mason, huffing.

"Well, maybe that and you leaving the lights on," his mother accused him. "You've been scared of the dark all your life, and you still never turn them off."

A tiny smirk played on Charlotte's lips. Amid the escalating chaos and worry, she found it oddly satisfying to see her tormentors exposed.

"Okay, let's save the finger pointing for another time," said Lucas, his eyes rolling. "Let's find Alexandria and get out of here."

"What about the others?" asked Marnie.

"We'll find them."

In unison, the rest of the group raised their eyebrows, failing to account for the others' absence. Keeping track of everyone's whereabouts was difficult because of the day's stresses. At that point, they realized the group's numbers had dwindled to half.

"Let's find her," said Marnie, the goosebumps on her neck becoming more defined in the moonlight.

Each push made the screen door's hinges shriek as they resisted the slam while they entered the house. Thoughts raced through their heads as their toes tapped against the linoleum.

Is Olivia playing another prank?

Did Alexandria have a tantrum and storm off?

Was Timothy just too overwhelmed and went for a breather?

Charlotte examined the dining room, Lucas close behind. Stars winked on the plates, reflecting the night sky onto the porcelain. The spoons showed her worried expression. With the silence pressing down, Lucas's ragged breathing betrayed his attempt at composure.

While in the den, Charlotte continued to glance at the chairs near the bookcases. The sight of Gemma sitting there showed her disappointment in the family's fragmentation. During challenging periods, their response has been to attack others or silence the problem instead of cooperating. What made the situation even worse was seeing Marnie and Mason running from the garage through the window, with Noah chasing after them, trying to catch them.

MARNIE FUMBLED WITH the keys while the crickets chirped once more. Beginning with the nearest car, she attempted to start it, but the engine only emitted a weak sputter. Noticing the slightly open hood, Mason's eyes grew as she tried again. He parted his lips as he raised it, discovering the battery's wires cut. As Marnie exited her car, she surveyed the other vehicles. In the darkness, the tires seemed to sink into black puddles, reducing their ground clearance.

Someone slashed the tires.

"No," Marnie mumbled to herself, a hopeless tear welling in her eye.

Beside the vehicle was a larger, darker puddle than the tire's reflection. This one mirrored the bushels visible above the surface. As she approached, a long section of intestines, resembling a hose, lay on the gravel near the torso. The stomach's contents spilled out, creating a mushy pile around his shoes.

A quiver ran through Marnie's chin as she examined the second part. Each of her shoulders had one of her boys' hands resting on them. The sight of the now-familiar bald head upset their stomachs. Agony and terror filled the vacant eyes of their father and husband in his last moments.

"Oh, my god!" she cried out, her heart breaking with the reality of her loss.

Mason and Noah clung to their mother. With each passing moment, their suspicion grew while they investigated the property. Every step became magnified with their echo creeping through the silence. The wind's touch cooled their necks, yet their furious blood still surged. Each sway of the branches saw them protecting each other, their guard becoming more tightened with the fear of attack. Dead leaves, falling closer, made them scurry, as if a grotesque spider approached.

Upon noticing the concession stands, they made a beeline for the sunflower butter. The chains rattled from the swings swaying from their swift movement. Marnie gasped as the shadow of her mother-in-law's cutout gleamed in the moonlight with fears that the silhouette was something more fatal. They stumbled on the uneven grass, causing blood to rush down their legs. With all his might, Mason flung the door open for his family. As the door closed behind them, they surveyed their small surroundings. Marnie's trembling hand dropped the rope she had just grabbed. Collaborating, Noah and his brother secured the item to a table leg by looping it around the knob and wrapping it many times for protection.

THE SMOKE ACTED AS their guide down the stairs. Charlotte's black fingernails dug into Lucas's olive sweater as she clenched his arm. The wooden supports of the pool railing gave way beneath their weight. Charred meat filled the air, making their foreheads sweat and eyes water.

The night light illuminated the calm waters as a buoy floated from the shallow to the deep end. In the deep end, a floating item had a red inner tube at one end and a yellow one at the other, each in a corner. Little blonde wisps escaped the balding scalp of the young woman. Her dark, vacant eyes spoke of a desperate plea for aid, a plea left unanswered as she met her end.

Losing his sister, Lucas broke down in tears. Charlotte shared the heartbreak, seeing her pained expression floating lifelessly. Even though some cousins weren't kind to her, it's questionable whether some would cry if the situation were reversed. Nonetheless, the pain one must've felt in their last moments was something she would never wish upon anybody. The approaching footsteps from upstairs barely gave them time to process the logic; each thump froze them.

With the sliding door open, they had no choice but to run. Disregarding the hill's steepness, their calf muscles were strained at the summit. A second look at Edward's body caused Charlotte to wince in sorrow. The jarring memory of his severed body lingered painfully as they walked across the gravel driveway. Sunflower petals bowed in shame as they moved closer into the brush, ignoring the path and running as fast and as far as they could to get away from the dangers on the land.

Upon Charlotte's arrival at the fence, the cows groaned. Lucas assisted her across the decaying wood, and together they navigated the uneven mud, sinking deeper with each step. Charlotte observed the house's tranquil appearance from a distance. To strangers, it looked idyllic, with vibrant flowers and the impression of a happy family within. Yet, life within that picture wasn't perfect at all.

Slipping on the cement, they arrived at Frieda's steps. Sweat made the metal railing slippery and hard to grasp. They pounded the door continuously, eyes scanning the property for anyone in pursuit. Each movement in the tall grass fueled their fear of an attack, mirroring Alexandria's fate.

The door creaked open, letting the pair force their entry. The sight of their panic erased Frieda's gentle smile. Her brow creased at the sight of their perspiration. Sensing their anxiety, her shoulders grew rigid.

"Honey, what's going on?" Frieda asked, closing the door behind them.

"There's someone at the farm," Charlotte said, catching her breath, her fingertips digging into the taupe wallpaper that was peeling.

"What do you mean?"

"Someone's trying to kill us," Lucas said, his eyes wandering. "Can we use your phone?"

He cut her off before she could answer. He proceeded down the hall to their living room. Her television set was fuzzy with the weekend rerun of *Wheel of Fortune*; even the white fuzz couldn't make Vanna White's purple sequin gown less saturated. A careless bump from his hip sent crossword puzzle books tumbling to the floor.

Charlotte's gaze drifted over the hallway's pictures. Frieda's happiness was more genuine and realistic with her family than in the Chester farm's foyer. Genuine laughter etched deeper wrinkles around their eyes. A decade seemed to have been shaved off Bennett's appearance; the weight of family stress was gone from him. Life and adventure flowed through Austin, a seemingly typical teenager. He beamed with joy, his father standing tall and proud, his happiness evident in his bright blue eyes.

"Dammit," Lucas screamed as he threw something against the wall. "Phone's dead!"

"What's wrong with your phone?" Charlotte asked, noticing the contestant solved the puzzle.

Family First was the famous phrase.

"I haven't a clue. The damn thing comes and goes."

"Why won't you get it fixed?"

A new round of the wheel brought cheers from the audience, ready for the next set of letters. From the open window, the speaker next to the television caused the fringe on the lampshade to shiver.

"Where's Bennett?" Lucas asked.

"Bennett is having his night cap."

"And Austin?" Charlotte asked.

"Would you two relax?" Frieda recommended, ushering them to the couches. "I already called for help before the phone went out. They should be here shortly."

"How long ago was that?" Charlotte asked as her body fell to the couch.

"About fifteen minutes. That repairman needs to do something about the damn static on my TV! He can get us some help when he gets here."

We need something more than antenna straightening! Charlotte thought, with the sound of the studio audience going in and out.

Lucas and Charlotte gazed into one another's eyes, their nerves were unable to keep them relaxed on the cushion. It felt like an eternity since the farm's power failure, and only then was Alexandria's body found, triggering a hurried dash to Frieda's. They don't know how long it actually took. As Frieda turned up the TV, Charlotte squeezed her cousin's arm to steady her nerves.

"S-so you didn't tell me how Austin has been," Charlotte said, her eyes peering back at the family photo.

"He's fine," Frieda said quickly.

"Just fine?"

"Yes."

Looking down the hallway, Charlotte saw the bedroom that was once occupied by Frieda's youngest. A decade later, the down comforter in the hallway picture remained unchanged: red and yellow plaid atop an indigo blue bedsheet. With one black marbly eye missing, an old teddy bear sat between two plush pillows, winking mischievously at her. The rocking chair's rhythmic sway caused only its back to be visible to her.

"It's such a shame that Austin has been so closed off for all these years," she said, noticing his drapes blowing by the open window.

A deep breath escaped Frieda's lips as she fought back a tear. The audience on the television let out a round of applause as the contestant in the blue position solved the puzzle; It's not every day somebody wins five thousand dollars.

"I know what it's like to be different," Charlotte continued, moving closer to the saddening mother. "I think he might be in danger."

Leaving the kitchen, Lucas's cousin found himself the subject of his cousin's worried stare. He took a steak knife and kept in his pocket, angled so it wouldn't touch his thigh.

"He wasn't always like this," Frieda said with heartbreak. "Austin was such a good boy."

"I know he was," Charlotte agreed.

"What happened?" Lucas asked as he went over to the window to shut the curtains.

"His father," Frieda choked. "He watched his father die, and it changed everything."

Chapter 24

Thirteen years ago was a busy weekend at Chester Farms. After a relentless rainy season that confined families inside, they were eager to explore. To prepare for tours, the establishment had its attractions fixed. Pits had to be drained from the kernels of corn that became miniature pools of muck that looked like chowder. Workers repainted the cutouts because the initial paint job was depressing, with the original finishings appearing smeared as though they were weeping throughout the storm.

Children ran through the maze, eager to get the blood pumping through their bodies after being cooped up watching reruns of Punky Brewster and Who's the Boss. Parents were relieved to get fresh air and try to take a break from their new cigarette addiction from their children driving them crazy. Freed from excessive attention, dogs chased rabbits that darted through the sunflowers.

Simon checked the rain-soaked fence for damaged planks, enjoying the view of his bustling business as he ran his hand along the rails. He prevented a couple of children from throwing rocks that landed twenty feet from one of Frieda's cows.

"Watch what you're doing!" he screamed at the kids.

The pair darted off like rats in their haste. As their small figures vanished into the yellow and green, they giggled.

"If you do it again, I'll see to it that you two are banned from coming here again!"

Simon proceeded down the path, his head shaking. He whispered to himself, needing to hire more staff; he hoped his business would one day flourish enough to employ more people than the few current employees and the occasional kind volunteers.

On the opposite side of the fence, a young man with baggy overalls and straps about to fall off his shoulders crossed his path. The sun played hide-and-seek amongst the clouds, illuminating the orange tones of his messy blonde hair while his hatchet winked.

"Hey, Mister Chester," said the boy, hammering a loose nail with the back of his tool.

"Hi, Austin," said Simon. "Busy day, I see."

"I can say the same for you!"

Four little girls followed closely, then vanished down another path. Their parents took a drag of a joint, allowing the marijuana to ease their anxieties while their children took in the land's simplicity. From the distance, Mason's yelp echoed as he tumbled into the pit; a fit of cackling laughter and a thick puff of smoke erupted from the couple.

"You're just a child. You need to enjoy it while you still can."

"Tell that to my dad," he said sarcastically.

"Yeah, he can be quite the hard ass."

With fear etched on Charlotte's face, the pair watched as she dashed through the undergrowth. With a giggle, Olivia pushed the flower stems behind her through the burlap, causing Alexandria to get hit in the face with flowers.

"Stop by any time, kid. I won't tell your pop," Simon said, his smile half-cocked.

Giving the kid a gentle nudge, Simon retreated back into the maze. He evaded two boys who attacked him with crude stick swords. Austin's mind reverberated with each clunk of the wood, envious of the carefree joy and innocence displayed by the kids at Chester Farms. No matter how many cow patties he scooped, nothing compared to the happiness radiating from his neighbor's house.

He wanted change.

"Austin!" his father yelled from the shed.

Dodging mud, he navigated a cow-filled path with only a few small dry patches. The sheep, seeking the closest stream formed by recent rain, leaped over puddles. Above him, two dozen pigeons landed on the roof of the crumbling red structure as they raced toward it.

As the barn door swung shut behind Austin, its exposed nails trembled as they punctured the planks. From his father's truck, Bennett heaved log after log, sweat beading on his flannel shirt.

"Yes, Father?" Austin said, the children's laughter muffled as the door shut.

"I'm going to need your help with the wood chipper today," he commanded, his voice stern as more logs fell close to the contraption.

Blood surged through Austin's veins. The glint of the blades mirrored his fear. During his last attempt at assisting with the chipper, he tripped while pulling a large log toward the chute. His body was close to toppling closer to his death, with the blades moving so fast and his life flashing before his very eyes.

He was seventeen.

For years, Frieda's support provided an excuse for him to avoid strenuous tasks. He could get away with collecting chicken eggs, cleaning animal droppings, or harvesting garden vegetables.

And he was content with that.

"Do I have to?" Austin asked, his voice strained.

"Yes," he said with assurance. "The Chesters are taking our business and we need to step it up if we need to survive."

Eustace held the Chesters responsible for their own lack of success relative to his own. Despite their business efforts, the allure of a sunflower farm and family playground surpassed everything. Everybody could have their fun petting farm animals and purchasing local produce. Not every farm had attractions based around sunflowers.

"Give them some slack. Maybe do some horse rides, or a petting zoo?"

"Look who knows how to run a business," Bennett said, groaning as he dropped another stack. "Let's just have him run the farm and we can run off and do nothing."

"I don't know everything," Austin defended. "I was just saying."

"Saying a bunch of bullshit, that's what," Eustace said, a giant brown wad of spit expelled from his mouth. "What gives you the right to speak to me like this?"

"Because I want to be like the other kids," Austin said, tears forming. "I want to have fun!"

"We can't afford fun!" Bennett hissed, slamming the tailgate to the truck. "That's not in the cards for us in this life."

A pitchfork in hand, Bennett rushed from the barn in a fit of anger. With a slam of the door, Austin checked the barn's roof. The ends of the wooden beams revealed peeking bundles of straw. Bits of cloth emerged at the seams, joining the small companions he made in his spare time. A red gingham swatch denoted a dress; his oversized blue flannel shirt went to her husband.

"Enough of the excuses. When we can afford the fun, we will have fun."

Eustace turned on the machine. A tiny roar grew into something that overpowered Austin's thinking, tuning out his sadness. Blades slid against one another, moving faster with each passing second. His father put a piece into the machine, starting a slow, destructive process. What was once a whole figure is now scattered on the ground in small fragments.

A breeze passed through the structure's uppermost aperture. Toward the beam's edge, one doll crept. Amidst the rotting wood and a cloud of sawdust, Eustace noticed the red gingham pattern becoming clearer, drawing his attention.

"What is that?" he asked, grabbing a long stick.

"It's nothing," Austin stammered, grabbing a piece of wood. "See, Dad. I'm ready to use this machine! I think I got the hang of this."

He put a log into the blade's path. Though slivers dug into his palms, his heart pounded as his fingers neared the machine. Eustace didn't care about that; he continued to reach for his doll on the beam. He grabbed the step stool and climbed six feet higher, bringing the plank within inches of his toy.

Austin didn't know what to do. The thought of his father learning about his playtime during work hours would distress him. To worsen the situation, involving dolls would be heartbreaking for him, given his belief that boys shouldn't play with dolls.

It was time to face the truth. It was time to tell him what he was doing behind his back.

Out of nowhere, a flock of pigeons flew past him, six of them rising from his knees and flying up to the beam. A scream escaped Austin's lips as he landed on the step stool, sending it tumbling forward.

"Austin! Help!" Eustace screamed as he tried to maintain his balance.

Austin plummeted to the floor after the ladder collapsed and its legs failed. Trying to lessen the impact on the equipment, Eustace extended his hands as he fell. The impact of his feet on the woodpile caused his bones to crack, and he slid closer to the machine. Pain shot through his lungs as he screamed, his face colliding with the blades. He thrashed to break free as the cut shot pain through his forehead. Each second fed more of his brain into the power.

Austin's arms shook with fear as he feebly attempted to move his father's lifeless body away from his deepening demise. Eustace's hefty frame was hard to maneuver through the woodpile because of his enormous arms and legs. The incessant corpse overwhelmed the wood chipper. Austin gave up and went to the chute. When the sawdust changed into blood and landed on his face, with guts and insides mushed before him, his guilt rendered him silent.

WITH THE GAME-SHOW'S end, the credits started. Tears welled in Frieda's eyes as she turned off the television, its screen dark. Charlotte sat in shock, observing Lucas, who never considered that watching his father die when he was young could lead to such silence.

"I'm so sorry that it happened to you and your family," Charlotte said.

"Thank you," Frieda said, dabbing her eyes with a tissue from her side table. "What hurts the worst is that I never got to tell him my secret."

"What secret?" Lucas asked, his eyebrow raised.

Frieda's breathing hitched. She looked back into the hallway; the family photo that showed the happiness in the group of four that was full of purity and love. The woman's chin quivered with regret at the sight of their smiling faces.

"There was one night that I was mad at Eustace. He could be quite an ass at times."

"Yeah," said Charlotte.

"I was out in the fields late one night. Your grandfather was also not in the best of spirits either. One thing led to another, and we spent the evening together."

A look of surprise widened the cousins' eyes. The letter Noah showed him earlier came back to Lucas's mind. It all became clear. Simon and Frieda's affair led Frieda to desire maintaining their friendship while creating distance.

"I'm so sorry," Frieda said. "I didn't mean to break your family."

Charlotte stifled her disappointment at the departed. Her supposedly honest relatives also harbored dark secrets. Each Chester harbored one that threatened their squeaky-clean image, leaving her palpitating.

"I also didn't get to tell Gemma something before she died. I wanted to find the right time to do so, but I was so scared."

What now?

"I needed a break from your family after that night, not just because I was mad for being unfaithful to my poor husband, but for another reason."

"What?" asked Lucas.

"I got pregnant with Austin."

Ideas filled her head. Though deeply hurt by the family's betrayal and dishonesty, other issues demanded her attention. Several people had disappeared, and some had been murdered. The equation just got an additional element.

Austin Grace was a Chester.

"We have to speak with Austin," Charlotte stated, hurrying from her seat.

With shared intentions, Lucas followed behind her. As they went down the hall, Frieda grabbed his sweater, trying to hold them back. In the youngest child's room, the rocking chair swayed gently, the blanket just brushing the floor. Anxiety pulsed through Charlotte as she seized control for the first time, determined not to have her destiny determined by the superficial judgments in one's image.

"Austin?" Charlotte said, her voice echoing in the empty corridor, carrying through the other bedroom and bathroom.

Moonlight reflected on the hardwood floors, making the gravel sparkle like glitter. With a whisper, the wind made the grass flutter. The rocking chair's wood creaked, revealing two straw dolls on the seat; one in a red gingham dress and the other in a blue plaid shirt. The room lacked the one person who could solve everything and possibly stop the mayhem.

Austin.

Chapter 25

The shack shook from the wind. Sunflower butter bottles fell to the floor beside Gemma's shaking cardboard cutout and Marnie's frozen expression. As Mason pulled the rope, his arms burned, and the frame groaned under the strain.

"We can't be in here forever," said Noah, sweat dampening his forehead.

"We can't go out there," said Marnie as she tucked her knees closer to her face.

"He's right," Mason agreed. "We're better with numbers."

The silence stretched time; it could have been minutes or hours. Perhaps the sun would meet them with Dexter and the will; he could send for help the minute he discovered Edward's mutilated corpse outside their door. The police could handle the assailant responsible for his death.

"You're right, hun," said Marnie. "Once we find Lucas, we run like hell."

"And Charlotte!" Noah hissed with annoyance, the stomp of his foot rattled the infrastructure.

His family's eyes widened in surprise as they looked at him. They were unsure whether the exterior or interior of the shop posed the greater threat.

"You all have treated her like shit ever since she's been a part of this family," Noah continued. "This is about life and death, for fuck's sake, and you still don't care about her."

"You didn't care about her either," defended Mason.

"I didn't have a choice. You and Olivia always had a way to threaten me if I didn't side with you."

"You always had a choice."

Silent and still, Noah felt the weight of his guilt. He realized he should have confronted his brother and sister, preventing Charlotte's suffering, as his brother had suggested. The anxieties of childhood consumed him, fearing exclusion for his nonconformity.

He didn't want to become Charlotte.

"Those days are over," Noah said with confidence. "Charlotte is just a part of this family as everyone else. I think she's better than most of us for being so strong for tolerating the crap we've thrown at her."

His proclamation made Mason and Marnie sigh in frustration. Their eyes rolled to the backs of their heads, unwilling to agree; just another person to cast to the side while they figured out how to get out of their predicament. Noah's eyebrows furrowed as he huffed and grabbed his brother by the neck, fingers digging deep into his skin.

"I'm not messing around. We find Charlotte and Lucas, then we get out of here. Got it?"

The fire in Noah's eyes made Mason's stomach lurch. This was not the person he had an enjoyment in pushing around. This person, in fact, was not one of the Chesters raised as part of the legacy.

Mason lost his grip, and the wind snatched the door. Overwhelmed by fear, Noah helped Marnie to her feet and escorted her from the structure. Behind him, Mason coughed, struggling for breath.

"Wait for me," he said, his eyes searching the rustling leaves, fearful of being left by himself.

Mason caught up, placing a hand on his mother's shoulder, hoping she'd approve. After all, she was the one of the people that fed the thoughts to him about their cousin; every comparison of her appearance to accusing her of grabbing the attention from his grandmother all came from Marnie first. Like he told his brother, he chose to inflict pain through leverage.

With the gravel behind them, the house grew smaller, disappearing into the night's darkness. The family's happiness, once so strong, is now reduced to a tiny memory, their family much smaller, with only flowers remaining as symbols of their love.

The stems were tall when they entered the maze when they looked around for any signs of movement. Petals swayed, attempting to guide them to the others. There were no other bodies to their left, only cleared rows, free of trinkets on the soft dirt patches. Looking to the right, the same thing, very hypnotic; the hard work put into the land was admirable with how pristine it was.

Approaching the first fork in the road was the first sign of movement; bundles of florals swayed. Fear and anxiety warred with their racing hearts, desperately hoping Lucas or Charlotte would appear. As black emerged from the yellow, there was a sense of relief, as it might be Charlotte. Patches of flannel revealed amongst the trench coat, with burlap peeking next to the flowers' faces.

The sight of the suncrow caused Mason's knees to tremble, reminding him of the project his cousins made years earlier. He ran faster to the right, his breath short as the path narrowed. The rough ground strained his leg joints. His basketball shorts snagged his fingers. A horrifying realization dawned on him as he looked behind.

Marnie and Noah went the other way.

The deeper Mason went into the maze; the path became more difficult to break out of. A chicken wire fence protected the flowers around the walkway from being cut. As he made contact with the wire, an electric shock surged through his arm, leaving him no option but to proceed down the path.

His inner voice repeated the scornful remarks he'd made, not just to his cousin, but to countless others. His head became lighter the faster he panted through the path, making the sunflowers appear like heads with each one laughing at him with judgement; all teasing him with the same insecurities.

The path was empty again when he looked behind. The realization that he had nobody around him to keep him strong and confident brought him into isolation. His footing became heavy with his next step not balancing his sprint. The ground became light in front of him, as he wasn't paying attention. As he lurched forward, his body felt heavy; the bridge he had dreaded for years loomed before him with ropes and planks provoking him with another failed attempt at not making it to the other side, a threshold to something deeper. Dirt showered down with him as he braced for his fall onto the corn, root fragments sprinkling down onto his scalp.

Upon hitting the ground, the gashes in his chest grew more severe, his limbs becoming entangled. His muscles flexed in pain, causing the constriction to become unbearable. Metal wrapped around his neck, with blades digging deep into his body, cutting into every bit of his skin and tearing every fiber of his clothing. His legs wrapped together with the back of his knees becoming stabbed with horrid pricks. The movement of his arms to try and release himself squeezed his veins, creating pulsating tension that was ready to burst. Intensifying waves of pain wracked his nerves as he struggled against his misery. Something trapped his mouth, preventing him from speaking as it squeezed his head, applying horrible pressure around his mouth. His eyelid was cut as he observed his surroundings, realizing he had landed in heaps of barbed wire.

Atop the pit, the suncrow perched, its gaze fixed on Mason below. It reached into the bushes; a wooden handle revealed itself through Mason's blurred sight with three prongs twinkling in the light. A pitchfork plunged into Mason's abdomen, emerging out his back. Blood seeped from the prongs, forming a small pool of his suffering in the pit. The sunflowers danced behind the figure with laughter, enjoying his misery as he sulked in pain that wouldn't stop growing, wouldn't stop ending.

THREE YEARS BACK, A beautiful birdsong filled the back patio. Behind the house, trees moved in the breeze as the last visitors arrived on Sunday after the news broke. The unexpected illness of Simon Chester caused the immediate and indefinite closure of Chester Farms.

Marnie sipped on her hot tea on the patio, attempting to relax and breathe in the fresh air while noticing her husband's increasing withdrawal from reality. Alexandria and Lucas attempted to lift his spirits by recalling his past pranks, but he only hummed in response.

"Dad, are you going to be okay?" asked Olivia as she went to his side, her arm rubbing his back to comfort his melancholy demeanor.

"I will be," Edward said, holding back his tears with a tightened chin.

Katherine rejoined the others, her face grim, leading Gabriel to the distant hammock. Gripping her son, she cherished every moment, brushing away sadness with a reminder of life's unpredictability. As she looked at Marnie, her sister-in-law ignored her sadness. The walls were coming up as though their mutual love for Madonna had never happened; she was a complete stranger to her.

Neil Diamond attempted to soothe the atmosphere by playing "Song Sung Blue" on the record player. Noah wrapped her arm around Charlotte, who dabbed the underpart of her eyes to soak up the sadness that consumed her with every passing minute as the cancer continued to spread throughout Simon's body.

"Everything will be okay," he said to his cousin, moving the stray hairs away from her face to see her quivering chin that reflected her breaking heart.

Trying to stay strong, Charlotte nodded as she heard Gabriel's sobs through the window. The profound loss she suffered at such a young age burdened her heart. The thought of Gemma facing life without her true love made her queasy.

Dexter exited the den, adjusting his tie as he approached the stove. Steam rose as he poured the water from the kettle into his cup. As the tea bag steeped, he caught glimpses of those his client was leaving and the legacy that would remain.

"I'm so sorry for your guys' loss," he said as he reached for the honey.

The rest of the family remained in silence, with only James and Gemma muttering a "thank you." Forced smiles continued to stretch across everybody's faces, with everybody trying to remain strong.

"We appreciate you coming, Dexter," said Victoria as she made her way around the area, her plate becoming emptier with each chocolate chip cookie being consumed by her family.

"Anything for you guys," he said, blowing the steam from the top of the mug. *"He's been more than just a client to me. He's like family."*

"You are a part of this family," Gemma said, trying to force a bite of the cookie into her mouth.

"You're always welcome here," James said, contributing to Dexter's warm smile.

"Thank you. I hate to bring this up, but since you're all here, I wanted to ask if you had any discussions about your plans moving forward with his assets."

Marnie joined the group, her arm around her husband in a comforting gesture. Edward embraced his wife's support as he reached for one of the last cookies.

"We've only brought it up here and there," Edward said, stepping in front of Timothy, who buried himself in front of his mug.

With the basketball placed on the bench, Mason closed the door behind himself. He slapped his tennis shoes together on the rug to remove the dirt before heading to the kitchen; his eyebrows shot up at the smell of sweets.

"Yes," James agreed. "Mom, have you put any thought into stepping down and selling the place?"

"You do owe it to yourself to take care of you," Victoria said, washing the mixing bowl in the sink, suds bubbling over the brim. "You could pay for everything and live comfortably, right?"

Gemma dried the remaining tears on her face. Ignoring the mounting dirt, she swept crumbs to the floor as her children repeated their pitch. As "Sweet Caroline" filled the room, the needle dancing on the record, her heart fluttered, remembering their years of love. Every success was made with him by her side. They endured and resolved all the fights. The family raised their children and created memories together in that very house.

"I think what Simon would want is for the business to go on."

James and Edward choked on their tea in disbelief. The birds abandoned their perch when the family noticed her unwavering look.

"But you could have enough money to pay everything off," said Marnie as she made her way to the refrigerator, her hand reaching for the Smirnoff. "You could pay a lot of our debts down too."

"We could use the help," Edward agreed meekly, trying to avoid admitting his shame. "The kids will be starting college before you know it, and we could use all the help we could get."

Their children's eyes grew wide. Their minds swirled with anxieties about their uncertain futures. All their plans that they expected to go off and make the memories could possibly be gone.

"You can't run the business forever," Victoria said, the faucet rinsing the suds from the bowl. "You need to think about the next step."

"I know it's not my place, but you should at least have some sort of plan," Dexter said as he placed the mug onto the counter. "What are your plans after you go?"

"You're our attorney and you don't even know?" James asked in disbelief.

"She didn't go through my firm."

"I already told you what I plan on doing with my money," she said, her knees cracking as she hoisted herself from her seat. "Charlotte asked for it first, so I'm going to give it to her."

Gemma playfully winked at Charlotte and chuckled at her joke. Her laughter echoed through the silence when the song ended, with nobody else in the family joining her. Disgust twisted Alexandria and Olivia's lips as they watched Charlotte shield herself from her family. Katherine's face lit up with a small smile as she remembered the moment from when they brought Charlotte to the farm and she had inquired, warmed by her mother-in-law's recollection as well.

"I-I'm going to talk with Grandpa," said Mason, his fist clenched as he crumpled the napkin in his grasp.

Family members left, each cousin taking a final glance at Charlotte before heading outdoors for some fresh air. Closing the screen door behind her, Charlotte went to the patio to enjoy the fresh air with her mother.

The closer Mason got to the den, the darker the corridor became. His eyes lingered on the family photo, remembering the immense pride Simon felt for his grandchildren after Mason's basketball team qualified for the state tournament the prior weekend. Beside Simon's bed, a nurse sat, watching the sunset's orange and blue glow. A cloud of dust trailed the group of cousins as they walked toward the sunflowers, his sister kicking at the gravel in the front.

Emaciation had wasted Simon's muscles, leaving little but bone as he lay on the bed. As his breathing grew heavy, his cheekbones appeared gaunt and his eyes sunk deep.

"Hi Grandpa," Mason said, his stomach twisting.

In the glow of the central fireplace, Simon's smile broadened, teeth shining bright. The nurse, needing to empty a bedpan, excused herself and headed to the bathroom. Glancing back down the hall, Mason saw his mother, whose head was in her hand, frustrated by the financial news. His past eavesdropping on their mounting debt had become her reality.

"Your parents will help us out," is all he heard Marnie say.

Simon coughed; his grip shivered when his bony fingers wrapped around his hand. A rush of oxygen through the tube bought him another minute of life.

"I'm so proud of you," he said, his palm cold and clammy.

Mason's mind raced, his heart fluttering with a rush of thoughts. He wished he had more time to say everything he wanted to him. He thought about updating him about the basketball team, being that he was one of his biggest fans. A nostalgic moment followed, recalling when they'd worked together on the cabin and Simon had let Mason pick the periwinkle blue to finish out the bedroom. However, another matter burdened him, one he couldn't articulate or share with anyone else.

"Grandpa, can I tell you something?" he whispered, his eyes looking around.

"You know you can tell me anything," he said wholeheartedly.

A dryness constricted Mason's throat. The back patio planks echoed with running feet after another kitchen door slam. Hearing his father's voice along with his aunt and uncle provided additional comfort.

"There's something that's been holding me back, and I don't know the right words to say it," he drawled.

Simon remained silent. As his grandson's armor cracked, he saw his guard weaken.

"I've been afraid of this family."

"Why would you say that?" Simon asked, putting effort into raising his eyebrow.

"I know how they treat some of these people," Mason answered. "Our parents try so hard to make sure everything's perfect. They even try to outdo each other."

"They were always like that." Simon coughed out a chuckle. "Your father can be so hard on you."

Mason paused, recognizing Simon's insight into the topic. Striving for perfection for so many years created unbearable pressure, compromising who he was. He struggled to have a fulfilling childhood because he always tried to live up to an impossible ideal.

"Which is why I need you to keep a secret for me."

"I'll take it to my grave," Simon said, his hand tapping his chest.

"I've tried all these years being something I'm not, and I'm getting tired of hiding. I need to tell someone that I'm not going to the University of Nebraska just for basketball."

"You're not?"

"No," Mason said, tears welling. "There's this friend of mine from summer camp years ago that will be going there as well. We've been friends for years and wrote to each other. One thing led to another; we became…more than friends."

For a split second, Simon's eyes widened before returning to his impassive expression. The oxygen machine hummed, then delivered a long, life-giving breath to his shaking lungs.

"I-I'm scared to say this to everyone here," Mason confessed, his nose sniffling. "I know how they've treated Charlotte over the years. I know how I've treated her. I just don't want to be a failure to them."

Mason felt Simon's weak pulse as his hand squeezed his again, the knuckles crunching. A single tear rolled down his cheek, yet his smile radiated warmth and affection.

"I don't think you are."

Relief washed over Mason. Love pulsed through him, making his fingertips tremble. For a moment, he felt a little lighter as his self-acceptance grew. Mason's fingers slithered around the cords to try to not pull anything out of Simon's body as he wanted to savor every minute he can with him in his long, final, tear-filled hug.

"I love you, Grandpa."

Chapter 26

The rocking chair's movement sent another chill down Charlotte's spine. Near the corner, a bouncy ball rolled slowly, dodging the attention-seeking jacks in desperate need for playtime. Disbelief washed over Lucas and her as they stood frozen, the trembling sleeves of Austin's flannel shirt gave a silent wave of uncertainty.

"Where's Austin?" Lucas asked, his breath quivering.

"He's not there? I thought he was," said Frieda, the corners of her blanket folded under her hands.

"Well, he's not. And we need to talk with him."

"And I thought you called for help?" Charlotte asked.

A slamming barn door broke the peace of the nighttime routine for the cows in the backyard. A single light shone through cracks in the siding, highlighting the accumulating dew on the pasture.

Pushing past Lucas, Charlotte startled Frieda, who retreated toward the door as she noticed Charlotte's attention. Charlotte's muscles strained as she struggled against Frieda's tight grip, a burning sensation searing her forearm as she pushed the woman out of her way.

"What the hell are you doing?" Charlotte asked, her grip slick as she tried to grasp the doorknob.

"He's just a boy!" Frieda pleaded with tears welling. "Please! He's just a boy!"

"And there's innocent people getting killed," she hissed, her fist clenching firmer. "Let go of me!"

Frieda's hold tightened, her other hand clutching at her. Threads strained at the seam of Charlotte's jacket sleeve as it pulled tight against her shoulder. His slender arms trembling, Lucas reached behind the woman to grab her shoulders, pulling her away from his cousin.

"What? Don't hurt him! He didn't do anything!"

The fierce stomp made the porcelain figurines on the mantle shake violently. The pans over her stove shook, like the building was experiencing a powerful earthquake. A flush crept over Charlotte's pale face as she struggled to keep her temper in check. A searing pain shot through her head as her knuckles connected with Frieda's cheekbone, sending her sprawling onto the floor from the sofa.

As Charlotte struggled to calm her trembling hands and angry breaths, Lucas' eyebrows rose in intrigue. His admiration for Charlotte grew because of a side of her they hadn't seen before. A surge of regret washed over her; if only she'd found the courage earlier, the family's path might have been altered. If Charlotte had been more assertive, maybe Olivia and Alexandria's antics toward her would have been less extreme. Had she not appeared so weak, Mason might have befriended her.

"Let's go."

The door burst open, and they dashed onto the gravel. With each step on the small pebbles, their ankles grew unsteady. Chickens fled to their coop when they jumped over their fence. The dogs began barking while James and Gabriel stared at their kin stumbling into the mud with each step. Their expressions of sadness contributed to their powerlessness.

The barn lights flickered when the door slammed. Along the workstation's corner, photographs of Eustace formed a shrine-like display above an array of power tools, nuts, and bolts. With trembling breath, Lucas peered at the truck situated across a clearing marked by wood shavings, where a chipper had once stood.

A figure lay stretched out along the wall, its limbs spread along the wood. Rubber bands held bits of straw at the wrists and ankles of the flannel shirt and denim pants, making them sway. Twine encircled its neck, and burlap fabric draped its round head. Two punctures marred a soldered nameplate of wood.

Eustace.

"Had to have a place to visit since there was nothing left of him to bury," said a voice behind them.

Charlotte's gaze returned to Bennett who appeared behind them at the door, her fingers shaking. Sweat and grime messed up the greasy ends of his dirty blonde hair. Calloused knuckles peeked through holes in the oil-stained rag, his fist clenched.

"Bennett," Charlotte said, her backside colliding with the rusted front bumper. "W-what are you doing here?"

"I live here?" Bennett asked, his eyebrow raising.

The wind howled past Charlotte and Lucas, a sound like the countryside's anguished shriek against their skin. Moths, drawn to the light's warmth, gathered near it, their wings creating shadows that emphasized Bennett's intense expression.

"Well, of course you live here," Lucas said. "What Charlotte meant is that you scared her. It's late."

"I could say the same for you," Bennett laughed, the rag pelted close to his boot as he moved to his workstation to reunite with a half empty bottle of Captain Morgan. "Why aren't you back at your house?"

"W-we need some help. Our phone's down and it looks like yours is too," Charlotte said as she noticed the field mice scurrying out a peephole near the scarecrow's feet.

"I know. The power sucks out here. I'm surprised yours isn't working, being that your family can afford top notch quality."

Brown liquid trickled down his throat from the tipped glass bottle. Bennett's eyes appeared through the glass; his disdain magnified. Charlotte noticed a chained padlock on the door when she looked behind him.

"You're right," Charlotte said, her hand squeezing Lucas's arm tight. "It's getting late. We should get going. Sorry to bother you and your mother."

Bennett smiled wider, the yellow in his teeth standing out more as it got darker. Bits of glass and wood mingled as the bottle shattered against the wall.

"You like my scarecrow?" Bennett said, slurring as he walked closer to the two.

"It looks great. Just like one of ours," said Lucas, his heart racing as he caught the size of Bennett's pupils getting bigger.

"Funny you mention that. I figured I take one of yours since your business took my dad's life."

"We heard what happened," Charlotte said as she saw the hurt behind his tough exterior. "But we were told that it was birds that spooked your brother."

"Speaking of Austin. Where is he?"

"He's doing what he needs to do," Bennett said, his finger swaying as he pointed at the two. "And it wasn't birds. It was your family's fault."

As Bennett approached, he stumbled. The Captain Morgan on his breath wheezed out, stinging Charlotte's nose. His anxious posture shifted as Lucas stood before Charlotte, shielding her.

"Charlotte, run!" Lucas said, his gut expelling a bit of air from Bennett's punch.

Frozen in place, Charlotte watched them wrestle. Paralysis seized her as she watched Lucas's arms shake while he fought the neighbor's powerful physique. Locked in, she couldn't escape without the key.

From under the scarecrow, the night sky was more visible through the siding. Tools rolling around made the planks rattle. Moving the legs of the figure, she kicked the wood, pulling it from the rusted nail that bonded it to the structure. With Lucas's constant pleas to flee, every kick made her cry. A final, forceful kick sent one board flying, knocking another loose.

Escaping the barn, her breath groaned with bits of regret that she let her cousin go without help. Each sound from the building sent a jolt through her as she struggled to stay upright in the mud. As she crawled under the fence back to her grandparents' farm, her denim skirt ripped. Tears welled, and the solitude consumed her as the sunflowers enveloped her, hiding her within their petals.

THE DEEPER MARNIE AND Noah ventured into the labyrinth, the more breathless they became. As the mother looked back, tears streamed down her face, realizing her other son wasn't there. Her mind raced, desperately hoping Mason had escaped unscathed. She was hoping he'd found Olivia, as she hadn't heard from her since breakfast.

"Help!" yelled Mason, full of agony, though his cry was weak.

A pang of sadness stopped Marnie's heart. The sound of his anguished cries, a cruel reminder of her dashed hopes, made her chin quiver in fear.

"We need to go back to him!" she said in a panic, her ankle twisting in the dirt from her abrupt stop.

"No, it's too late," Noah said with regret. "That thing probably got him."

"It did! He hurt my baby!"

Noah's sweaty hands lost their grip, and they slipped apart. Torn between his own suffering and his brother's, Noah witnessed a final, fading breath after another cry.

Noah stumbled after their connection ended. His foot hit a piece of rubble, making him fall down. The taste of dust in his mouth parched his tongue as he coughed. Having a dead stem stuck behind his teeth caused the back of his throat to feel scratchy. Looking back, he noticed the source of his tumble was a piece of wire, illuminated by the moon's light that was unraveling. Behind Marnie, a massive piece of plywood was caving in. Creaking hinges made Marnie freeze, lost in mystery.

"Mom, watch out!"

Marnie saw a giant wooden sunflower approaching her. She felt a gut-wrenching urge to dodge to the side. Her nose, and the curved yellow edges nearby, burrowed into the earth just a few feet from her. A fierce pounding in her chest, on the right side, signaled the arrival of panic. As she sprang up, a scream escaped her lips; she ran for safety, leaving her son behind. The thought of protection flooded her mind, not knowing where to find it, who to trust in obtaining it.

"Mom, wait!" Noah said, his gut tight.

As his mother ran farther, Noah began to step more carefully. One after the other, Christmas lights blew like firecrackers, causing Marnie to jump as though she were a startled cat. A tiny yelp escaped her lips with each piece of glass that landed on her head, like a nervous dog. She sped up, tripping over a wooden cutout that fell as she passed another wire.

"You need to stop!" Noah said, pleading as he felt helpless to control her panic.

Noah's steps grew unsteady as he slid across the turf on the wood, like a surfboard. Marnie glanced back at her crying son, her eyes widening, but she didn't heed his cries.

Marnie went on, past the merry-go-round, through the open area, her mind controlling her body as it wanted to keep running. Noah's only thought was to hold her back, and he quickened his pace to do so to catch up with her struggling run. As she went under the main swing set, she noticed the planks and chains were gone, her foot landing on a third wire.

She stumbled back when a wire slithered under her soles. Seeing his mother fall made Noah jump. A log from the top of the swings, released when the wire gave way, swung down like a pendulum, striking Noah hard in the ribs. His muscles grew heavy, and he fell backward. His consciousness drifted as the yellow blurred, the flowers fluttering away.

Marnie wept once more, her son's eyes closing with the realization that she failed another one of her children. Her breath hitched as her hands shook. She heard a tiny buzz in her ear, reminiscent of a fly. As she peered into the flowers, a blinding light overwhelmed her with only the shadows of the disk and florets crowding her, sparking hope that a divine being had arrived to save her within the crops. She needed a break from the painful images of her family's suffering.

Her cheek was scratched from the sudden prick that came from the light, her heart stopped from the pain. Touching the annoying surface wound, Marnie raised a curious eyebrow just before another injury struck her. The sight of blood made her chest heave with panic with the petals fluttering around her with warning.

And another.

And another.

Grimacing, she shielded her eyes, attempting to see through the betrayal of the bright light. Her eyes quickly noticed the buzzing sound escalating into a revving engine, while small bits multiplied as the wood chipper uprooted sunflowers, leading to the blades destroying the plants. The chute ejected seeds, hitting Marnie and causing her wounds to deepen and bleed. Backing away from the machine, her back touched the other end of the path, tickled by the shock of wire shoving her back.

Marnie screamed in terror as she ran straight ahead. With each step, the machine pulled the cord, preventing escape as its parts embedded in her sweater and jeans. Blood mingled with sweat and tears streaming down her face, the taste of iron causing her to choke from her short breaths. Benches ignited from a firework explosion at the base as she passed, her heart stopped as the wood flew in front of her. Blinded by a seed in her eye, she screamed, unable to see the nearby cabin and feel any hope.

While crossing the open patch, Marnie's blurry sight struggled to confirm that the chipper had finished grinding flowers. Relief washed over her with the new scratches ceasing to add to the existing wounds. The tension of her skin as she neared the porch caused her skin to burn from close to one hundred scratches. She wept as she noticed the extensive damage to her jeans; the indigo dye faded to purple, revealing her sliced thighs and knees. Reaching for the doorknob to find a first aid kit, she saw that her forearms looked as if a cheese grater had mutilated them. As she pulled the doorknob, her shoulder strained; her eye widened as she saw a string attached.

A sudden burst from the kitchen caused the front window to shatter. Wooden siding and shingles rained down on the plants scattered across the fields by the burst. Marnie's body fell back to the ground, her limbs sank into the dirt as she became weaker. Questions flew through her mind as to why she had to go through all of this pain and misery. Every wound and burn that covered her body made her feel helpless with nobody in her family out there to save her. With the thought of only Lucas and Charlotte still out there, she hoped for salvation, but every second of searing pain brought reflections of every wound she inflicted on others. The view of the cabin diminished as the small gable roof rained upon her with each plank, burying her in her pain and misery.

Chapter 27

A stumble interrupted Charlotte's journey back to the Chester's house. The screams frightened her, and she retreated toward the gravel road. Motors blaring made the sunflower petals tremble. The collapse raised concerns about the suncrow's likely victims.

Who's still out there? Somebody please be out there! Please, get this bastard!

She ascended the incline, cutting through the undergrowth to get to the tallest peak. Only the creaking branches accompanied the lone rope's silent sway, quickening her pulse. Each time a branch hit her face, she worried about Lucas and hoped he'd escaped Bennett's stupor unharmed.

Patches of green and yellow peeked through the dark land. The fierce fire at the cabin's center was a stark reminder of her lost memories, leaving her speechless. The absence of movement was deeply disturbing, hinting at something wrong. She couldn't have been the last one standing on her family's property; she wasn't prepared to face this being.

"Pretty scary, isn't it?" Gabriel said, appearing behind his sister.

"Dammit, don't do that!" Charlotte said, nursing her chest from halting.

"Yes, pipe down. She needs to stay alive for both of us," James appeared on her other side, patting his daughter's shoulder.

Disbelief rendered Charlotte motionless. His jokes were more appreciated when he was alive. As she looked down the path, she saw Edward's lower half again and bit her lip, fighting back her father's sarcasm.

"I-I don't know what to do," Charlotte said, her fingers trembling. "People are dying and I don't know what to do."

"I know," James said somberly. "I wish I could be there to protect you from this horrible person."

"Do you know who's doing this?"

"We don't," Gabriel said with regret.

"I thought you could see all," she said with pained sarcasm.

"We can, but only on the farm," said James.

"What do you mean?"

"We're stuck on this farm, and can only see what happened here," said Gabriel.

"So, Austin did it? You remember him?"

"It could be," James said. "I wish we could help you more."

"What we could tell you is that there are people that liked you more than they gave you credit for," said Gabriel, squeezing her shoulder.

"He's right. People aren't what they say they are in this family. Just like you. You're stronger than what you've shown these people."

"What're you trying to say?"

The porcelain clattered downhill. A gasp escaped Charlotte's lips as she surveyed her surroundings, her breath quickening. Everything in the field was the same as when she'd checked it out before. The collapse reduced all attractions to their bare frames. Despite the lessening flames, there was no activity from the cabin. Moonlight shone on plates beneath a draped white tablecloth at the labyrinth's start. A chair shifted, its base tilting toward the silverware. On the table's surface, three small lights grew faint, failing to illuminate anything.

The dinner table.

"Please stay with me," Charlotte said as her chin quivered in fear. "I'm scared to be alone."

With a yearning for contact, she put her hands to her shoulders. The rough denim of her jacket, its threads frayed, scraped against her palms as she tugged at it. She looked at her sides. Her stomach lurched as she felt her father's and brother's absence, especially at this critical moment.

"Oh, come on!"

With her hands exploring the branches of the trees, she felt sharp twigs, sending jolts of pain through her fast-thinking brain. She cringed at her loud sneeze, silently wishing it hadn't happened. Nothing around her can give her a fighting chance to defend herself, giving her no other choice but to take a deep breath to calm herself down.

"You can do this."

She took another breath, only to hear the self-soothing words she'd used to cope with her cousins' relentless taunting.

"Forget what they said before. You're strong."

The shivers gradually subsided. Her shoulders dropped.

"You're a tough bitch."

All of Charlotte's insecurities fizzled away. Bursts of inner light washed away the darkness inside her. Past the gravel, the table's outline sharpened. Despite lingering memories of the night before, a rush of blood washed away her fears and insecurities. She became a new woman. With newfound confidence, she could see the shadows lurking within the chairs.

Weak at the knees, she watched as her uncle Timothy, salt and pepper hair and mouth agape, seeds spilling from his lips, revealed himself. Her confidence wavered as she saw the dried blood running from the corners of his eyes to his jaw.

Looking at the other person brought tears to her eyes. Olivia's skin was melted over her clothing like candle wax on a holder. The sight of pink facial muscles made Charlotte nauseous, bile threatening to erupt. The sunflowers trembled in fear as a boastful cry resounded throughout the field. Once again, the terrified little girl became frozen as Charlotte's hands covered her mouth.

Looking at the head of the table where she once sat the night before, a figure straightened themselves out from their bowed position. Burlap brightened in the light, and the white lines in the plaid flannel shirt stood out from the blurred adrenaline. Lost in the sunflower brooches' mesh, Charlotte peered into their awful, dark depths, hearing whispers from the fabric. With its hands slowly lifting the table, her creation stood on two feet as she retreated. The table's collapse caused a cascade of clattering plates, silverware, and bodies hitting the ground.

Charlotte sprinted back toward the house, fighting the urge to look back. She glimpsed the suncrow approaching as she passed cars through their reflection. When she spotted a glint of the scythe swinging down, her eyes grew wide, shredding the hem of her skirt and cutting into the bottom of her calf as it advanced toward her Achilles. Another swing from the suncrow forced her to dodge. With a trail of blood, Charlotte limped into the garage and house, her nemesis still fighting with the object stuck in the doorway.

A quickening breath and rising panic made Charlotte feel her head grow light. She struggled to turn the lock, her fingers slipping on the wet doorknob. With rapid action, she ripped off two inches from the bottom of her skirt and applied it to her wounded leg, grimacing in pain. Realizing her solitude filled the air, making it feel heavy. Doubt clouded her mind as tears streamed down her face, questioning her ability. Beyond the kitchen, the patio appeared shadowed, adorned with potted plants moving on the railing. The leaves moved in the faint breeze, their stems lightly brushed. Two people stood by the largest window, their faces impassive, but their eyes spoke volumes of support.

James and Gabriel.

Charlotte marched into the kitchen, and after wiping her trembling hands on her skirt, she took off her jacket and slammed it on the table. Clasping the block's largest knife handles, she peered into the blade's reflection, a final show of forced bravery with her tears dried along the bits of earth on her cheeks. Entering the dining room, she scanned her surroundings, holding her breath to detect any movement.

In the dim light, the central fireplace in the den was dusty. The ashes in the chamber evoked memories of her family, who once filled that room. Every seat on the couches was filled with those she had loved or despised growing up. Either way, they were people that were in her life that held a place in her heart. Memories of playing slap jack with Mason and Noah, and Timothy teaching her "Chopsticks" on the piano stayed with her and gave her the strength to carry on. Even looking at the bookcase, every time she and her grandmother talked about a new book for the other to read, with Victoria occasionally joining in on the club with her enthusiasm matching every time there was a book Gemma found; there would never be another recommendation.

No more.

Another spine-tingling chill. Down the hallway, she saw the light twinkling on the floor. The broken glass and picture frames caught and reflected the moonlight. Noticing the open side door, she collapsed, realizing she wasn't alone.

Restored power caused the lights above her to flicker. The needle skipping on the record made her cringe. A thick throat left Charlotte with a dry mouth and nothing to swallow. As the suncrow attacked from behind the sofa, she felt straw fibers in her nose as they punched her.

As Charlotte hit the piano, her shoulder popped, sending the knife tumbling into the bookcases. The suncrow hurled Charlotte into a stack of magazines, shattering three shelves and sending books tumbling to the floor. Sliding across the old hardcovers caused Charlotte's hip to ache and her breathing to become labored. Kicking at her enemy, her legs thrashed, but this only pushed the enemy closer to the sofa. With pain distracting her, the suncrow jumped back and enveloped Charlotte's body, wrapping their gloved hands around her throat. Her breath escaped, accompanied by the cracking of cartilage in her neck.

Charlotte's fingers trembled as she fiddled with the very pages she read throughout the years. Going through the covers, her hand sank deeper, like an abyss of literature. As she neared the floor, her fingertips felt lighter, a faint prickling sensation near her nail barely registering. Her tears obscured her vision; her father held her brother on the couch, unable to alleviate her misery. Their words echoed in her mind as she reached for the knife's handle. Her limbs felt heavy and useless as she tried to lift her arm, her fading strength barely enough to graze their leg.

With a pained flinch, the suncrow removed their hand from Charlotte's neck. Charlotte rolled over, using her family's strength to push them off her, using *Prince Caspian* to smack them across the burlap to knock them out.

Coughing for air, Charlotte tried to regain her balance. The hallway was spinning with bits of glass reflecting in the light like a disco ball. Fresh air started to bring her back, making the world spin less as she limped out the door. Running on the gravel, her ankles burned, her heel aching for respite.

Yellow petals danced in her wake, a cheering entourage as she sped into the maze. Having turned left at the road's first fork, she found the path smaller, the suncrow absent. In silent prayer, Charlotte wished for the misery to cease or for it all to be a dream with no one, not even Gemma, dead. She'd even settle for this being a hallucination as an inmate in an insane asylum; at least she would be medicated.

The deeper she went into the labyrinth, the more the loose dirt hampered her progress. As she neared the pit, she worried she couldn't cross the bridge. Before turning around, a bit of light caught the corner of her eye. Curiosity propelled her closer, her jaw dropping at the sight of Mason trapped in the wire. Following the razors encasing his form, blades sinking into his body made her stomach churn. Even Charlotte recognized the regret and mystery behind the sadness etched on his face.

She turned and ran toward the dissipating smoke. All that was left of the playground was a pile of rubble. Only ashes and memories remained from the cabin. Leading up to the fire was a lineup of scarecrows strung up on their perches. A plank in hand, she felt her palm tremble with the pain of splinters. Each scarecrow brought back memories of family—some with cousins, some with aunts and uncles, and others just with their immediate families. The sight of the entire army made of straw and burlap caused urine to trickle down her leg.

The last one in the row was strung uniquely. This lacked a flannel shirt, ripped denim, or any straw. Razor blades glinted in the moonlight, a familiar sight to those in the pit. As Charlotte neared, the weight of her sadness increased, and she dropped the wood upon realizing it wasn't a scarecrow, but a person.

Marnie.

Marnie's fingers dripped blood, creating damp patches in the dirt below. The clothes that were once clean were now soaked in various bodily fluids. Embedded in her skin, black seeds sparkled like little sequins.

"Marnie," Charlotte said, her hand touching her aunt's knee.

A weak gasp from Marnie shocked her niece. With frantic movements, Charlotte attempted to untangle the wire around Marnie's waist. Each labored gasp from Marnie, regret etched on her face as she looked at Charlotte, produced tears which revived the dried bloodstains.

"I'm so sorry," Marnie mumbled, the razors wiggling in their places as Charlotte continued to free her.

Marnie let out a groan as the wire became loosened. From the open gash in her stomach, intestines spilled out onto Charlotte's arms, cascading down her body and pooling around her sneakers.

"No!" Charlotte said, her hand pushing Marnie's stomach back inside, ignoring the guts nauseating her.

As the final pang of pain consumed Marnie, her eyes rolled back with the lowest rib grazing Charlotte's pinky finger. Marnie's blood and gore filled Charlotte's mouth, making her gag. As Charlotte released her, the woman who'd set many fires against her now saw her own flame extinguished.

The muddy field path left Charlotte numb as she tried to make her way along it. Lights in the barn windows illuminated her path, making the flowers glow. A low moan from Freida's cows was the first ordinary sound she'd heard in hours. Her eyes became flushed by the blinding light that made her dizzy.

Charlotte's empty stomach recoiled in horror at the image of her aunt and uncle lying in the barn. Bruises covered Victoria's face and arms; blood trickled from her lips; and her pale body was clad in bloodstained jeans. The image of Edward's death, the sorrow on his face before the fatal blow, seared into Charlotte's memory as she looked at his torso. As she gazed at Edward, her eyes welled with tears; his sweater and pale blue shirt was torn, and his khaki pants were baggy on his gaunt frame. A section of tissue, emitting a foul odor, clung to the fabric close to the embroidered black design on the shirt pocket.

James Chester.

"Daddy," Charlotte said, gagging from the stench that made her head ache.

She's reached her limit with all of this being too much. Despite a weekend of conversations with her stepfather, Charlotte couldn't handle confronting his decomposing corpse alongside the other deaths. A sudden person startled her, jolting her body as she tried to run back to the door.

Noah.

Inches of rope encircled her cousin's torso. Noah's head rested on the wall, his dark yellow bandana getting damp from the saliva drying in his mouth. As consciousness returned, he thrashed, his eyes blinking open, then snapping wide with a look of fright. He made a circular motion with his head, wanting her to turn and avoid danger.

WHAP!

The intense pain in Charlotte's head disrupted her equilibrium. She felt her muscles growing heavy, longing to collapse. Splinters dug into her knees when she gave into her struggle. The stench of her stepfather went unnoticed as she collapsed onto the soft, scratchy straw beside him. Only blonde hair and pale skin were visible beneath the spinning light above. With a groan and a scream of the person's name, Noah succumbed; her smile grew menacingly proud as another family member fell prey to her scheme.

Victoria.

Chapter 28

Six Days Ago

WHEN THE CLOCK STRUCK five, families began their departures, heading home to prepare for dinner. With strained backs and knees, workers checked their watches, eagerly expecting the upcoming three-hour respite. The intense heat caused them such misery; their parched throats and throbbing heads cried out for relief. Maintaining the trails caused calluses to form on their hands because of the hard work.

Dust swirled around the tires of a BMW like a genie as it drove up the driveway. Looking around at the children, Victoria observed the insurmountable amount of joy that flooded the farm; something that would've been nice for her and her brothers to have more of growing up. Seeing two siblings play with bubble wands instead of feeding the chickens in the coop made others envious. Bags of candy corn consumed by them was something she desperately craved back then instead of the mandated celery and carrot sticks provided by Frieda's garden.

As she moved through the garage, the building's walls muffled the sounds from outside, shifting from excitement to the ordinary. Blue jays and cardinals chirped outside the kitchen windows. A subtle breeze found its way through the screen, caressing Victoria's neck and drifting over the videotapes and Nintendo.

Her sneakers tapped on the linoleum as she walked past each portrait on her way to the living room, evoking memories captured in each photo. Her eyes first fell upon a photo of herself and her red tricycle; its ribbon streamers and her pigtails danced in the breeze. Seeing her brothers at the bottom of the driveway, feet in the creek, brought a smile to her face. A small laugh emerged when she remembered James's clumsy fall into the water, a moment captured just seconds before in a photo.

Upon entering the living room, Victoria's eyes fell upon the extensive collection of books on the shelves. A stack of worn Berenstain Bears *books, their corners frayed from children's use over the years, sat on the bottom shelf. Dust coated a lone toy trunk on the other side, neglected from years of disuse; her brother's old tractors intermingled with her father's wood-worked cars.*

Settling onto the bench, she dabbed the piano keys, playing "Chopsticks" at a slow tempo. Her first church recital, complete with the congregation's applause, remained a cherished memory that brought her joy for years. Though years had passed, she played with the ease of a seasoned pro, her fingers flying across the ivory and black keys.

"Victoria, what a pleasant surprise!" said her mother, coming out of the office.

Victoria's stiffening fingers produced a grim, unpleasant clatter from the keys. A deep breath helped her focus, reminding her of her visit's purpose.

Remember why you're here.

"Hi Mom," Victoria said, her fingers tucking into her jean pockets.

"What brings you out here? How are Timothy and the kids?"

"We're okay."

The room fell silent, the front yard full of children running around. Playing softly overhead, Neil Diamond's music evoked Simon and Gemma's legacy for the patrons. An employee rushed onto the grass to chase three preteens who were throwing gravel at the side of the house, while six pebbles tapped on the window. Hoping for a break, birds circled the yard, seeking refuge from intrusions.

"I-I have something to ask you," Victoria said, her body falling onto the couch.

"Of course," Gemma said, following behind her. "Now, go on and tell me. You're making me nervous with all this silence."

Stay strong.

"So, we're in some trouble," Victoria said, fighting the tiny quivers on her chin.

"Trouble? Like with the law?"

"Not exactly."

Gemma's blue eyes welled up with worried tears, shining like a pool's surface. She drew closer to her daughter and put her arm around her. Wrapped in her mother's embrace, Victoria's body temperature rose. The rapid beat of her mother's heart made Victoria nervous.

"Timothy's business has been struggling."

"How so?"

"Like, there is no business," Victoria said shamefully.

"Oh, no!" Gemma said with regret. "I'm so sorry!"

"We've been behind on all our bills. My reduced work hours during the off-season are causing us to fall behind. And now the kids' tuition bills are due."

"Damn."

"I feel like I'm drowning in debt, and I don't know what to do."

Victoria's shirt was wet with tears at the neckline. With a mind racing to solve the insurmountable number of bills, her fingers trembled, each number a reminder of her financial struggles. Admitting her debt made her feel immobilized, as though she were drowning in quicksand. She didn't know what to do or where to start.

"Have you thought about getting another job? Has Timothy found a new one?"

Victoria experienced a sudden unsettling feeling in her stomach. Victoria expected her mother's reply, but was hoping for a different outcome. Help had never been freely given upon request. Her assumption that this time would be different was naïve.

"We haven't. Back-to-school sales are about to start, so my hours will come back."

"And Timothy?"

"He was told by his old boss that they are working on something else and told him to be available when they're ready to launch."

"How long ago was that?" Gemma asked, her eyebrow raising.

"Six months."

Gemma shook her head in disbelief as she struggled to get back to her feet. Her nostrils flared as a large breath of air passed through them. Seeing her daughter's tears, her face flushed with frustration.

"And you could've found jobs to tie you over until then," Gemma said, her voice shaky. "You two aren't thinking right."

"But just this one time."

"Sweetie, I will help you out if something was an emergency. I don't count this as one, especially since you had the time to figure out something and try to make it work. Instead, you chose to wait it out and make your problems bigger."

"You don't understand, Mom," Victoria said, taken aback.

"Do you think anybody came to your father's or my rescue when we were in trouble? We had to figure it out on our own. If I didn't think you could handle it, I wouldn't have this talk with you. And besides, your father and I didn't have a gambling problem either."

Victoria's blood boiled. As her fingers contacted her palm, a crackling emanated from her fist. Her toes curled inside her shoes, grounding the soles.

"Okay, you've been unfair to all of us. I'm going to go right out and say it!"

Gemma's jaw hit the floor in astonishment. She walked over to the other side of the couch and retrieved the blanket, the fabric's corners clashed as she folded it.

"Really? And why is that?"

"You never want to give any money out to those that love you."

"I will not repeat myself," Gemma said with impatience. "And if you value my love by the amount of money we give you, then you have another thing coming."

"Fine. You never want to talk about money, either."

"Yes, I do."

"Then why do you keep joking about Charlotte getting everything when you go?"

With the blanket's edge dangling from the couch, Gemma let out an irritating cackle. As she brushed dust from the piano, she observed the particles floating off like birds taking flight.

"And that's what I'm going to do!" Gemma said facetiously.

"You've got to be kidding me. Her?" Victoria scoffed.

"I told you guys. She was the first to ask, so she gets it."

"She was just a kid!"

"And that's what makes this all perfect! You keep asking, and that's what I'm going to say until the day I die."

"What a bunch of shit!"

"You know what's a bunch of shit? My daughter coming by after not calling to check on me. The child that only stops by for the holidays and then wants to talk about money. Also, how much of this debt came from your gambling? You also said that you'd stop going to the casino."

"That's none of your business," Victoria hissed.

"And you want me to bail you out without learning your lesson?" Gemma said, her feet clamoring as she opened the side door. "Now that I think of it, Charlotte has been the most responsible with her money and has worked her way out of her problems without asking for any help. Maybe you should take note from her!"

"So, you're going to give it to her? She's not even a part of this family!"

"That's my business. Besides, she's my granddaughter, and I'm proud to call her that! And it's none of your business who gets the estate. You'll find out when that day comes. In the meantime, enjoy my company since it seems like you care if I was dead more than alive. I've got to get back to work, so let yourself out!"

Victoria's hair swirled as the door slammed behind her. Anger and fury have replaced the tears of sadness and embarrassment. Approaching the family photo, she glared at her husband, furious at his lack of urgency in business, which was crippling them. As she stared at Edward, her body heat rose as she pondered the words that would be spoken when his family discovered, fearing their competitive nature would make her feel small. She wasn't prepared to see them; she wasn't prepared to see any of them. Especially the one at the end, their outfit standing out and expression different from the rest of the Chesters' smile. The one person who her mother seemed to see something special in, even though Victoria didn't see her like the others.

The more furious Victoria became, the more everyone in the picture seemed as invaluable to her as her niece. These people were no longer important to her. She aimed for a fresh start, financially free, and resolved to eliminate any interference. Despite her affection for them, getting her guarantee was paramount.

Chapter 29

Creaking boards intensified Charlotte's throbbing headache. A heavy, sawdust-filled air made her muscles ache. The light above her flickered, adding to the difficulty of her already blurry vision. The long night of running had sapped her of all energy, both physical and mental. Her family's taunting words about her loss replayed in her mind.

"I knew you wouldn't get out of this," said Alexandria.

"You're a shame to this family," said Edward.

"I knew it was the alcohol talking when I thought you could do this," said Marnie.

"You are the most worthless person I ever met in my life. She should've gotten you!" said Olivia.

A wave of shame washed over Charlotte, making her spine tingle. Her lone tear traced a path down her cheek, leaving her dehydrated. A wave of nausea washed over her. A burning sensation in her ankles woke her up with rope tied at her calves. The discovery of her restrained wrists filled her with despair.

Another look at her stepfather sent a surge of panic through her, making her fingers tremble. His corpse showed no skin, almost no muscle or tissue remained, exposing broken ribs and limbs from the accident. James's insides have blackened from the months below the earth. Because the casket was closed at his funeral, Charlotte never saw his face; this reunion with his physical form, however, was something she would never forget, the stench of decay clinging to her lungs.

In the seat facing hers was the person who had caused all the trouble that day. The same person who once brought joy to the family. Its eyes gleamed with a mocking wink, boasting of its victory, its straw limbs rigid and airy. The sight of their corpse did nothing to raise Charlotte's heartbeat.

"Don't you think it was pretty genius?" said her aunt, startling Charlotte as she grabbed her shoulders from behind, rocking the chair on its wooden legs.

The woman's buggy eyes caused Charlotte's breath to catch in her throat. The more she saw Victoria's bloodshot veins, the less remorse she detected. Her gritted teeth betrayed the anger in her smile. A day of chasing her family left dirt-caked sweat trails on her face.

"You're crazy," Charlotte whimpered.

Victoria laughed in pain, shaking her head in disbelief as she tried to make sense of her thoughts. Running her fingers through the matted blonde hair, she separated the blood-caked ends.

"You want to know what's crazy?" Victoria said, her hand grabbing onto Charlotte's disheveled braid. "You're not even a part of this family and Mom still plans on giving you all her money!"

Noah's eyebrow went up as he fought to breathe steadily, his mouth now covered with duct tape. Limp from the restraints on his exposed nails, his wrists dangled against the wall.

"Seriously?" Charlotte said in disbelief. "Even I know she's fucking joking!"

"No, she wasn't! I know it!"

As her aunt touched her cheek, Charlotte gasped for breath. In a wave of anger, her jaw joints cracked. The fury from her family's ridicule had become personified into physical pain.

"So, you kill everyone over a joke?"

Victoria murmured words of encouragement to herself. Scanning the barn, her eyes lingered on each part. Using contradictory phrases, she bit her lip, attempting in vain to justify her actions.

"She wasn't joking."

"She couldn't have given it to her."

"They're your family."

"They had to go. They all had to go."

Charlotte's feet scrambled in the dirt. The fibers in the rope dug deep into her wrists, burning into her skin as she tried to wriggle out of her restraints. Her shoulder screamed in pain from the gash that continued to moisten with her tears. She had never witnessed such a multitude of different voices projecting before her. The outwardly composed individual had unleashed the deepest, darkest recesses of her psyche.

Charlotte's eyes followed a rope that looped around a worktable behind Victoria. The braided fibers snaked up the walls, coiling around the planks like a colossal anaconda before reaching the roof. At the highest point of the building, it hung next to a woman with little slack.

Earth fell on her head as the planks above groaned and shifted, the dry flakes irritating her eyes and causing them to wince. Seeing white tennis shoes and blue scrubs made her heart skip a beat. The woman's terrified expression sent shivers down Charlotte's spine, urging her to free herself from the ropes.

"Mom!"

The ropes binding Katherine's hands and feet caused burns on her pale skin. Her tears cleaned the dried blood that had once trickled from her temple. The stance was rickety from confinement and nothing to nourish her. With a hopeless gaze at her daughter, bound and gagged, she felt the crushing weight of her failure to protect her.

"They all have to go."

Chapter 30

Flapjacks toppled from the stack Victoria carried as she set down the plate onto the dining room table. Mason barged in, knocking Alexandria backward onto the couch as he shoved past her. A suppressed laugh escaped Noah's lips as he winked at Charlotte, savoring their karma's return.

Oh, for fuck's sake!

"Okay, who's ready for breakfast?"

"I'm not that hungry," Charlotte said, holding her arms across her chest for protection.

Don't get upset, honey. Remember what I told you. You need to remember that she doesn't belong here.

"You need to eat," Lucas said, placing his arm on her shoulder. "We have a busy day today."

The sound of Mason's fists hitting the table made Marnie massage her temples in frustration. The clatter of silverware accompanied the morning ritual of preparing for nourishment. Unable to hold back any longer, Mason speared the pancake pile and retrieved three giant pancakes. A generous pour of syrup created a cascade over his breakfast, engulfing the three strips of bacon in sugary delight. Olivia meticulously picked through the stack, choosing the thinnest and smallest piece, which she handled with delicate care, earning an eye roll from Noah.

Everybody took their turns with dishing up their breakfast. Marnie rushed back to the kitchen, grabbed a small, sharp knife, and began carving the green-skinned apple she had taken.

Look at these people. Why did they let Mom treat us like she did?

Charlotte watched the portions shrink. Her eyes tracked her cousins, engrossed in their meal, oblivious to her grabbing. She disregarded her earlier comment, then helped herself to two pancakes, two sausage links, and bacon.

With her chair settled, a silent exchange of glances passed between the people present. Lucas winked at Charlotte, amused by the amount of food on her plate. As mouths snapped, food being chomped with each bite, she was free to eat without restraint.

I can't believe one of these idiots will get her money.

"Mason, you ass, you took the last of the pancakes!" Alexandria said as she craved seconds; the tiniest one was just not enough for her.

Mason disregarded her anger, shrugged, and stared at her while taking a huge bite and devouring it with the intensity of a lion tearing into an animal carcass.

"So, how's everybody been holding up?" Edward remarked, seeking to shift the conversation toward a brighter outlook."

They don't need it. Not as much as I do.

Nobody responded right away; their mouths were full of food and only Noah let out a tiny cough to clear his throat before shoving food down it.

"I know that this has not been the easiest week for any of us," Victoria added as she gently placed her fork onto her plate; the clanking made Marnie cringe once again. "But they say that with death, it brings an opportunity to reunite and mend relationships."

Or break them. This is all her fault!

Olivia scoffed in disbelief. She patted her lips with the napkin, trying to keep her rouge lipstick perfect.

"You've got to be kidding me," she hissed as she threw it onto the table.

"I'm not," Victoria countered, raising her eyebrow. "I know you're all close already, but isn't it nice to be together as a family?"

"That's true," she agreed. "But not all of us here are family."

That's right. Just like I told you.

Charlotte stopped, nearly gagging on the pancake in her mouth. She reached over to her glass of orange juice, her fingers trembling as she tilted the glass. Her lips puckered as she swished around the liquid in her mouth.

Edward said sharply, "Olivia, we will not talk about this again."

"Yes, we will!"

Yes!

As Olivia rose from her chair, her hip bumped Alexandria, causing a sticky substance to brush her cheek.

"Watch it!" Alexandria said, wiping it away, the fibers of the napkin sticking to her.

"How come she gets to come here and get what's rightfully ours?" Olivia carried on, as if Alexandria wasn't even there.

"Yeah, I think that everybody that has been in this family from the start should only get it," Mason added, his mouth full of pancake.

"Well, that's not your say, is it now?" Lucas said, staring daggers at him.

"What is it with you guys and money?" Edward said, his tone raising. "Is that all Grandma meant to you?"

"No, but it would be nice if she gave us a little something," said Alexandria, dipping her napkin in her glass of water to dab onto her syrup stain.

Why would you need to? You ruined your car. You're failing school. You're wasting my money! I'm so tired of lying about you. We even had to lie about you getting into nursing school!

With each mumbled word circling the table, the voices grew more insistent. The family members were having conversations that felt like alliance negotiations. Everyone except Charlotte, who gazed at Edward with sadness. With wide, disbelieving eyes, Victoria scanned the table, her chin twitching as family members voiced their thoughts.

"You don't deserve that!"

"Uncle James is dead. Why is she still here?"

"Mutt."

"I really want that Nintendo. I call dibs if it doesn't go to anybody."

Everyone's distracted. Now's my chance!

"Enough!" said Victoria, her fist pounding on the table, causing the glasses to teeter.

The water in Alexandria's cup spilled onto her lap. A grunt of irritation escaped her as she rose from her chair and stormed out of the room. Her anger was palpable as she stomped up the stairs, her every step shaking the light over the dining room table, silencing the complaints.

"I can't believe what I'm hearing!" Victoria hissed, her fist trembling. "I thought you were joking last night, but I guess you all feel the same way."

Mason and Olivia lowered their heads, shrinking back as if they were a dog being reprimanded for ruining furniture.

"If Grandma saw the way you're acting and how you view her, she would have an absolute cow! How dare all of you treat Charlotte this way? She is family, regardless if Grandma said it or not."

Yeah, right!

Victoria grabbed her plate and ventured into the kitchen. The redness in her face faded away as she turned her blonde hair to face them. She hurled the plate into the sink, sending it crashing into a pile of shards. A slamming door followed shortly after the jingling of keys as she reached for her purse.

VICTORIA TOOK A COUPLE of breaths. Satisfied at her successful, undetected departure, she watched the windshield fog up. A stolen cigarette from Charlotte's pack was lit, its ash falling onto her lap as didn't care about taking one from her despised niece. Her hands couldn't

stop shaking; the family was acting out of character, and the trap was set for them to continue to implode, making it easier for her plan to come to fruition.

"This isn't right," she said to herself.

They're my family.

As she watched her niece stroll along the arches, a single tear formed in her eye as she gazed in her rearview mirror, Charlotte's fingers brushing the leaves.

"Poor girl."

I can't wait to mutilate you, just like how you've destroyed my mother.

With a jingle of keys, she started the car. The engine's rattling indicated a badly needed oil change. Changing gears, she backed up and then shifted into drive to proceed down the incline. Driving helped her reconnect with herself, focus her thoughts, and leave her relationships behind.

When she reached the bottom, thick dust gathered over the car, with gravel crunching under the black rubber. She steered to the right, reaching a speed of thirty miles an hour. With her hand outside the window, the breeze cooled her sweaty palms while the sunflowers transitioned into maples. This wasn't the way she wanted this weekend to go; she wanted things to go by more smoothly, like shooting fish in a barrel. What she wanted was the assurance of her debts being paid. She couldn't risk anyone else obtaining it. For her to guarantee it, the entire family would have to go.

Out the window went the cigarette; it fell onto the pebbles as the car sped away, leaving it behind. The player fought to start after she put in the cassette tape. A cheerful melody of guitars and violins opened I Like It, I Love It, introduced by Tim McGraw. In time with the music, her hand tapped the steering wheel.

A figure sprinted across the road without warning. Victoria's heart leaped into her throat as her foot slammed on the brake, sending the car sliding five feet before stopping. As the person in jeans and a flannel shirt ran further into the dusty woods, their form blurring, her eyes grew wide. To identify the person, she shifted the vehicle into park after pulling over.

"Hey!" she said, clearing her throat.

The person didn't stop. Their footsteps broke branches, the sound echoing through the woods.

Having indulged in nicotine, Victoria was unprepared to run, and sighed in frustration. With unsteady ankles, she struggled to keep her balance on the loose gravel before descending the steep incline into the ditch. She struggled to run; her lungs ached, burdened by a full stomach and racing thoughts. Despite her emotions, the individual persevered, their presence diminishing to a tiny point.

Dodging branches, Victoria made her way into the forest. She felt a searing pain in her thighs, about to experience a cramp. The once defined grains in the bark have become indistinct and blended. As she climbed the small hill, she needed a break, especially with the person gone.

A massive, decaying log laid at the incline's top. She leaned onto the wood; the bark flaked to the ground next to her heels. Stray hairs, escaping her haphazard ponytail frizzed around her face—a style Charlotte would appreciate. In the canopies, birds chirped and fluttered their wings near her. She stared at her hand, anticipating the end of her double vision. Next to it was a hollowed opening. Curiosity aroused, she investigated, discovering an anomaly. The navy paint was running and peeling off the chipped corners. Unpolished and rusty, the clasps revealed a lack of care.

A chest.

A branch broke behind her, and she gasped. As she turned, the sunlight filtering through the leaves became suddenly blocked. A figure confronted her; its red flannel shirt had a tear at the elbow. Mud caked the knees and shins of their denim jeans. A stick held a polished, bent metal plate at the top.

The shovel hit her face, throwing her backwards past the trunk before she had a chance to utter a word. Muddy leaves cooled her face; mud painted her forehead. With her eyelids drooping lower, the shaded area darkened. With the ceaseless spinning, her energy dissipated, consciousness fading, leaving only the figure who struck in sight.

"Austin!" Victoria said, panting, with thoughts racing. "What're you doing here?"

Austin's chest heaved violently. Despite the rage on his face, there was a childlike courage, a readiness to confront a terrifying foe. He recoiled from her antagonizing smile as she wiped her lip.

"Pathetic," she said, her laugh malicious. "You're just as much of a coward as you were when I babysat you. If you wanted to finish me off, you should've."

Paralyzed by fear, tears streamed down Austin's face. Victoria's commanding presence reminded him of his father's habit of assigning him unwanted tasks. As she shifted from mother to her needed persona, the deer scurried away from her menacing glare.

"Stay out of my way, or I'll make sure you watch every minute of your mother's death as I kill her slowly," Victoria said with her teeth gritted.

As Austin ran over the mound, his steps faltered. With a satisfied smile, Victoria watched him vanish into the bushes. A deep laugh escaped her lips as she returned to the chest, her tongue tracing their outline. The secret her family kept, a pact between her and her brothers, echoed in her thoughts. As she opened the top, her eyes widened as flannel and denim revamped her entire image. Sunflower brooches twinkled in her irises, severing the connections she had to become the thing she needed to get what she desired the most, no matter how many branches in her family tree needed to be cut.

Chapter 31

Back and forth between Charlotte and Noah, Victoria paced as they stared at each other in silence, disturbed. Restrained, they were unable to prevent their aunt from causing more harm. The rafters creaked with Katherine's trembling legs trying to maintain her balance. A whirlwind of thoughts filled Charlotte's mind; how could a family be so intent on harming her, yet so blind to their own culpability?

"So, you kill all of us and then you get the money?" Charlotte asked somberly. "Is that your plan?"

"That was always the plan," Victoria said, her fingers twiddling in the air with counts of numbers.

"And what will the police think when they see that you're the only one in this family still alive? Don't you think that will be a little fishy?"

"I'll figure out a way," Victoria panted maniacally. "I've done this before. Yes, if I got out of this before, I could again!"

Concern and suspicion clouded Charlotte's gaze as she looked at Noah, her eyebrows raised. Katherine's nostrils flared at the sight of his agony; the nurse inside of her eager to come to his aid. The tension of the rope around her neck made her whimper helplessly.

"What do you mean you've done this before?" she asked.

A small laugh erupted from Victoria, growing stronger and stronger until it became a raging roar. A proud smile shone on her face after her first kill as she approached her brother. As she raised

James's decomposed body, the sound of cracking bones filled the air; her head tilted against his skull as if she were about to capture a striking photograph.

"T-that can't be right," Charlotte said as her eyes bounced between hers and her mother's, who also shared mutual confusion. "Dad and Gabriel died in a car accident."

"That wouldn't have been possible if someone hadn't loosened his brake line!"

Charlotte and Katherine's faces were wet with tears. Victoria enjoyed the suffering she inflicted upon them. The news setting in with the fresh development becoming sweet in her mouth as Charlotte choked in her panic.

"They didn't deserve to die!" she said, gasping. "None of them did."

"He was the oldest child. I needed to make sure everything was going to plan."

"Money isn't going to fix your problems!"

"It will!"

Charlotte's sadness morphed into anger, marking a new phase in her grieving process. Ignoring the searing pain in her hands, she struggled against the ropes, attempting to escape alongside Noah.

Victoria ambled to the other side of the barn, reaching for a white, starched cloth covering a machine. Dust wisped in the air when she revealed the contents, her enthusiasm matching a model on The *Price is Right* showcasing the new car. Cobwebs hung between the gaps in the rust-covered machine. Blades on an open chute winked at Charlotte. Dried blood spattered the hole's exterior, triggering a memory shared from earlier that evening.

"Is that the wood chipper that killed Eustace?" Charlotte asked, the tip of her finger dipping into her skirt pocket.

"The one and only!" Victoria said, skipping around the contraption. "What poetic justice that Frieda asked for Mom to hold on to it after her husband died so the memory wouldn't haunt her when our family was responsible for killing him!"

"Wait. It was an accident. Nobody killed him," Charlotte said, dumbstruck.

"That was only what *they* saw," Victoria exclaimed with pride as her hands grazed the metal surface of the chute. "Birds scared the little brat, but who told the boys on our property to go after them? Who gave them the idea of throwing rocks at them to give them a little scare?"

"You're sick!"

"Not sick, a failure. Eustace wasn't supposed to die that day. If it weren't for Austin not being man enough to do the work, it would've been him falling into this baby and not his dad."

A look of confusion passed between the three prisoners. They frantically thought of reasons Victoria might justify killing a young child. What role did Austin play in preventing her from accessing her funds, given he's a stranger to the family?

"Why him?" Charlotte asked, her fist clenching.

With a switch flip, the machine let out a grumpy hum. Slowly, the blades stirred as the thing awoke from its long slumber. A sudden, ear-splitting screech of grinding metal filled the air as Victoria fetched a chair to sit opposite her niece.

"You know, I missed these days of telling you guys bedtime stories," Victoria said with enthusiasm. "How about one more?"

The closer Victoria came, the wider Charlotte's eyes became. The powerlessness terrified her, her heart pounding with fear; seeing her aunt three feet away with the suncrow in the background distorting her perception.

"I mean this when I say that Grandma and Grandpa loved each other very much," Victoria started.

Charlotte's mouth released a copious amount of spit that landed on Victoria's face, leaving a slow trickle of saliva that ran from her nose and dripped off her chin. Enraged, Victoria's hand slammed against Charlotte's, sending her chair's front legs airborne and cracking the back legs.

"I know about Grandpa's affair," Charlotte groaned in pain.

"I'm serious," she continued as she sat back down and wiped her chin dry. "They worked hard for everything we had and let nothing bring them down. Early in the farm's business, the stress got the better of them. Like every other couple, their marriage was tested, and Grandma was being a little hard on Grandpa. One night, he stormed out to do some projects she asked of him where he ran into Frieda who was also sharing the same feelings. One thing led to another, and something happened."

"How did you find out about it?" Charlotte asked.

"Your dad, Edward, and I were out there and saw the whole thing. I was just as upset as you were. You think of your parents as the perfect couple and that they will never leave, and when one cheats, it feels like a part of your soul gets damaged and everything seems like a lie."

Charlotte and Noah scuffed a bit of laughter. While her statement held some truth, they both suspected her soul had been damaged long before this.

"Your dads and I promised to keep this a secret, and we did. We all forgave Daddy when we saw the letter from Frieda saying that this wouldn't happen again. It was something that we erased from our memory until nine months later, when Frieda gave birth to Austin. I didn't want to believe that he wasn't a Chester and your dads kept telling me that Frieda and Eustace probably got back together without a sign that he was aware of her indiscretion. But watching that kid grow up was like looking into a mirror. He had Daddy's eyes and his crooked smile. He looked so much like James."

A soft engine purr accompanied the increasing speed of the machine's blades. The couple minutes of shaking off the grogginess of neglect has brought on a taste for something to break apart.

"So, you try to kill him so he doesn't get any money either? I'm guessing that was part of your stupid plan," Charlotte hissed.

"Exactly," Victoria confirmed, clapping with sarcasm at her assumption. "It's enough that someone like you is still here, but at least you've been a part of this family. You may be a mutt, but that boy is a mutt from the gutter, and I'd be damned if he gets a dime from this family's hard-earned cash!"

"Well, you've done the slowest killing in history." Charlotte's gut rolled with a chuckle. "I don't know if your greed has clouded your grasp on reality, but Austin is still alive and has been for quite some time."

"True, but he is now too unfit to inherit anything. The little moron can't even speak a full sentence!"

Charlotte's smile returned to normal again. The laughter subsided. As Victoria moved to the chair, her pride shone in her smile. Approaching the rope, a little skip caused the heels of her shoes to click together.

"Okay, story time's over. Let's put the rest of you to bed!"

Victoria slackened the rope tied to the wall. She leaped higher, extending her arms to lift Katherine from her standing position. Looking down at her daughter's frantic wriggling in her chair, Katherine's eyes enlarged. Victoria cackled with glee as Charlotte's mom dangled, legs quivering, suffocating in mid-air.

"Mom, no!" Charlotte screamed as she jumped in her chair, the legs snapping further.

Veins throbbed in Katherine's temples as her face reddened. In her chair, Charlotte swayed unsteadily, her chest heaving with hopeless hyperventilation, aggravated by the ropes. A sight of her stepfather fueled her determination to stop her aunt from murdering her parents.

As Noah extracted his arms from the overhead nails, a terrible groan escaped him, audible from beside her. Rising to his feet, the discombobulation and slowness of his journey to Victoria affected him. Disgusted, Victoria had to let go of the rope to defend herself; Katherine and her daughter fell simultaneously as the chair's front legs tipped, the wood splintering and Katherine breaking an ankle.

As the ropes binding her torso came loose, Charlotte was able to free her arms. Seeing her mother collapsed, surrounded by hay, her heart pounded, spurring her to free her ankles. Once released, she inched toward her mother, then looked at Noah, whose strength was pitted against Victoria. Unbinding Katherine, she saw the rope's marks and her limp body, and tears streamed down her face.

"Mom, please don't go," she said as her finger begged for a pulse. It was weak.

A terrible grunt from Victoria pulled Charlotte's attention as she shoved Noah against the wall where he was bound. His arms slumped, and Noah's eyes widened in pain. As she freed him from the nail embedded in his rib, blood seeped from the wound onto the board. Blood trickled from his mouth; his knees threatened to give way. With gritted teeth, Victoria pushed him back in, allowing the nail to penetrate him once more.

As Charlotte watched her cousin weaken, his blood slicking his tennis shoes, a surge of anger coursed through her. His body fell to the floor and his eyes became vacant, barely focusing on her as she charged after her aunt. Charlotte's punches, though painful, drove her on, each one a consequence of her torment and a strike back against those who wronged her. Charlotte's unexpected display of courage knocked Victoria's teeth out before she fainted.

Heavy breaths from Charlotte's flared nostrils carried the metallic tang of Victoria's blood. With the return of pain, her hands shook, and her need for distraction was high. Crawling toward Noah, she removed two more inches of denim from her skirt, stuffing it against his injury to stem the bleeding. Pain etched Noah's face as the blood flow slowed, his complexion turning pale.

"Don't worry, I'm going to get us out of here," Charlotte said, the denim soaked in her fingers.

A boot connected with the side of her head, knocking her to the floor, the impact making her dizzy. Her rage escalating, Victoria pulled Charlotte's weakened form closer to the wood chipper by her hair. The splinters tore at her trembling fingers as she struggled to dig. Pulled upright, the menacing blades taunted her as Victoria propelled her closer to the chute, Charlotte's stomach plummeting.

BANG! BANG! BANG!

A protruding nail scratched Charlotte's knee as she fell from Victoria's distraction. The overload of blades and engine being met with the door toppling down sent waves of pain to her brain.

A burly shadow revealed itself as it stepped into the light. His red and black plaid shirt hid a chest heaving with vengeful breaths. His fists clenched, he looked at the wounded bodies around him, his bushy eyebrows raised.

Austin.

Fear flickered in his eyes as he confronted her daunting posture. With hands on hips, Victoria prepared to reprimand him like a child. With blood wiped from her chin, she licked her lips, poised to fight another.

"You just don't know how to take direction, do you?" she said, antagonizing. "You really must be stupid."

Austin stared back at her. His expression, like marble, remained unbreakable.

"Now I'll just have to kill you and your pathetic whore of a mother!"

A tremor ran through Austin's hands as he resisted the return of his former terror. The machine's roar evoked painful memories of his father. Tears formed as he relived the bits of his body raining down on him; he could even recall the taste of his blood.

"You'll have to go through my friends first," he mumbled.

"Friends?"

"Yes, my friends."

In the blink of an eye, a crowd enveloped them. Disappointment etched their faces as they stared into Victoria's wide, startled eyes, glimpsing her troubled soul.

Her family.

Victoria's hands shook as her niece and nephews encircled her in a protective hand-holding barrier. Timothy shook his head when he saw the person in front of him, not the same one he married as his arm cradled over Alexandria, who grieved at their reality. Gemma and Simon moved closer, only inches from her trembling chin. Their silence spoke volumes, delivering the harshest punishment. As Victoria's face softened, her murderous look disappeared. Her innocent eyes triggered a flood of childhood fear.

"You guys. I'm so sorry," she said with tears welling. "You know I had to do this. I just had to."

The spirits didn't respond.

Marnie and Edward held Mason and Olivia close.

James and Gabriel squeezed each other's hands.

Charlotte, regaining her bearings, was confused to see Victoria frozen in front of Austin. Taking another blink, her family appeared, showing the reason for Victoria's distraction, allowing Charlotte to crawl over to her mother. Katherine's face was tear-streaked, her color returning as her eyes painfully blinked open, a sight that broke her daughter's heart. With unwavering focus, Charlotte retrieved the noose, her feet tapping lightly the floorboards on her way back. She tossed the slack into the chipper's gears before looping the rope around Victoria's neck, who was still shocked and distracted.

The machine's horrendous humming and the shortening slack jolted Victoria from her guilty trance. Her eyes traced the rope's descent into the machine; a gasp escaped her lips as she saw the other end was around her neck. Austin's charge forced Victoria's head against the engine as he pushed her into the metal.

A torrent of blood flowed from Victoria's new gash on her temple; her yelp was inaudible over the machine's roar. Lightheadedness weakened her legs, and she hardly noticed Austin and Charlotte exchanging a nod before gathering around her. The metal bit into her wrist as they grabbed her, shoving her into the chute and cracking her shoulders. As the blades sliced into her fingers, then her knuckles, then her palms, she emitted a shriek of pain.

"Those hands will no longer inflict pain," said Austin, pushing her closer.

"This body will no longer kill," added Charlotte.

Bits of flesh from the machine splattered Charlotte's head. As the blades relentlessly cut into her forearms and elbows, Victoria's head moved wildly.

"Please, no!" Victoria said, her mouth spitting out blood.

Another shadow appeared from the door. The pale outline firmed as the light revealed it, its faint footsteps nearly silent on the wood. Bruises marred his face, and his shaggy hair was tousled in every direction. Blood trickled down his chin, staining his torn sweater.

Lucas.

"Baby!" Victoria said with relief, her teeth coated in pink. "Help me out of here. These two killed the whole family. Look what they're doing to me!"

Lucas's eyes observed the bags under her eyes, and the blades approached her upper arms. As she begged to be spared, his mother's neck grew weaker, struggling to support her head. With blood streaming down her mother's hairline, Charlotte tried to stay calm.

"They killed Daddy and electrocuted your sister," Victoria continued, her eyes squeezing tight from the pain.

Lucas's eyebrow went up. Seeing his family taken away caused his fingers to ball into a fist. The reality of the one who ended their lives is the one who brought life into their world.

"How did you know Alexandria was electrocuted?"

Victoria froze, with nothing more to say. Her lack of blood has resulted in unreliable storytelling. A look at her son petrified her, her knees giving way under the force of his grip on her hair.

"This face will no longer tell lies," he said before shoving it toward the blades.

As Victoria screamed one last time, the three of them moved away from her. Tremors wracked her body as the blades carved into her brain, leaving her limbs powerless against the pain. The engine emitted wisps of smoke, leading it to exert more effort as it attempted to dig deeper into her skull while her shoulders joined in. When the power to the machine failed, blood drenched the three, penetrating every fiber of their clothing, leaving Victoria's body dangling inches over the floor.

Relief washed over Charlotte as she hugged her cousin, their wet arms slipping into a tight embrace. Each inch of Charlotte's body ached, the day's events returning to haunt her with every agonizing moment.

"I'm so glad you're alive," Charlotte said, feeling their heartbeats return closer to normal.

"Me too," Lucas said, his breath warm against her head.

"I thought you were a goner with Bennett."

"Yeah, he was tough."

"He can be quite the drunk," Austin added, patting Lucas on the back. "Ever since our dad died, he wanted somebody to blame."

"I can tell. He's quite the son of a bitch," Lucas said with sarcasm.

"Yes, he is," Austin agreed.

A quick laugh passed between them. His strained smile couldn't hide the lingering pain from Charlotte. He seemed burdened by a sadness reflected in his eyes, an unshakeable grief.

"Thank you for saving me," Charlotte said, reaching out to squeeze his forearm to warm up his smirk. "And I'm sorry she killed your dad. I didn't know how horrible of a person she was."

"None of us did," Lucas added, his mouth tightened with guilt.

"I know you didn't," Austin said. "At least there can be some closure in knowing what happened."

"Exactly."

Echoing coughs in the barn startled Charlotte. Gasping for air, Noah's body shook, prompting the other three to join him. Charlotte's arm hit a chair, sending a figure crashing to the floor.

"You should get help," Katherine said, her voice raspy while she removed her scrub top to apply more pressure, revealing her black tank top, which provided minimal warmth from the nighttime breeze.

"Mom. I'm so glad you're okay," Charlotte said, wrapping her arms around her.

Quickly escaping her daughter's grasp, Katherine resumed her professional demeanor. Her eyes welled with tears, a mother's pride swelling as she admired her daughter's bravery.

"I'm glad you are too. Please go get help. He needs an ambulance."

Katherine tilted Noah forward, using the shirt to ease the pressure on his back. With the increased pressure on the wound, her biceps tensed, removing a bit of Victoria's flesh clinging to her from Charlotte's hug.

"We can take our tractor to the Mackenzie's up the road!" Austin said, grabbing her arm to usher her out.

"I'll check the house to see if there's anything we can use!" Lucas said as he sprinted ahead.

"He'll be okay, right?" she asked with concern.

"Yes, if you get help quickly."

As she departed, Charlotte gave a small nod. The fresh air hitting her face invigorated her, acting like a caffeine boost. With the rising sun, its shadow eclipsed the moon's last light. With a graceful, celebratory bow, the flowers perked up from their fearful disposition and returned to their calm routine. Taking one last look at the barn, she caught a final glimpse of the chair she tipped over, noticing the suncrow laying in Victoria's blood; the last bit of blood it was going to soak up was coming from the one that gave it life over the last week.

Chapter 32

M^onday

SIRENS WAILED ACROSS Chester Farms. First responders navigated the difficult terrain with stretchers while police conducted a comprehensive search of the sunflower fields. The employees helped clean up the aftermath, disheartened by the toll the labyrinth took on their bosses' family. All that volunteer work painting plywood was now being used to inflict harm.

As Charlotte sat in the ambulance, her hair matted with her aunt's dried blood, mist descended on her face from the firefighters dousing the cabin ashes. With a tight grip on her mother's hand, the girl gazed into her mother's eyes. The rope burns served as a constant reminder of nearly losing her, fueling Charlotte's determination to never let that happen again.

"I'm so proud of you, Charlotte," Katherine said, her smile sincere.

Their heartbeats pounded in sync as Charlotte's grip tightened. The distance between them had lessened, and her period of isolation was over.

"We're proud of you."

A pained Katherine turned, her neck straining, startled. The sight of her lost husband and child left her speechless. With a smile mirroring his father's pride, Gabriel put his arm around James.

"What the hell?" Katherine said in disbelief. "Is it really you?"

"Yes, Mom. It is," said Gabriel, holding back tears.

"I-I don't understand. You're dead."

"Don't remind us," James said with a wink. "We didn't know why we were here either."

"I think I know why," Charlotte said. "Unfinished business."

"Yes, and now it's time for us to go."

With tears streaming down her face, Charlotte struggled to wipe them away with her sling. Her chin shook, unable to confront the fact they were leaving.

"I don't want you to go," Charlotte said, her throat thickening. "There's so much to catch up on."

"And we'll still get to see it," Gabriel said. "We'll always be there with you. But it's time for us to move on."

Charlotte snuggled close to her mother, feeling her mother's tight hold, hearing Katherine's racing heart pounding in her ear. A second loss was hard to accept; their hands shook with the struggle.

"Remember that you should never question yourself ever again," said James, his teeth beaming. "You can do anything as long as you have a little courage."

"Yeah, and don't take shit from anyone," Gabriel added.

Charlotte's mother held her close as she laughed through another fresh bout of tears. Her heart and blood thrilled to the words, like a shot of adrenaline. She blew her nose and opened her eyes, only to find they'd vanished.

Forever.

From every direction, stretchers with black bags appeared. Charlotte got up and walked toward them, each person's location helping her to identify them. She forgot the hurtful words, letting forgiveness heal her, focusing only on happy memories, real or imagined; the ridicule was not the way she wanted to remember them on her own path to healing.

Except for one.

Flashes peeked through the barn door on the horizon, while photographs showed evidence of her aunt hanging with half of her body by the wood chipper. The pretense of their close friendship, once a comfort, now disturbed her. All her past professions of love were lies; she's one of them who poisoned their minds.

Paramedics pushed another stretcher toward her. With the wheels rolling over uneven gravel, paramedics hung blood bags over Noah, whose torso was wrapped in tight bandages. Lucas stood by his side; his limbs were heavy with fatigue, but his face jacked with adrenaline.

"How're you doing?" Charlotte asked with concern, her eyes following the tubes intertwining around his body.

Noah's mouth twitched slightly. With a thumb raised, he winced in pain as he lifted his arm. As the paramedics lifted him into the vehicle, relief washed over Charlotte. Lucas found solace in the ambulance's corner, relieved others escaped his mother's fury, though grieving the loss of his nurturer.

"I'm sorry my mom did this," he said with remorse. "I didn't even know."

"None of us did. It's not your fault," said Charlotte.

"Just know that if I knew, I would've stopped this earlier."

"I know you would've. Just because she's your mom doesn't make you a bad person. But promise me you won't be an asshole like her."

Another group of employees passed, eliciting a small huff of amusement from Lucas. A cloud of dust filled the air, weighing heavily on Charlotte's lungs. Another car pulled into the driveway with difficulty, having to avoid other cars. Pressing down on the gas pedal, the car veered up the slope to park beside the dining table where sunlight gleamed on a bald head.

"Hey guys!" Dexter said, his jogging suit sagged with the seams drenched in sweat as he sprinted around everyone.

Lucas stood in front of his cousin. Despite Dexter being family, the weekend's length and the number of surprises were enough to last everyone a lifetime.

"I'm so sorry for what happened to you guys," Dexter said as he caught his breath.

The rest of the group stayed silent.

"I have Gemma's will," he continued, his voice becoming apprehensive. "And I'm going to assume that this is the rest of the family, so we don't have to wait for anyone else before we can start."

Charlotte's fingers tingled. This entire problem started because of something inside the manila envelope. Hearing all the greed that started the pain made money such a sore subject; it left a sour taste in her mouth.

"Can you just summarize it? I don't care about the specifics," Charlotte said, cradling her arm.

"I don't either," Lucas agreed. "Not after all this."

Ripping open the top, Dexter gave a somber nod. He examined the papers, his eyes searching for information. His mouth uttered silent words, too drained to piece it all together.

"I, GEMMA CHESTER OF sound body, mind, and spirit, will release all my assets to the one person I trust will split into the rest of the family. This family is not about hatred. We are not about separation, so my intentions were to give the assets to one person, knowing that they would do the right thing and split it amongst the family. To keep the peace of fighting between who gets what, I know this person is levelheaded, and has handled all situations responsibly and respectfully throughout her childhood. I love you all equally, but I enlist all my trust in my dearest daughter.

Victoria, don't let me down."

Gemma Chester 9/22/1980

"WELL, I'LL BE DAMNED," Charlotte said, scuffing a tiny laugh.

"I guess she would've gotten her way without a single person being harmed," said her son, shaking his head in disappointment.

"What do we do now, Dexter? That bitch is gone, so what happens from here?" asked Charlotte out of curiosity.

"Well, it goes to Lucas, of course. He's her only family left."

Lucas's eyes grew wide. He never imagined inheriting the entire estate, but his mother's descent into madness was equally unbelievable. The entire property being all his and the success of his grandparents' labors was now in his pocket. Looking at his family being taken away in body bags was a dark and heavy weight on his soul. He noticed someone on a bench, watching sunflowers near his house, as cars drove away.

Austin.

"Can I ask you to do something, Dexter?" Lucas said tentatively.

"Of course."

"I want to split the money between Charlotte and Noah, but I want my share to go to Austin Grace and his family."

"The Graces?" Dexter asked, perplexed. "May I ask why?"

"Because he is just as part of this family as the rest of us, and they deserve their share for all the pain they've endured."

"As you wish," Dexter said, his grin tight as he continued to face their exhausted disposition. "I'll let you be."

"Wait," Charlotte said, grabbing Dexter's shoulder. "I have something to ask too."

A concerned look crossed Lucas's face as he looked at his cousin. A gentle breeze caressed their necks, softly blowing their hair across their faces.

"I would like to ask that my share goes back to the business. I don't want it."

Katherine's eyes grew with surprise. Silent and wrapped in a blanket, she shielded herself as shadows fell from the passing clouds. A surge in blood pressure led to pain in her neck.

"You don't want it?" Dexter asked.

"That's correct," she confirmed. "Of course, I could always use the money to better my life, but I just remembered something that Grandma and I talked about a long time ago. And besides, I want to invest it into something that will carry on her legacy."

"Are you sure, baby?" Katherine asked, holding back her shock.

"I've never been more sure in my life," Charlotte said, her smile beaming.

"And we can figure out who will take over after we take some time to heal," Lucas joined.

As Dexter walked toward Austin and his mother, he gave a brief nod; Austin's arm was around her shoulder. Three water bottles in hand, Bennett sat outside the Chester house, his headache intensified by the bright light that made him squint while they await for the police for questioning. With a pat on Lucas's back from Charlotte, they observed the Graces' response to the inheritance; Frieda's relief at easing her retirement struggles was clear. Bennett glanced over at the two of them, acknowledging them with a mutual apology, a peace offering of forgiveness before joining his family for a hug of relief.

A smile spread across Katherine's face. Her overwhelming pride in her daughter was something she cherished and wanted to remember. The warmth in Charlotte's body radiated as she patted her back.

"Ready to go?" she asked.

With a nod, Charlotte embraced Lucas. Unwilling to release their hold, they remained locked together. Thinking of their separation from their family, their only family, caused them to tear up.

"Please keep in touch," she asked, sniffling.

"Of course," he said, raspy. "You're only going to the hospital!"

"I know, dumbass! After this blows over. I don't want to lose you. You're my family, and I love you so much."

"I love you, too."

The distance between them grew, and their smiles became strained. As they entered the ambulance's back, the doors closed. With a final flourish of petals in the wind, the sunflowers said goodbye. Charlotte noticed something different about the caution tape buckling near the dinner table.

The family's spirits filled all the chairs.

Saying goodbye to the departed filled Charlotte with a warm sensation in her stomach. Their smiles and joyful atmosphere touched her. As the car neared the bottom, the dust increased, causing the spirits to vanish. Then she thought of Gemma telling her something when she was younger; the thing that motivated her to not take the inheritance.

"MY DEAREST, CHARLOTTE, let me tell you a secret to life. Having the money we worked for can certainly make life easier, but be careful. Money can give you things that you may not need or create habits that could bring out the worst in you, or even create new problems."

"But Grandma, you seem to have everything you need."

"I would've had my life full without all this money as long as I had the people I love and those that love me."

"Can't you have both?"

"You can. What I'm saying is that money is the root of most evils, and it brings out the worst in all of us. We need it, but all of us want more than what we need. Just be careful, okay?"

"I promise."

SHE WILL ALWAYS WONDER if she'd made the correct choice about the inheritance. Her exhaustion might have been the reason behind her choices. For whatever reason, she chose what felt right at the time.

She stole one last look as the vehicle departed to see if anyone else was there. Vengeful and focused on their mission, the killer's chest rose and fell, their arms folded across their chest. In the road, isolated from their family because of their crime, they stood watch over their secret that was once secured in the chest down the road. Charlotte had no more feelings of fear; not a single tingle in her spine, no lurching in her stomach, nothing. As she moved away from Chester Farms, her fears subsided, and the vulnerable part of herself that allowed negativity to affect her disappeared.

"Is there a radio you can turn on?" Charlotte asked, her voice dragging with exhaustion.

Proceeding up the incline, the ambulance passed the neighboring farms. Charlotte felt increasingly weary as the grass swayed, full of peace in the open countryside. The presence of her mother, the most important person to her, filled her with such peace that her eyelids grew heavy as she lay beside her; the one that will provide strength for years to come.

Man, I feel like a woman!

Acknowledgements

There are always so many people to thank for *Petals of Peril* coming to fruition. Of course, I appreciate my friends and family for their support. My husband has always been one of the biggest ones to thank. Without him being there for me as I worked tirelessly through every draft and edit, I would go crazy! I also want to thank my readers for being supportive over the years. You guys are the best people out there!

To my dear friend Josue, thank you for taking me in when I had nowhere to go all those years ago. You always were the type of person who would take the clothes off your back to keep others dry before yourself. Your kindness has inspired me to become a better person, and the legacy you've left behind in this world has been one of living authentically and full of kindness and bravery. I think of you often.

This story was a love letter to the part of my childhood that spent time in the country back in the nineties. Writing all the references from the music to the toys I played with was a real treat, and I'm thankful to share that joy with all of you.

About the Author
Brady Phoenix

BRADY PHOENIX IS A self-published author. With a love for 1980s and 1990s slasher movies, his goal is to add diversity to the horror genre through his work. When he is not writing, he enjoys long nature walks, hanging out with his husband and two cats, along with reading and supporting the self-publishing and horror community.

    Facebook- @Brady Phoenix
    Instagram- @AuthorBradyPhoenix
    Bluesky- @bradyphoenix.bsky.social
    TikTok- @AuthorBradyPhoenix

Also by Brady Phoenix

Cardinal Rules
Nun Taken
Troll
Petals of Peril

www.ingramcontent.com/pod-product-compliance
Lightning Source LLC
Chambersburg PA
CBHW051124190726
48290CB00006B/1672